Tipped in Blue

Best wishes,
Lynda F. Beasley

Tipped in Blue

A Novel

Linda F. Beasley

iUniverse, Inc.
New York Lincoln Shanghai

Tipped in Blue

Copyright © 2007 by Linda F. Beasley

All rights reserved. No part of this book may be used or reproduced by any means, graphic, electronic, or mechanical, including photocopying, recording, taping or by any information storage retrieval system without the written permission of the publisher except in the case of brief quotations embodied in critical articles and reviews.

iUniverse books may be ordered through booksellers or by contacting:

iUniverse
2021 Pine Lake Road, Suite 100
Lincoln, NE 68512
www.iuniverse.com
1-800-Authors (1-800-288-4677)

This is a work of fiction. All of the characters, names, incidents, organizations, and dialogue in this novel are either the products of the author's imagination or are used fictitiously.

ISBN: 978-0-595-41918-0 (pbk)
ISBN: 978-0-595-86263-4 (ebk)

Printed in the United States of America

Inspired by a life; for Katherine's four daughters, Carolyn, Judy, Linda and Barbara.

Chapter 1

▼

The '47 Nash carried them up old highway 41. They headed north with three little girls and a marriage that had gone as sour as the milk in Linda's baby bottle.

"Miles," Katherine said, "we have to stop at a restaurant to get fresh milk for Linda."

When Katherine said restaurant, she meant one of those little hole-in-the-wall, run down places along the old road going north. Katherine hated stopping at those small dumps with signs that read *Eat Here*; she felt their food wasn't fit for anyone to eat. The shacks were gray and dirty with litter thrown around and there was usually a dog or a man loitering about; sometimes both. However, she couldn't be too choosy about where to stop because that's all there was along the lonely mountain roads.

It was April 16, 1950, Miles' 31st birthday, when they started on their journey. Katherine found herself having to face something she didn't know if she could. She was also 31, twenty-two days older than Miles, facing the biggest challenge in her life so far. She was going to be without the stability of her home, her relatives, her heritage, and her dear Aunt Etta; she had always relied on that stability because she lacked it emotionally. Aunt Etta had raised her since her mother's death and she had been Katherine's source of security and love.

Katherine had battled with her nerves since she was a teenager; at the same time, she had an inherently strong will to survive. She not only wanted to survive herself, but she wanted her marriage and family to survive; she was willing to forgive and forget many things to keep it all together. Now that she was leaving the warm south, and all that was the very heart of her, she was determined to give it a good try. Up to this point, her determination to find and keep the love she had so desperately searched for since she was a child had kept her going during the most painful and stressful times in her life. Katherine was going to have to call on that strong will and determination over and over again in the cold north.

"Miles, Linda needs some milk and Carolyn and Judy need to go to the bathroom. When are we going to stop?"

"We'll stop soon. I just want to get up the road a piece. I think the brakes are going bad," Miles said. "I'm going to have to use the shift to slow down. I hope this old jalopy makes it to Michigan."

Miles always drove junky cars; he could never afford a new car so his spare time was filled with keeping an old jalopy running. He was a good mechanic due to his training in mechanic's school early in their marriage and then in the army motor pool; however, lying on the cold damp ground took its toll on his back and arthritis had begun to form in his spine. Although Miles loved to drive, sitting in the car seat for long periods of time gave him a terrific back ache.

Highway 41 was the main route that carried travelers north. It was a two-lane road that wound around the Great Smoky Mountains. There were so many twists and turns that it sometimes felt as though you were coming right back at yourself. In many spots it was evident that the flimsy guardrails had been run down; it was anyone's guess if there was a car sitting at the bottom of the valley. If a car had gone over, it would be there forever because even a heavy-duty wrecker could not get it up the steep mountain side.

"I want to see, I want to see," Carolyn screeched.

"Me too," Judy's little voice echoed. Both girls stretched their necks out the window just to see if they could catch a glimpse of a car crunched between the trees. Katherine would not look; she could not stomach the thought of accidentally going over the edge. She was very squeamish about that kind of thing, almost to the point of being fanatical. Now that she knew the brakes on the old Nash were bad, she felt even more anxiety about this trip; she yelled even more at Miles to slow down around the hairpin mountain curves. He was always a fast driver and sometimes he would do it just for the sake of teasing her and making her scream. At times she wasn't sure if his laugher was out of having fun or if there was something more sinister about it; the only time he seemed to act that menacing was when they were in the car. Even though they had a few verbally aggressive arguments, most of them in the latter part of their marriage, Miles never became physical with her. That's why she felt disturbed by the ominous look in his eyes when he did this; she tried hard to ignore the suspicions running through her mind about why her husband enjoyed frightening her so much.

Miles and Katherine were headed for Michigan with the dream of a better life than they had in Chattanooga. The auto industry was growing and offering dreams for hire; dreams of good jobs, dreams of more money and better opportunities for all.

Miles' younger brother, Larry, twelve years his junior, was the first one to investigate the prospects in Michigan. He had been reading about the industry in the local paper and talking to his buddies about it for months. Finally he decided to go north to see what all the talk was about. It seemed like a good opportunity so he moved his family up north. Larry called Miles frequently telling him about the good things that were happening in that area, trying to persuade Miles into making the move too. The Detroit area was growing fast because of General Motors and the Ford Motor Co., and the great migration from the South transplanted hundreds of families. It was becoming very common to hear a southern accent in the Detroit area. Miles saw this as a good opportunity to get a fresh start; he knew his job at the Lava Co. was on shaky ground, and so was his marriage. Katherine agreed to make the move for the same reasons.

Miles, his full name was Robert Miles, was a good worker when he first got the job after he was discharged from the army; unfortunately, his restlessness, and the influence of the women employees, took its toll on his work ethics. It wasn't long before he started going in late, missing days and even lying to Katherine about going to work. Miles had already gotten a few warnings from his foreman so he knew if they didn't go to Michigan now, he would have to look for a new job in Tennessee very soon.

Katherine listened to the hum of the tires on the old road as she held Linda on her lap; she tried to be patient waiting for Miles to stop, although patience was not one of Katherine's finer points. She tried not to say anything because she didn't want to start another argument; it was all she could do to keep quiet. As the drone of the tires lulled her tired spirit, many things ran through her mind. The same things kept coming up over and over again; feeling guilty about leaving her Aunt Etta, leaving her roots, all of Miles' broken promises, the hope that this move would make a difference, and the doubt in the back of her mind that it wouldn't. She let out a sigh as she pushed in the cigarette lighter and waited for it to pop out. Katherine lit her cigarette and blew the smoke out the window.

Carolyn, eight years old, and Judy, six, were getting antsy in the back seat. Katherine couldn't hold back any longer.

"Miles, Linda is hungry," Katherine snapped again. Frustrated, she turned away and propped her elbow against the open car window frame. The warm April breeze blew against her cheek and gently tossed her hair. She slowly closed her eyes as the rhythm of the road made her drowsy. Suddenly she was back in their small kitchen in the house in Fairview, a suburb of Chattanooga.

"Honey," Katherine remembered Miles saying, "I think this will be good for us. There aren't any good jobs here. We can get a new start up north."

Katherine didn't know how to feel about her husband's suggestion. She was close to her family. She relied on them for help with the kids; more importantly, for emotional support. How could she move so far away from them? How could she tell Aunt Etta she was leaving, especially since her aunt had done so much for her? How could she handle being so far away and all alone if trouble started again?

"Do you really think this is going to be good for us, Miles?" Katherine had asked him. "Do you really think things will be different up there? Will *you* be different up there?"

"Yea, baby," Miles said as he grabbed her around the waist from behind. "Yea, I'll be different. I'll be good. This will be good for us, I can feel it," she remembered him saying as he gave her a big squeeze with his head on her shoulder.

Katherine gazed off into space as they stood in the middle of the kitchen. She tried hard to convince herself that this was going to be a good move; however, her teary eyes shed some doubts. The quiver in her stomach told her that she wasn't at all sure about the whole thing. Miles continued to hug and kiss her, but she paid little attention. She thought about what Aunt Etta had said to her.

"Katherine," Aunt Etta's voice echoed in her ears, "you can't leave your troubles behind. They're like an old mama cat; they'll find their way back."

And that's what Katherine was afraid of as the old Nash carried them closer to the growing automotive land of opportunity. She was afraid Miles would start up his old habits of staying out late, bar hopping and picking up women. She kept her eyes closed trying to shut out all those old memories; hoping beyond hope that if she kept them closed long enough they would not open up to a future of the same old habits.

Miles finally stopped at a shabby little café; Carolyn and Judy jumped out. He loved his girls; however, if the truth be told, he had wanted all the kids after Carolyn to be boys. Katherine had been willing to keep trying for a boy; she felt if Miles had a son, he would be more content at home; sadly, Miles hadn't been content for a long time.

"Do you want to go with us?" Katherine asked.

"No, I'll stay here." Miles said; Katherine thought he seemed exceptionally restless.

"Mama, look at the dog," Carolyn giggled as she spied an old mutt lying beside the wooden porch.

"Don't get too close," Katherine ordered. As the three females stepped onto the porch, the dog lifted his head to see who had made the footsteps; however, he didn't make any effort to get up. Katherine put her free arm around Carolyn and Judy to shelter them as they passed by, just in case the dog decided to attack. Katherine was suspicious of all strange dogs.

"Could I get this baby bottle washed out and fresh milk put in it please?" Katherine asked the waitress. "We're on the road traveling north and it spoiled on us."

April in the south was usually warm and this year spring had been especially hot.

"Sure," said the waitress, "give it here."

"Where are your bathrooms?" Katherine asked. The waitress turned and made a motion that let her know they were around back.

"You girls hurry up and go to the bathroom," their mother instructed, "and stay away from that dog!"

Carolyn and Judy walked toward the back of the building kicking at the pebbles on the ground. As they kicked, clouds of hot, dry dust wafted in the air and floated down to rest on their shoes. They could see the old gray doors marked *MEN* and *WOMEN* with white paint; obviously the painter had done his job in a hurry because the paint ran half-way down the slats. They did not like to use the bathrooms at these old places; they smelled so bad and frequently had a burned out light bulb. The floor was usually wet, either from an overflowed toilet or someone with bad aim who had urinated on the floor.

Katherine looked at the waitress and asked, "Do you need a key for bathroom?"

"Yea", said the waitress as she reached under the counter and pulled out a key that was attached to a large wooden paddle.

"Don't forget to bring it back," she said as she snapped her gum.

"We won't," Katherine retorted as they exchanged one of those snotty glances that only two women can do.

She called out, "Carolyn, come get the key." Carolyn ran back and took the key from her mother's hand.

Katherine glanced in Miles' direction. She saw him get out of the car and walk around a bit; she figured his backed ached. She watched him light one of his Camel cigarettes and stare down the road. He looked uneasy.

Katherine hurried to use the bathroom too and then headed toward the car. Carol and Judy skipped excitedly.

"Look, daddy, mom bought us some candy." They held up their little hands to show him their treats. Linda squirmed in Katherine's arms as she reached for the clean bottle full of fresh milk.

Miles took another drag off his Camel and mumbled, "Come on, Herbert; get your ass here." He picked a piece of tobacco off his tongue as he paced anxiously. Katherine heard him, but she was busy getting the kids in the car.

"We're all set, Miles," she announced. "Hadn't you better use the bathroom before we start out?"

"Yea, I guess I'd better go while we're here," he said as he flicked the end of his cigarette on the ground. Katherine watched him limp away.

"You have to get the key from inside," Katherine called out as she lit a cigarette.

"Yea, okay," he called back.

Katherine stood outside and waited for Miles; it was too warm to get back in the car. As she stood in the sunshine, she attracted the stares of some other male customers.

Katherine was a medium height, about 5'5", and very slender. As a result of her bad nerves, Katherine had been a poor eater ever since childhood; and, having three children hadn't affected her figure at all. She wore a housedress that was snug at the midriff with a flared skirt that gently fluttered in the gentle breeze. It was white with blue flowers, which accented her blue eyes. She loved blue, it was her favorite color and she wore it whenever she could.

Her dark brown hair was shoulder length and the slight breeze blew it back away from her face, which added a flair of sexiness to her stance. She had a small mouth, which caused her rather large teeth to be slightly crooked; however, they weren't visible right then because she wasn't smiling.

As Miles walked back to the car, Katherine called out, "Any sign of Herbert and his friend?"

"No," Miles answered back, clearly irritated.

"I bet I know what happened to them, and so do you. They probably stopped off at the bar," she goaded him.

Miles knew she was probably right.

Chapter 2

▼

Both Katherine and Miles were worried and in foul moods; neither one wanted to get into an argument while they were cooped up in the small Nash with no way to get away from each other; they both kept quiet.

They had been traveling about an hour when Katherine broke the silence.

"I wonder where in the hell Herbert is? What are we going to do if he doesn't get there when we do? Where will we sleep? We won't even have a chair to sit on. Do you think he is going to get there on time?" she demanded.

Herbert, Miles' youngest sibling, and his friend, had agreed to follow Miles and Katherine up north with a rented truck full of their furniture. However, somewhere along the way Herbert and the truck dropped out of sight from Miles' rearview mirror.

"He'll be there," Miles yawned, he tried to make light of it.

"He'd better be," Katherine shot back.

"I'm getting tired. I'm going to look for a turnout to pull off and grab a few hours of sleep," Miles said.

A turnout, a spot in the road that had been cleared of trees or brush or a natural open spot, was common on narrow two lane roads, particularly in the mountains or heavily wooded areas. These clearings were useful when a car needed to turn around or pull off the road for any number of reasons. Some people used them to stop and have a picnic or simply to sightsee.

Miles and Katherine didn't have enough money to take their time and spend one night in a motel. They had to drive straight through while Miles took little catnaps along the way. In 1950, there were no expressways going north so it took two days to make the trip to Michigan. Katherine could not help him with the driving because she had not learned how to drive yet. Miles had taken her out on some of the lonely roads a few times back home, but she couldn't get the feel for the clutch and Miles ended up yelling.

"Okay, take me home! I've had enough! I don't want to drive anyway!" she yelled back. That was the end of the lessons.

Consequently, Miles had to drive the entire way up north; now he was sleepy and his back ached. He came upon a turnout and stopped. Practically before Katherine got the car door opened and the seat moved forward, Carolyn and Judy jumped out of the car. They ran over to the edge and looked down the mountain side.

"Nope," Carolyn said to Judy as they leaned over the guardrail on their tummies looking for a car, "I don't see one."

Katherine yelled franticly, "You girls get away from there! Do you want to slip and fall? God, that would kill you."

"Miles, you could have looked for a place on the other side of the road you know," she said glancing at him as she shut the door and walked over to where the girls were.

Miles ignored her look and took a long drag off his cigarette.

"Now you girls play over here away from the edge," Katherine snapped, pointing to an area with a little grass growing up between the stones.

Miles finished his cigarette and tossed it out the window; he moved his seat back to get comfortable. He rested his head between the top of the seat and the window frame and closed his eyes. Before long he was breathing long deep breaths; he was on his way to a deep sleep.

"Come hold Linda while I get a blanket out of the trunk," Katherine called to her oldest daughter. Carolyn came running over and took Linda in her arms.

Katherine headed back with a blanket and some oversized plastic keys on a thin plastic key ring, Linda's favorite blankie and a stuffed teddy bear. Carolyn handed over her baby sister and ran off to play with Judy while Katherine situated herself on the blanket. She wanted to keep Linda awake now so she would sleep when they got back on the road. She knew the baby's schedule was all messed up but it was so much easier riding in the car with a sleeping baby.

Katherine had her cigarettes in her pocket so she pulled out the pack and lit one. She looked out over the scenic mountain view. How beautiful the mountains were. It was about 4:00 in the afternoon and the sun had only slightly peeked out from behind the clouds. The overcast conditions were perfect to show the beauty of the Smoky Mountains. A sunny day would have filtered out the haze and it would have been mostly transparent; instead, it was thick and full of color. To Katharine, the smoky haze looked like a veil, a veil that she never wore since she and Miles slipped off to the justice of the peace to get married one hot June afternoon. The veil reflected blue, not just any blue, but smoky, china blue; the color that the ancient Chinese craftsmen got from using cobalt to decorate their fine porcelain. The tulle-like covering rested along the top of the ridge and was bluer and thicker than she ever remembered. Perhaps she simply never took the time to really look; but then, she never expected to see the mountains from this view, which was behind her.

However, today she looked and it all looked different; she couldn't turn her eyes away; she couldn't even get her breath enough to take another puff on her cigarette. It seemed like it would have been a sin to mix the smoke of the cigarette with the china blue smoke that rested in the valleys and atop the ridge. The mountains tugged at her. The smoky veil reached out to her, it held her like the arms of her Aunt Etta, her brothers, and her cousins; indeed all of her relatives saying, "Don't go, please don't go." She felt the veil wrap around her like a warm, blue security blanket that she wasn't ready to give up yet. She wanted to grab it and hold on; the way Linda held her favorite blanket. Katherine wanted to feel warm and secure again, a feeling she hadn't had for many years. She wanted the ache in her stomach to stop too. She found herself admitting that she really didn't want to leave her home or the mountains. At the same time, how much was she willing to give up in order to save her marriage? At this moment she realized there was going to be an awful lot of adjusting.

"Oh, I hope this works," she sighed.

Katherine looked over at Miles sleeping in the car. The top of his head had slid down and was sticking out of the car window. She could see the breeze slightly blowing his sandy blonde hair. Miles wasn't a tall man, about 5'9" with a slim frame, probably the perfect weight for his age and height. He had large ears that stuck out quite a bit, which he got teased about as a kid, and he had a large Indian nose, which he inherited from his Cherokee, great great grandmother. He had never been teased much about his nose and he was rather proud of it. He had a funny little sway to his walk, evidence of his back problems, and a playful bounce when he was in the mood for some fun. Miles was a big talker with an even bigger smile. His voice was very deep and rather gruff and he attracted a lot of ladies with these charms; Katherine was one of them.

She sat on the blanket feeling detached from her surroundings as she gazed out over the mountains. She found herself thinking about sitting on Aunt Etta's front porch swing, which all front porches in the South had. She and Miles sat on that swing for hours; that was where they did most of their courting. As she sat and thought about the front porch swing, she rubbed her forehead and wondered how in the world did she ever get here from the easiness of that swing? Katherine's daydreams turned into thoughts about the night it all began with her and Miles.

Hazel was Katherine's best friend. She had a date to go to Lake Winapasoka, an amusement park in Chattanooga, and she told Katherine she would get her a blind date.

"I don't know," Katherine hesitated.

"Come on, Kat," Hazel said, "I'll bring Miles for you. He can be lot of fun, you'll see. Just give him a chance."

Sometimes her friends called her Kat and her father always called her that; however, she hated it no matter who said it.

Katherine knew Miles so it wasn't exactly a blind date. As a matter of fact, he always teased her, in a flirty kind of way, when she was over at Hazel's; she pretended to be annoyed.

"Okay?" Hazel asked again.

"Well, all right," Katherine answered, "but he'd better behave himself."

Katherine and Miles started going out pretty steady from that night on. They spent most of their time together on Aunt Etta's front porch swing, much to the dismay of her Aunt June. Aunt June, Aunt Etta's sister, and Uncle John made their home with Aunt Etta their entire married life. Aunt Etta was a spinster so Uncle John was the only man in the house. Aunt June was a fiery redhead with a hot temper and she let Katherine know she was not happy about giving up her swing for courting purposes.

Katherine took a puff on her cigarette and slightly smiled as she remembered. She could still hear Aunt June yelling.

"I'd like to drink my iced tea outside on the swing where it is cool. Ettie, can't you do something about this," Aunt June barked.

"June, what would you have me do? This is her home too, and it is a respectable way to court," Aunt Etta responded in her soft, kind way.

Katherine remembered how Aunt June sulked on the couch with her arms folded across her chest while Uncle John went about reading the paper ignoring the whole thing.

She enjoyed remembering Uncle John. Katherine thought he was the nicest man in the whole world; he must be made of pure gold to put up with Aunt June.

Katherine began to feel guilty. Her aunt had given up a lot for her. Aunt Etta had never married, even though she could have; she had raised Katherine after her mother, May, died in 1931. They had formed a bond and now Katherine felt remorse for breaking it.

The blue veil floated through the air and gently twirled around Katherine. It was as though the mountains coaxed her to journey through her past before they would let her move on to the future. It carefully tugged at her thoughts and pulled them even farther back in time, perhaps farther back than she wanted to go, but now she was there.

She thought about her parents, May and Sam Williamson. They had divorced when she was five, which was the beginning of her journey down a long and bumpy road. Katherine had two older brothers, Raymond, the oldest, and Dennis, her favorite.

May got the house in the divorce settlement and she and the three kids lived there for a while. Sadly, May could not come to terms with the divorce; she became restless and edgy. Two years after the divorce she sold the house and started traveling. Raymond was old enough to be on his own, so he found a job and stayed in town; May packed up Katherine and Dennis and away she went to try to kill the pain.

Katherine got up from the blanket and lit another cigarette and looked over to see what Carolyn and Judy were doing. She saw that they were playing safely away from the edge of the cliff; she walked around to stretch her legs. Despite Katherine's many shortcomings, she was a very protective mother; she always made sure her children were safe.

"Let's see," she muttered to herself, "where all did we go? We took the train to Chickasha, Oklahoma; then there was Minneapolis, Minnesota; then Des Moines, Iowa. Oh yea, I went to school with the Indian children in Albuquerque, New Mexico. Boy, I'm surprised I can still remember that."

Katherine became sullen as she began to think about her mother. She wondered why she did all of that traveling. She didn't remember it being that much fun or anything special, just long rides on the train. She remembered her mother sitting awful still and quiet and not paying her much attention.

"Mommy, why didn't daddy come with us?" she recalled asking her mother in her little six-year-old voice.

"Because he wanted to stay with that lady from the bus stop, that's why," May sneered.

Katherine didn't know how to describe the look on her mother's face; she just knew that it made her look ugly. She recalled trying to sit very still so she wouldn't cause her mother any more trouble than possible; Katherine knew that her mother was terribly blue so she usually didn't say anything about her stomach aches.

During her travels, May married two more times; however, Katherine couldn't remember their names. At the same time, she did remember her mother not feeling well; they finally returned home after three years, with May's pain still intact.

Katherine hadn't thought about her mother's other marriages very much; but now she was annoyed at herself because she couldn't remember their names.

"I should be able to remember that, I was certainly old enough," Katherine muttered. "If I can remember all of the cities and states that we lived in, I should be able to remember the names of the men my mother was married to."

"I must remember to ask Dennis the next time I talk to him," she promised herself. A fleeting thought crossed her mind.

"I wonder if there's a particular reason why I can't remember." She was frustrated at her lack of recollection.

Katherine shook her head and the mysterious thought was gone as quickly as it came. However, most of May's unpredictable and irrational behavior was remembered by her daughter, but with a much softer regard; she placed most of the blame on her abandoning father.

Eventually May and her children settled back in Tennessee where they rented an apartment in the small town of Ridgemont, a city that bordered Chattanooga. To make ends meet, May worked as a seamstress at one of the better dress shops in Chattanooga; however, her health was not good. As the months went by, she worked fewer and fewer hours. Dennis was fifteen at the time; he quit school and went to work to help his mother financially. Katherine was eleven and began to look frail and show signs of nervousness, like her mother. This went on for a year; all the while May's health slowly slipped away. Soon she was unable to keep up the apartment; she and Katherine moved in with Aunt Etta. Dennis did not make the move with his mother and sister. He kept his job and moved in with his best friend, Buddy Dobbs.

Aunt Etta's house looked large from the outside, but it only had two bedrooms. She and May shared one of the rooms, while Aunt June and Uncle John had the other. Katherine had no other place to sleep but the couch.

Aunt June had her only child, a son named Johnny, while Katherine and her Mother had been on their travels. "There must have been an extra bed in Aunt June's room for Johnny," Katherine muttered. Consequently, it became a full house.

Katherine finished her cigarette and shuddered at her next memory.

Chapter 3

▼

May lost her battle with pneumonia a short four months after she and Katherine had moved in with Aunt Etta. May had said all along that she never wanted to be taken to a funeral home so her body never left the house. It still laid in the very bed that she and Etta had shared. Etta called the doctor and the undertaker late that morning.

"What is taking them so long?" Aunt Etta complained as she wrung her hands and paced the floor.

"Doc Polk probably had some other stops to make on his way over here, Ettie," June reassured her. "Besides, Mr. Carter can't do anything until the doctor certifies her. I expect they'll be here soon."

They glanced at Katherine, who sat on the couch too afraid to move.

"No child should have to go through this; knowing that their mother is lying in the next room, dead," Katherine heard Aunt Etta whisper. The two women heard a car door slam and they rushed to the window. It was Dr. Polk.

"Finally," Aunt Etta gasped; she opened the door and let him in.

"I'm sorry I'm late Miss Tomas, but some of my patients are so hard to get away from," he bellowed. He glanced around the room and nodded at John and June. "Mr. and Mrs. Dune." His eyes continued on until he stopped at Katherine. His mood became more somber as he comforted her.

"I'm sorry about your mama, honey." He walked over to her and patted her hand. Katherine looked at him with a watery stare.

"Well, where is May so I can get this done?" He roared, in a mater-of-fact way.

Aunt Etta motioned for the doctor to follow her and they both disappeared into the lifeless chamber.

Katherine sat on the couch with her hands in her lap; she softly cried. She could hear voices talking back and forth and she could hear the clinking of the doctor's instruments. By the time they came out of the bedroom, Katherine had begun to cry harder. Her shoulders heaved back and forth and the mucus from her runny nose mixed with the tears to wet her lips.

"Mommy, Mommy," Katherine whimper in-between the sobs. She tried to be as strong as a twelve-year-old could be; at the same time, she couldn't believe she would never see her mother again. She couldn't understand why her mother had to leave her. Her father left, then her closest brother, Dennis, left; now her mother left. She couldn't understand why in such a short time her whole family left her; she was confused.

"Now, Miss Tomas, give this death certificate to Mr. Carter when he gets here."

"I will, Doctor, thank you," Etta said politely as she looked down at the death certificate; the date caught her eye, April 13, 1931.

"Pneumonia is a hard thing to cure. May waited too long; the infection was too advanced for the quinine to do any good; there wasn't anything else I could do," the doctor explained; he looked around the room at the sadness.

"We understand, Doctor. Thank you for all you tried to do," Etta said softly as she showed him to the door.

Aunt Etta, Aunt June and Uncle John were in the corner of the dining room; Katherine heard whispers. She stared at them through her teary eyes as a knock came at the door. It was Mr. Carter, the undertaker and his apprentice, Willie Key.

They were an odd pair Katherine thought. Mr. Carter was very tall, about 6', and a big man, not fat, just big. He must have weighed around 285 pounds. He had blond hair and light brown eyes, and his face was round with a kind smile. His size made his presence very evident and the black suit made him look rather like a whale, but a gentle whale. Willie, on the other hand, was short and thin with dark hair all over him. Katherine thought he looked like a gypsy. He wore a black suit that he obviously had outgrown, but it was neatly pressed. In his excitement at getting to apprentice with Mr. Carter, he always ran ahead, and usually got in the way.

Aunt Etta went to the door and greeted them. "Come in, Mr. Carter. Hello, Willie. Can you give us a minute please?"

Aunt Etta turned to Katherine and knelt down on one knee.

"Now, dear, we don't think it is a good idea for you to stay in here while Mr. Carter does his work. I want you to go outside; you can sit on the swing, okay?" Aunt Etta suggested.

"Okay," Katherine answered as she scooted off the couch and went outside. However, she didn't sit on the swing; she stood at the opened window and listened to the gruesome conversation.

"A real shame for this to happen to a woman of forty-three, a real shame," Mr. Carter said.

"Here's the death certificate, Mr. Carter. Now remember what we talked about," Aunt Etta reminded him.

"Yes, I remember, Miss Tomas; I know May wanted to be laid out at the house and that will be just fine," he said.

"May didn't leave much money, just a little for her two younger children to divide. Doing this here at the house will help a lot," Etta explained.

"I understand."

"Do what?" Katherine wondered as she continued to listen at the window.

"I'm happy to oblige May's last request," the undertaker said. "Now, Miss Tomas, we're going out to the hearse to get the embalming table. Can you clear a space in the kitchen close to the sink for us please?"

Katherine ran to get on the swing when she heard the screen door open. She watched the funny pair take a large metal table out of the hearse. She wondered what that was for. As they carried it through the front door, Katherine heard her aunt yell out.

"Mr. Carter, do you need the kitchen table too?"

"No, I think the table I brought is big enough for her. She's a small woman."

Katherine shuddered. She wondered what in the world they were talking about. She went to the window and peered in.

Mr. Carter and Willie carried the table into the kitchen along with the embalming tools. Katherine watched Mr. Carter disappeared for a few minutes; he reappeared carrying her mother; he held May very close and tight to his chest so that her head and arms would not flop around. Katherine covered her eyes.

"Miss Tomas," he said turning his head around but standing in such a way as to block the view of the body, "you and Mrs. Dune go into the bedroom and pick out something nice for me to put on May, will you? Pick out her favorite dress so she will look real nice. You and Mrs. Dune can fix her hair and put a little lipstick on her when we get done."

When Katherine heard the undertaker's request, she rushed into the house and ran straight to the bedroom; for the moment, she forgot about where she was.

"I want to help pick out mama's dress," Katherine announced through her tears.

"Katherine, dear, what are you doing in here? I told you to stay outside. You shouldn't see this; it's not right for you to see this," Aunt Etta exclaimed.

"I want to help," Katherine cried. Aunt Etta couldn't help but give in to this little girl's request.

"Okay, you can pick out your mama's dress, but don't look out the door," Aunt Etta ordered. Katherine shook her head in agreement.

"Miss Tomas, do you think we could have a little music in here?" Mr. Carter called out. "I do like to listen to music when I work. It helps me to relax; it keeps me from tensing up. You know what I mean, don't you?"

Katherine thought that was a very good idea. If there was some music, loud music, then she wouldn't hear the sickening noises coming from just outside the bedroom door. Before Aunt Etta had a chance to decide what music to start, Mr. Carter appeared in the doorway. His appearance startled everyone and only made the situation more ghoulish.

He wore a large, black, rubber apron that tied around his neck; it went almost to the floor with another tie that went around his waist to keep the apron close to his body. Katherine thought he resembled a mad scientist; furthermore, she didn't want to know what the long black rubber hose, which he held in his hand, was used for.

He asked again, "Can we have some music?"

"Yes, I think we all could use some music," Aunt Etta said; she walked past him into the living room. Aunt Etta first thought to turn on the radio, but she changed her mind and decided to wind up the old Victrolla. The RCA Victrolla was one of the few items that had been saved when May sold off everything and moved in with her. May loved to wind up the old box and listen to her favorite tunes.

"Put on *Vagabond Lover*," Katherine suggested. She knew how much her mother loved Rudy Vallee.

"Okay, honey," Aunt Etta said as she placed the record on the turntable. Katherine watched Aunt Etta turn the crank on the side of the box and place the needle on the plastic disk. Out came that wonderful, megaphoned voice. Katherine closed her eyes and cried for her mother.

Aunt Etta sat down next to her hurting niece. "Katherine, honey," her soft voice soothed, "you know I made your mother a promise. I told her that I will take care of you until you are grown. She also made me promise not to let your father take you away; and I won't. You can stay with me as long as you want."

Katherine hugged her aunt and fell asleep in her arms.

"Okay, Miss Tomas, we're finished," Mr. Carter called out. His booming voice startled Katherine awake.

The two men had worked for a few hours; they cleaned up their work area leaving no trace of the gruesome task that had been done there. With no autopsy necessary, and the simplest embalming process used, it didn't take very long to prepare the body.

"Bring me the clothes that you picked out," Katherine heard him shout.

Aunt Etta delivered the dress that she had picked out. It was made of silk and it had a yellow background with white flowers all over it. It had a large white collar, which always framed May's face so prettily when she wore it. The two morticians dressed the body as gently as a parent would dress a child; they left her lying alone and peaceful in the kitchen.

"Katherine, now you stay in here while we get things set up in the other room," Aunt Etta told her weary niece. "Do you hear me?"

"Yes," Katherine moaned. She heard furniture being moved around. She heard the front door open and close; she heard the two men grunt from carrying the weight of the coffin. She wanted to peek out the door, but she couldn't muster up the nerve.

Finally, she decided to look. An eerie sight overwhelmed her as she watched Mr. Carter and Willie carry her mother's dressed body to the coffin. She could see her mother disappear in the red, velvet, lined box.

"Okay, ladies, we're finished here. You can fix May's hair and make-up," Mr. Carter instructed.

Aunt June went into the bedroom to get May's powder and lipstick. "Katherine, do you want to come out now?" she asked.

"I don't know," Katherine whimpered.

"Well, maybe in a few minutes," Aunt June said; she didn't see that Katherine followed her out.

Katherine stood a good distance from the coffin; she was afraid to get too close. She watched her aunts prepare her mother. She watched them comb May's long red hair. June put some powder on her thin face; May had lost a lot of weight during her sickness. Etta put some of May's coral lipstick on her purple lips. She always wore coral lipstick because she thought it complemented her red hair. The vision of May's red hair, her yellow dress, and the coral lipstick against the red, velvet, lining of the coffin radiated hues of flames. Not the flames of a hot temper like her sister, June, but vibrate flames of passion for life that she once held, before the depression took over. The enthusiasm and warmth that everyone loved about her had gone out, and it was going to be missed.

"Mama looks pretty," Katherine said softly; Aunt Etta gave her a hug.

"Do you want to help me straighten up the kitchen a bit?" Aunt Etta asked. "Maybe that will help you get your mind off things."

Katherine quickly shook her head in agreement. She sat motionless and watched her Aunt Etta work. Katherine couldn't help but think about what the man with the black apron had done in the kitchen just a few hours ago. However, it didn't seem to bother her aunt, she simply went about doing what she had to do.

Before long, the relatives and other visitors started arriving. Etta, June and May were three of eight sisters. By early evening all the rest of them had arrived, Lilly, Margie, Ila, Jimmie, Louise and their only brother, Terah. In true southern fashion, they all came with food, some with a casserole of some kind and some brought a desert. Aunt Etta was happy about that because she hadn't had any time to cook; her kitchen had been preoccupied. As the neighbors, relatives and friends sat around and talked, Aunt Etta, Aunt June, Uncle John and Johnny slipped away into the kitchen to get a bite to eat, but not Katherine. Etta tried to persuade her.

"Katherine, honey, come over here and eat a little bit."

She tried to eat, but she simply ended up pushing the plate away. "I'm not hungry."

"But, honey, you are going to get sick if you don't eat. I wish you would have just a little bit of this cake Mrs. Yates brought over. Maybe you would feel better if you ate a little bit," Aunt Etta coaxed.

"I don't want anything. I feel sick," Katherine whined as she got up and went into the living room.

Since her parents divorce, and having to cope with her mother's restlessness, Katherine had begun to develop a problem with food. She wasn't anorexic, but any kind of traumatic episode caused an eating problem for her.

She flopped down on the couch and bent down to pick up her cat, Snowball. Snowball had been out of sight for the last few days; however, now she was out roaming from room to room investigating all the people.

After their travels had come to an end and they were settled in an apartment, May picked up a free kitten for Katherine. Aunt Etta allowed her niece to bring the cat with her when she and May came to live at her house. Snowball was a white, fluffy, longhaired cat, a little plump, with big round blue eyes. Katherine loved the fact that the cat had blue eyes just like hers.

She and snowball sat on the couch and watched every new arrival. With each person came another casserole, or cake, or plate of cookies. Aunt Lily brought a huge pot of chicken and dumplings. Katherine listened to the family gossip.

"She just never got over Sam leaving. She died of a broken heart as sure as we're standing here. Sam running off with that woman he met at the bus stop, what ever her name was, is what killed her; yes, a broken heart for sure!"

Young Katherine heard the poignant tell told over and over all evening. Her impressionable mind was implanted with the idea that a person could indeed die of a broken heart, and she would forever believe that's what killed her mother.

Katherine began to feel sleepy and wished everyone would just go home. But once the visitors started coming, they never left. Southern tradition dictated that several people stay all night to sit up with the body. This gave the family a chance to get some sleep.

Katherine didn't want to hear any of them talking anymore. All of this was just too much for one day. As each mourner finished paying their respects, they would go over to her, hug her, and tell her how sorry they were, and that everything would be all right. That made her angry; she wanted to shout, "How can everything be all right. My mother is dead, and I haven't seen my father in a long time; he's with that woman from the bus stop." Her twelve-year-old mind wondered why he wasn't there with her; what did she do wrong?

"It's time for bed, Katherine. You can sleep with me tonight," Aunt Etta announced; she went into the bedroom and turned on the light. Katherine could see in the room; however, she didn't want to go in there; her mother had died in there. She sat on the couch for a few minutes too afraid to walk around the coffin. She gathered up her courage and made a mad dash for the bedroom with her cat at her heels.

Aunt Etta shut the door and changed into her nightgown. "Katherine, get changed now," she said as she walked over to the four poster bed and pulled the covers back.

"I don't want to sleep in this bed tonight, Auntie. That is where mama died," Katherine whimpered.

"I know it must be hard for you, dear; but there is no where else for you to sleep. You have to sleep here with me," Etta explained as she helped Katherine slip into her nightie. "You don't want to sleep on the couch in the living room, do you?"

"No!" Katherine said emphatically.

She and Aunt Etta got into bed at the same time and Etta pulled the string. She had a ceiling light, which had been made to turn on and off with a pull chain; the room had not been wired with a wall switch when the house was first built. For convenience, she had Uncle John tie a string on the end of the pull chain and made it long enough to drape down and tie to the poster nearest to her head. That way, all she had to do was reach over and pull on the string to turn out the light after she got into bed. On any other night, Katherine would have gotten a big kick out of such a simple little invention; however, tonight she lay stiff as a board not even noticing how the light went out. She couldn't relax. She was tense and stiff wondering if she was lying on the same side of the bed that her mother had been laying when she died. She thought about asking Aunt Etta, but then she thought that maybe she really didn't want to know after all. Then she wondered if Aunt Etta had changed the sheets; she hoped that she had. It was hard lying in the same bed in which her mother had died that very morning, and knowing her mother was lying in the coffin in the living room freshly embalmed. Katherine closed her eyes tight, said a little prayer; finally, her exhaustion gave way and she drifted off.

Morning came. More visitors came and went; more food was brought. Mr. Carter checked in on them to see if everything was all right and went over the funeral plans with Aunt Etta.

"Have you talked to Pastor Shives?" Mr. Carter asked as he inspected the corpse to make sure everything was in place and to see how the body was holding up. Pastor Levi Shives was the minister of the Methodist church in Chattanooga, which had been the Tomas family church for decades.

"Yes, he was here last night for prayers," Aunt Etta informed him.

The funeral was going to be held in the Rock Springs Methodist Church in Rock Springs, Georgia, with the internment in the family plot next to the church. Rock Springs was just over the Tennessee line and the family's ancestry went back and forth between Tennessee and Georgia in that immediate area since 1837.

The following morning dawned and Katherine was relieved it was time for the funeral. She couldn't wait to get the coffin out of the living room; she was so tired of the company, the food and the chatter. She couldn't wait for it all to be over.

"Aunt Etta, I see Mr. Carter coming," Katherine yelled as she saw the black hearse turn the corner.

"Here come Aunt Lilly and Aunt Jimmie too," she called out.

"Okay, honey," Etta returned; she put on the jacket that matched her black dress.

Mr. Carter, Willie and Pastor Shives came in the house and greeted everyone.

"Are we all set here, Miss Tomas?' the pastor asked.

"No, more will be coming," John answered instead.

Within the next twenty minutes the rest of May's siblings had arrived.

As he moved to one side of the casket, Mr. Carter whispered softly, as if he was in a church.

"Okay, let's all gather around May for one last viewing; perhaps each one can say their own goodbye."

His hands were clasped behind his back; his glance spanned each one of them. Etta, June, Katherine, Lilly, Jimmie, Ila Louise, Terah and their spouses stood in a half circle in front of May's coffin. Solemn and still they looked at May and wondered why they lost their sister at such a young age. Etta stepped forward and laid her hand on May's cold hands.

"Goodbye, May, honey, you have a home in heaven now." She wiped away the tear that ran down her cheek.

June and John stepped up arm and arm as June held a handkerchief to her mouth to muffle her crying. They looked for a few minutes then stepped back because June wasn't able to speak. Lilly and Russell Stevenson were standing closest to the head of the coffin; with one short step they were next to May's head. Lilly reached in the casket and gently stroked May's fiery, red hair; she said goodbye to her sister. Jimmie and her husband, Bryon Engle, went up next. She bent over May.

"God bless you, May, I'm so sorry." She stepped back.

Everyone heard her apology and they all knew what it was for. Margie and Bennett Williams were next in line. May and Margie were the two oldest and they had been very close growing up. It was Margie that knew about May's hopes and dreams.

"May, dear, I hope you are finally at peace," Margie whispered, she choked back the tears.

Terah Tomas clung to his wife's hand as they went up to the coffin. Terah was the only boy in the family of nine children. Terah and Rudy stood motionless in front of May as he tried to hide the tears from his wife and sisters. Ila and Clive Gracy took their turn beside the coffin. Ila patted May's hand and fussed with the handkerchief that had been placed in between her fingers.

"I'll miss you, May, honey. I'll see you in heaven." Her voice began to crack so she stepped back in line.

Louise was the baby of the family and she was the last of May's siblings to say goodbye. Louise had a hard time letting her oldest sister go because May had often times been a mother figure to her. Louise's husband, Leon Jones, put his arm around his wife's shoulder as she buried her head in his chest.

"Good bye, May," which was barely audible through her sobbing.

Katherine was the only one left to say goodbye. She felt afraid, she didn't know if she really wanted to go closer to the casket, but she wanted to say goodbye to her mother. She was frozen in place, unable to move. However, her dear Aunt Etta came to her rescue; she moved closer and took Katherine by the shoulders.

"Come on, honey, I'll go with you." They walked up to the casket together.

"Goodbye, mommy," Katherine said as her tears began to flow.

Etta and the rest could hardly bear the sight of this little, thin, twelve-year-old having to tell her mother goodbye. It was such a sorrowful moment and none of them would ever forget it.

Mr. Carter and Willie moved around in front of the group and began preparations to close the lid of the coffin, which would snuff out the flames of May's existence forever. Willie walked back and forth tucking the red velvet lining in around the edges of the coffin like a fireman checking to make sure that all of the flames were out before he could leave the scene; Mr. Carter slowly lowered the lid and locked it. The pastor prayed that May's soul would finally be at peace.

By the time the little ceremony had been completed the pallbearers had arrived. They filed in and moved around the coffin and took hold of their respective gold handle. Aunt Etta's house has a very high porch with many steeps steps; the six men looked awkward as they held tightly to the coffin handles and struggled down the steps to the hearse.

Uncle John rode in the front seat of the hearse with Mr. Carter, while Aunt June, Johnny, Aunt Etta and Katherine rode in the black Cadillac with Willie. Katherine's brother, Raymond, brought his own car so he and Dennis rode together directly behind the Cadillac. The rest of the family followed along in their own cars. The funeral procession wasn't very long, just the hearse, the car for the family and several others. The trip to Rock Springs would have normally taken about thirty minutes, but going slow in the procession made the trip about fifty minutes.

Katherine sat in the nice comfortable car and stared out the window. The route took them through town but she didn't pay much attention. They rode past the town's only theater and the marquee caught her eye. It read *The Road to Singapore* staring William Powell. She didn't know where Singapore was and she didn't know who William Powell was, but she thought that sounded nice. She would have liked to be on the road to somewhere; anywhere but on this road going to the cemetery to bury her mother.

Rock Springs was just as beautiful as it sounded. It was a rural town and the church sat in the middle of a wooded area; it was built like the typical New England church, rectangular and painted white with a tall steeple.

The sun was bright that day; as it shown down on the white-washed church, it caused an awe-inspiring glow, which was contrasted by the dark green trees of the forest. The bright blue sky was its heavenly ceiling.

Azaleas were planted around the church and they were in full bloom. The shocking pink blossoms were striking against the white building; the trees that were closest to the church, as well as the ones that lined the clearing, dripped with Spanish moss. Katherine sat with her face pressed against the car window and watched this scene come closer and closer. It looked like a dream. She was glad that her mother was going to be buried at this spot, and at this time of the year; she thought nowhere in the world could spring be more beautiful than in the South.

The vehicles pulled up to the church and stopped. The doors of the hearse opened, which signaled everyone else to get out of their cars. The mourners stood around and talked while the pallbearer performed their task.

There was a slight breeze and it felt good against Katherine's face. She could feel her hair being tossed as she watched the Spanish moss gently sway; for a brief moment she felt relaxed.

"Yes this is a prefect spot for mama," she whispered.

Everyone filed in after the coffin. Katherine could smell the wonderful azaleas as she walked past them; she took one last whiff and then a deep breath before she went into the church. It was a typical country church inside with a simple cross at the front of a plain altar. There were wooden pews and a wooden floor, both of which looked quite worn, but that was comforting to Katherine. The thing that struck her the most was the breath taking stained glass windows. She hadn't noticed the windows when she looked at the church from the outside; however, from the inside they were lit up by the sunshine and, oh, how mesmerizing they were. Before she knew it, the service was over.

The pallbearers carried May's coffin down the church aisle, out the door and toward the cemetery. A wrought iron fence, which was badly in need of repair, surrounded the entire cemetery. It was obvious it had been there a long time and hadn't been tended to as well as the churchyard, which was unimportant as the mourners filed through the rickety gate.

May's grave had already been dug by the black gravedigger, who was standing off to the side waiting to finish his job. This was the first funeral Katherine had ever been to and she was sad, fascinated, curious, and appalled all at the same time. Everyone gathered around May as the minister said a prayer. They watched as the pallbearers lowered her casket into the ground with the straps that had been lying across the deep, dark hole. Pastor Shives read May's favorite bible verse, John 14:1.

Katherine heard the preacher say, "Let not your hearts be troubled." All anyone ever wished for May was that her heart not be troubled.

The service was concluded when Pastor Shives read a verse which Etta had requested; one which she clung to for comfort because she knew her sister couldn't help her illness. Pastor Shives read Psalm 116:15, "Precious in the sight of the Lord is the death of his saints."

Before leaving the graveside, each person picked up a handful of dirt and tossed it into the hole. It sounded like rain on a tin roof as the dirt peppered the top of the casket. Katherine was curious, but not curious enough to walk closer to look in. Etta walked over to the grave and picked up some dirt.

"Katherine, get a hand full," she coaxed.

"No. I don't want to do that," Katherine winced.

"Yes, come on now, I think you should do this. It's tradition," Etta explained.

"Hold my hand so I don't slip and fall in the hole," Katherine said as she held Aunt Etta's hand so tight that it hurt her aunt's fingers.

She reluctantly picked up a handful of dirt, tossed it in and watched it slide across the top of her mother's casket. As Katherine looked over the edge of the hole, she shivered; she jumped backwards and nearly fell.

"Okay, honey, let's go to the car now, you've been through enough today." Aunt Etta put her arm around Katherine's shoulder.

Katherine was glad to hear those words; she was glad it was all over. Exhausted, Katherine slept on the way home.

The black gravedigger filled the hole with dirt and placed a spray of flowers on the mound to finish his job.

Chapter 4

A scream from Judy jarred Katherine out of her memory and she was glad to be free of it. She looked over at the two girls to see what they were doing. To her relief, it had been a playful scream.

Katherine got up to stretch her legs; she lit a cigarette and walked closer to the car to see if Miles was still asleep; he was. He hadn't been asleep very long so she left him alone. There was a boulder near the blanket so she sat down on it to finish her cigarette. She was hungry and all she could think about was Aunt Etta's carrot cake. Katherine's memory found her back in her aunt's kitchen.

After her mother's funeral, Katherine settled in at Aunt Etta's and tried to make it feel like home. School would be out soon and she would have all summer to play, forget, and move on; happily, she was on her way to doing just that. Katherine liked Aunt Etta's house; she was especially glad that it was in the city; she didn't like the country. The house sat on a hill and there were at least fifteen steps to climb to reach the large porch. It was an old house, which appeared to be large, but once inside, it was surprising to see that the rooms were very small. The ceilings were very high and covered with white tin squares that had been stamped with a most delicate floral pattern. The floors were covered with large area rugs and waxed hardwood was visible where the rugs did not cover. Katherine liked the creaking sound the floors made when she walked on them.

The living room was long and narrow; it served as the main sitting room at one end; the dinning room was at the other. Aunt Etta kept her china cabinet in the living room directly across from the couch. Katherine loved to sit on the couch with her cat, Snowball, and look at the china cabinet. Etta kept the glassed in area filled with colorful ribbons and bows, which she respectfully plucked from funeral arrangements that were left at the church after the services were over. Katherine sat for hours and stared at the ribbons and thought about what she could make with them. Mostly she thought about making hats. She thought that was funny because she didn't even like to wear hats, but she liked to think about making them.

There was a door on both sides of the china cabinet, which lead into the two bedrooms. The four-poster beds were always neatly made because the inside of the rooms were visible from the living room. At the far end of the living room sat the fine mahogany dinning room set; on the farthest wall hung an oblong mirror, which was suspended from a long gold rope attached near the ceiling. The mirror lay at a tilt so that the table setting shown in its refection. Aunt Etta had inherited the china cabinet, dining room set and the mirror. The Tomas siblings were not too happy about their sister receiving the furniture, but she was the only one that didn't have a husband to buy her nice thing like that, so they kept quiet.

The kitchen was at the very back of the house and stretched almost across the whole width of the structure. There was a door adjacent to the three, double sash windows, which led out onto a screened in porch. Aunt Etta kept the trash out there. Katherine didn't like to take out the garbage because there were usually large black ants crawling all over the greasy bags. She hated bugs.

Evidence of Katherine's contented adjustment showed in her little habit of skipping from the front door all the way to the kitchen for a snack when she got home from school. She had even adjusted to sleeping in the bed where her mother died. Katherine liked it when Aunt Etta let her pull the string to turn out the light; it made her feel special; and she longed to feel special to someone.

At the same time, Katherine began to build a special relationship with her cousin, Johnny, eight years her junior. They got along very well; he was as gentle and easygoing as his father, dear Uncle John; Katherine loved Uncle John. Aunt June was another story; she was quite high strung. However, Katherine managed to keep from upsetting her too much and the household was congenial. This was good for Katherine; the stability had a calming effect on her and her stomach.

Katherine especially loved the evenings when she and Aunt Etta sat close to each other on the couch; Katherine snuggled while her aunt read passages from the Bible. This was a favorite time for both of them; this was the closest Katherine was ever going to get to having a mother again, and it was the closet her aunt was ever going to get to having a child.

Aunt Etta was a wonderful cook and very accomplished in crocheting and embroidering, and she was an avid reader. Katherine never showed much interest in crocheting, embroidering or reading, but she did enjoy cooking and baking;

she caught on very quickly. Her favorite thing to bake was Aunt Etta's carrot cake. It was a luscious dessert baked with large pieces of walnuts, and frosted with a smooth cream cheese frosting. Katherine liked it served with peach ice cream. She thought it should only be served with peach ice cream. It was preferable to have homemade ice cream, and the only thing that would be more heavenly than that, was to have homemade snow ice cream. Snow ice cream was made by actually mixing newly fallen snow with the heavy cream to make the delightful dessert. Of course, snow ice cream was a rare treat because it seldom snowed in Tennessee; but, if it did, she and Aunt Etta would make snow ice cream. Either way, she loved Aunt Etta's carrot cake. The smell of it baking warmed her; it became the smell of home.

One day, about three weeks after school started in the fall, Katherine waited in the schoolyard for the school bus to come and take her and her friend's home. She heard someone call her name.

"Katherine," she heard; she turned around to see who had said it. She didn't recognize anyone, nor could she decipher where the voice came from.

"Katherine," she heard again. This time she could tell that the voice came from a shinny, black, 1931 Cadillac with a man and a woman sitting in the front seat, and a little boy in the back. The man leaned his head out the window and motioned for her to come over to the car. She didn't know who this man was, or so she didn't think she knew him, but then again, maybe she did. Her little friends asked her who that man was.

"I don't know," she replied as she tried hard to search her memory. She began to suspect who it was, but it had been such a long time.

"Katherine, come over here for a few minutes. I'm your daddy. Don't you remember me?" Sam called out as she turned toward him looking confused.

"If that's your daddy, why don't you go over to him?" her little friend asked. Katherine shrugged her shoulders.

"I don't know," she said looking at the ground and kicking at the few pebbles that were scattered about.

"Come on, Katherine, I just want to talk to you, that's all." Sam spoke gently as he tried to ease her fears.

Katherine didn't know what to do. She was a little afraid; then again, she was a little curious, especially about the little boy in the back seat.

"Come on," he coaxed.

She stopped thinking about the little boy and started toward the car; she was perplexed that she didn't remember her father looking like that. After all, she was only five when her parents divorced. Katherine knew her mother had kept a few pictures of her dad; however, she had torn up most of them. Katherine stood a few more moments and thought *is this the man that made mama so upset and made her cry all the time?* Her young mind remembered the face on the torn up pictures as they were thrown across the room; now she realized that it was the same face looking at her from the car window. She took her time walking over to the car where Sam had his arms stretched out of the window ready to take hold of her hand. She stopped when she got close enough to be just short of his reach.

"Hi, Kat, honey," he said with a big smile, which showed a mouth full of big, white teeth. *Kat*, she thought to herself, *who's that?* Why is he calling me Kat? No one ever called me that before.

"What do you want?" she asked, still standing just outside of his reach.

"I just wanted to come to see you and see how you were doing, that's all," he answered, trying to sound like a concerned father.

She stood silent for a few seconds looking down at the ground; finally she got the nerve to speak.

"Mama died," she said with her head lowered; she looked up from beneath her brow and sniffled.

"I know, honey, and I'm real sorry about that. Are you doing okay at Aunt Etta's?" he asked, still trying to sound concerned.

"Auntie says she died of a broken heart."

Sam didn't know what to say; he looked over at his second wife, Lillian. They looked at each other for a few moments. They knew they were adulterers; Lillian had known Sam was married. They also knew their infidelity had broken up Katherine's happy home. It may not have been a happy home for Sam or May, but it was happy to a five-year-old little girl. They tried to shrug off the guilt as Sam attempted to lighten up the moment.

"This is your stepmama, Lillian," Sam said as he introduced his second wife.

Lillian leaned over him so she could be closer to the window. "Hi, Katherine, I'm glad to finally meet you."

Katherine felt her insides tighten up. Her little mind thought *so that's her, the lady from the bus stop; the lady that took my daddy away, the lady that caused my mama to have a broken heart.* She really didn't want to say anything to this lady; she simply looked at her.

"Can you say *hi* to your stepmama?" Sam said sternly; the question sounded more like an order.

Katherine managed to squeak out a soft little, "hi," as she glanced in the car window. As she did, she saw something that she hadn't noticed before; Lillian was holding a little boy. *Two little boys* she thought to herself.

Lillian saw this glance and promptly took advantage of the moment.

"These are your two half brothers, Sunny," pointing to the boy on her lap, "and Stanley," turning her head toward the back.

"Say, hi, to your sister, boys," their mama coaxed.

Sunny fidgeted in Lillian's lap but Stanley managed a soft little, "hi." He sounded no more enthused than Katherine had.

By this time Katherine's mind raced. *Brothers! No one ever told me I had brothers!* Just as Katherine tried to register all of this new information, the school bus pulled up.

'The bus is here, I have to go," she said hurriedly.

"Okay," Sam called out. "Can we come to see you again tomorrow?"

Katherine thought about his request. "I guess so, if you want to." She headed toward the bus.

"Oh, Kat," Sam called out. Katherine stopped and looked back at him.

"Let's keep this just between us. Don't say anything to your Aunt Etta about me coming here, okay?"

Katherine didn't reply. She turned and ran to the bus and up the steps.

She had a very uneasy ride home. All sorts of questions ran through her head. Why did her daddy suddenly show up? What did he want? Why didn't someone tell her that she had brothers? Why was he coming to the schoolyard instead of Aunt Etta's house? And why didn't her daddy want her to tell Aunt Etta? She hadn't felt this confused in a long time; she didn't like it. But, for now, she didn't say anything to Aunt Etta, and the next day her father was at the schoolyard.

Sam parked by the bus pickup. He continued to do this a couple of times a week; Lillian and the boys were always with him, and with each visit, Katherine began to feel more comfortable around her stepmother and half brothers. They were so nice to her that she began to feel less and less angry with her dad and stepmother; slowly the past felt farther and farther away. She liked the attention that Sam and Lillian showed her; she actually looked forward to the schoolyard visits, and she still had not told Aunt Etta anything about it.

After about a month, Sam stopped coming to the school. From then on, Lillian and the boys came alone. One day early in October Lillian popped the question.

"Katherine, how would you like to come and live with us? Would you like that?"

Katherine was stunned. She didn't know what to say. She didn't know what to think. She looked at Lillian with her mouth opened.

"I don't know. I don't know what Aunt Etta would say," Katherine replied a little perplexed.

"Well, why don't you think about it for a while? Your daddy has a good job so we can provide for you a lot better than your Aunt Etta can. You can have your own bedroom and we can get you some pretty new dresses," Lillian said, clearly trying to tempt her young mind with all the things she knew Katherine didn't have, but wanted.

Katherine was wide eyed as she thought how great it all sounded. It was time to get on the bus so she started to leave.

"Now you think about what I said, okay?" Lillian called out.

"Okay," Katherine yelled back. She bounced away feeling giddy with the idea her stepmother had planted in her head.

Chapter 5

▼

Whatever plans Sam and Lillian had concocted, it worked. Katherine sat on the school bus and thought about whether she should say something to Aunt Etta, or not. If she was going to live with her daddy, she was going to have to tell her Aunt. Katherine remembered the promise Aunt Etta had made to her mother. She remembered her mother making Aunt Etta promise not to let Sam take her away. But surly Aunt Etta wouldn't mind if she wanted to live with her daddy. "After all," Katherine said to herself with a smile, "he said he loved me and wanted me to be with him." She began to formulate a plan of action if her aunt protested, which Katherine knew she surly would.

Katherine sat on the boulder and stared off into the blue haze; she felt sad. She knew she was heading toward something very painful. Were her actions those of a spoiled child or simply a desperate child seeking love from her father? Sam had filled her head with such wonderful promises, she just couldn't refuse; and Sam's charm was irresistible.

Sam was a tall thin man with sandy blonde hair and blue eyes. His face was narrow with a slightly long thin nose and he had a big warm smile. He wore round, wire-rimmed glasses, which made him look handsome and scholarly; when he wore his straw hat he was the sharpest man on the block. It was easy to see why Lillian had been attracted to him. Sam worked hard and provided well for his family; he did mechanic jobs on the side at night. He loved the newly invented automobiles and he enjoyed working on them, and he was good at it. If anyone in town needed a good mechanic, they called on Sam. He was also a big fisherman; he loved nothing better than to catch a mess of fish and invite all the neighbors over to share in a fish fry. He and Lillian were also fond of square dancing. They belonged to a dance group that met once a week, usually at one of the members' houses, one that had enough room to hold at least four pairs of dancers. If the caller was not available, Sam would oblige.

Sam loved the children from his first marriage; actually, he had loved their mother too; sadly, May had become so difficult and so depressed that they turned away from each other. She had turned away from him in the bed and he had turned away from trying to be patient with her.

Actually, Sam had no intention of violating his marriage vows; but that day at the bus stop, when Lillian began to flirt with him, and made him feel desirable, he realized that he liked the feeling; he had missed it. It didn't take long for Sam to become totally under Lillian's spell; he was in love again. He knew it wasn't right with society; he knew it wasn't right in the eyes of God, but he simply couldn't help himself. He agonized over breaking up his marriage and what it would do to the children; however, in the end, he chose Lillian.

Sam suffered terrible pangs of guilt during the first several years of their marriage, but he was able to bury them deep inside as long as he had young, lovely Lillian. As long as he had her he could take the disdain and hatred he got from May's family, the Tomas'. He could take the whispers all around him on Sunday morning when he and Lillian sat in the pew; he could take it when the preacher looked him right in the eyes when the message was about adultery. He was even able to dismiss from his mind the three children he left behind; however, the one thing he could not do was say *no* to Lillian. No matter how strong he had been in his life, Lillian was his one weakness.

Lillian, on the other hand, was not weak at all. She was a mere twenty-five years old when she and Sam met, fourteen years younger than him, and she held her head high with arrogant confidence. She had a stylish short bob hair-do and a young, slim figure; Sam was smitten with her.

Lillian's family was very upset that she got involved with a married man. Her two sisters, Corrine and Po preached at her constantly about the wrong she was doing. Lillian threw her nose up in the air and let them all talk. She knew what she wanted and nothing was going to stop her from getting it, even if someone got hurt along the way. She knew Sam was teetering on the edge of breaking up his marriage anyway, so she became determined to give him the extra push he needed to end it. She and Sam married in 1940; from then on he catered to her every whim.

Katherine sat on the rock trembling. The memory of her father catering to her stepmother drove her crazy. She hated it, simply hated it! She simply couldn't understand why her father always pampered Lillian, but not her. She closed her eyes and gritted her teeth. She felt sorry for herself, so, so sorry. Those thoughts had haunted her for many years and they fueled her feeling of inadequacy to the point of neurosis. Katherine had tried to forget. She had tried to put it behind her. She had tried to move on and be happy, as a teenager, as a young woman, and then as a mother. Sadly, she never could come to terms with the fact that her father let Lillian treat her the way she did. Katherine took a long drag on her cigarette and she mumbled to herself.

"It wasn't right. I was his only daughter. It was a damn, dirty shame that he let it happen."

Chapter 6

▼

As bad as they were, her memories continued. The wind picked up and blew the cigarette smoke back in her face. She hoped the mixture of the cigarette smoke and the mountain haze would cloud her memory, but it didn't; her painful journey went on.

It was the day that she decided to tell Aunt Etta about the schoolyard meetings and her desire to go live with her father.

It was mid October and Katherine sat at the kitchen table having breakfast before catching the school bus. Aunt Etta sat down at the table with her.

"Katherine, it's almost Halloween. What kind of costume would you like to wear?"

She had been so preoccupied the last few weeks that she hadn't thought much about what kind of costume she wanted for the Halloween party in town.

"I don't know," she said looking down at her cereal bowl. Etta tried to lift her mood by making a suggestion.

"How would you like to be a princess?"

The suggestion worked; her eyes widened with a smile. She liked that idea. She would like to be a princess. In fact, she had always fantasized about being a princess. That would be perfect.

"Yes, Auntie, I would like to go as a princess. Can you make the costume?" Katherine asked with excitement in her voice.

"I can get Aunt Lilly to help me," Etta told her, "and you can even help. You need to start learning how to sew anyway."

This conversation seemed to put Katherine in a much better mood. She finished her cereal and decided not to say anything to Aunt Etta about leaving.

"Here is your lunch," Etta said, holding a brown paper bag. Katherine hurried over and took the bag out of Etta's hand. She reached up and gave her aunt a hug good-by, just as she did every morning. As their cheeks touched, so did their thoughts. Katherine knew she was going to have to tell Aunt Etta very soon about what was going on, and Katherine could see that Etta knew she had something to tell. As Katherine pulled away from the embrace, their eyes met for a brief moment; in that moment they saw into each other's souls; they silently agreed to talk later.

Katherine sat on the school bus trying to decide when she was going to tell Aunt Etta; she decided that definitely she would tell her after school. At lunchtime Katherine ate her lunch in a hurry so she could go outside on the playground to see if her father or stepmother had come for a visit on such a wonderful autumn day. She didn't see either one anywhere; she felt surprisingly disappointed. She wanted to tell Lillian and her father about her choice of costume for the Halloween party and to ask them if they were going to be there. She was even thinking about costumes for her half brothers. She thought Stanley could be a cowboy, he was plenty big enough for that, and since Sunny was still so little, he would make a good puppy dog. She wanted to tell them her ideas. After school was out for the day, Katherine quietly rode home on the bus; she had so much to think about. Her thoughts went back and forth between how to tell Aunt Etta about her father and about the upcoming Halloween celebration. Her twelve-year-old spirit chose to think more about the latter.

Chattanooga always had a huge Halloween celebration in the middle of town. The police blocked off all the roads leading into town so there was no automobile traffic and people could walk around on the streets safely. The city council planned activities and games for the children and various groups planned to have treats and cider for refreshments. The children participated in a costume parade, which went down the main street in town; this was the highlight of the whole celebration.

Katherine was anxious to get started on her costume. She hoped that Aunt Lilly could help. Lilly worked in a fashionable dress shop in town and was up on all of the latest fashions; if anyone could give some good advice on what would be appropriate for a princess' dress it was Aunt Lilly. She also did some sewing, so she could help with that part too. Katherine softly gasped as a thought popped into her mind.

"Maybe Aunt Etta will let me use some of the ribbons in the curio cabinet to decorate my dress. Those beautiful ribbons would make it look like a real princess' dress."

She couldn't wait to get home to tell Aunt Etta about her idea. Suddenly her mood changed; she remembered she had planned to tell her aunt about something else when she got home. Oh, but it was much more fun to think about her costume than to think about the confrontation that awaited her.

One of the girls that Katherine had become a good friend with, Aline Narcissus, moved over to sit next to her on the school bus.

"Hi, Katherine," Aline said. "What are you doing sitting here all by yourself?"

"Oh, nothing, I was just thinking about my Halloween costume, that's all," Katherine responded as she scooted over so Aline could sit down.

"Oh yea, what are you going to be?" Aline questioned as she slipped into the seat.

"I'm going to be a princess," Katherine said with her nose up in the air hoping her friend would feel jealous.

"Really?" Aline gasped with envy in her voice.

"Yes I am. My aunt is going to make it for me. What are you going to be?" Katherine asked her little friend.

"I think I will go as an old lady. I can use some of my grandma's old clothes. That will be easy and it won't cost anything," Aline replied with a sigh, thinking that Katherine's costume idea sounded so much better.

Aline came from a family that tried to make a living off a small farm outside of town; they were considered country folk. With the depression coming on and money tight, Aline's family had to make the best of things. Katherine's little friend knew this and she was willing to compromise her Halloween costume this year. Katherine, on the other hand, did not like compromise; she took special pride in the fact that her family was considered city folk; already she had realized the importance of appearances.

Aline Narcissus was a happy, ebullient child in spite of her family's economic situation, and no where near as moody as Katherine. The school bus pulled up to the first stop and Aline jumped up.

"Well, I've got to go, I'll see you tomorrow, Katherine." She hopped off the bus and skipped down the road toward her farm.

Katherine watched her until the bus pulled away. The closer the bus got to her house the tighter her stomach became. She thought about how she was going to bring up the subject with her aunt. How was she going to start? She didn't want her aunt to think that she didn't love her or that she wasn't happy with her. She didn't want to hurt her aunt's feelings; at the same time, she really wanted to do this. Surly Aunt Etta would understand that she should have all of the things her father and stepmother promised her.

Katherine arrived home first, as she always did; Aunt Etta didn't get home from her job at the post office until a little past 4 o'clock. Aunt June always had an after school snack prepared for her when she got home; that was mainly because she gave her son, Johnny, a snack at that time. Katherine sat at the kitchen table and took her time with her juice and cookies while she waited for her aunt to get home. The cookies and juice didn't set too well on her stomach; it had been in knots all day. Katherine sat quietly, fidgeting with the crumbs on her plate going over and over in her mind how she was going to start the conversation. She fed Snowball some of her cookie crumbs as she looked around the room; she liked living with her aunt; however, she really, really wanted to go live with her dad. Maybe Auntie was wrong about her dad being so bad. He didn't seem so bad. So far he had been pretty nice; she hoped her aunt would understand.

Katherine was deep in thought when the sound of the front door opening caused her to jolt back to reality. Aunt Etta walked in the house and took off her jacket. She headed toward her bedroom to hang it up because there was no coat closet in the living room.

"Hello, everyone."

"Hi, Ettie," June responded, preoccupied with cleaning up Johnny after his snack.

"Hi," Katherine said softly.

"How was your day at school, honey?" she asked walking past Katherine and into the kitchen

"Fine," Katherine whispered as Etta disappeared around the corner.

"Aunt Etta," Katherine called out in a low voice.

Etta was in the kitchen but she heard the soft summons. She walked out with a glass of juice. Katherine could see that her aunt was stiff, that she suspected something bad. Etta took a deep breath and sat down at the table. Katherine caught June stealing a glance at them as she and Johnny went out on the porch to sit on the swing. She and Aunt Etta were in the room all alone.

"Did you call me, dear?" Etta questioned gently.

"Yes," Katherine said; she couldn't look up.

"What is it Katherine?" Etta asked; she reached out and placed her hand on Katherine's little hand.

"I know something has been bothering you, honey; tell me what it is."

Katherine didn't know how to start. She hesitated, still searching for the right words. She looked up at her aunt and their eyes joined in the uneasiness of the moment. She still said nothing. It wasn't that she was second-guessing her decision to go live with her dad; it was that she was afraid of her aunt's reaction; she was afraid of seeing the hurt on her aunt's face. With one last pause, Katherine got up the courage to speak.

"I've been having some visitors at my school," she said so softly that her aunt barely heard her.

Etta pulled her hand off of Katherine's and questioned her with suspicion.

"Visitors? Who?"

"Daddy," Katherine said in a whisper. Etta took in a gasp of air.

"Who? Your father?" she screeched. Etta's mouth hung open; she was stunned. She asked Katherine the question again just to make sure she heard it right.

"You mean your father has been coming to your school in secret to visit you?"

"Yes, and Lillian, his new wife, and my two half-brother too," Katherine confessed shyly.

"What? His new wife? He brought that woman to your school to visit you?" Etta said in a voice that was a pitch higher than normal.

"Well, of all the things that I thought could have been bothering you, I never would have guessed this. I can't believe it," Etta said with disappointment. "How dare Sam Williamson sneak around to see you after all of the misery he put you and your mother through? How dare him, and not even to call and ask me if it was okay." Aunt Etta shook with anger. "And the nerve of him to bring that woman from the bus stop with him; the nerve of that man!"

There was an uncomfortable silence.

"Katherine, I can't believe you kept this a secret from me. Why didn't you tell me?" Aunt Etta asked, clearly starting to shake. "How long has this been going on?"

"About a month; right after school started," Katherine informed her.

Katherine saw how upset her aunt was and she hadn't even told her the most important part yet.

"Well, why did they start coming to see you? What do they want?" Aunt Etta was obviously puzzled. Katherine stared at her aunt; she was afraid to say the words.

"Well," she paused for a few seconds, which felt like minutes, "they want me to come and live with them," Katherine finally blurted out.

"They what!" Aunt Etta shouted.

June had been listening from the porch; at hearing Etta shout, she now stood in the doorway.

"They want you to live with them?" Etta repeated in disbelief.

Katherine sat motionless waiting for her aunt to calm down. With as controlled a voice as she could, Aunt Etta reminded Katherine of a sacred promise.

"You know, Katherine, your mother wanted you to stay with me. Her dying wish was for me to raise you, not your dad. I can't go against your mother; it wouldn't be right. I just can't. It is out of the question," Etta said as she sat at the table with her hand over her mouth; she fought back the tears.

Katherine knew her aunt was upset but she went ahead with her arguments.

"Why can't I go live with them? They said that they wanted me to come live with them so they can give me all the things that I should have. Daddy has a good job and he can buy me things," Katherine said selfishly. "And I can get to know my half-brothers too."

"Katherine, I can't let you do that."

"Please, please can I go to live with them?" Katherine begged; she looked at her aunt ready to turn on the tears.

"Does your brother, Dennis, know about this?"

"No," Katherine admitted.

"I want to talk to him. He knows what your Mother's wishes were. I want him to know about this. I'll call him after supper," Etta stated more forceful than Katherine ever remembered her aunt being.

Katherine couldn't figure out why Aunt Etta wanted to call Dennis. He didn't have anything to do with it. She knew she had one last argument so she jumped at the chance to use it.

"You and Elmer might want to get married some day. I don't think he wants me around anyway. This way you two can get married and be alone," Katherine told her shocked aunt.

"Why, Katherine, why would you say such a thing?"

"I know Elmer doesn't want me around. I've heard you guys talking," Katherine said.

"Katherine, that's not so," Aunt Etta said, aghast with the realization that her niece had over heard her and Elmer's conversations.

"Yes it is, auntie, you know it is," Katherine shot back.

Even at her tender age, Katherine had already begun to learn how to make someone feel sorry for her, and to cast guilt, when appropriate, to get what she wanted. It was true that Aunt Etta has spoiled her; however, it wasn't enough to fill Katherine's need for the precious attention she craved. At the same time, Katherine still searched for her Knight in Shinning Armor; the one she had fantasized about from the time she sat on the train with her mother, wanting someone to carry her away to happiness; in her young mind, her dad was that knight.

Etta was powerless next to Katherine's pleading, and Katherine could see it. However, just in case she needed more persuasion, she figured that she had one more option. If Aunt Etta called her brother, Dennis, she would simply have to get him on her side. He could help persuade their aunt to let her go.

It was true that Etta and Elmer Best had casually talked about marriage and a family; and it was true that he had asked Etta why she felt she had to raise Katherine instead of one of the other sisters. Etta knew that he didn't like the idea of starting off a new marriage raising someone else's teenager. Actually, she hadn't seen as much of Elmer in the past year because of May and Katherine moving in with her, the funeral, and then getting Katherine adjusted. He was not fond of the whole idea; at the same time, they stayed interested in each other.

She and Elmer had met while singing in the church choir five years prior to May's death. Etta and Elmer were in their late twenties when they began to develop a relationship. Elmer was a veteran of WWI and Etta admired him for having served in the Great War.

When WWI started in Europe in 1914 there were rumors that the U.S. would eventually inter the war. Elmer, a young man at that time, continuously thought about enlisting in the army if indeed the country did go to war. In 1917, when Elmer was twenty years old, President Woodrow Wilson issued his declaration of war and Elmer Best enlisted in the U.S. army. After his basic training, he was stationed at Fort Oglethorpe, Georgia. The day after Congress declared war, President Wilson issued a proclamation that essentially restricted the conduct of alien enemies in the United States. There were twelve regulations to this proclamation with the twelfth one being the most serious, which stated in part ... *an alien enemy whom there may be reasonable cause to believe to be abiding or about to aid the enemy ... will be subject to arrest ... and to confinement in such prison or military camp.*

The Department of the Treasury and the Department of Labor performed the arrests and then the prisoners were transferred to the War Department. Most of the people arrested were officers and seaman serving aboard German naval and merchant vessels anchored in American ports, but also arrested were wealthy German aliens as well as citizens of German descent and Austro-Hungarian aliens. Originally these prisoners were held in a camp in North Carolina; however, when that camp was closed the War Department opened the War Prison Barracks #2 at Fort Oglethorpe. There were two other Prison Barracks, but Fort Oglethorpe held the largest population of enemy aliens of the three prisons. Because of the large population of prisoners at Fort Oglethorpe, the War Department stationed 32 commissioned officers and 452 enlisted men as guards. Elmer Best was one of those guards. When Elmer enlisted in the army he thought, even hoped, that he would be sent to Europe. He wanted to see combat. He never imagined that he would be stationed just twenty miles from his home; but, he did his duty admirably.

To his surprise, as he developed relationships with the prisoners, he realized that most of them were not enemies of the United States at all. He was astonished to learn that many of the prisoners were thankful that they were in the war camp, which ironically protected them from irate citizens that thought they were enemies of the United States.

WWI ended on November 11, 1918, and the war prison barracks ceased its operation on June 30, 1920. Elmer had served his four years and he was discharged from the army. To his surprise, he had become interested in a young German girl who had been arrested along with her parents. She was just fourteen when she came to the camp and during the four years as her guard, Elmer had grown very fond of her. After the camp had disbanded and all of the prisoners had left, he missed the young German girl. He thought about her often; he even thought about investigating her whereabouts, but something stopped him. He knew that Germans were not looked upon very kindly at that time and he didn't know if he wanted a girlfriend, or possible wife, that society treated that way. He didn't know if he was strong enough to handle the prejudices. He decided to keep his desire for her a secret and move on with his life.

Elmer had been absorbed in securing his job and Etta had been preoccupied with helping sick family members, so their relationship moved slowly. Gradually, Elmer began to think about settling down with Etta and she was happy with the thought of a life with him. That was when May got sick and moved in with her. Of course, Etta could not say *no*. She had been raised with the value system that *family takes care of family*; there wasn't any other decision to be made.

Katherine sat on a rock on the side of the road and remembered how she and her mother got to Aunt Etta's in the first place. She was appalled at the memory.

It was at the end of May's travels; she had called home to her sister, Jimmie, in a panic.

"I'm dying, Jimmie, I'm coming home." Katherine overheard her weak mother say on the phone.

Jimmie took her sister, Katherine and Dennis in the first night they got back in town. May coughed the entire night and all the next morning. Jimmie couldn't stand it; she called her sister.

"Ettie, you have to come and get May and the kids." Jimmie shrieked. "All she does is cough; I think she might have tuberculosis. She can't stay here." Young Katherine listened to her horrified aunt arrange to put them out.

"I don't know where you're going to put them, Ettie, but come and get them!" Jimmie demanded. As they waited to be picked up, Katherine watched in disbelief.

"Byron, get these sheets outside; burn them in the fire pit," Jimmie ordered her husband. "Haul the mattress to the dump."

Katherine felt like a leper. She was humiliated for her mother and brother.

As it turned out, May had pneumonia instead of tuberculosis. Jimmie carried a stigma with the family for the rest of her life, despite her apology as May lay in the coffin.

Katherine turned her memory to another who did not want her.

Elmer tried to understanding Etta's feeling that she had to do this for May and Katherine. Although he didn't like it, he tried to be patient. However, his annoyances sometimes got the best of him; Katherine overheard how Elmer felt about things.

"Henrietta, I understand family loyalty, but why do you have to be the one to take them in?" Elmer questioned. "Why can't one of your other sister's take them?"

"No one else wants to take them. What can I do, Elmer? I have to help May and Katherine; it's only right. You understand, don't you, Elmer?" Etta pleaded.

Katherine didn't know if Elmer understood or not, but she didn't see much of him in the months to come.

Etta composed herself after the shock of Katherine's announcement.

"Why don't you go outside for a little while, I have to think about this. We'll talk about it after dinner. I'll call Dennis and see if he can come over tonight."

Katherine grabbed Snowball and went out the back door. She still didn't know why Aunt Etta had to talk to Dennis. She sat down near the garbage cans; this time she didn't notice the big black ants. Katherine heard Aunt June come in the front door.

"Did I hear her right, Ettie?" June said in astonishment. "Sam wants her to live with him and his new family?"

Etta nodded her head.

"Well, you're certainly not going to let her go, are you? Why May would turn over in her grave if she knew what was going on here," June expressed with disgust at the thought that Etta might even consider it.

"No, June," Etta said with a sigh. "I can't let her go with Sam. I promised May that I would never let her go with him."

"Ettie, you're going to have to be strong and tell Katherine NO! I told you that she was getting too spoiled. You have to be more firm with her. You let her get away with too much and it's not good for her. I knew she was getting too spoiled, I told you so," June preached at her.

Katherine sat on the back porch; she was angry at Aunt June for discouraging her aunt from letting her go, and dismayed that Aunt Etta might listen to her. Katherine heard Aunt Etta call her brother.

"Dennis, can you come over tonight after dinner? There is something I want to talk to you about," Etta explained. "We'll take when you get here. Good, see you later."

Etta's house was very quiet at dinner. Everyone finished eating quickly and got up from the table. Etta, as though in a trance, carried the dishes into the kitchen and started to wash them. The clinking and clanking of the pots and pans could be heard over the uncanny silence of the house. Etta didn't notice the noise or the silence; she was deep in thought wondering what to say to Dennis.

Dennis arrived early that evening curious about what Aunt Etta had to say. When she explained what Katherine had told her, he was just as surprised as everyone else.

Dennis had been boarding with a friend, Buddy, ever since his mother and sister had moved in with Aunt Etta. He hadn't wanted to move away from home; he missed his mother and sister. Quitting school had not been something he had wanted to do either. In fact, he wanted very much to graduate from high school so he could make a good life for himself. However, he felt an obligation toward his mother so he did what he had to do for his family. His positive attitude kept him from letting the situation get him down. He worked a full time job and also took night classes to learn the heating and cooling trade. He was a hard worker for such a young age; he was only nineteen, and he had the free spirit of a nineteen year old. At the same time, Dennis cared for his sister and he wanted what was best for her.

"I'll talk to dad; I'll explain how this move would disrupt her," Dennis explained, with his distressed sister listening.

"Good," Aunt Etta said. "You know, Dennis, your mother wanted Katherine to stay with me. Do you remember that?"

"Yes, I remember."

Dennis was not a tall man; neither was his brother Raymond for that matter. They both took after their mother's side, which did not produce very tall people.

He was on the stout side, not skinny, but not fat. He had a very sweet smile, which showed two deep dimples; girls loved to tease him, which made him smile bigger, and made his dimples deeper. His eyes were blue, like Katherine's, and they sparkled most of the time. Dennis was mild mannered, much like Sam, and a total opposite of Katherine. He was full of life, mischievous, and even a little reckless; he held no bitterness toward anyone, not even his dad. He enjoyed life too much for that; and Katherine loved him very much.

Aunt Etta looked into Dennis' jovial blue eyes. She had a certain connection to Dennis because he was the cause of her breaking her first promise to May. Etta had made three deathbed promises to her sister. The first one was that she raise Katherine; the other two were that what little money she left was to be used for Katherine's education and for Dennis to start a new life when he got married. Raymond was already married, so May did not allow him a portion of the money. Shortly after May's death, Dennis approached his aunt and asked if he could have his inheritance to buy better transportation for work. To her dismay, she couldn't say no to Dennis any easier than she could Katherine; she let him have the money.

To Etta's utter disappointment, he bought a motorcycle with a sidecar instead. She was so upset with herself for giving in to Dennis that she paced the floor for days. To her way of thinking, a motorcycle was far too extravagant and way too dangerous. Now his money was gone and he might get hurt; plus, she had broken her promise to her sister. Now she was faced with the possibility of breaking yet another promise; this one was much more serious.

Dennis got up to leave. Katherine walked out on the porch with her brother; she wanted to catch him alone. She pulled him close to her and spoke in a hushed voice.

"I really, really want to go live with dad. Will you help me talk Aunt Etta into it?"

Dennis stopped and looked at his sister. "Katherine, why do you want to do this? You're doing fine here," Dennis questioned.

"Because ... dad wants me," Katherine said. Dennis stood motionless; he saw the longing in his sister's eyes.

"Let me talk to dad first, okay? See you later." He ran down the steps and out the wrought iron gate.

The tension in Etta's house that evening was so thick it could have been sliced with a knife. There was no sitting on the couch together reading Bible verses. There was no playing the old Victrola. And there was no listening to the nightly radio programs. All was quiet and uneasy; everyone thought that going to bed would bring some relief from the stifling strain. Etta and Katherine got ready for bed in silence. As they lay in bed together, Katherine softly asked, "Auntie, can we work on my costume tomorrow?"

"We'll see."

Katherine got very little sleep that night.

Chapter 7

▼

Katherine puffed away on her cigarette hoping to calm her nerves. She felt incredibly guilty about causing her aunt so much anguish when all Etta had tried to do was love her like a mother, and do what was best for her. She tried time and time again to let this part of her past stay in the past; however, she simply could not do it. Her brother had told her many times to let it go; Miles lectured her over and over again.

"That's spilled milk, Katherine. Stop talking about it," her husband scolded.

If she could have, she would have escaped this torture and floated off across the valley that lay out in front of her; she would have disappeared into the china blue haze. Unfortunately, the harder she tried to forget, the more vivid her memories became.

"Has Dennis called yet?" Katherine asked anxiously.

"No," Aunt Etta answered.

"I wonder what is taking him so long."

"He'll probably call soon," her aunt said as she tried to occupy both their minds. "Let's work on your Halloween costume."

"Okay," Katherine groaned.

"Katherine, Elmer is coming over after dinner; we have something to talk about. I want you to give us some time alone, okay?" Aunt Etta gently asked.

"Okay," Katherine answered; she wondered what her aunt wanted to talk to Elmer about.

Aunt Etta and Elmer went outside and sat on the porch swing with a cool glass of sweetened tea. Katherine wasn't about to be left out; she plopped herself down on a chair next to the opened window.

"Well, Henrietta, why shouldn't she go live with her father? That's where the child belongs. It's a good thing that her father wants to own up to his responsibility. I don't understand why you want to prevent it," Elmer lectured.

"Yes," Katherine mumbled. She realized Elmer wasn't so bad after all.

However, Elmer saw this as the perfect opportunity to release Etta of her obligation; he could move ahead with his marriage plans and be free of the child.

"But, Elmer, May made me promise not to let Katherine go live with Sam. She was so adamant about it. I feel guilty about going against May's wishes. I don't know what to do." Etta's voice cracked with worry.

"You know, Henrietta, we could get married and start our life together, just the two of us. Katherine will be fine at her father's. I know your sister asked you to raise her, but May was practically out of her head with fever. She was still angry with Sam when she made you promise that," Elmer said as he pleaded his case. "Besides, it's not fair for the dying to extract deathbed promises from the living, Henrietta. The future is just too uncertain for that. I know you meant well promising your sister that you would raise Katherine, but it wasn't right to put the burden on you. I've said that all along. You have your life to think about too. You have our life to think about. It's not selfish for you to think about your future, our future. You want us to be together, don't you?" Elmer's persuasions made Etta feel guilty.

"Yes, Elmer, I want us to be together," Etta responded. There was a moment of silence and Katherine fingered they sealed their desire with a kiss. She also skipped away from the couch as she thought one hurdle had been won.

Katherine and Aunt Etta continued to work on the Halloween costume as they waited to hear from Dennis.

The Monday before Halloween Sam sat at the school bus stop. Katherine was excited to see him. As she walked over to the car, Sam waved and she waved back.

"Hi daddy," she said eagerly. "Are you alone?" She walked around the car and got in on the passenger side.

She loved that car and she hoped all her little friends saw her in it.

"Yes, Lillian was too busy with the boys so she didn't come today," he replied.

"Kat, I got a visit form your brother, Dennis. He told me that you finally told your aunt about us visiting you and that we offered to have you come live with us. He also said that Etta is very upset and is opposed to it."

"Yes, she is. She said that mama made her promise to raise me, and she wants to do what mama asked," Katherine explained.

"Well, I understand that, but you should have some say in this too. I am your father; if you want to come live with me, I think you should get to. Don't you?" Sam said in a most shrewd way.

"Yes, I do, and I told Aunt Etta that too. I told her that you said I can have my own room and you will buy me things; that you have a big backyard, and I will have my half-brothers to play with."

"Oh yea, Daddy," she said quickly as she suddenly remembered something, "I forgot to ask you if I can bring my cat, Snowball?" Katherine looked straight at her father; her eyes were as big as blue saucers. Sam knew this wasn't the time to refuse her anything.

"Of course you can bring your cat. I'm sure your step-mama won't mind," Sam said, not as sure as he tried to make it sound. Katherine felt his demeanor change for a moment.

Sam shrugged off his worry and smiled happily for Katherine's sake. He knew he had Katherine's support; all he had to do was get Etta's, and he hoped Dennis would be able to help with that.

"Well, I think when Dennis talks to Aunt Etta things will get worked out. I think he will be able to persuade her to let you come live with me," Sam told his daughter, sounding confident.

"Me too," Katherine agreed.

Katherine sat in the front seat feeling sure that her father was right about everything; she had found her Knight in Shinning Armor.

"Are you going to be at the Halloween parade next week?" she quizzed her father. "We're going to be there; it's going to be fun. Why don't you come and bring my brothers?"

"Well, maybe we will. I'll talk to Lillian. I'd better go now; your bus will be here soon," Sam said in a rush.

"Okay." Katherine jumped out of the car. She hoped Dennis would be over that night. She got their wish.

Aunt Etta sat at the table with a cup of tea when Dennis walked in. Katherine ran over to him. "Hi, Dennis," she screamed.

"Hey, sis." He sat down at the table with his aunt.

"Well, Dennis, what did Sam say?" Aunt Etta inquired.

Dennis stared at the teacup. There was a pause, a long pause. He fiddled with his aunt's teaspoon.

"Well, Dennis, what did your father say?" Aunt Etta asked as she took the teaspoon out of his hand. Katherine intently watched her brother waiting for him to answer.

"You know, Aunt Etta, dad really wants Katherine to come live with him. He wants to take care of her. He sounded real sincere about the whole thing," Dennis told her. "Maybe it wouldn't be such a bad idea."

Dennis said these words without looking at her. Aunt Etta was completely taken aback by his response. She took her time before she answered.

"Dennis, you know your mother wanted me to take care of your sister. You know how she felt about this. I'm really surprised you would consider anything else," Aunt Etta whispered. Katherine could see her eyes slowly begin to budge with tears.

"Your father didn't care about you two when he left; do you really think he cares now? Dennis I'm surprised at you," Aunt Etta responded with a quivering lip.

"Well, he realizes he should have kept in touch with us; he wants to try to make it up to us," Dennis continued.

"Is there something else, Dennis?" Aunt Etta questioned suspiciously. "What do you mean when you say *us*?"

Dennis paused for a long time. Katherine sat on the couch with Snowball and watched him.

"Dad said if I wanted to save some money that I could board free with him for a while," Dennis finally blurted out.

Katherine sat up straight; her eyes popped open wide. She couldn't believe what she heard. The thought of her brother also moving in at their father's house was wonderful.

Aunt Etta took a moment to register what Dennis said; she sensed the muscles in her throat tightening up. She had felt there was going to be something disastrous about this visit and she was right. She sat at the table hearing Dennis throw these words at her; he might as well have thrown daggers at her heart. She could feel the love, pride, and devotion for these two children slowly ooze from her wound; a tear from each eye rolled down her cheek. The silence was unbearable. Aunt Etta stirred her tea and Dennis sat sheepishly quiet; Katherine squirmed with excitement.

"Is that what you want to do, Dennis?" Aunt Etta asked softly.

"I don't know. I guess I was thinking about it," he said, still not looking at her.

"Well, Dennis, I just don't know." Aunt Etta paused not knowing how to finish the conversation. She had tried to look at every possible side of the situation; she had tried every possible argument. Nothing worked. She felt defeated. All she could do now was what any mother would do, and that was try to make sure the two children would be treated well.

"Did you talk to Sam's new wife?" she quizzed.

"Yes," Dennis answered.

"Was she nice to you?" Aunt Etta said softly, her voice cracked.

"Yes, she seemed real sincere about having Katherine come live with them."

"You know, Dennis, people are not always what they seem. You can be fooled."

"I know." Dennis tried to sound like he had thought the whole thing through and was satisfied.

"They are happy about me coming to live with them and it will work out just fine. I know it," Katherine interjected.

"Katherine, do you really think you are going to like it there, I mean with your dad's new wife and children?" Aunt Etta asked Katherine in a voice that resonated defeat.

"Yes, Auntie, I do. I think it will be fun."

Aunt Etta looked at Dennis. "Doesn't Sam want to talk to me? Didn't he say anything about meeting with me to talk about this?" she asked her nephew.

"No, he asked me to take care of the arrangements," Dennis said sounding guilty; at the same time, in control.

"Oh, I see. Well, I want to think about it some more. I can't make this decision just yet. We'll talk about it later," Aunt Etta said as she got up from the table; she picked up her teacup and took it over to the sink. Dennis got up and walked toward the front door; Katherine followed him.

"Are you really going to live there too?" Katherine asked in an excited whisper.

"I've been thinking about it. Yes, I think I will give it a try," he answered her.

"Great, it will be fun, us living together again." Katherine was almost unable to contain herself. Dennis gave his sister a hug good-by and then ran down the steps.

June went into the kitchen to see what her sister was doing.

"Ettie, are you really going to let Katherine go to Sam's?" June gasped.

"June, what can I do? They want to go and Sam is their father. He does have a legal right to Katherine," Etta sniffed; she saw Katherine walk back into the living room.

"Besides, Katherine has made up her mind that she wants to go; if I don't let her she will hold it against me forever. There's nothing else I can do, June. I've lost them both," Etta sighed, she wiped her nose with her handkerchief.

"Well, Ettie, I can't say that I agree with you. It wasn't supposed to be this way. May didn't want it to be this way and you know it. You're just spoiling Katherine again," June said shaking her head.

"June, I can't talk about it any more tonight," Etta pleaded. June turned and stomped away. She gave Katherine a disgusted look as she passed by.

Etta slowly walked into the living room and sat down. John sat in his favorite chair and read the paper; nearby, Katherine played with her cat.

"John," Etta said softly, "You haven't said a word about this. What do you think?"

John put down the paper and looked at Etta; he answered her in a whisper.

"Etta, I feel bad for what you are going through, but I don't see that you have any other choice. Katherine has made up her mind and she will throw it up to you some day if you don't let her go."

Katherine strained to hear her Uncle John; she had a satisfying smile on her face.

CHAPTER 8

▼

Halloween night arrived and Katherine was excited about putting on her princess costume. Aunt Etta had finished the dress using pink and white ribbons from the curio; she used an extra long, blue ribbon as a sash around the waist forming a large bow with long streamers in the back. When Katherine put the dress on she felt like the princess that she had always dreamed about being. She had two reasons for being excited that evening. She liked the Halloween Costume Parade and Aunt Etta had given her permission to go live with her dad. Everyone at Etta's house had become edgy, except for Katherine. She thought her life was just great; she was getting what she wanted and she was happy.

Etta tied the sash for Katherine and fluffed up the big bow.

"Katherine, you have a home here for as long as you want it; but, if you leave this house, you can never come back."

This was a harsh statement coming from Aunt Etta, but she had suffered a hurt deeper than she knew how to handle.

Katherine stood in front of the mirror primping and admiring herself. After one last look, she turned and looked at Aunt Etta, just to let her know that she heard her.

"Okay," was all Katherine said; she left the room.

Aunt Etta had asked Dennis to make arrangements to take Katherine to the Halloween celebration. He said that she could go with him and his girlfriend. That pleased Aunt Etta because she didn't feel like being around a crowd of people, and she certainly didn't feel like celebrating. However, two days before Halloween Dennis called his aunt.

"Aunt Etta, I got scheduled to work on Halloween, I won't be able to take Katherine to the celebration."

"Oh, Dennis, Katherine is going to be so disappointed," Aunt Etta replied.

"What's he saying, Auntie?" Katherine demanded.

"Hold on Dennis," Aunt Etta said as she turned toward Katherine. "Dennis had to work; he can't take you to the celebration."

"Who's going to take me, Auntie?" Katherine screamed. Aunt Etta shushed her and said good-by to Dennis.

"Will you take me?" Katherine cried when her aunt had hung up the phone.

"Katherine, I don't know if I can make it this year," Aunt Etta told her looking weary. "Aunt June and Uncle John are going. Why don't you go with them?"

Katherine sat on the couch and pouted; she didn't want to go with Aunt June. She didn't want to go with her outspoken aunt; she knew Aunt June was very mad at her for wanting to leave. She didn't want to give her hot-tempered aunt the opportunity to say anything to her. Katherine got a cunning idea; although she knew her aunt wouldn't go for it, she knew the suggestion would get her what she wanted.

"I suppose I can call Daddy. I know they are going; maybe he will come and get me," shrewd little Katherine suggested.

Aunt Etta, Aunt June and Uncle John stood silent and exchanged glances.

"No, I don't think that is such a good idea," Aunt Etta quickly said. "Your dad hasn't even contacted me about when he is going to move you," she complained. "I can't believe he hasn't talked to me yet." Aunt Etta shook her head with disappointment. "Well, anyway, I guess I can take you." Aunt Etta gave in to her wariness; Katherine smiled.

"Ettie," June interjected, "why don't you ask Elmer to come over and go with you and Katherine. That would make you feel a lot better, don't you think," June said, pleased with her idea; Katherine liked that idea too.

Elmer was delighted that Etta called him. He had been a lot more congenial toward her since she had decided to let Katherine go to her dad's; he figured he could handle a threesome a few more times. Etta confided in Elmer that she was edgy because she knew Sam and Lillian were going to be at the party, and that Katherine was sure to find them. What Etta didn't know was that Sam and Lillian weren't expecting her to be there.

The plans had been made and the time had arrived to leave for town; Katherine stood at the front door waiting for Elmer to get there.

"Where is he, Aunt Etta?" Katherine asked impatiently.

"He'll be here soon, Katherine. Just settle down." Aunt Etta called out from the bedroom as she put on her sweater.

Johnny came out of his parent's bedroom with his costume assembled just right. His mother had made him the cutest train engineer suit complete with blue striped overalls, a blue striped engineer's hat, and a red bandanna around his neck.

"Johnny, you look great!" Katherine complimented.

Johnny felt very proud. He wanted to be a train engineer when he grew up; he felt like he was wearing a uniform more than a costume. Now that he was ready, he was excited about leaving for the parade too. Uncle John and Aunt June waited around until Elmer arrived so they could leave together. He finally showed up and the jolly clan filed out the front door, down the steps and out the gate, with Katherine and Johnny jumping with glee.

The family always went to the celebration in Rossville, Georgia rather than the one in Chattanooga, Tennessee because it was within walking distance.

Late October in the south was still on the warm side, and that particular Halloween night was very mild and balmy. There was a brisk, breeze blowing and playful whirlwinds caught what leaves had fallen and twirled them around on the sidewalks and streets. Dusk had just passed and darkness crept up on the merry makers. Each house had jack-o-lanterns sitting out on their porches; the breeze made the flames inside the pumpkins waver, casting eerie shadows and strange flickerings all about. The kids loved the spooky atmosphere and the adults loved the children's ebullience for the moment. As they walked along, more and more families joined the march toward town; the excitement was contagious.

Aunt Etta and Elmer walked slowly behind the group. Katherine ran back every now and then, just to make sure she didn't get lost. She over heard some of their conversation.

"Everything is going to work out just fine. You wait and see," Elmer said sweetly.

"I hope so. And I also hope I don't see Sam and that woman tonight," Etta quipped.

"You know, Henrietta, you don't have to talk to Sam if you don't want to. We'll try to stay away from them," Elmer responded firmly, as though he was her protector.

"Well, I don't expect he'll want to talk to me anyway since he hasn't already. I don't understand a man like that. It makes no sense to me," Etta sighed.

"Well, let's not let that spoil our good time, okay?" Elmer patted her hand.

"I'll try not to."

They finally reach the barricades that protected the center of town and moved passed them into the excitement of the City Square. Adults milled around while tribes of costumed figures ran here and there. Aunt Etta, Elmer, and Katherine moved slowly through the crowd inspecting each booth that had been set up. The first one they came to was sponsored by the Ladies Auxiliary from the First Baptist Church of Rossville. They were dressed as pioneer women and most of the little kids didn't see much difference in their appearance. The ladies sold glasses of apple cider for a nickel apiece. The booth directly next to them was set up by the Historical Society where Cowboys sold spiced fried cakes. The smell of the warm cinnamon wafting on the breeze made everyone's mouth water; a line had already formed at that booth. As they walked along, Etta scanned the crowd. She didn't see any sign of him.

The local Boy Scout Troop had their booth set up and they sold apples for two cents each. The troop had decided to dress up as Cherokee Indians because they had been studying the local Indian history; they were the talk of the gathering. Also, there was a sign next to the booth saying that the troop would be cleaning up the area after the celebration as a way to work for their community service badge. The Boy Scout troop was the pride of Rossville and Johnny had been asking his parents if he could join it when he got a little older.

Aunt Etta and Elmer stopped a few times to greet some friends and fellow church members; Katherine spotted some of her schoolmates. She hadn't left Etta's side yet; she clung to her aunt's skirt as she tried to get past her timidness.

There were a fair amount of kids dressed as ghosts, and the way the wind blew, the sheets flapped and fluttered in the air creating an illusion, in Katherine's mind, of real ghosts. It didn't help to calm her fears any with the mischievous ghosts coming up behind her and bellowing, "BOO!"

Etta was on edge too; she went stiff as she looked out over the expanse of heads and there it was; the straw hat that she hoped she wouldn't see. There were a lot of straw hats, because that was the popular hat of the day, but this one had a distinguishing red and blue band on it. She knew of only one man that wore a straw hat with a red and blue band on it; that was Sam. She began to breathe fast. She stretched her neck to see if she could see the woman standing next to him.

"What are you looking at, auntie?" Katherine asked.

"Oh, nothing, honey," Etta replied, as she continued to look. Etta quickly ducked down as the straw hat turned in her direction. Elmer felt the change in her demeanor.

"What's wrong, Etta?" he asked.

"I think I see Sam over there," she said pointing with a nod of her head. Elmer, as well as Aunt June, Uncle John and Katherine, looked in that direction.

"Now just stay calm, Henrietta. Even if we do run into them, everything will be just fine," Elmer reassured.

"Ettie, did you see that woman with him?" Aunt June questioned with extreme curiosity.

"I could see a head next to him; she must be short," Aunt Etta explained.

"Oh, I think I see him too," Aunt June squealed; she ducked down so she wouldn't be seen either. Katherine stood on her tip-toes to get a look, but it was futile; she couldn't see above the adults.

"Ettie, do you remember the last time we saw that straw hat," Aunt June reminisced.

"Yes, that was a long time ago," Aunt Etta answered.

"Remember, you, me, and May went to Lake Winabasoka for the day," June started her story.

"Where is that?" Katherine asked.

"It's an amusement park in Chattanooga. Your mother loved to go there. You were with us that day; but, you were too young to remember," Aunt Etta explained.

"It was a warm summer day and everything was going well; that is, until May saw Sam and Lillian together," Aunt June continued. "Remember how mad May got; how she ran over to Sam and yanked his straw hat right off his head? She threw it on the ground and stomped the daylights out if it."

"Yes, I remember, "Aunt Etta said. "Poor May was so hurt; she never got over seeing them together."

"What did daddy do?" Katherine asked.

"He tried to calm her down; he told her she shouldn't act like that around you," Aunt Etta told her.

"You know, Ettie, May didn't make it easy on Sam. She even stalked him at work for a while; poor thing made quite a spectacle of herself over that man," Aunt June admitted. "Well, enough of that," she concluded.

Katherine was going to ask more questions when her friend, Aline Narcissus, ran up to her.

"Katherine, you look like a real princess."

"Thanks, Aline, you make a good old lady," Katherine returned. Aline laughed.

"Come on. Let's go over to the candy booth," Aline suggested.

"Go on and join the other children, Katherine," Etta said as she gently pushed Katherine toward Aline. Katherine's fears gave way to her excitement and she ran off to be with her friends.

While the girls walked around, Katherine finally spotted her dad and stepmother. She forgot all about her aunt's conversation and excitedly ran up to them.

"Hi, daddy, this is my friend, Aline."

"Do you like my princess dress?" she asked holding the dress out to the sides and twirling around.

"Yes, it's very pretty," her dad responded. "Are you two having a good time?"

"Yes, and I can't wait until its time for the parade. That's my favorite part," Katherine said as she took hold of Sam's free hand.

Sam held Stanley's little hand in his other one; Lillian held Sonny.

"Why, Katherine, you look just beautiful," Lillian managed to say through her fixed smile.

"Thanks, Aunt Etta made it for me," Katherine said, glancing across the square.

"Oh, she did? Is your aunt here?" Lillian gasped as she looked in the direction of Katherine's glanced.

"Yep, right over there," Katherine answered.

Lillian glared across the square half thinking out loud. "Oh that's just great."

Sam pretended not to hear her.

"I thought Dennis was bringing you. What happened?" Sam inquired.

"He had to work tonight," Katherine explained.

"I see," Sam said. Lillian glared at him.

"I suppose Etta is going to want to talk to you about Katherine since we're all here together, don't you think?" Lillian said with disgust.

"Yes, I suppose so, but what else can I do. I can't ignore her. Let's just do this and get it over with, Lil, okay?" Sam was irritated with her bitching.

Katherine didn't understand their demeanor. "Is something wrong, daddy?" Katherine asked.

"No, no, Kat. Everything is fine. You two go on and play now. We'll see you later," Sam said as he waved them off.

Katherine and Aline ran toward the apple bobbing barrel screaming as a couple of ghosts flew by taunting them with ghoulish howls.

The costume parade was about to start so all the parents and on-lookers began to line both sides of the main street in town. The city council had hired a small bluegrass band called The Paul Douglas Band; they had played all night in the gazebo in the Town Square while couples danced to their tunes. Now they turned their attentions to the parade and began to play a peppy little melody to accompany the gleeful marchers.

There were cowboys and cowgirls, hobos, and angels passing by the spectators. There were old ladies and old men, train engineers, and devils smiling and waving to the crowd. There were witches and outlaws, dozens and dozens of ghosts and, of course, one very happy little princess.

The onlookers stood on the curb and marveled at all of the wonderful costumes while Katherine waved back and forth at her dad and aunt; she felt wanted, she felt worthy. The Halloween festivities were over for another year.

The marchers disbursed at the end of the route and slowly filtered out finding their respective families. Katherine walked up to Aunt Etta.

"Wasn't that fun?"

"Yes, that was wonderful," Aunt Etta said as she spied Sam and Lillian coming up behind Katherine. Aunt June and Aunt Etta stared at them; Lillian stared back; Katherine jumped around with anticipation.

No one spoke as the foe approached. Elmer moved closer to Aunt Etta, Uncle John moved closer to Aunt June, and Sam took hold of Lillian's arm like suspecting opponents feeling the need to protect their women. Neither side knew if there was going to be a battle or a truce, but both sides seemed ready for either one. Sam and Lillian walked up to the small group; they kept safely outside of each other's personal space.

"Hello, Etta," Sam said.

"Sam," Etta retorted.

Sam looked over Etta's shoulder and said, "John, June, how are you?"

"Not bad, Sam," John replied.

Sam nodded his head at Elmer since he didn't know him to call him by name.

There was a terrible awkwardness with everyone being so close to each other. Katherine picked up on everyone's uneasiness so she started the conversation.

"Auntie, Daddy wants to know when I can move in with him."

Etta dreaded the sound of those words. She didn't have an answer for Katherine and she didn't know what to say anyway; she didn't say anything.

"I was thinking two weeks would give everyone time to make the arrangements, don't you think?" Sam looked at Aunt Etta right in the face.

There was one thing that Aunt Etta wanted to say to Sam while she had the chance.

"Well, Sam, you know this isn't what May …," she was interrupted.

"I know what you are gong to say, Etta, but that's over now and it's time for Katherine to come live with me." Sam said sternly, so sternly it almost hurt her feelings.

Elmer didn't like it that Sam spoke that way, but he didn't say anything because he was all for the move. Uncle John didn't like it either, but he knew Sam had a legal right to his daughter; Aunt June didn't like it but she was too steamed to say a word. Of course, Lillian liked it because it let them know who was in charge; she enjoyed seeing defeat on the faces of these two women.

"Well, I'll have Dennis come over to pick up Katherine and her things. He'll let you know the exact day," Sam finished.

Sam tipped his straw hat to all and turned to walk away.

"Why couldn't he have left us alone?" Aunt Etta snapped. "He had to go and mess everything up,"

"It will be okay, Henrietta," Elmer said as he took her hand in his.

"Yes, Auntie, it will be okay," Katherine agreed.

It was a successful Halloween; everyone felt contented as they casually walked home and reminisced about their favorite costumes and who scared whom.

As they got closer to home, Etta's house became visible; she stopped abruptly.

"Not again!" she shouted. Everyone laughed.

The group walked up to the front of her house only to be confronted with the same prank that was played on them every year. Without fail, every Halloween night someone took Etta's gate off of its hinges and put it on top of the telephone pole. The neighborhood kids, as well as the adults, always got a big kick out of this joke. Each year everyone tried to figure out who did it and how in the world they got the gate up so high. John wasn't amused; now he had to call the fire department to bring over one of their tallest ladders to get the gate down. Everyone else laughed and giggled and pointed; it was a humorous ending to their Halloween celebration.

The next two weeks went by very quickly; Dennis had been in touch; Aunt Etta helped Katherine get her things packed. With all of her moving around, Katherine didn't have that much; however, May had left some thing. Etta had them stored in her basement and Katherine was going to leave them there for now. One item, which was going to stay with Etta, was May's favorite possession, the old Victrola. There was a beautiful cedar chest that had been a wedding present for May and Sam. May had packed away some wonderful hand embroidered linens, which she had stitched herself, along with some table cloth and napkin sets, and some perfectly matched doilies. May was an impeccable embroiderer and she had mastered many different stitches, which included the chain stitch, the cross stitch, a perfect French knot, and a satin stitch that was matched by no one. May had embroidered a table cloth for an accent table, which was four feet in diameter. It was a dark flax color with rolls of matching lacey crocheting around its circumference, which May also did beautifully. Evenly spaced on the table cloth were three embroidered floral bouquets of pinks, blues, yellows, and greens, which were represented by the most exquisite satin stitch May had ever done. This cloth also lay packed away in the cedar chest in Etta's basement.

Next to the chest sat two ladder-backed chairs, which May had bought during a brief period of working at a furniture store when she had returned home. They were well made chairs and Etta decided to keep them for the home Katherine would have some day.

Dennis arrived on the moving day and began putting Katherine's things in his car. It was so odd to Aunt Etta, Aunt June, and Uncle John that Sam had not come over to help at all with the move. Even if it meant being uncomfortable or having a confrontation, he should have been there to help his daughter. But with Sam, that was par for the course. It didn't seem to bother Katherine, though; she was excited and couldn't get her things in Dennis' car fast enough. In fact, she was so elated that she was completely oblivious as to how dejected her aunt felt. However, Aunt June noticed and several times put her arm around her sister's shoulder.

"Well, I guess we're all set, Aunt Etta," Dennis called out. "We'll be going now."

Dennis and Katherine stood at the front door waiting for their aunt to respond.

"Give me a hug, Katherine." Aunt Etta grabbed her and hung on so tight that she almost smothered her.

"Now you be good and go to church. Read your bible verses and give me a call sometime, okay?" Aunt Etta choked back the tears. She pulled out her handkerchief and held it to her nose.

"Okay, I will, Auntie," Katherine called out as she got into the car.

The car pulled away from the curb and slowly rolled down the street. Katherine turned around and looked out the back window. She saw her dear aunt sit down on the bottom step and bury her head in her lap.

Chapter 9

Miles had been asleep for a couple of hours and that was all he wanted. Katherine got up from the boulder and walked over to the car.

"Miles," she nudged his shoulder, "It's been a few hours. You want up now, don't you?"

Miles roused up and looked around. He yawned and stretched with one arm sticking out the window; he groaned.

"Well, I guess we'd better get started. I want to get out of these mountains before it gets dark."

He got out of the car to stretch his legs and wake up a little more. He lit one of his Camel's and walked over to a clump of bushes. Katherine called to the girls to turn around when she saw Miles peeing without fully hiding himself. Miles finished and turned around and yelled out an order.

"You girls better go to the bathroom now; I'm not going to stop until I get to Cincinnati."

Katherine helped the girls find a good spot and all three squatted down. They finished, packed up, and piled into the car.

"Miles, I don't see how we can get to Cincinnati without stopping to get the girls something to eat," Katherine said, thinking to herself that the kids will get irritable if they are hungry.

"Well, we'll see how far we can get. Let's go," Miles said impatiently.

It didn't take the children long to settle down and fall asleep to the rhythmic sound of the highway. Katherine was glad; it would be quiet for a few hours. She fidgeted as she positioned Linda comfortably in her lap.

"Why are you so quiet?" Miles finally asked.

"Oh, I just got to thinking about Aunt Etta; how I left her once and now I'm leaving her again," Katherine answered with a quivering lip.

"For crying out loud, Katherine, are you going to start that again? Bringing it up that you left your aunt when you were twelve doesn't help anything; and as for leaving her now, we're trying to make a better life for ourselves. I think she understands that."

"I guess so. I suppose I was thinking about all the times that I hurt her," Katherine replied sniffling, trying to get a reaction out of him.

"Damn it, will you stop it. That was a long time ago. You have to let all that go. I'm trying to do something that will be good for us and our future. You can't keep bringing up the past like that," Miles snapped, not giving her the reaction she was looking for. However, she didn't stop the direction of her thoughts.

"I can't help it. I can't forget how I hurt her; and I can't forget what happened afterwards. I don't know how my dad let it happen; I just don't understand," Katherine said, nearly crying.

"Katherine, I don't want to talk about this again. Besides, you seemed to have gotten along with them pretty good since we've been married. Why keep going on about what happened so long ago. Talk about something else," Miles demanded; he wanted her to change the subject.

"Okay then. Let's talk about where your damn brother is with our furniture. Where the hell do you think he is? I bet he has stopped at every little, stinking bar along the way since we left Chattanooga," she blurted out.

"Do you think we are going to have any furniture when we get to Michigan?" Katherine said as she released her anger.

That wasn't the conversation Miles was looking for. He was sorry he hadn't humored her on the first subject rather than let her get started on his brother.

"Damn it, Katherine, are you looking for an argument?" Miles said with a look that implied *knock it off.*

"No, I don't want to argue, I want my furniture," Katherine shot back. She sulked as she leaned back in the seat and stared out the window. As the car sped along so did her memory; she was forced to finish the visit with her tumultuous past.

Katherine got settled in Lillian's old sewing room. It was small but adequate with a double bed and a fair size dresser. There was a window that faced the wooded back yard; Katherine liked the view. The view she had at Aunt Etta's was of the house next door, which was so close she could see in the neighbor's windows; consequently, looking out at a large wooded lawn was very pleasing to her. Lillian had hung a pair of pink Priscilla curtains at the window, which fluttered softly in the breeze when the window was opened; they made Katherine feel feminine. She thought she was going to be very happy here.

Katherine was busy putting away her clothes and things and she didn't notice that she hadn't seen Snowball anywhere. She figured the cat was exploring the house; she would look for her later.

Dennis finished moving Katherine rather quickly so he sat and talked to his dad for a while. Their relationship had stayed on pretty good terms. Dennis' personality was largely responsible for their amicableness and he was looking forward to moving in with his dad almost as much as Katherine.

"Is it still okay for me to move in here, Dad?" Dennis asked as Katherine plopped down on the couch next to him.

"Sure son. Just give us a week to get the basement straightened up," Sam said quite agreeably.

"Okay. That will work out for me too."

Dennis and Buddy left and Katherine was alone to start adjusting to her new home. She finally missed her cat and started looking around for her.

"Have you seen Snowball?" She asked her stepmother.

"Why, no. Isn't she in your room with you?" Lillian said without looking at Katherine in the face.

"No, she isn't," Katherine answered; she started going from room to room searching for her cat.

"Maybe the cat got out when the boys had the door opened moving your things in," Sam said to his daughter when he heard her and Lillian talking about it.

"I don't know. I didn't see where she went," Katherine whimpered.

"Maybe she did get out," Lillian mocked; she glanced at Sam; he ignored her look and took his daughter by the hand.

"Let's go outside and look around," Sam said like a loving father. After they explored the immediate area and found no traces of the cat, they came back in the house.

"Well, let's give it a little time. If the cat did get out, I'm sure she'll come back later." Sam comforted his daughter.

"Katherine, did you put a bag over the cat's head when you left Etta's? You know you're supposed to put a bag over a cat's head when you move it so it won't see where it is going. Otherwise, it will try to find its way back," Lillian quizzed her stepdaughter.

"No, I guess I forgot," Katherine admitted, sounding upset with herself.

"Oh, well, we'll just have to wait and see if it comes back," Lillian scolded. She cunningly placed the blame on Katherine.

Sam put his arm around Katherine's shoulder. "I'm sure Snowball will come back. Now don't you worry, Kat," Sam comforted.

Katherine got settled at her new home. Despite her worry about Snowball, she enjoyed the next few days being with her dad and playing with her two stepbrothers. She got registered at her new school and walked down to the bus stop a few times to get familiar with the area. She hoped there would be some girls her own age close by to play with; she missed her friend, Aline Narcissus.

Aunt Etta had a hard time adjusting to Katherine being gone. She hoped Sam and Lillian would to be good to her. Aunt Etta was one of the few people who knew how fragile Katherine was, how easily her dreams could be crushed. Sam didn't know what Katherine had gone through after he left. He didn't know what an unstable few years she had with her mother. He didn't know what a fierce need she had for love and affection. And, he didn't know how quickly she could size up a situation and change her mind about what she wanted.

The cat finally showed up and Katherine thought things would be perfect just as soon as her brother got there. Katherine knew Dennis was supposed to move into the basement soon, but she hadn't seen her father or Lillian fixing it up yet.

"Daddy, when are you going to fix up the basement for Dennis?" Katherine asked her father at dinner. Lillian gave her stepdaughter a dirty look.

"I know; we have to get started. Lil, are you ready for me to start?" Sam asked as lovingly as possible; Katherine thought it sounded more sheepish than loving.

"No, I'm not ready. You know, Sam, Katherine's bedroom was my sewing room, so I thought I would make a sewing room in the basement. I really don't want to have Dennis and his friends down there getting in my way when I'm sewing." Lillian complained. "You know you never discussed it with me."

"I know, but I didn't think you would mind. It isn't going to be that long anyway, just long enough for Dennis to get done with school, which will be in the spring," Sam explained.

"Well, I have another idea," Lillian said rather cunningly. "We'll discuss it later." Katherine wondered what her other idea could be; she would just have to wait and see.

Dennis had chosen the day and had all of the arrangements made to make his move. He never asked his dad, but he assumed that there was an extra bed in the basement; in fact, he hoped there was one because he didn't have the money to buy one. He took it for granted that the furniture would be there, so all he was concerned about was packing his clothes and a couple of small belongings. Dennis had called his dad to ask if the day he had chosen would be okay. Sam said it was; everything was set for Monday week. Dennis had actually wanted to do it on Sunday but Lillian wouldn't hear of it; they were going to have company for dinner on Sunday afternoon.

Lillian had been fussing around the house since Snowball came back; she didn't like all the cat hair; unfortunately, Katherine got her first hint of what was to come.

"Katherine, come on and get up. We're having company for dinner and I want some cleaning done before church," Lillian ordered; she awakened Katherine early Sunday morning.

Katherine was still half-asleep and she wasn't sure she heard correctly. It was still dark outside so she thought it was still the middle of the night.

"Come on, I said, get up right now." Lillian grabbed Katherine's arm.

Katherine was confused, even a little scared. Why was her stepmother making her get up while it was still dark, and to do housework? Katherine stumbled into the living room rubbing her sleepy blue eyes while they tried to adjust to the lamplight.

"What are we doing up in the middle of the night?" she mumbled.

"I said I want to get some cleaning done before church and you're going to help me, that's what," Lillian snorted with sarcasm.

Katherine could hardly believe what she was being asked to do; she turned toward her bedroom.

"Where are you going?" Lillian huffed.

"I'm going to get dressed," Katherine said in a low, nervous voice.

"You don't need to get dressed," you impetuous child, "just come on and start running the carpet sweeper over the area rugs. When you are done there, take the small rugs outside and beat them with the whisk. I want all of the cat hair off of everything."

Lillian went into the kitchen and sat down at the table; she had a cup of coffee while Katherine worked. This had been one of Lillian's ulterior motives for wanting her stepdaughter to come live with them. She wanted help with the housework and she didn't want to spend money on a housekeeper. At the same time, the way Lillian went about getting Katherine to help was evidence of something very dark about her personality. She sat at the kitchen table enjoying watching this young girl work in her nightgown in the wee hours of the morning. Sam and the boys slept soundly and unaware in the next room. When Katherine had finished with the sweeping and whisking, she headed toward her bedroom.

"Where do you think you are going?" Lillian questioned.

"I'm all done," Katherine whined.

"No you're not. The kitchen floor needs to be scrubbed before everyone else gets up," Lillian ordered.

"I don't know how to scrub a floor. Why are you making me do this?" Katherine whimpered.

"Quit being such a baby. Your aunt spoiled you rotten; that is going to change in order for you to stay in this house," Lillian said as she grabbed Katherine's arm and led her to the kitchen.

"Get a bucket from the pantry and fill it with soap and water; here is a sponge. The only way to get it really clean is to get down on your hands and knees. That way you can get in the corners real good," Lillian instructed.

Katherine carried the full bucket of water into the kitchen as best she could. It was almost too heavy for her thin, little arms to handle, which made the water splash from side to side spilling out onto the floor. Lillian gave her a disgusted look and snapped.

"Be more careful and don't make a mess. I'm going to lay down on the couch. I want this floor done before 7:00; that's when your dad gets up," her evil stepmother barked.

Katherine glanced up at the clock and saw that it read 6:00. She looked at the large kitchen floor and wondered if she was going to be able to get it done in time. Bewildered, she got down on her bony, little knees and grabbed the sponge; she looked at the bucket and then at the sponge wondering what she was supposed to do with it. She quickly dipped the sponge into the water. Katherine got the sleeve of her robe all wet, which upset her so much that she dropped the sponge on her lap and got the front of her robe wet as well. She was agitated to the point of crying as she tried to roll up her sleeves. Slowly she began to wash her first floor, a chore not fit for a princess. It was beyond her young mind to understand why she was being made to do this. As she worked, she glanced up and saw Snowball sitting in the doorway looking at her. Dare she wish that she and her cat were back at Aunt Etta's, and so soon after making the move that *she* wanted? Katherine worked fastidiously and finished scrubbing the floor with ten minutes to spare.

"I'm all finished. What do I do with the water?" she called out to her stepmother.

"Keep your voice down," Lillian scolded. "Take it outside and throw it to the side of the house and put the bucket and sponge away."

Katherine did as instructed and walked into the living room where Lillian was laying.

"Can I go back to bed now?"

Lillian lay on the couch with her eyes closed. "Yes, go ahead, but you'll have to be up in a half hour to get ready for church,"

Katherine started walking toward her bedroom when Lillian called out.

"Oh, Katherine," there was a pause, "why don't you start calling me *Mother*?"

Lillian half opened her eyes to catch a glimpse of Katherine's reaction. Katherine looked at her and then turned and went into her room. She lay in her bed thinking about what Lillian had just asked her to do. "I didn't even call Aunt Etta *Mother*. Why should I call her *Mother*?" Katherine mumbled to herself; she dozed off.

A half-hour came very quickly and Katherine crawled out of bed to the voice of Lillian calling everyone to breakfast. Sam, Sunny and Stanley were all bright eyed and chipper as they waited anxiously for Lillian's famous breakfast of eggs, country ham and red-eyed gravy; Katherine sat at the table and yawned.

"What's the matter, Kat, didn't you get enough sleep?" Sam asked; his daughter yawned again. She looked at her dad contemplating whether to tell him why she was tired that morning. As Lillian took biscuits out of the oven, Katherine could feel her straighten up and stare at the back of her head. Although she felt her father would not have approved of the way she had been treated, she quickly decided that it was best to forget about the whole thing. Katherine figured the events of that morning were a one-time thing; she shrugged it off to think about more pleasant things.

"Snowball kept waking me up, that's all," she fibbed.

Lillian sat down at the table and placed a plate full of baking soda biscuits next to the gravy; she cast a glance at Katherine that said *it's a good thing you answered that way*. Sam happened to see the look and wondered what was up; consequently, he decided to forget it too.

The following week Dennis stopped by his dad's to look over the basement.

"Dad, I'm moving in next week," Dennis said as he stared at Lillian's sewing machine and dress form. "Do you want me to help you move these things?"

"No, no. I can get them later; don't worry, son," Sam answered. "Let's go upstairs and talk a little while."

Sam sat at the table with his two children while they ate a piece of delicious apple pie, Lillian's specialty. He fidgeted something awful. Everyone noticed the sweat beads.

"What do you hear from Raymond?" Sam asked Dennis.

"I talked to him last week. He's buying a restaurant," Dennis said.

"Oh, I thought he had a good job at the bank," Sam said.

"He said the bank was cutting his hours, and that Mary Jo was not happy about that."

"I don't like Mary Jo," Katherine interrupted. "She thinks she is better than anyone else."

"Anyway, Raymond decided now was the time to make a move," Dennis continued.

"Where did he get the money for this restaurant?" Sam asked, very curious.

"He got it from Aunt Etta," Dennis informed the shocked group.

"Etta has enough to loan Raymond that much money?" Sam said, amazed.

"I didn't know Etta had that kind of money," Lillian interjected.

"Well, she gave it to him," Dennis answered; this time he fidgeted in his chair while Sam and Lillian exchanged glances.

"What is the name of the restaurant?" Katherine jumped in.

"I can't remember right now, sis," Dennis answered.

"Well, I hope it works out for him," Sam said, concerned for his oldest son.

"Me too," Dennis agreed. "I guess I'll go now. I'll be back next week with my things."

"Okay, son," Sam avoided eye contact with Lillian.

Katherine rushed in from school. "Is he here yet?" she yelled.

"No, but he should be here soon," Sam answered as he anxiously looked out the front window. Finally Dennis drove up.

"Where've you been, son?" Sam questioned.

"I got called in to work for a few hours. Mr. Hatfield needed his car right away!" Dennis worked at a garage just over the Tennessee line in Georgia. He came by mechanics quite naturally, just like his dad.

"I was worried," Sam replied nervously; he put his hands in his pockets so he wouldn't fidget with them.

"Sorry, dad, I didn't think it would make that much difference," Dennis apologized.

As Dennis spoke, Katherine ran up and gave him a big hug around the waist.

"I'm so happy you're going to live here with me," she whispered.

"Me too, sis. Now let's get busy and get this stuff unloaded," he said.

Dennis and Katherine had an armful of clothes as they went in the back door and started down the basement stairs, assuming that was going to be Dennis' bedroom. Lillian stood in the kitchen and watched the whole scene; Katherine saw her turn toward Sam with a sharp look. She saw her father close his eyes and take a deep breath.

"Hold up, Dennis," Sam instructed.

Dennis stopped on the first step, obviously strained from the heavy load.

"You two bring the clothes in here," Sam said as he walked into the living room.

Dennis and Katherine looked at each other as they followed Sam; they were perplexed why they were to take the clothes any place other than the basement.

"Hey, Dad, what's up? Why are we doing this?" Dennis asked; he struggled to hold the bundle of clothes without dropping them.

Sam stood silent; he put his shaking hands in his pockets again. He tried to look at his children but couldn't; he quickly cast his glance to the floor. Slowly he began to explain.

"Well kids, the arrangements are different, at least for now. Lil wants to use the basement for her sewing room. Dennis, you'll have to share the room with Katherine," Sam blurted out.

Sam still did not look at Dennis or Katherine. His shame kept him from looking at his children face to face.

"But, Daddy, where will Dennis sleep?" Sam's young daughter queried.

Sam stared at Katherine; he could feel Dennis' stare. Sam could see out of the corner of his eye that Lillian stared at him too, all awaiting his answer.

"Well, you two will just have to share the bed for a while, I guess."

Katherine and Dennis stood mute. They thought their ears had deceived them. Could their dad really be saying they were going to have to sleep together?

"So come on you two. Let's get all of Dennis' things in the bedroom before it gets too late," Sam blurted out quickly; he wanted out of this painfully awkward moment.

Dennis and Katherine stood frozen; they wondered what in the world their dad was talking about. He never said anything about this. Katherine stood beside Dennis waiting for him to make the first move. She didn't know what to think; but one thing was for sure, it didn't sound like the proper thing to do. Sam saw Dennis' hesitation and coaxed him to continue moving his things in.

"Come on, son, it will work out."

"Well, I'll just sleep on the couch for now. Can't I do that?" Dennis suggested.

"That's a new couch. I don't want anyone sleeping on it and breaking down the cushions," Lillian yelled from the kitchen.

"Dad, I can't sleep with my sister. How can you expect me to?" Dennis pleaded. "I wouldn't have given up my room at Buddy's if I had known this. Why didn't you say something?"

"I thought I could work something out before you got here," Sam tried to explain. "Just give it a try for a while. Maybe things will still work out," Sam begged.

"Come on, dad. You want me to sleep with my sister?"

"I'll try to get things worked out, I promise, son. Let's see how it goes."

"Just for a while," Dennis whispered in his dad's ear; Katherine heard.

Lillian stood in the kitchen with the two little boys and watched the whole episode from afar; she knew enough to stay out of the way; the smirk on her face expressed her satisfaction at being able to control this morally twisted situation. She wanted to make sure she had control over Sam's kids, which would enable her to keep the control she had over her husband. Lillian was not about to give up the dominance she had in her marriage, especially because of two kids Sam had with another women. She smiled with satisfaction that things were going just the way she wanted them to go.

Dennis couldn't believe that his dad actually expected him to sleep with his sister. The thought of it made his face wrinkle with repulsion. That was sick. That was too close to incest for him to be comfortable. He knew of some families that participated in such things; in fact, he had one acquaintance that did sleep with his sister, and for sexual reasons. Dennis had never been interested in that kind of activity, and he wasn't interested in it now. Just thinking about the sleeping arrangements angered him terribly.

And yet, curiously he didn't object anymore that evening. Katherine, even though she thought it was a very strange arrangement, wasn't all that upset. She had been used to sleeping with someone so the thought of another person in the bed didn't bother her; her naiveté prevented her from even thinking about anything sexual. Katherine didn't say anything to her dad that night either. The family sat in the living room listening to the radio; everyone sat very quiet and tautly awaited bedtime.

Katherine changed first and jumped into bed; Dennis came out of the bathroom where he had changed. Dennis had been used to sleeping in his T-shirt and briefs but he didn't feel comfortable wearing that to bed with his sister. He slipped on a pair of athletic shorts, which he had left over from middle school gym class. Dennis turned out the light and got into bed. They lay on their backs feeling tense and looking up at the ceiling, which was gently lit by the full moon shinning through the pink Priscilla's. Snowball jumped up on the bed and gingerly walked around trying to find a place to lie down. Finally she decided on a spot right between Katherine and Dennis.

"Dennis," Katherine said in a whisper, "Why do you think dad wouldn't let you make a bedroom in the basement? That's what he said at first, wasn't it?"

"I don't know, sis. I think Lillian had something to do with it. Maybe she didn't like the idea of me coming to stay here in the first place. I don't know why dad didn't make her let me stay in the basement. I don't know why he can't speak up. I do know that this isn't right! We shouldn't be sleeping together, and don't you tell anyone!" Dennis ordered. "Ever!"

"Okay. I won't," Katherine said in a whisper.

"You know what she made me do this morning?" Katherine continued.

"What?"

"She made me get up at 5:00 to clean the house. I had to sweep the rugs and scrub the kitchen floor before we got ready for church."

Dennis raised up on one elbow and looked at his sister.

"What! She made you do that before sunup? And what was she doing while you cleaned?"

"She laid on the couch and went to sleep."

"Does dad know this?" he asked.

"No, I didn't tell him. I didn't want to cause any trouble," Katherine explained.

Dennis flopped back down on his pillow. They lay very still, deep in thought.

"Well, sis, I don't know how long I'm going to be here. I don't think this is going to work out."

"I don't want you to go, Dennis. I want us to be together," Katherine urged; she grabbed hold of Dennis' arm, which made Snowball jump to another spot.

As she grabbed his arm, there was a strange familiarity about the feeling. She didn't know why she was comfortable with having a man in bed with her. She did not necessarily have sexual feelings, but something evoked a strange awareness.

"I know, but this just isn't right Katie. A brother and sister shouldn't be sleeping together," Dennis said, admonishing their act.

Katherine knew it wasn't right, but she felt so safe. What Katherine didn't remember, what she had buried deep in her subconscious, was her relationship with Mr. Peterson. Mr. Peterson was one of two men May had married during her travels in the Midwest. May had been desperate and lonely on the road; she made two regretful mistakes, and Mr. Peterson was one of them. After May married him, she and the kids moved into his tiny one bedroom apartment in Oklahoma. Dennis slept on the couch and Katherine slept in the bed between her mother and Mr. Peterson. This seemingly concerned man had come along at one of May's weaker moments and convinced her that he wanted to provide her with security and companionship. To her dismay, he was interested in much more. After a one-night honeymoon, he insisted that Katherine, then seven and a half, sleep in their bed between them. May knew this was a questionable request; however, she wanted to please her new husband. Katherine slept quite comfortably and soundly lying next to Mr. Peterson so May went along with it at first; she ignored the pangs of suspicion in her gut. Her suspicion grew into fear; as her fear grew, so did Mr. Peterson's attention toward Katherine; he began to cuddle and hug her more each night. She knew it was only a matter of time before Mr. Peterson would cross the sacred line. One night while they got ready for bed, May suggested that Katherine sleep in the other room so that she and her husband could have some time alone. In a rage, Mr. Peterson objected; a huge argument ensued as piercing accusations flew. May accused him of wanting her daughter instead of her and Mr. Peterson accused her of being jealous. The next day May took her children and headed for the train station. However, Katherine, even at her tender age, knew they had argued over her; she knew her mother didn't like her lying next to her step-father, but she was too young to understand why. The only thing she knew was Mr. Peterson was very nice to her when she would sit next to him and let him hug her. There were only four people who knew about that incident; Mr. Peterson, who was lost in Oklahoma somewhere; May, who took the secret to the grave; Dennis, whose memory was very vague; and Katherine, who involuntarily buried the memory deep inside her where it would go invalidated forever.

"It wasn't supposed to be this way, Katherine, and you know it. Lillian shouldn't make you get up before the sun to do house work. Dad should put his foot down about all of this stuff," Dennis complained. "He doesn't want to loose that young wife, that's why he doesn't say anything." Dennis laid on his back staring at the shadows on the ceiling.

They lay in the bed side by side daring to think that they made a big mistake. Dennis already missed the privacy and independence he had at Buddy's, and Katherine missed the gentle kindness that she had at Aunt Etta's. Now they had new lives to adjust to and neither one seemed too thrilled about it anymore. Dennis couldn't help but remember what his aunt warned him, "Some people are not what they seem." Aunt Etta was right.

Chapter 10

The pre-dawn cleaning tasks had stopped for the time being; however, Lillian continued to be harsh with her stepdaughter. At the same time, she sensed that she'd better not go too far as long as Dennis was around; she could feel him looking over his shoulder at her, which made her completely incensed that the little prima donna had a protector. She began her mission to rid herself of the predicament that caused her to be annoyed, like a splinter that gets in your heel, and every time you step down you're reminded that it's still there. Lillian started throwing little remarks at Dennis about freeloading off of them. Dennis never acknowledged her insolent remarks, but he heard them loud and clear; that only made him more determined to find a new place to live. The only thing that made him hesitate, even the slightest bit, was the uneasiness he felt for his sister's welfare; he kept searching for a place to rent while he kept an eye on Lillian.

"Katherine, I want you to be careful around Lillian. I don't trust her," Dennis told his sister. "And remember what I told you, don't tell anyone about us having to sleep together; do you hear me. I don't want anyone calling me *cesty*. Everyone calls Ernest that; of course, they have a good reason; but I don't want that to get started about me!" Dennis lectured his sister.

"Okay, Dennis, I won't. I told you I won't," Katherine insisted. "Dennis, why don't you tell dad how you feel?"

"I don't want to cause him any aggravation," Dennis explained. "I don't know why I should care; look what he is causing us. It's not our fault he married a difficult woman. We shouldn't have to pay for it. God knows, we've paid enough." Dennis exhaled to gain some composure.

"Just be careful, Katherine," he warned.

Katherine had come to her dad's house already spoiled by her mother and aunt; however, the new situation caused other negative aspects of her personality to awaken. Her desire to be loved, which brought her to this point in the first place, was again sorely neglected; this fueled her insecurity and increased her stomachaches. Katherine's argumentativeness and complaining became more evident. The resentment she felt toward her dad for not protecting his little princess from the evil stepmother was born.

In the mean time, to get her mind off of her present predicament, Lillian began to think about something else. She began to get curious about what items May had left behind.

"Katherine, come here. I want to ask you something. Didn't your mother have a Victrolla? I seem to remember your dad talking about buying a Victrolla for one of her birthdays," Lillian asked as sweetly as she could. "Do you still have it?"

Katherine was surprised at her question; just the mention of the old Victrolla brought back melancholy memories of her mother and all the old and wonderful records she played. Katherine remembered being told when she was a little girl that she would sit by the music box for hours and listen to the megaphoned notes that came out of it; when the spring wound down she would lie on the floor and kick and scream until her mother wound it up again. She enjoyed thinking about the Victrolla and her mother.

"Yes, I still have it," Katherine answered.

"Why didn't you bring it with you?" Lillian asked, handing Katherine a cookie.

"Aunt Etta likes listening to the records that Mama listened to. She said she would keep it for me along with the other stuff," Katherine said with a mouth full of cookie.

"Other stuff? What other stuff?" Lillian quizzed. Katherine thought for a moment.

"There's a cedar chest and mama packed away some linens, doilies, and some tablecloths," Katherine said pausing to think about what else was in her aunt's basement.

"Was there anything else?" Lillian inquired; Katherine thought some more.

"There are two chairs, a table, and a lamp. That's all I can think of," she said as she took a bite of her cookie. "Auntie said she would save them for when I get married some day." Lillian watched her finish her cookie while she made plans.

"Wouldn't you like to have the Victrolla here so you can listen to all of those records yourself?" Lillian handed Katherine another cookie. "After all, it does belong to you. I'm sure if you told your aunt you wanted it, she wouldn't mind letting you have it now. Don't you think so?" Lillian coaxed.

"I don't know," Katherine replied somewhat uninterested.

Katherine didn't know if her aunt would mind or not. She hadn't thought about it until now. She knew Aunt Etta loved playing the Victrolla in the evenings; it was special to her because May had loved it so much.

"I guess it would be nice to have it here," Katherine surmised. Lillian could see that Katherine was starting to agree with her; she seized the opportunity,

"Why don't you call your aunt and tell her you'll come over tomorrow and pick it up? I can drive you over there after school," Lillian said as engaging as she could.

Lillian knew if she got Katherine over to Aunt Etta's house right after school, she wouldn't be home from work yet and wouldn't be there to protest. Lillian hadn't planned on Aunt June being home though.

Katherine dialed her aunt's number; it was early evening so she knew Aunt Etta would be home.

"Hi, Auntie." Katherine sounded happy and alert.

"Katherine, dear, how are you?" Etta returned with such kindness and love that Katherine got chills at the very sound of her voice; to her surprise her mouth started squiring saliva as she thought she smelled carrot cake.

"Are you making a carrot cake, Auntie?"

"Why, yes, I am. How did you know?"

"I don't know. I just thought about a carrot cake that's all."

A comfort came over Katherine as she remembered being at Aunt Etta's house; she felt a longing to be there.

"Aunt Etta, why haven't you called me?" Katherine asked.

"Why, Katherine, I call every week. Lillian always says that you're not home," Etta explained. Katherine gave her stepmother a dirty look at discovering her ploy.

Lillian ignored the look and nudged Katherine's shoulder.

"Tell her you would like to come over and pick up a few of your things tomorrow," Lillian whispered in her ear.

Katherine's face wrinkled up and her eyes squinted as she tried to hear what her aunt said, and at the same time make out what her stepmother tried to convey to her. She finally realized what Lillian wanted her to ask.

"Auntie, can I come over tomorrow and get a few of my things?" Katherine watched her stepmother as she mouthed more instructions.

"What things are you talking about, Katherine?" Aunt Etta felt a twinge of suspicion.

"I was thinking about getting the Victrolla. I would like to listen to it."

Lillian continued to sit by Katherine; she fed her dialogue like a line coach in a play and Katherine was the actor who had forgotten the script.

"Tell her that your dad will buy you some new records if you have something to play them on; and you want it because it reminds you of your mother," Lillian said in a whisper; her eyes wide with excitement at the thought of pulling off the ruse.

"Katherine, what did Lillian say? Is she telling you what to say?" Aunt Etta asked. Katherine could hear an emotion in her aunt's voice that she had never heard before.

"Katherine, do you really want the Victrolla?" Aunt Etta said in a shrill. She hated the idea that May's things were going to be in that women's house. Why the very idea of that woman touching May's things made Aunt Etta sick to her stomach.

"Yes, I do. I would like to listen to it," Katherine assured her aunt.

"Well, Katherine, of course you can come and get it."

"Okay," Katherine said, feeling the thrill of getting her way, even though it wasn't her idea. The look on Katherine's face told Lillian that Aunt Etta had agreed.

"Tell her you'll come over one day next week after school," Lillian coached.

Etta heard her again; she gritted her teeth almost to the point of making her jaw hurt; she waited for Katherine to repeat the command.

"I'll be over one day next week after school."

"All right, dear; but, I want you to wait until I get home from work", Etta stipulated. "I want to see you."

"I will, Auntie. Goodbye."

"What did she say?" Lillian slyly asked Katherine.

"She said she wants me to wait until she gets home from work so she can visit with me." Katherine thought she would like that too.

All Lillian said was, "Oh," but she thought was, "fat chance."

Lillian waited a few days before taking Katherine over to her aunt's hoping to prevent any resistance from the Tomas family. Although resistance didn't scare her, she wanted to make sure she could get Katherine back over to the house some other time for the rest of the treasurers.

"Let's go over to get the Victrolla today," Lillian suggested as Katherine came in from school. Katherine looked up at the kitchen clock.

"Okay, but it's a little early. Aunt Etta won't be home yet; can't we wait a little while?" Katherine pleaded.

"No, I want to go right now. I have to get back to get dinner for your father. You know how he likes his dinner right on time," Lillian answered, incensed that Katherine questioned her.

Katherine knew better than that. Her father never said a word about when he liked his dinner. He always came when Lillian called.

"I don't think daddy will mind dinner being a little late tonight. I want to wait so I can see Aunt Etta."

Lillian's first impulse was to snap at Katherine, maybe even back hand her for being insolent; however, she wanted Katherine to be in a halfway decent mood when they got to Aunt Etta's house.

"I want to go now; the boys are being good, Katherine," Lillian said firmly.

Katherine wanted to argue some more; but, Lillian's stare was so full of daggers that Katherine winced at the thought that one might actually pierce her. She puffed up and pouted all the way to the car.

Lillian had asked Sam to leave the car that day because she had some errands to run. Sam would often leave the Cadillac for Lillian while he took the bus to work. He didn't mind because she was always in an exceptionally good mood when she had the car all day; that meant he would have an exceptionally easy evening.

Katherine was already perched in the front seat when Lillian opened the car door; she placed Sunny in her lap. She put Stanley in the back seat and hustled herself in the driver's seat; away they sped.

Katherine sat quietly and wished that her aunt would be home. She felt excitement at the thought of at least getting to see her old house, at feeling the warmth, the warmth she now missed; the warmth that she had taken for granted … and wanted back.

"What else did you say was in the basement?" Lillian asked; Katherine went through the list again.

"You know, your dad bought all of those things for your mother; now that she is gone, they really belong to him," Lillian rationalized in her greediness.

"Aunt Etta says they belong to me," Katherine shot back.

"Same difference," her stepmother returned.

"So, your dad says your Aunt June has a temper. Is that so?" Lillian asked.

"Well, I guess so," Katherine answered. Lillian actually felt excited about the prospect of riling June's Dutch tenacity. She sped up.

Katherine cleared her mind of anything unpleasant; she enjoyed the familiar surroundings that she suddenly missed so much. Lillian pulled up in front of Aunt Etta's house and turned off the motor. Katherine jumped out and ran up to the gate. She touched the twisted iron and looked up at the telephone pole; she smiled remembering the funny prank always played on her aunt on Halloween. Katherine ran up the many steps; she pushed on the door expecting to run right in; she found it locked.

Aunt June peeked out the little window in the door; after an uncomfortable few seconds, she pulled it open.

"Hi, Auntie June," Katherine chirped, pushing past her into the living room.

Aunt June didn't acknowledge her greeting as she watched Lillian come up the steps. The two women's stare at each other was cold; they were as rigid as a beam of steel as Lillian brushed past the door.

"June," Lillian said, not as a greeting, simply as an acknowledgement that she had entered someone's home, which her manners demanded; she took pride in her proper social manners no matter where she was.

June didn't answer; she turned and shut the door.

"What do you want, Lillian," June demanded.

Lillian took her time answering as she looked around the room, inspecting and calculating; itemizing.

"June," Lillian said as she walked over to the curio to have a look. "It's not what I want; it's what Katherine wants." She threw a glance at June; Katherine noticed and knew Aunt June didn't like it.

"Katherine, why don't you go down to the basement and start gathering up the records," her Aunt suggested.

Katherine did just that; however, she paused on the steps for a few minutes; she knew what was about to unfold.

"Lil, you don't fool me for one minute. I know this wasn't Katherine's idea. Maybe you think you can fool Etta, but you can't fool me," Katherine heard her aunt snort.

"I'm not trying to fool anyone, June; Katherine wanted her mother's things, that's all," Lillian responded.

"I don't like your kind in this house," June spit; she tried to keep her voice down. "You couldn't leave well enough alone, could you? It wasn't bad enough that you lured Sam away from May; you had to coerce Katherine away from Etta too; now you think you have to have May's things. There are words for a woman like you, but I'm too Christian to say them!"

Lillian responded in a low stern voice as well; Katherine strained to hear.

"Look, June, don't go and get all holier than thou with me. May was a wacko and you know it. She put Sam through hell with all her ranting and raving; accusing him of all sorts of things when none of them were true. He was good to her, he tried to be patient, he provided well for her and the kids. All she did was give him grief. Your family just chose to ignore it."

Katherine heard footsteps come towards the basement door; she slipped a little farther down on the steps.

"Well, if you hadn't been flaunting yourself at that bus stop like the floozy you are, Sam never would have been led astray. No decent woman hangs out at the bus stop," June shot back at her.

"I wasn't flaunting myself. I took the bus to work every day like a lot of people, women included. I was using my education; and by the way, Sam was looking. If it hadn't been me, it would have been someone else. He was tired of putting up with your sister; she wore him out with her constant nagging, and endless needs," Lillian said with anger.

"You've hurt this family enough. Sam's leaving crushed May; it led to her death.

A whore at the bus stop led to my sister's death."

Katherine couldn't believe her aunt said such a thing; at the same time, it was okay. She felt proud that Aunt June stood up for her mother. Now, she had one reason to dislike her stepmother.

"Where do you get off calling me a whore, you frigid old bat? You Methodists sit up here on the hill looking down at everybody thinking you're better than us, when you have the same problems, the same crazy relatives, and the same secrets as the rest of us. Maybe you should look inside your own house before you start blaming everyone else for your troubles," Lillian preached.

Just then Katherine called out from the basement. "I need help with the Victrolla; it's heavy."

"Okay, I'll help you," Lillian called out. "Where are the rest of your things?" Lillian asked hurriedly.

"Over hear," Katherine motioned; she opened her hope chest.

"Oh, what a beautiful tablecloth," Lillian gasped.

"My mama made it," Katherine said proudly.

"Maybe we can get that the next time," Lillian suggested.

Lillian came up the steps struggling with the weight of the Victrolla; with Katherine's help, she managed to get it to the car.

"Open the trunk, Katherine." Lillian slipped the Victrolla in just before she dropped it. Katherine placed all of the records in the trunk and Lillian slammed the lid down.

"Bye, Aunt June," Katherine waved; Aunt June forced a wave back.

Chapter 11

▼

Katherine's head started to nod as the long, straight, northern highway got monotonous.

"Why don't you close your eyes while the kids are asleep?" Miles suggested.

"I guess I should; but, I can't get Herbert off my mind. I'm worried he won't arrive when we do. I'm anxious to get everything in the house, aren't you?" Katherine asked her husband. Miles didn't answer; he simply fidgeted in his seat.

Katherine was tired, but she was almost too anxious to sleep. However, she laid her head back and dozed in and out of consciousness for the next several miles.

With the car quiet, Miles was left to drive undisturbed. He loved to drive; it was his refuge.

Miles had the gift of gab; he loved to tell stories. Katherine's description of him was *a big bull shitter*. He would get involved in conversations with just about anybody and spend hours laughing and joking; just bull shitting. However, the last few years neither he nor Katherine laughed very much. Their many troubles had gotten the best of them, which was one of the reasons they had made the decision to move. Miles sincerely hoped that this move would be good for his family. He would have a better job, more money, and he and Katherine could make a new start; at least that was the reasoning his brother used to get him to move. Miles hoped that it would turn out to be true.

Miles was the second oldest child of Doc and Julia Mangrum. His sister, Lulabell, known to everyone as, Lula, was the oldest, then Miles (Robert), Herbert, Larry, and the youngest, Harry. Their father, Doc, was a ruff man, tall and lanky, with deep-set eyes, and weathered thick skin; he was a drinker. Often times he got rough with Julia and the kids; when he wasn't home making things difficult, he was running around with other women. Julia, a very slight woman, was devoted to taking care of her children and tending to their little farm. Miles helped his mother when his dad was gone frolicking with what stray female he could find.

Miles got along well with his mother; being the oldest boy, she depended on his help a lot. He had seen his dad push her around many times and he didn't like it; he didn't like seeing his sister and brothers whipped either. As for himself, he never made much fuss about being flogged; he kept it all inside not wanting his dad to think he was a weakling, that he couldn't take a good whipping. Besides, it wasn't his nature to moan and complain, he'd rather laugh and joke around, which made it appear that he was oblivious to the hurt his dad inflicted on him; however, his mother knew better.

Miles didn't like to see his mother and siblings abused; he thought many times that he would never be that kind of husband or father; he would never run around on his wife or whip his kids. As Miles got older, he began to distance himself from his dad in order to avoid the mental and physical abuse.

Miles didn't want to turn out like his dad; but, as the apple does not fall far from the tree, Doc's influence on Miles, whether sub-conscience or not, would be far greater than he had hoped, or planned.

The drinking and cavorting finally caught up with Doc; he died when Miles was just fourteen years old, leaving his frail mother to care for the family alone. Miles and his brothers and sister watched their mother weaken under the strain; she died two years later. This put Miles' sister in a very difficult position. She was already married to John Snider, Bun for short, with two babies of her own, and now she had her four younger brothers to care for.

Lula was a good woman, very devoted to her family, and Bun was a good husband. A lot of young married couples would not have taken in four young males, but she never even thought twice about it; it was clearly the right thing to do. During the time she had her brothers in her home, she had two more babies. One by one her brothers grew up and moved out. Her baby brother, Harry, was only eight when their mother died, so he grew to think of Lula as his mother, and she thought of him as her own son. This situation kept the family very close and Lula continued to act as surrogate mother to her brothers throughout their adulthood. It would have been hard to find a finer woman than Lula Snider in the Chattanooga area, except for Etta Tomas, of course.

Miles was sixteen at the time of his mother's death and since she was no longer there to insist that he stay school, he quite; Miles decided it would be better for him to get a job and help his sister. He worked at local garages learning more about auto mechanics, which he very quickly accepted as his life's occupation; he liked it, and he became good at it.

As a young man, Miles began to get better acquainted with his cousin, Hazel, and her friends; he especially enjoyed going over to her house. Miles and his friends liked to hang around Hazel and her friends; one of Hazel's friends was Katherine. Katherine found it exciting being around Hazel; she was everything Katherine had been taught not to be. Hazel was loud; she smoked, drank beer, and really knew how to flirt with the boys. But as brazen as Hazel was, she was a pleasant person and Katherine had fun when she was around her; so did Miles.

Miles had gotten acquainted with Katherine over a period of a few years. He goofed around with the two girls, even flirted with Katherine. However, Miles' flirting didn't get him very far at first. Katherine didn't take his flirting seriously; in fact, she rejected his attention. She didn't know what to make of all the fuss he made over her. She couldn't decide if he was actually attracted to her or if he was seeing how easy she could be; one thing that Katherine was *not*, and that was easy!

Miles knew he had his work cut out for him if he wanted to get close to Katherine; he was shown from the start that she was a deeply complicated woman. Miles decided he was up for the challenge and her rejection didn't stop him; it only made him more determined to win her over. As time went on, his desire became more serious. He knew Katherine would never accept a date at his request so he convinced his cousin, Hazel, to set up blind date for them; that was the beginning of their romance.

Katherine aroused enough to feel the wind gently blowing her hair. The pleasantness sent her memory dashing back to when she and Miles spent some of their dates at an amusement park in town. Her head was flooded with memories of warm, balmy, breezy night when they laughed and enjoyed each other. She could smell the hot, buttered popcorn that was sold at the little red wagon: her mouth watered at the thought of the candy apples and how the deep, red candy crackled when she took a bit. The sounds of the carnival music filled her ears and she could see the tallest Ferris Wheel in the world going around and around. Katherine smiled as she remembered how Miles rocked the car when they got stopped at the top; oh, how she would scream. The louder she screamed, the harder he rocked. They were happy then.

That was ten years and ages ago. Now, she and Miles were headed for yet one more attempt at deliverance. Katherine could feel the cool air and she wondered if she was going to like the climate in the north. She rationalized that saving their marriage would be worth having to cope with the winter months. *Oh well, summer is near; I won't have to think about winter for a while,* she thought.

Katharine straightened up and looked around. "Any sign of Herbert?" she asked.

"No," Miles muttered, clearly irritated as he looked in the rearview mirror. "Herbert, where in the hell are you with the damn furniture?"

Chapter 12

"My stomach hurts; I feel sick," Katherine groaned as she rubbed her abdomen. "I think I'm car sick."

Miles had tried for the past ten years to cope with his wife's bad stomach; he tried to manage all the whining and complaining, all the fussing and blaming; however, a few years into their marriage he began to have a hard time. He never figured out exactly how to handle his wife, even after he sought advice from Aunt Etta, and even the pastor. Their suggestions helped only to a point; he didn't know what to do after that. He answered her with what he thought only seemed obvious,

"You've got yourself all upset thinking too much about the past again. That's all you have done since we left Chattanooga. You have to let all that go or your stomach never will get better," Miles crabbed; he tried very hard to be patient; at the same time, he came off as being disgusted.

"You could be nicer you know; that might help. I need someone to be nice to me," she whined as she rubbed her stomach.

"Awe, come on, Katherine. We're trying to get a new life started. You don't need to keep carrying on like this. Enough is enough," Miles snapped.

Miles knew it didn't matter how nice he was to her; it wouldn't help her stomach. There was too much going on in there; too much of the past was still present. Once she got the nerves in the pit of her stomach flared up, it could go on for days, sometimes weeks and months. Miles had to cope with it the best way he could. He had done a pretty good job in the very early years of their marriage; however, his patience had worn thin some time ago, which largely contributed to their marriage problems.

The girls had learned at an early age to keep their distance from their mother when she was in that state. They sat in the back seat and looked out the window at the strange surroundings of northern Kentucky; they ignored her grumbling.

"We're going to have to stop soon so the girls can eat. I couldn't eat a thing; *ick*, just the thought of food turns my stomach," Katherine moaned; she rubbed her stomach again.

"Has Herbert caught up to us yet?" Katherine asked.

Miles had hoped she wouldn't ask for a while; unfortunately she did.

"Nope! I haven't seen him yet."

At that moment she was too miserable to bother with Herbert. Her stomach pains took her back to another time when her stomach gave her so much trouble.

Six months had gone by since the fateful moving in day; things were still tense when everyone was home together. Much of the time it was very quiet except for the sounds of the Victrolla playing in the living room. Everyone enjoyed listening to it; that made it easy not to talk to each other.

Though miserable, Katherine and Dennis continued to sleep together. They didn't understand why they submitted to such a thing; it continued to be their deep, dark secret. To her discredit, Lillian continued to bask in the misery of her stepchildren.

"Did you find a room to rent yet?" Katherine quietly asked Dennis.

"Not yet, but I have a few prospects," he answered. "Listen, Katherine, I know Lillian is watching me like a hawk. How is she treating you when I'm not around?" Dennis knew the thorn that his sister and stepmother stuck in each other's side had begun to fester, and things were getting worse.

"She's still mean, but she doesn't do it around daddy," Katherine informed her brother.

"Just stay out of her way, okay?"

"I will," Katherine responded.

In the meantime, Katherine did housework chores, cooked, and watched her half-brothers while Lillian arranged her social calendar.

Sam and Lillian were very active people; they belonged to a square dancing group and spent many afternoons fishing. Actually, Katherine liked that part of her new life, except that she was always the babysitter, and she hated fish. Otherwise, she found it exciting. Katherine had never done those kinds of things at Aunt Etta's house; their activities mainly revolved around the church. Even though Sam, Lillian, and the kids attended church regularly, their activities went beyond the bounds of the church, and she enjoyed that too.

At the same time, Katherine was filled with a sense of emptiness and a sudden longing to be back at her aunt's house. Dare she admit that she changed her mind; dare she think what she couldn't say out loud, that she wanted to go back to her aunt's house? It was all she could do to shake these feelings from her young mind; unbeknownst to her, that strong, determined, and conniving psychic, that lay right behind those blue eyes, had already made the decision; she was going to get back to Aunt Etta's, one way or another. In the mean time, she was going to have to manage.

There was one thing, though, that did help a little, just a little, and for just a little while; that was her acquaintance with her cousin, Vesta Cannon, daughter of Auntie Po.

"I'm so glad you came over to help me watch the boys, Vesta," Katherine said after their parents left to join their square dancing group.

Katherine liked Vesta; she was positively captivated by her persona. Vesta was loud, bold, and even a little sexy; everything Katherine wasn't.

"What do you want to do, Vesta?" Katherine asked. "Do you want to play a game, or listen to the Victrolla?"

"I have something else planned, Katherine." There was a mischievous gleam in Vesta's eye.

"What do you mean," Katherine asked. Just then she heard a commotion at her bedroom window. Vesta jumped up with excitement and ran into the room; Katherine followed her.

"What's going on," Katherine screamed as her cousin grabbed a boy by the shoulders and pull him right through the window. They fell past the pink Priscilla's and on to Katherine's bed.

"What are you doing? Are you crazy?" Katherine scolded Vesta.

"We're going to have some fun, Katie," Vesta giggled; she and the boy began to kiss.

Katherine stood dumbfounded at what she saw. She had heard her aunts talk about girls that were promiscuous with boys; she heard what awful names they were called. Katherine hated to think that her favorite cousin was one of those girls.

"Vesta, you must stop right now!" Katherine shouted.

"Katherine, maybe you should go in the other room now," Vesta managed to get out between the feverish kisses.

Katherine did just that. She ran into the other room hoping that her dad and Lillian would not get home early and catch Vesta in the act. Katherine wondered what they doing in there, and in her bed. She wasn't sure what the sounds meant that she heard coming from her bedroom; Katherine heard moans and grunts; she heard the bedsprings squeaking. Poor Katherine was just beside herself.

"Vesta, come out of there!" Katherine called out; there was no answer. "Our parents might be home any minuet." Katherine nervously paced back and forth from the bedroom door to the living room window.

"Vesta," Katherine called to her, "you shouldn't be doing that!"

There was no answer. The bedroom door was not latched so Katherine pushed it open just enough to peek in. Then moonlight allowed Katherine to see her cousin and the boy with most of their clothes off; she gasped at seeing the lovers. Vesta's legs were spread wide with the boy lying between them. The small amount of light allowed Katherine to see an untanned buttock moving up and down rather vigorously. Katherine shot back away from the door. What was she seeing? What were they doing? A picture of the boys bear buttock flashed in her mind again. She had never seen a male without his clothes on, at least not to her knowledge. She hadn't even seen Dennis without his clothes on, despite their strange sleeping arrangements; at the same time, somewhere in the back of her mind, it didn't really surprise her when she saw the square hips and the bigger thighs. Katherine began to get agitated, but she didn't know why. Her stomach began to churn; she started pacing again. Katherine stared at the front door hoping her father and Lillian would not come walking through before Vesta and the boy were finished with their vulgar activity.

"Where'd he go?" Katherine quizzed as Vesta opened the door and came out alone.

"He's gone," she answered in a slow, satisfied way.

"Where'd he go?" Katherine asked again, this time in a higher pitched voice.

"He went out the same way he came in, you silly," Vesta laughed.

Katherine ran to the bedroom and looked around; she noticed her bed covers were thrown completely off the bed.

"He went out the window?" Katherine quizzed in amazement; Vesta nodded. "We're going to have to get this bed straightened up before my dad gets home, Vesta," Katherine ordered. The girls worked together to straighten the bed.

"You shouldn't be doing that; you're going to get caught, you know," Katherine scolded.

"I'm not going to get caught, unless someone tattles on me," Vesta said a little snotty. "Besides, it feels good; I like it, and *he* likes it."

"He'll do anything I want if I keep doing that; he'll stay my boyfriend," Vesta reflected.

Katherine was quiet; her insides quivered. "I'm not going to tell anyone. I won't tattle, Vesta. But you can't do that anymore in my bed," Katherine ordered.

"Oh relax, Katie. I've got to do something exciting or I'll go crazy," Vesta said with a yawn. "Besides, someday you'll want to do that too, you'll see."

However, Katherine wasn't so sure about that. Right then all she thought about was getting the bed straightened up before her stepmother got home and saw the mess.

Sam and Lillian arrived home with Auntie Po and Uncle Dale. Vesta left with her parents good and tired and ready for bed. Katherine hated the thought of getting in her bed. Changing the sheets would help, but she couldn't change the sheets now; Lillian would suspect something.

While Katherine lay in bed she heard the front door open. She figured it was Dennis. It was and within a few minutes he climbed into bed.

"Aren't you asleep yet?" He asked her.

"No, I can't sleep," Katherine responded.

"Are you sick or something?"

"No, I'm just not sleepy," Katherine said.

She pondered whether to tell Dennis about what Vesta had done; she decided she would be too embarrassed. Besides, she told Vesta that she wouldn't tell anyone. Her young mind ran in circles.

"These sheets feel funny. Why are they all loose? They need to be tucked in better or something." Dennis fidgeted to get comfortable.

Katherine lay stiff as a board, her eyes wide opened with fear of being found out.

"I don't know. I guess I didn't make it good enough this morning," Katherine said trying hard to act like nothing had happened.

Dennis squirmed a little more. "Well, go to sleep. It doesn't matter." He turned over and said no more.

Katherine didn't know why she was so afraid that someone might find out. She didn't do anything wrong. At the same time, she felt she would be judged the same way as Vesta if it became known what went on in her bedroom. She knew Vesta would be thought of as a tramp; she didn't want to be thought of that way as well. Katherine hoped that Vesta would not do that again, but to Katherine's dismay, as long as there were square dancing nights, there were boys climbing through the window.

Katherine lay awake many nights as images of what she saw ran through her mind. Something bothered her; she didn't understand why she was so restless and quivery inside. It was as if something was trying to come to mind. A bit of Katherine's elusive past was calling. She had buried any memory of her stepfather, Mr. Peterson, but he was still very much alive and creating havoc in her sub-conscience. He had been far too attentive to her. Katherine's conscience mind had forgotten that he had lain too close to her in bed; her mother on the other side. She also forgot that he didn't attempt to hide himself from her as he dressed, and undressed. Katherine tossed and turned as these memories attempted to resurrect themselves. They never actually did; they only got as far as her stomach, the culmination spot of all of her emotions.

As agitated as she was, Katherine thought about how Vesta said the boy would do anything for her as long as he got to touch her that way. Though Katherine didn't realize it, she began to slowly and methodically grasp the relationship between men and sex; she tucked this information away for future use.

Chapter 13

It was spring and Dennis finally found a flat to rent; one he could afford. The flat belonged to Clovis Windom, who had a sister named Alice. Dennis met Alice through mutual friends and they hit it off right away. Alice had an air about her, which some might call stuck-up, but Dennis was smitten with her. Alice's family was not from any higher social group than Dennis', but she certainly thought so; Dennis felt proud, as well as surprised, that she was also attracted to him. He had been complaining to Alice that he was not happy at his dad's, but he certainly did not tell her why. Alice had mentioned to him that her brother might have a flat for rent, and at a low price. Dennis pursued that lead; to his delight, Clovis agreed to rent it to him.

Now all Dennis had to do was get up the courage to announce his plans. He knew Katherine was going to be very upset, and in his gut, he knew his being gone was going to make Katherine vulnerable to their stepmother. However, he felt he had no other choice.

Dennis understood that his sister had been through a lot in her short thirteen years; she had a birthday while at her dads. She had a difficult time when their parents divorced, and an equally hard time when their mother took them traveling around the country; especially hard for her was adjusting to two stepfathers.

Dennis knew, although the memory was somewhat vague, why his mother left Mr. Peterson. At the same time, he also knew that something tawdry had gone on behind the closed bedroom door while his mother was married to her third husband, Dan Walker, an Englishman she met in Oklahoma.

Dennis recalled sneaking a peek in the bedroom when the door was ajar and saw his stepfather cuddling Katherine in the bed; he could see his arm around her as he kissed her cheek. He winced when he remembered seeing Dan's hand under the covers. Dennis felt cheap even thinking about it.

Although May's brother and sisters knew she was married twice while on her travels, they never knew what went on between her two pedophile husbands and her daughter. Dennis felt if they knew everything it would change how they remembered his mother; furthermore, he certainly did not want to give his dad and Lillian any ammunition in validating that his mother was indeed unfit. He was too good of a son to allow his mother's memory to be defiled.

Dennis felt that bringing up these events would only disturb Katherine, since it seemed she had buried all her memories; resurrecting them would be futile. He tried to be compassionate toward his little sister's needs; however, all things considered, he stuck to his decision.

"Dad, I'm moving out."

"What? Why do you want to do that, son?" Sam asked, genuinely surprised. That disgusted Dennis for he fully expected his dad would have seen it coming. He wanted to say, *Dad, you're not really surprised are you?* He wanted to tell him the real reason why he was moving out; however, the words wouldn't come; he lied.

"Dad, there just isn't enough room here. I found a flat at a really good price; and it's close to my school." Dennis skirted around the real reason.

Katherine listened from her bedroom; she began to cry.

"Well son, have you told your sister yet?" Sam asked.

"No, not yet. I'll tell her in a minute," Dennis replied, clearly dismayed at having to handle that task.

"You'd better go tell her," Sam sighed; Dennis walked toward the bedroom. Lillian watched him walk away with a hint of a smile in the corners of her mouth. Katherine looked up as Dennis entered the room.

"Hey, sis."

"I heard what you told dad. I don't want you to move out Dennis. I don't want to be here alone. I'm afraid," she whined, obviously upset.

"Katie, you don't have to be afraid. I'll stop by every week to check on you, okay?" Dennis reassured her.

"No, that's not okay! I want to go back to Aunt Etta's!" Katherine blurted out. She had held back saying those words for a long time; it felt so good to say them now in front of her brother. She stared right at him, their blue eyes stuck to each other like magnets, neither one being able to pull away at that moment.

"Katherine, let's give this a little while longer, maybe it will work out. With me gone, maybe it will be better." He broke the stare and looked down at the floor. "Besides, you remember what Aunt Etta said; if you leave, you can never go back."

Katherine stared out her bedroom window. "I know, but if you talk to her she might change her mind."

"I don't know about that. She was pretty upset when you left," Dennis remembered. "I think you broke her heart."

Katherine stared at her brother; she didn't acknowledge any blame.

"She'll listen to you, she always does." Katherine augured back.

"Katherine, I can't do that right now," Dennis said as if exhausted. "You're just going to have to make this work for now."

"I can't. I want to go back to Aunt Etta's."

"Katherine, I can't do that right now. I've got schoolwork to do. I have to concentrate on that right now." Dennis left the bedroom and Katherine; tears finally burst forth and streamed down both her cheeks.

Katherine ran to the front door and watched her brother leave. She headed back to her bedroom; but, not before she shot a dirty look at her stepmother; she was the one to blame for this whole mess.

Katherine grabbed her cat and snuggled; their blue eyes met.

"Don't worry Snowball; Dennis will get us back to auntie's. You'll see."

Chapter 14

"I wonder where Dennis has been." Katherine said to Lillian. "It's been two weeks since he's been by to visit."

"So what," Lillian shot back "Come on, you need to fold these clothes." Lillian snarled as she forcefully grabbed her stepdaughter's arm.

Katherine tried to cope with the abuse; at the same time, she couldn't understand why her dad didn't defend her from her stepmother, his only daughter. Even though Lillian wasn't mean in front of Sam, Katherine felt that her dad knew what was going on; it was beyond her comprehension why he wouldn't stop his wife from being so nasty to his only daughter; his little princess. Her knight in shinning armor hadn't been her dad after all. Katherine's longing for that special, chivalristic love increased the ache in her heart, which found its way to her stomach.

The summer wore on and numerous fishing trips and fish fries kept the family occupied. The only reason Katherine tolerated any connection to fish was that Lillian was always nice to her around their friends. That group was socially more influential and Lillian wasn't going to do anything to ostracize herself from them. However, every once in a while, when the time was just right, she gave her stepdaughter a look, just to let her know the change in her disposition wasn't permanent.

Even so, there was one person that knew what was going on.

"Lil, why do you treat Katherine that way?" Po asked. "Why do you do those things?"

Lillian didn't answer her sister when she was confronted.

"Katherine is just a little girl. You shouldn't be that way with her," Po scolded.

"She's just a spoiled brat," Lillian mumbled under her breath.

Po gave her sister a disgusted look. She was careful about not bringing up the subject too much; she didn't want to make matters worse. Po instructed her daughter, Vesta, to keep an eye on things when she and Katherine were together.

Vesta came right out and asked Katherine if her stepmother was mean to her. Katherine shrugged her shoulders and shook her head yes.

"I don't know why daddy doesn't do something about her beating me, Vesta," Katherine said in a low, angry voice.

"She beats you?" Vesta asked, aghast at the thought. "Does she do that a lot, Katherine?"

Katherine paused for a moment; she didn't answer the question; she went on with her complaints.

"Why does he let her do that? I'm his only daughter. Why doesn't he stop her?" She said as he began to cry and rub her stomach.

Vesta wanted to help, but she didn't know what she could do.

"Maybe you could spend the night with me sometime." Vesta hoped her suggestion would make Katherine feel better.

"Yes, I would like that. When can we do it?" Katherine was excited with the idea.

"Well, I'll ask my mom if it would be okay."

"Good," Katherine said. "I hope we can do it soon."

"I can't wait for school to start. That way I won't be here all day with Lillian," Katherine confided in her cousin. Vesta shook her head with understanding. Just then she noticed some odd.

"Katherine, where are your shoes?" As she thought about it, Vesta realized that all summer Katherine had only been wearing house slippers or going barefoot. Katherine didn't answer; she looked down at her feet.

"Where are your shoes?" Vesta asked again.

"They don't fit anymore," Katherine finally responded. "Lillian said she is not going to buy me any new shoes until school starts.

"What?" Vesta winced. She made a mental note to tell her mother.

Vesta and her parents were getting ready to leave the last fisherman's feast. As she went out the door, Vesta turned and looked at Katherine; she privately thought she had some shoes that might fit her cousin; she would bring them over the next time they visited.

Dennis' weekly visits had turned into once a month. When he did stop by, he got an ear full.

"Dennis, you have to do something. Lillian beats me; she treats me more like a maid than a daughter," Katherine confessed in the sanctuary of their bedroom.

"What does dad do when she treats you like that?" Dennis inquired. "Does he tell her to stop?"

"She never does it in front of him," Katherine explained through her snivels. Dennis thought for a few minutes; he wasn't sure what to do. He figured that Lillian was certainly capable of such behavior, but he also knew that his sister was capable of being overly dramatic.

"Well, have you told dad about it?" Dennis continued to question; he had a very hard time believing it was as bad as his sister let on.

"I've tried to, but he doesn't seem to listen, or he tells me to go and play," she answered with her sniffles getting louder and harder.

"And she won't buy me any new shoes. My shoes don't fit anymore," Katherine, added with a burst of theatrics even Gloria Swanson would have been proud of.

"Okay, Katie, I'll talk to dad." Dennis tried to comfort her.

Dennis talked to his dad before he left that day; however, Sam simply played down everything.

"Of course we'll get Kat some shoes before school starts. She hasn't been wearing shoes this summer because she told Lil she likes to go barefoot." Sam seemed perfectly satisfied with his wife's explanation.

Dennis accepted his dad's word about the shoes but never mentioned the physical roughness that his sister told him about. He decided to let it ride for a while.

Dennis had come to the last fish fry with his new girlfriend, Alice. Having a girlfriend was something very new for him; he felt anxious and delighted at the same time. Dennis proudly meandered through the crowd with Alice on his arm while she artfully strutted at his side. Alice was very good at socializing; she was able to charm everyone at the gathering; everyone except Katherine. She didn't know what to make of this woman her brother paid so much attention too; attention she usually got. She didn't like this one little bit.

The guests at the summer gathering were quite impressed with Alice even though she had a bit of a snooty air about her. She carried herself very well; she was dressed to a tee, she enunciated very nicely and sat like a perfect lady. Lillian hated her too. It was hard to imagine that Katherine and Lillian had anything in common, but they did; they both could do without Alice.

The last few weeks of summer sped by and Katherine had been reminding her stepmother that she needed shoes for school. Lillian kept putting it off saying there was plenty of time. Now the time was here and still Katherine had no shoes to wear to school.

Registration day went by with Lillian telling Katherine it would be okay to register late. Katherine was furious that her stepmother wouldn't take her to get some shoes; she didn't want to start school late. She wanted to tell Dennis, but he hadn't been around lately. Katherine thought she could say something to Vesta, but she hadn't been around lately either. She thought she could tell Auntie Po, but she hadn't seen her in a while; that left her dad. Katherine didn't know if it would do any good; however, she decided to try.

"Daddy, I need some shoes for school!" Katherine almost yelled at Sam just a day before school was to start; oddly, he seemed aloof, like he didn't even comprehend what she said.

"We'll get you some, Kat. Don't worry."

"When? School starts tomorrow!" Katherine shouted.

"Kat, calm down. I'll talk to Lil," he said, sounding uninterested.

Katherine stomped away and went to her bedroom to pout. She had gotten so anxious that she was just beside herself. She couldn't get anyone to help her.

Katherine hopped she would see Aunt Po or Vesta soon; they normally visited often; however, they remained absent.

Where have Aunt Po and Vesta been lately?" Katherine got no acceptable answer from her stepmother, which irritated her more that they weren't around to help her get some new shoes; Katherine decided she was going to have to get in touch with Dennis, or maybe even Aunt Etta. Somebody was going to have to help her get some shoes!

It was by chance that Katherine answered the phone one afternoon.

"Dennis, where have you been? You're going to have to get over here! *She* still hasn't bought me any shoes! I haven't started school yet!" Katherine bellowed into the receiver.

This took Dennis by surprise. He assumed his dad would have seen to it by now.

"Okay, sis, I'll be right over," Dennis said. Though he really didn't have the time, Dennis put his books aside, jumped on his motorcycle and headed over to his dad's house.

Chapter 15

Katherine sat in the front seat of the old Nash enthralled in her memory of when her brother finally came to her rescue. She wanted so much to say something, but Miles had told her to change the subject. Most of the time, even though she had wanted to change the subject, she was totally unable to do so. It was beyond her ability to let it all go; most of the time she kept talking about it despite Miles' order.

Miles glanced over at her; he knew without a doubt she was deep in her past. He thought he might try to start a conversation; he also knew if he did, she would drag him back into the past with her. He turned his eyes toward the highway and concentrated on looking for a gas station. Katherine, however, was back at her stepmother's house waiting for her rescuer.

Dennis banged on the front door. Katherine ran to let him in before her stepmother had a chance to even hear the knock.

"I'm so glad you're here," Katherine gasped as she hugged her brother.

"Are you okay?" Dennis asked, looking down at her shoeless feet.

Katherine shook her head yes and turned her eyes toward the kitchen. Lillian came walking in the living room with a surprised look.

"Dennis, I didn't hear you come in. What are you doing here?"

"I want to know why Katie is not in school," Dennis demanded.

Lillian was at a loss for words; she was not used to being confronted.

"Why won't you buy her some new shoes for God's sake?" Dennis bellowed.

Lillian was still without words while she tried to come up with a plausible explanation. Dennis and Katherine stood side by side staring at her. Wide eyed she replied as innocently as possible.

"Why, Dennis, what are you talking about?"

"You know what I'm talking about!" Dennis said disgustedly.

It was all he could do to not voice the rest of his thought, which was *you bitch*; Lillian could read his mind.

"I think you should calm down, Dennis," she demanded.

"I'll calm down when you get Katie some shoes and get her in school," he snapped.

They stared at each other for what Katherine thought was an awfully long time. Lillian could not respond with a good reason; there wasn't one.

"I just haven't had a chance to get to the store," she said trying to reason with him, but that was useless; it was actually ridiculous that she even tried.

"Enough of all of this nonsense. You are going to take Katie to get some shoes today so she can go to school tomorrow," he ordered.

He could see she didn't take to being ordered around very well; that didn't bother him at that moment. Lillian stared at him, contemplating how far she should push him.

"Aren't you?" Dennis demanded again. His anger and forcefulness shook Lillian into an answer.

"Yes, we will go a soon as Sam gets home. That's what I was planning to do anyway."

Dennis knew that was a lie and looked away in disgust. This was a lot for him to handle. He had never been put in this kind of situation and he surprised himself that he was able to stand his ground.

"I think I'll stay here until dad gets home," Dennis said, in total control.

Needless to say, Lillian was incensed. The fact that Dennis seemed to have control over the situation irritated her to death. No one ever got the better of her and she was obviously seething. She stomped back into the kitchen.

Now that Lillian was out of sight, Katherine whispered to her brother.

"Have you talked to Aunt Etta?"

"No, I haven't had a chance yet," he whispered back.

"Well, when are you going to do it?"

"I don't know, Katie, we'll see! I've got to take care of this right now," he snapped.

Katherine didn't like her brother's tone; she sat on the couch and pouted.

While Dennis waited for his dad, he began to look around the room. He noticed that the old Victrolla still sat in the living room; record jackets were propped up at the side of the table as if they were next to be played. His eyes moved across the room to the dining table and he suddenly recognized the tablecloth. He became curious and his eyes continued to move around the room and down the hall as far as he could see. He knew his dad and Lillian's bedroom was down there; he got up and walked toward the room. Dennis got to the doorway and peered in at his mother's hope chest.

"Katherine, what are all of mom's things doing here? I thought they were put away at Aunt Etta's for you."

"She made me bring them here. She said that they really belonged to dad because he bought them for mom," Katherine explained.

"What? That's ridiculous." Dennis' thoughts were interrupted as his eye caught a glimpse of his dad's car pulling in the driveway. Dennis waited anxiously for his dad to get out of the car and into the house. Lillian also saw Sam pull in; she got ready too.

"Dad," Dennis exclaimed as Sam walked through the front door.

Sam looked up in surprise. As their eyes met, Lillian rushed past Dennis and gave Sam a big hug.

"Hi, dear. I'm going to take Katherine shopping for shoes. You know she has got to go to school tomorrow. We'll have dinner a little late tonight."

Dennis stood next to the Victrolla, which he was nearly pushed into as Lillian flew past him. Sam was surprised by the whole situation.

"Come on, Katherine, let's go. You can wear a pair of my shoes. I know they are a little big, but you can manage," Lillian said unbelievably sweet.

Katherine glanced back to see her dad and brother dumbfounded by the ordeal; however, she was finally going to get some new shoes.

Katherine admired her new purchase; she was distracted when the phone rang. Lillian answered it.

"Hi, Kenny."

Katherine looked up. Kenny was their cousin on their mother's side; she wondered why he would call her dad's house.

"Sure, you can talk to Sam. What's the matter?" Lillian quizzed; he apparently didn't answer. Lillian seemed taken aback by what he said, but she called Sam to the phone.

"Yes, Kenny, what is it," Sam asked. Sam became obviously upset.

"Well, I'll go over right away," Sam responded.

"What's going on?" Lillian demanded; Katherine wanted to know too.

"Okay, I'll talk to you tomorrow, Kenny." Sam hung up the phone.

"Dennis had a motorcycle accident. I guess it's pretty bad." Sam explained. "Kenny just got him home from the hospital."

"Is he going to be okay?" Katherine squealed; she began to cry.

"Well, Kenny says his back is a mess; the hide was scraped off; he hit his groin pretty hard on the gas tank. I don't know, he'll probably be laid up for quite a while," Sam said, clearly distraught with the thought of his son being injured.

"Are you going over to see him?" Lillian asked.

"Kenny is staying with him tonight. Dennis took some pain pills so he's asleep now; he'll probably sleep all night. I go see him on the way home from work tomorrow."

"I want to go with you," Katherine whined.

"I won't have time to come home to get you, Kat. You'll have to see him later."

Katherine didn't like being left out; she was furious that she couldn't go with her dad. He brother was her protector and she couldn't have anything happen to him.

To Katherine's delight, and Lillian disgust, Sam arrived home the next day with his injured son in tow.

Sam helped Dennis into the house and headed straight for Katherine's bedroom. Dennis never lost a step because he figured that's where he was going to be anyway. He nearly fell out of his dad's grip and onto the bed. Now he hoped he could get some sleep.

Katherine stood at the bedroom door and stared at her brother; she was glad that he was back in the same house with her. Sam went into the kitchen where Lil was sitting.

"Who do you think is going to take care of him?" Lillian snapped; Katherine listened.

"He couldn't stay alone, at least not tonight. He needs some help; we can at least do that. It's only for a few days." Sam was more forceful than normal.

Lillian heard the tone and didn't say anything more. The banging of pots and bans could be heard all the way to the bedroom.

Dennis slept all that evening and most of the next day; Katherine periodically looked in on him. By the afternoon he was starting to feel a little better, but he still was more comfortable lying in bed. He could hear the voices of Katherine and Lillian, though he couldn't make out the words. Katherine had left a crack in the door and he could see out into the living room; he watched Snowball walk past and jump up on the sofa. He was in a relaxed, twilight state as he stared out the through the slight opening. Dennis was shocked into awareness when he saw Lillian walk up and grab the cat. With one swing of her arm, Snowball went flying across the room with a loud cry.

Chapter 16

▼

"Get off the sofa you stupid cat!" she yelled out.

Dennis had never seen Lillian be mean to the cat before, actually he had never seen her be physically mean at all; he was stunned. He began to put Katherine's stories together with what he saw; he felt very uneasy, and guilty for not taking Katherine's accusations seriously. He tried to focus on what he saw and what he should do, but lying in the quiet room allowed his weariness to get the better of him; he was dozing again when he heard a loud disturbance. This time he struggled to get up.

"Keep that damn cat off the furniture!" Lillian screamed. Katherine picked Snowball up in her arms.

Dennis appeared in the doorway just in time to see Lillian grab Katherine by the arm and whirl her around. The jolt made her loose her grip and the cat went flying again. To his dismay, Dennis clearly saw his stepmother slap Katherine across the face. At that moment he realized no matter how dramatic his sister was, she was undoubtedly being abused.

"Lillian, what are you doing? Stop treating Katherine like that right now," Dennis shouted.

"Mind your own business, Dennis. You're not even supposed to be here," Lillian shot back.

"This is my business. You stop abusing my sister."

"If she needs correcting, I'm going to correct her," Lillian shouted.

"Stop slapping her like that, I said; or else," Dennis demanded; actually, he was not in a position to threaten anyone with the pain he was still in. Katherine ran over to her brother and gave him a hug. She helped him back to bed where he nearly clasped. A few days later he left his dad's house.

"I'll talk to Aunt Etta," Dennis whispered in Katherine's ear.

Even though Katherine had only had her brother for a few days, she missed him all over again. While her stepmother continued to mistreat her, she wondered daily if Dennis had talked to her aunt.

In the mean time, Katherine got to see her sweet Auntie Po; however, it wasn't a pleasant visit. Aunt Po sat at the kitchen table slumped over with her head in her hands. Katherine heard Lillian ask how Vesta was doing. At the very mention of her name, Aunt Po burst into sobs. "Okay," Katherine muttered, "what is wrong with Vesta?" She stood by the kitchen door for a few more minutes hoping to get an answer. Aunt Po cried so hard that she could hardly talk.

"I can't believe this has happened to my little girl," Aunt Po blubbered. "I can't believe Vesta is going to have a baby."

Katherine was stunned as she heard those words. "A baby," she gasped. "Vesta is going to have a baby?"

Katherine wanted to know where Vesta was, but she was afraid to interrupt. She continued to stand behind the kitchen door, to stunned to move; she wondered if she would ever see her cousin again; she didn't.

The winter was very ruff on Katherine. She continued to be abused behind closed doors and she continued to wonder why her father would not put a stop to her mistreatment; why he didn't save his little princesses.

Dennis continued to push his aunt to take Katherine back without much success; however, he continued to try. Dennis found out that the Truant Officer had been called out to the house several times because of Katherine's poor school attendance, which made him furious. Dennis paid another visit to his dad's.

"Katherine, why has the Truant Office been out here? Dennis demanded. "Why aren't you going to school?" With a closer look, Dennis realized that Katherine had her foot propped up on the coffee table.

Before Katherine could answer his first question, he asked another. "What's wrong, sis?" Dennis bent down to get a closer look.

"I stepped on a bone in the back yard," she whimpered.

As Dennis' eyes neared her foot, he became extremely alarmed. What he saw made him angry. Katherine's foot was red and swollen. The spot where the bone had penetrated the tender flesh was yellow with puss oozing from the hole; red lines inched out around the wound.

"Katherine, how long has your foot been this way? This is infected! You need to get to the doctor!" Dennis nearly screamed.

"I know. *She* won't take me," Katherine whined. "I can't even go to school. That's why the Truant Officer was sent out."

"Where's Lillian?" Dennis demanded. Katherine limped behind her brother in search of their stepmother; they found her in the pantry, ironing.

"What's the deal? Why won't you take Katherine to the doctor? Her foot is badly infected."

Lillian was surprised by Dennis' forcefulness. She didn't say anything right away. Dennis demanded an answer.

"I'm putting ointment on it. It will clear up," Lillian said. "You know, Dennis, doctors are expensive. We just can't run to the doctor for every little thing."

This made Dennis even angrier.

"This is no little thing. Her foot is bad; she could get gangrene," Dennis yelled.

"I'll take her when I have a chance," Lillian said as she set the iron down to turn the shirt she was pressing.

This was one of the few times, probably the only time, Dennis lost control; he seized the opportunity and grabbed the iron. He thrust it forward and stopped a few inches from Lillian's face. It was so close she could feel the heat from the smooth, flat surface; she froze.

"You'll take her today!" Dennis demanded between gritted teeth; his eyes glared out from his red face.

Dennis' actions surprised even him; but, he had simply had enough. The pressure of recovering from his accident, continually trying to talk his aunt into letting Katherine come back, Katherine continually pestering him about it, and the genuine concern for his sister had pushed him to his breaking point. He wasn't going to be meek any longer.

Lillian was stunned. She didn't move. She didn't know what Dennis might do next; she had never seen him like this. Lillian thought he might actually burn her. She stood very still and stared at the iron for a few seconds then looked at Dennis, still keeping one eye on the iron.

"Okay, okay. We'll take her when Sam gets home," Lillian submitted.

"That's right, and I'm going to wait right here to make sure of it," Dennis roared. He was so livid he could hardly stand. He placed the iron back down on the ironing board very slowly never breaking his stare from Lillian. She could feel the extent of his rage; she knew she dare not challenge him.

Katherine sat on the sofa and watched her brother fight for her. She welled up with tears, partly because she afraid and partly because she was touched by her brother's concern for her, and partly because of her father's lack of concern.

Katherine had no idea the indelible impression that event made. Her subconscious recorded the sight of her brother holding a hot iron at her stepmother's face in her defense; in her eyes, this would forever be Dennis' shinning moment. Katherine's overworked emotions culminated in her poor little stomach and she began to feel sick.

Dennis went back into the living room with Katherine; he sat down where he could see Lil through the kitchen door. She felt the uneasiness of his stare; she was not used to that kind of treatment and her temper was as hot as the iron. She wanted to strike back at him; at the same time, his actions were so out of character she held back for her own protection. However, she was not going let him totally get the best of her; she continued her ironing.

Dennis looked at his sister. "Don't worry. You're going to go to the doctor as soon as Dad gets home."

Katherine admiringly smiled at her brother; he was indeed her savior.

Sam got home and was thrust into the middle of the commotion. He seemed to genuinely be unaware of how serious Katherine's foot was; that was no excuse as far as Dennis was concerned. It was beyond Dennis' comprehension that his dad was so ignorant about what was going on in his own house, oblivious to the secrets his wife kept from him. Dennis insisted he and his dad take Katherine to the doctor while leaving Lillian at home with the boys. Since Lillian did not resist, he told his son okay. The two men helped a limping Katherine out to the car. Alone and free of Lillian, Dennis thought this would give him a chance to confront his dad.

"You know, Dad; I don't think it's working out having Katherine live with you."

"What do you mean, son?" Sam asked dead serious.

"What do I mean?" Dennis responded in disbelief.

"Come on, Dad; you must know Lillian and Katherine are not getting along! I saw Lillian slap her across the face with my own eyes!"

Sam was silent. Katherine sat in the back seat waiting for her father to scold Lillian and stick up for her. Dennis gave him a chance to explain, to redeem himself; he did neither.

"Well, I know Lil can be a little rough on Katherine sometimes, but you know Katherine can be difficult too," Sam said.

He tried to rationalize by acknowledging Katherine came to his house already spoiled by her aunt, and her age didn't help matters either. Perhaps Katherine did antagonize her stepmother with her teenage moods, and Katherine was on a mission to get back to her aunts, but that was not the answer the siblings wanted to hear from their dad. Katherine being difficult was no excuse for Lillian's treatment of her.

"Dad, Lillian should be more patient and understanding. Katherine has been through a lot; she doesn't need this kind of treatment. Why are you allowing it?" Dennis quizzed.

His silence answered the question. Tears welled up in Katherine's eyes again; she couldn't understand why her father didn't love her enough to stand up for her, why he allowed his wife to beat her, why he didn't save his only daughter. Tears rolled down her cheeks as she ached inside. Sam added one more notch on her fragile belt of betrayals.

Dennis realized trying to reason with his dad was pointless. "Dad, I think maybe Katherine should go back to Aunt Etta's. What do you think about that?" Dennis questioned. Katherine anxiously awaited his answer.

"Etta said she couldn't go back if she left," Sam remembered.

"I know, but I'm going to talk to her. She might change her mind," Dennis said.

They pulled into the parking lot of the doctor's office, which was actually Dr. Butterfield's house doubling as his office. The trio ceased their conversation with Sam never answering Dennis' question.

Chapter 17

Dennis took off on his motorcycle; he was on a mission. He pulled up to his dad's house; without thinking, he jumped off the bike and run up the steps. He rushed through the door.

"Katherine!" He yelled as he quickly scanned the living room and kitchen. "Where's Lillian?"

"She went next door. Why?" Katherine asked, surprised at his demeanor.

"Get your things. You're going back to Aunt Etta's." Dennis rushed toward her bedroom. "Do you have a suitcase or some bags or something to put some clothes in?"

Katherine was stunned. She stood in the middle of the room not knowing what to do; she watched Dennis open her drawers.

"Quick, Katherine, before Lillian gets home."

"What? I'm going back to Aunt Etta's right now?" She gasped.

"Yes, yes. Here, help me get your things."

It finally sunk in that Dennis was serious; she was going back to her aunt's. Katherine quickly ran to the kitchen and got a few brown paper bags; she ran back to the bedroom and stuffed her clothes in them. She looked up and saw Stanley standing in the bedroom doorway watching her and Dennis. She was supposed to be babysitting him; Lillian had taken Sonny with her to the neighbors.

"Where are you going, Katie," five year old Stanley asked.

Katherine didn't answer him. She had actually grown fond of Sonny and Stanley. They were sweet little boys and they had nothing to do with the way their mother treated her. Katherine had developed into a very good babysitter and the boys were comfortable with her as well.

She and Dennis kept stuffing clothes into the bags. Finally, the bags would hold no more.

"That's it, let's go!" Dennis commanded.

As Katherine ran into the living room, she noticed the Victrolla.

"I want my Victrolla; oh yea, and my cedar chest."

"We'll have to come back for them," Dennis said in a rush.

Katherine didn't want to, but she let it go. The important thing was to get out now. As she ran past the dining room table, she looked at the tablecloth that her mother had embroidered.

"Well, this isn't going to stay," she said, determined to take something with her.

Katherine grabbed the edge of the cloth and yanked with all her might. The table cloth came whirling off the table and the vase of flowers, which sat in the middle, went flying, shattering against the wall and splashing water all over the room. The tablecloth flipped about as Katherine ran away; the centrifugal force caused the cloth to wrap around her as if it were offering protection, like a mother covering her child to shield it from harm; as if May had reached down from heaven to protect her daughter.

Katherine bent down and scooped up Snowball. She and Dennis ran out the front door leaving little Stanley standing in the middle of the room all by himself.

Lillian sat at her neighbor's kitchen table with a cup of coffee; she saw a motorcycle whiz past the window. Katherine knew her stepmother saw them, their eyes met momentarily; with a smile on her face, Katherine felt the thrill of escape.

Dennis sped down the road toward his aunt's house with Katherine, Snowball, and Katherine's few possessions stuffed in the sidecar of the speedy Brown. This was the first time she had been in the sidecar, and if she hadn't been so excited about going back to her aunt's, she would have been terrified. She didn't think about her fear, she couldn't wait to get to her old house with the curio full of pretty ribbons. Katherine looked up at Dennis, who was intently concentrating on his driving; she might as well have been looking at a young knight covered in armor, hastening her away from the evil kingdom toward her realm of happiness. Unbeknownst to her impressionable subconscious, this act would be used to judge all the future men in her life.

Dennis pulled into Aunt Etta's driveway. Katherine ran up the steps and through the front door; a feeling of *being home* shot through her.

"Auntie," Katherine yelled as she ran toward her aunt.

"I'm so glad you let me come back," Katherine cried.

Snowball jumped out of her arms as if she felt at home too; Katherine wrapped her arms around her aunt's waist.

"How are you, Katherine, dear?" Aunt Etta asked as she inspected her niece.

She saw a bruise on her cheek and knew instantly that she had made the right decision, despite Elmer's disagreement.

"I'm okay now, Auntie. I couldn't wait to get away from there." Katherine broke her hold on her aunt and whimpered. "I couldn't get my hope chest or Victrolla. Do you think we can go back and get them?"

"Yes, we'll find someone to pick them up. We'll think about that later. Let's get your things in the bedroom right now."

"Dennis, how did Sam take the news that Katherine was coming back to Etta's?" Uncle John asked.

"Well, neither dad nor Lillian was home when we left," Dennis confessed.

"Oh," Uncle John grinned, "I would like to be a fly on the wall when they get home."

Uncle John was glad Katherine was safe from any bad treatment; he gave her a welcoming hug. At the same time, he and his wife were concerned about how Elmer was going to accept this. Aunt June paced the dining and living rooms feeling extremely tense. She could see that her sister was clearly happy to have Katherine back home. It was undeniably a mother-daughter relationship, which validated the move.

That night Aunt Etta went to choir practice with Katherine in tow. Elmer was less than happy to see the two females together.

"Elmer, dear, can we talk after practice?" Etta asked softly.

"Sure," Elmer nodded as he glanced at Katherine; he knew it was about her.

Etta sang uninhibited, free of the betrayal she had committed; Elmer forced the notes from his throat.

"Okay, Henrietta, what do you want to talk about?" he questioned when practice was over.

"Dennis came over today."

"Oh," Elmer said with suspicion.

"He told me things were getting worse at Sam's and asked if Katherine could come back to live with me," Etta explained as she cuddled her niece.

Elmer started to get edgy. "Well?"

"I told him yes, Elmer," Etta blurted out.

"Why did you do that?" Elmer shouted.

"I couldn't stand thinking about her being treated that way any longer. She's just a child. She doesn't deserve that, Elmer," Etta argued as she hugged Katherine.

"I know, Henrietta, but why does it have to be you? Why can't it be one of your sisters? You have a big family."

"She's the closest to me. I was with her when she was born; I'm like a second mother to her. I know that we want a family of our own, but would it really be so bad having Katherine live with us? It's not like she's a toddler; she doesn't need constant attention." Etta tried to convince him.

"I know, but why can't one of your sisters take her? Why does it have to be you?" Elmer asked again, this time more emphatically.

"May asked me to look after her, and besides, my sisters have their own families."

Etta didn't mean to say that because it just validated what Elmer had been saying all along.

"That's right, they have their own families and they don't seem to care whether you do or not. None of them want to take her; they don't want the responsibility or the inconvenience."

Katherine buried her head in her aunt's stomach; she knew Elmer didn't want her. She held on tight to Aunt Etta, hoping that she wouldn't let her go.

"We can make it work, don't you think?" Etta said, trying to sound more positive.

Elmer paced in the hallway. "No, Henrietta, I don't think it will work. I don't want to start off with a teenage daughter, especially one that has such an influence over you. I would always be second to her needs."

"No, Elmer, no you wouldn't," Etta said; she released Katherine and rushed over to her beloved. "You would always come first, I promise." Etta tried to satisfy his doubt.

"Henrietta, I don't think this is going to work. Maybe it wasn't meant for us to be together."

"No, Elmer, that's not true! We were meant to be together; I want us to be together. We're getting married in a month. We have the wedding all planed. Everything's all set," Etta pleaded. "Elmer, please think about this. I don't want to throw away our life together, do you?"

"No, I don't; so see if one of your sister's can take Katherine," Elmer said in a most cruel way.

Poor Etta was bewildered; she was surprise that Elmer could be so heartless toward her niece, and her.

"I can't do that."

"Why not?" Elmer insisted.

"Because, I promised my sister that I would look after Katherine," she repeated.

Elmer was frustrated by her resistance.

"Elmer, I love you. Can't we work this out?" The tears rolled down her cheeks.

"I don't know, Henrietta. Perhaps we should postpone the wedding," he said somberly.

"No, Elmer. I love you. Please, let's try to work this out. We don't have to make this decision right now," Etta implored.

"It was already decided when you let Katherine come back. You knew how I felt about it and you did it anyway," Elmer barked out.

"Katherine is a child, we are adults. She couldn't do anything to help herself, we had to help her," Etta said in a way that exemplified the fine Christian woman she was.

"*You* had to help her, not me!" Elmer barked. "I have to go now."

Etta was stunned and Katherine was bewildered. They walked in the house, Etta's eyes obviously red from crying.

"Ettie, what's wrong?"

"Elmer wants to postpone our marriage," Etta blubbered.

"Oh, Etta, I'm so sorry," June said; as she gave her sister a hug, she cast a stare full of blame toward Katherine.

Etta tried to compose herself and get ready for bed. She and Katherine lay quietly in the dark.

"Aunt Etta, I'm sorry I messed up your wedding," Katherine whispered.

"Try not to think about it, Katherine. Elmer should have been more understanding," Aunt Etta expressed, clearly disappointed.

"I knew he didn't want me," Katherine sniveled.

"Now you listen, Katherine; I want you and that's all that matters," Etta said softly. "Don't you worry about it; he'll come around, I can feel it."

Katherine hugged her aunt.

Chapter 18

▼

Dennis visited his aunt and sister frequently after the move; he brought his girlfriend with him, which didn't thrill Katherine. Dennis wanted the family to get better acquainted with Alice; he even introduced her to the porch swing. Of course, Katherine perched herself on her normal eavesdropping chair.

"Okay, Dennis, is your sister finally taken care of?" Katherine heard Alice ask.

"Yes, she'll be fine," Dennis said.

Katherine peeked through the curtain and saw Dennis try to hug Alice.

"What did your dad say about the whole thing?" Alice asked; she pushed his arm away.

"Well, I haven't actually talked to him about it yet," Dennis answered; he tried again to put his arm around her.

"Don't you think you should talk to him about why you did what you did? After all, you are close to your dad. You want to keep you relationship with him, don't you?" Alice quizzed. Katherine wondered why Dennis' girlfriend had to butt in on their business.

"I guess so, but I'll talk to him later," Dennis answered.

Dennis hadn't talked to his dad yet. He had been afraid to confront him; and a good thing, because Lillian was beyond furious; Sam was perplexed. He couldn't believe Dennis would deliberately take his daughter away without talking to him first; he was surprisingly hurt. His stomach was going to bother him for a long time.

Katherine slid away from the window as not to be found out.

"Aunt Etta, when can we get my hope chest and Victrolla back?" she inquired.

"I talked to Uncle John about it. He said he would get Uncle Bennett to go pick them up. He's got a flatbed that should work just fine." Aunt Etta explained.

"Okay," Katherine said, satisfied with the plan; she ran to answer the phone.

"Hello."

"Aunt Etta, it's for you. It's Elmer," Katherine yelled.

"Of course you can come over, Elmer. I would like that," Etta said as she hung up the phone. Katherine anxiously looked at her aunt.

"Katherine, Elmer is coming over tonight; I would like to have some time alone with him, okay?"

It was a warm, balmy evening and Elmer and Etta sat outside on the swing with the normal little nosy body in place. There was an awkward silence as the swing chain squeaked against the eyebolts, which attached it to the porch.

"Well, Etta, did you get any of your sisters to take Katherine?"

"No, Elmer I didn't. I had no intention of asking anyone else to take her. I thought you knew that; I never told you that I would," Etta said calmly and innocently.

"I thought you realized that I wanted you to get someone else to take her," Elmer said rather coldly.

"I know you said that, but I told you there was no one else. I really thought you understood that," Etta explained more clearly.

"And I thought you understood I didn't want to start out with a ready made family!" Elmer barked, clearly trying to control his emotions.

"Etta," Elmer finally said, "I thought it was the right thing to do when you let Katherine go to her dad's; the way I see it, that's where she belongs. I had no idea you would let her come back," Elmer explained. "I can't start out with a fourteen year old girl; I don't want to start out that way." Katherine heard the stinging words.

"Etta. I'm afraid I'm going to have to call off the wedding," Elmer finally said.

Katherine was too young to understand the hurt that her aunt felt; however, she felt the pain of not being wanted; she felt the ache of rejection.

"Elmer," Etta choked out of her throat. The next sound Katherine heard was Elmer's car door shut.

Aunt June looked over at her niece; Katherine knew her red-headed aunt was mad at her. She didn't mean for anyone to get hurt; she just wanted to stop being hurt. Unfortunately, the hardy seeds of guilt had fertile ground in Katherine's young stomach, and it had already started to sprout.

Chapter 19

Katherine was uneasy. The guilt of the past, the resentment of the present, and the uncertainty of the future made her twitch in her seat while the old Nash continued to make its way north. Miles looked at her; he had seen that look before.

"I feel so bad about leaving my aunt. She's going to miss the kids so much."

Katherine was painfully aware that she was leaving her protector, her defender, and her guardian angel. Her emotions were all jumbled up like ingredients in a mixing bowl. She hated to leave Tennessee and her aunt, she hated to leave her friends; but she wanted to be a supportive wife, she wanted her girls to have a father, she wanted a husband; mostly, she didn't want to be alone.

The north scared her; the farther away she got from the smoky blue drape of the mountains, the more chilled she felt. The cold weather and snowstorms scared her, and not having anybody to turn to scared her even more. What would she do if things didn't go well with her and Miles? It took a lot of courage for her to head off to a strange place so far away from what was familiar.

A little voice came floating up from the back seat. "Why didn't Aunt Etta ever get married?" Carolyn asked.

The girls had heard their mother say many times that Aunt Etta was an old maid.

This gave Katherine all the encouragement she needed. Katherine turned around so she could see the girls in the back seat.

"My aunt was a dear soul. She raised me all by herself. She could have gotten married, but *he* didn't want me, and my aunt wouldn't marry him if he wouldn't keep me," Katherine explained, clearly indebted to her aunt.

Katherine held back the tears that appeared to be ready to bust forth, a scene she had practiced many times. She was very good at playing the moment, even to her daughters, and they had already been programmed to fall into the trap of feeling sorry for her; Katherine didn't care where the sympathy came from, as long as she got it.

"That wasn't very nice," Carolyn said in her nine-year-old innocence.

"She gave up a lot to raise me. And now I'm leaving her," Katherine sniveled.

She continued to tell the girls the story since she had a captive audience.

The girls and Miles had heard the account of her childhood many times, and they would hear it many more. Those two years left deep, permanent scares in Katherine's mind, almost to the point of psychological damage; most certainly emotional damage; and anyone who knew Katherine, knew this story.

Katherine lit a cigarette and looked out the windows. She was quiet for a time before she asked the burning question.

"Where do you think Herbert is? She looked at Miles waiting for an answer.

Miles sighed, disgusted that she brought it up again.

"I don't know where the hell he is. I'm sure he is not more than a few hours behind us." Miles nervously looked out the rearview mirror. "Don't worry about it."

"Don't tell me not to worry." Katherine argued; she hated to be told not to worry; it always ticked her off. "I want to be sure we are going to have some furniture when we get there; and it's getting cold, our bucket of coal is in that truck. How are we going to keep the girls warm?" Katherine nagged.

"Kat, he can't be that far behind us. He'll be there." Miles tried to appease her.

"This is bull shit! He should have stayed closer to us," Katherine snapped back.

"Damn it, stop it now. I told you he would be there. Drop it, damn it!"

They continued to bicker back and forth until Miles finally pulled into a gas station and jumped out. He figured the only way to stop her was to put a break in the line of fire. The girls sat quietly in the back seat; they had become accustomed to their parent's frequent curse filled arguments. Katherine didn't like that he bailed out. She hadn't gotten to say all she wanted too; it would have to wait until he got back.

"I'm hungry," Carolyn whined in the back seat.

"I know, we'll stop soon," Katherine reassured her children.

Katherine looked at the two little ones in the back and wondered how they were going to adapt to their new world; to the little southern family, the north really was a new world.

They waited for Miles to get back, but Carolyn's questions sparked Katherine's memory again. In Carolyn and Judy's short life they had already heard their mother's stories many times; however, Katherine never admitted that she was a difficult teen, only that she was spoiled by her angelic aunt. In Katherine's mind, admitting to being spoiled legitimized all of her actions, no matter what triggered them.

Katherine settled in at Etta's and she was happy when Uncle Bennett went to retrieve her hope chest.

"Where's the Victrolla?" Katherine asked Uncle Bennett.

"Mrs. Williamson said she put it in the shop for repairs; she'll let you know when it is ready."

"Fat chance that's going to happen," Aunt June mumbled.

Things went back to the way they were before Katherine had moved. Aunt Etta made arrangements for Katherine to start piano lessons again; Etta and Katherine sat in the evenings and took turns reading passages from the Bible, and June went back to lecturing her sister.

"Ettie, you're spoiling that girl."

Aunt Etta did spoil her, but she felt such pity for her niece. She felt Katherine had been through so much, she just couldn't scold or punish her; she couldn't add to her pain. Aunt Etta tried to heal her niece's wounds with love and kindness. However, Aunt Etta's love couldn't heal everything and Katherine's eating habits began to worsen; her resistance began to decline.

"Katherine, you're going to have to eat better," Aunt Etta pleaded with her.

"I'm not hungry." Katherine pushed her plate away after only a few bites.

Katherine's need for constant attention and expressions of love nearly exhausted Aunt Etta. Invariably, during Katherine's mood swings, it always came out that she couldn't understand why her father never stuck up for her. His lack of protection was beyond her understanding, or forgiveness. As Katherine's health, physical and mental, continued to fall apart, all the worry fell on Etta's shoulders. Devotedly, she stuck by her unstable niece, loved her, cared for her, and guided her more lovingly than any natural mother.

"Etta, you're quiet tonight," Aunt June mentioned at the dinner table.

"Mable Dixon said something that bothered me," Aunt Etta revealed.

"What?" Katherine interrupted.

"I told the ladies about helping to plan Dennis' wedding. Then, Mabel asked me if it was going to be difficult for me. I told her I wouldn't want to put a damper on Dennis special day, and that I would be okay." Everyone at the table was quiet. They knew Aunt Etta had a difficult time losing Elmer.

"Then she had the nerve to tell everybody that she heard some gossip at White's Emporium. Irene, a teller at the bank, told the checker that their manager was going to be gone for a while; he was going on his honeymoon," Aunt Etta told everyone. "Well, her manager is Elmer." Etta was visibly shaking.

"Somebody ask who he was marrying and Irene said some young German women; apparently he met her while he was in the Army."

"Then, everyone looked at me and asked if I knew who she was; of all things, how would I know who she was?" Etta snorted.

"I told them no; finally they changed the subject." The family finished dinner in silence.

Katherine was not particularly happy about her brother's upcoming wedding. After all, where did this stuck-up woman named Alice come off taking her brother away from her? She had him back, and now he was leaving again; *she* was taking him away.

Katherine's and Alice's personalities collided fiercely, and they wasted no opportunity to piss off each other. At the same time, Katherine was well on her way to learning the art of manipulation and how to get the reaction she wanted; she saw that it worked quite well; at the same time, Alice was very good at it too. She could achieve her goal just as well as Katherine, only Alice's timing was better. Alice knew when to lay it on thick and when let it go; Katherine had trouble with that part.

The wedding came and Aunt Etta and her sisters succeeded in giving Dennis and Alice a very nice ceremony and reception. The entire Tomas family was present with all of its extensions, along with several members of Alice's family, even her questionable brother. Raymond brought his wife of three years, MaryJo Travis, and if the family thought Alice acted high and mighty, she didn't even come close to Raymond's wife. MaryJo never thought the Tomas' were high class enough for her.

Katherine heard her aunts complaining about MaryJo, and her snooty attitude.

"How dare her think she is better than us," Katherine voice to her aunts. Being made to feel not good enough added to Katherine's many scars.

The Tomas' were a proud family and they didn't take kindly to being made to feel they were beneath anyone. It was a documented fact that their ancestors came directly from colonial New England. Their relatives were among the first pilgrims that came to America from Holland; they were aboard the second wave of ships that crossed the Atlantic searching out religious and political freedoms. The Tomas' migrated south and even helped to settle the region of Woodstation, a very prominent area during the development of Tennessee; the family still had a fair amount of influence in the town. Perhaps they didn't have as much money as the Travis family, but they certainly carried their own weight in business, church, and moral conduct; at the same time, MaryJo's arrogant attitude pushed the restraint of the family's integrity. Consequently, compared to MaryJo, Alice was quite tolerable.

Now that Katherine was back with the Tomas', she became privy to all of the family affairs. When she learned Raymond borrowed her inheritance, and hadn't paid it back, she began to harbor resentment. Aunt Etta reassured her that he would pay it back when he could; however, that wasn't good enough, the wait added to Katherine's anxiety and her feeling of betrayal by yet another man.

"Katherine, what are you doing out here on the swing all by yourself?" Aunt Etta asked.

"I was just thinking, Auntie," Katherine said.

"About what?"

"Why didn't daddy love me enough to stop her from being mean to me?"

"Katherine, you've got to let that go now. You must put that behind you and move on. You're young; you have your whole life ahead of you. You must stop it," Aunt Etta implored her troubled niece.

Katherine stared off into space; she wondered who would turn out to be her knight and when would he come and rescue her?

Chapter 20

Aunt Etta decided she couldn't wait any longer; she placed the call.

"Dr. Polk, can you come over and see Katherine. She's been sick with a cough for a few weeks, and now she's worse; she running a fever," Aunt Etta informed the doctor.

"I can be over there in the morning, Miss Tomas," the doctor replied.

In the mean time, Aunt Etta prepared a home remedy learned from her mother.

"June, we're going to make mustard plaster, that might help Katherine breathe better," Aunt Etta instructed.

"Oh, no, Ettie, that stuff is terrible," Aunt June complained.

"I can't help it, June. I think Katherine might have pneumonia. I've got to do something." Aunt June turned up her nose.

"John, you go to the store and get some dried mustard and a can of turpentine?" Aunt Etta ordered. "I have some onions on the back porch. June you can get them chopped."

"I'll find some white, linen cloth while we wait for John," Aunt Etta said.

Uncle John walked in the door and Aunt Etta grabbed the supplies out of his arms.

"Okay, June, put the onions in the pan." Aunt Etta added the dried mustard and enough turpentine to make a paste.

"This is hot enough; spread the pieces of cloth out on the table," Aunt Etta instructed. She and Aunt June pressed the paste between two pieces of cloth until they had several flat compresses.

"Etta, I can hardly breathe because of the fumes; this stuff smells absolutely horrible," Aunt June complained; she held a towel over her nose.

"I know, June." Aunt Etta picked up the plasters and headed for the bedroom.

"What is that smell," Katherine asked in a weak voice. "It's terrible."

"Katherine, I have to put this on your chest; it will help with your breathing and the fever," Aunt Etta said as she opened Katherine's nightgown.

Aunt Etta then placed a hot water bottle on top of the plasters in order to keep the paste hot. Heat made the effects of the mustard more effective; it also made the house reek.

"This can only stay on for twenty minutes," Aunt Etta informed her niece. "If it stays on too long, it can burn the skin."

"Take it off now," Katherine ordered; her aunt ignored her. After the smelly twenty minutes, Aunt Etta gently rubbed Katherine's chest with castor oil to make sure all the mustard had been cleaned off. She repeated this ritual every few hours.

Along with the mustard plaster, Etta placed a few drops of camphor oil in some warm water and placed it beside Katherine's bed; she knew camphor oil was good for opening the sinuses and relieving congestion. Etta hoped the oil would give Katherine, and the rest of the family, some relief; her coughing throughout the night kept everyone awake.

Dr. Polk arrived early the next morning. The smell of the Tomas house made him stop in his tracks. He knew what it was; he had visited many houses where the people used folk remedies; he tried to ignore it and went right to the bedroom with his black bag in tow. He found a thin, sixteen-year-old girl lying in the bed, soaking wet with sweat from the fever.

The doctor examined her very slowly and carefully, making sure he heard every little rattle in her chest. Aunt Etta stood at the bedroom door and watched, much the way she had when the doctor examined Katherine's mother. She prayed to God that Katherine would not join her mother at such a young age. The sound of a harsh cough brought Aunt Etta back to the sick room and she heard the doctor calling out to her.

"Miss Tomas, I want you to get some cool water in a basin, and a towel."

Etta ran out to the back porch and pulled some cool water from the old pump, which still worked, even though the house had been equipped with running water for a few years now. The water from the pump was always cooler than the water from the tap.

"I want you to put cool compresses on Katherine's forehead to try to wane the fever. I don't need to tell you Katherine's condition is serious. She has double pneumonia; both lobes are infected and her breathing is extremely labored."

"Doctor, do you think she will be okay?" Aunt Etta said almost at the point of crying.

"Well, Miss Tomas, I don't know if she'll be okay. Pneumonia is a very dangerous and tricky thing; we can't do much to treat it," Dr. Polk said walking around the bed staring at his patient, obviously feeling powerless to help her.

"The only medicine that might possibly help is quinine. I don't know if it will; I can't guarantee anything. All we can do is give it a try; the rest will be up to her."

Dr. Polk sounded unsure; at the same time, he dug in his bag and pulled out a small cardboard box.

"This is quinine powder. It has to be mixed with water and you have to get Katherine to drink it. I must tell you, it taste very bitter so she will probably resist." He wrote the directions on the top of the box and handed it to Aunt Etta.

"If it is going to work at all, you have to make sure she drinks most of it with every dose." The doctor knew Katherine would have a hard time getting the acrid medicine down.

"Also, try to get her to drink some plain water and broth, otherwise she is going to get dehydrated; we don't want that to happen, it would only make things worse. The next few days will be critical; only time will tell whether she'll be strong enough to fight off the infection."

"Should I keep putting the mustard on her chest, Doctor?" Etta asked.

"Well, I'll tell you. I don't know how much that really helps. That's just an old folk remedy. Some say they have good luck with it. I don't know. If you want to keep putting it on her, well then go ahead. I guess it can't hurt. Just be careful with it; it can burn the skin, you know," the doctor instructed.

"She is awfully weak; let's hope she has a stronger constitution than her mother," Dr. Polk said as he sighed and patted Aunt Etta's arm. "I'll check back with you in a few days."

All that night Etta sat in a chair by the bed watching Katherine; she kept the towel on her forehead cool and the mustard plaster fresh and hot. She talked to her.

"Come on, honey, stay strong until this passes. You have to keep fighting. I love you honey," Etta whispered through the night.

Katherine drifted in and out of consciousness. She knew she heard voices, but she couldn't decipher who's they were.

By the next evening, Katherine out of her head with fever. She thrashed about as she fought her aunts attentions.

"Don't touch me! Don't touch me!" Katherine screamed with her eyes closed. "Get away!"

Aunt Etta, of course, tried to ignore Katherine's ramblings; she tried to calm her down.

"Now, honey, stop that. I'm just trying to cool you off," she said gently. It was all she could do to overlook her niece's foul blather.

"You bitch, leave me alone," Katherine screamed as she pushed Aunt Etta's hands away.

June wanted to be mad at Katherine for being so nasty to Etta, but she kept telling herself Katherine didn't know what she was saying, that fever can make a person talk out of their head. She felt bad for her sister.

"Ettie, come out of the bedroom and rest. I'll sit with Katherine for a while."

"June, I appreciate the offer, but I can't leave her now."

"Well then, I'll bring you some coffee and a biscuit, and you are going to eat it!"

Etta sat by the bed, ate her biscuit and drank her coffee. She was drained; her exhaustion weakened her control and she broke down and sobbed.

Katherine heard noises; however, she couldn't decipher them. At the same time, she felt the love of her aunt very near; she drifted into a deep sleep.

Chapter 21

The third day was the worst. Katherine's fever went higher and her ramblings gave way to unconsciousness. Etta kept hope that she would pull out of it, but the rest of the family got prepared for a funeral. Sam never came to see his daughter, but to Aunt Etta's extreme surprise, he called that morning.

Aunt Etta continued to sit by her niece, praying. She asked Pastor Shives to come over; she hoped he would get there in time.

"Come on, Katherine, honey, come on and wake up," Aunt Etta begged.

To Aunt Etta's surprise, Snowball jumped up on the bed and laid down by Katherine. The cat had been nowhere to be seen for the last few days; Etta tried to use the cat as a way to rouse her niece.

"Katherine, Snowball came to see you. See, here's Snowball right beside you."

There was no response; she tried again, still no response. Etta had a very bad feeling; however, she refused to allow herself to give way to thoughts of death.

As she expected, Dennis and Alice came over that evening. Aside from the normal concern he had for his sister, he seemed overly burdened. Of course she knew he was worried about his sister, but there was something more; even Alice seemed tense.

Pastor Shives had come by to pray and discuss funeral plans, and get an idea of what day would be best to have the funeral. Aunt Etta was disturbed by his assumption; she would not even discuss a funeral; she had not given up hope yet.

The evening wore on; Aunt Etta put a fresh, hot mustard plaster on Katherine's chest and a cool towel on her head. She got up to stretch a bit; she was weary, her face sagged from exhaustion.

"Would you like a cup of tea, honey?" Jimmie asked.

"Not right now," Etta uttered as she rubbed the back of her neck.

"Ettie, do you have any particular …" at that moment Aunt Etta interrupted Jimmie; she lifted her hand up as if to hush her.

Aunt Etta quickly turned around and looked at Katherine; she listened intently. She heard it again; the slightest moan came from what had been the lifeless body lying in the bed. She ran to the bedside. Aunt Etta fell to the side of the bed and grabbed Katherine's hand.

"Katherine, Katherine! Honey can you hear me?"

To her surprise, Katherine opened her eyes. Aunt Etta's astonishment gave way to relief and she began to wail uncontrollably, all the while giving thanks to God. The rest of the family ran into the bedroom only to find Katherine awake.

"Can I have a drink of water?" Katherine's weak voice asked.

"Of course, honey." Aunt Etta was barely able to lift the glass of water. She raised Katherine's head and allowed a little bit of water into her mouth. Katherine opened her mouth just enough to let the water seep in between her parched, cracked lips. She didn't keep her eyes opened very long, but it was evident that she was back with the living. Katherine took a deep breath; it was the first time she had been able to do that in two and a half weeks. She moved her arms, then her legs; life had returned to her limbs.

"Jimmie, Jimmie, call the doctor. See if he can come over to see Katherine," Aunt Etta shouted.

Jimmie ran to the phone and placed the call. Everyone was so astonished they barely knew how to react. First they hugged each other, then they cried, and then they gave thanks to God; then they smiled, kissed each other, and laughed with joy. Calls were made to Dennis, Raymond, Pastor Shives, and of course, the undertaker.

Etta sat a while longer, devotedly holding Katherine's hand. She fondly wiped her face with the cool towel. Etta didn't know what saved her young niece; was it the mustard plaster, the quinine, Pastor Shives' prayers, or her prayers? What ever it was, she knew it wasn't Katherine's time to go. She also realized this frail, fragile girl was tougher and stronger than anyone knew. Etta gave Katherine a few spoons of broth and she fell asleep.

The pneumonia left Katherine very weak, and her poor eating habits did not help; Aunt Etta remained worried; and she still hadn't told Katherine the bad news.

"Katherine, let's go sit on the swing. I want to talk to you," Etta suggested.

"Okay," Katherine agreed. The front porch had become a special place for her and Aunt Etta. They talked for hours on the squeaky swing.

"Tell me again who came to see me when I was out of my head," Katherine insisted.

"Well, let's see; all your aunts and uncles, the preacher and the doctor."

"Who else?" Katherine wanted to know.

"Of course, Dennis and Alice, and Raymond."

"Raymond came?" Katherine asked with surprise.

"Yes, and he sat by your side for a long time. He was very concerned about you," her aunt told her. This made Katherine happy beyond words. Her blue eyes sparkled as her aunt told her about all the people who visited her.

"I remember something smelling terrible," Katherine said.

"Oh yes, it smelled terrible all right. That was those stinky mustard plasters that I put on your chest," Aunt Etta explained. "You should have seen Aunt June; she was covered in the smelly paste and she cackled her complaints like an irritated chicken." Etta and Katherine giggled as the image entered their heads.

"I think I remember something tasting terrible too," Katherine recalled.

"Yes, that was the bitter quinine powder. I couldn't get you to drink it. You kept knocking it out of my hand," Aunt Etta told her.

Each little story, and retelling of each story, filled up an empty spot inside Katherine; a spot that should have been filled with love a long time ago. Katherine's feelings of worthiness and deservedness were being fed by her aunt's stories; she hungered for them.

The next question made Etta agonize. "Did my daddy come and see me?"

Etta took a long pause. She didn't want to answer. "No," she finally said.

Katherine didn't say anything more.

"Katherine, I have something else to talk to you about," Aunt Etta said changing the subject.

"I talked to Dennis the other day." Etta didn't want continue, but she had to. "He and Alice are moving to Florida."

"What!" Katherine shouted. "Why are they moving there?"

"Well, honey, he had a chance to get a good job there; he simply couldn't pass it up. Good jobs are very hard to get these days. We're all very proud of Dennis; he is going to be very successful in the heating and cooling business," Etta explained.

Katherine heard the words but they didn't justify her brother moving away.

"I don't want him to move. Why does he have to move?" Katherine whimpered; her eyes began to fill with tears.

"Katherine, we can't do anything about it; you'll just have to get used to it," Aunt Etta explained.

"When is he going?"

"Well, actually, he will be moving this week," Aunt Etta said.

"This week? So soon? Is he going to come and see me before he goes?"

"Oh, I'm sure he will," Aunt Etta reassured her niece; and he did.

Three weeks passed and the doctor had visited Katherine several times. He came for another visit during the fourth week. He was concerned.

"Miss Tomas, Katherine is not gaining her strength back. I don't like that. She is so thin and pale," the doctor observed. He seemed to be thinking about something. Etta waited for him to continue.

"I think it would be good for Katherine to get away for a while; go to a warm, sunny climate. Is there anyplace you could send her for a while? Do you have any relatives south of here that could take her in?"

Etta searched her mind. None of the relatives lived any farther south than Ringgold, Ga.; well, there was one.

"Katherine's brother just recently moved to Jacksonville, Florida."

"That's perfect. Ask him if Katherine could come and stay with him for a while?" The doctor said, making it sound more like an order than a request.

Etta stared at him for she was actually surprised at his suggestion. She never thought about Katherine needing to recover somewhere else.

"That would be great, Auntie. I would like to go to see Dennis," Katherine interrupted.

"Well, I guess I can ask him. Do you really think that is what she needs, Doctor? "Yes I do. She needs to be someplace warm and sunny; she needs to get out and walk and run on the beach, and have some fun like a normal sixteen year old. It's already warmer in Florida and it's going to be a few more months before it warms up here; she can't wait a few more months, Miss Tomas. She needs to get her strength back now before her health is permanently damaged," the doctor lectured.

"Okay, doctor. I'll call Dennis right away," Etta said with urgency in her voice.

"Good. Let me know what happens, okay?"

Etta walked him to the door. She felt a sense of urgency as she told Aunt June and Uncle John what the doctor advised.

"Well, Ettie, then you'd better call Dennis and see what he says," Aunt June practically ordered.

"But you know, Ettie, they are newlyweds. How do you think Alice is going to take to having her sister-in-law staying with them?" Aunt June sounded doubtful.

"All I know is that Dennis is the only one that can help his sister right now. I hope Alice will understand." Etta tried to sound hopeful that it would work out.

Katherine had no qualms about leaving her aunt's home in order to be with her brother. She listened intently while her aunt called Dennis to explain the situation.

"I know you have a small apartment, Dennis, and I would never impose upon you like this is it wasn't very important," Aunt Etta pleaded.

"What's that? Yes, Katherine can stay alone," Aunt Etta obviously answered Dennis' question.

"What is he saying?" Katherine whispered.

"Alice got a job and you'll be home alone during the day," Aunt Etta repeated.

"The doctor thinks six weeks would be enough time," Aunt Etta explained.

"Okay, Dennis. Goodbye," Aunt Etta said as she hung up the phone.

"What did he say?" Katherine asked, excitedly.

"He said he'll call me tomorrow. He has to discuss it with Alice."

"Ump," Katherine mumbled, "why does he have to do that? Can't he make the decision?"

Dennis and Alice were still newlyweds and enjoyed their independence. At times Dennis missed home; however, Alice was perfectly happy being away from the intimacy of the family; she especially liked not having to share Dennis with them, particularly his baby sister.

Jacksonville, a classier area and close to the state capital, was all new territory for Alice. She felt she could start fresh and make connections with a more influential group of people, a group that didn't know her roots. Alice knew she and Dennis had to start out at the bottom of the economic ladder; at the same time, she was impatient about being able to move up the rungs and out of the tiny flat. Dennis worked hard to keep his new bride pacified; now he had to convince her to have a houseguest.

Chapter 22

"Hello." Aunt Etta answered the telephone. "Well, that's wonderful news, Dennis. I'll call you back just as soon as I can make arrangements. Okay, honey, goodbye."

When Katherine heard the one-sided conversation, she threw herself into a whirlwind of excitement. She was packed and ready to go in no time; however, the hustling made her pale and short of breath.

The family had made the decision to have Uncle John to drive Katherine to Jacksonville. He was a gentle man and Katherine felt very comfortable around him. At the same time, the excitement of preparing for the trip made her tired and she fell asleep very soon after they got on highway. After her nap, Katherine awoke refreshed and began talking to her uncle. He listened to her chatter until she finally got on the subject of her brother, Raymond.

"Do you think Raymond will pay back my inheritance?"

"Oh, I'm sure he will, Katherine; when he gets the money he will," Uncle John said reassuringly.

That pacified Katherine for the time being. John was surprised just how much Katherine remembered and how much detail she recalled; and just how in depth her memories were. He thought they were too vivid for her own good; she had placed Aunt Etta and Dennis dangerously high in her ivory tower, leaving no room for forgiveness for Sam, Lillian, or Raymond. He began to worry about her bitterness at such a young age.

They made good time. "It won't be long now," Uncle John said excitedly.

Katherine was elated. She couldn't wait to see her brother. She hadn't seen him in nearly a month, which seemed like forever.

It was warm and the sun was bright when Uncle John pulled into Dennis' driveway. Katherine barely waited for the car to stop when she jumped out and ran toward the door. Just as she got to the porch, Dennis opened the wooden screen door; they met in an embrace.

"Hi, sis."

He tried not to let it show that he was shocked by her appearance. She was so thin and puny; her blue eyes were sunken in with dark circles under them. Alice came out behind Dennis and greeted Uncle John and gave him a hug; she said hello to Katherine and gave her almost a hug. Alice could put on a gracious act any time she wanted. She offered Uncle John a cup of coffee and then he headed back to Chattanooga.

Dennis got Katherine settled in; she didn't even mind when she found out she had to sleep on the couch. The trip had tired her out so she fell asleep very early. Dennis and Alice wanted to listen to the nightly radio show but they didn't want to wake Katherine; they decided to go to bed early too. Dennis grabbed the afghan, which was thrown over the back of the couch, and gently covered his sleeping sister; he followed Alice into the bedroom.

Shortly after Dennis and Alice went to bed, there was a knock at their door.

"What is it, Katie?" Dennis said; Katherine could hear the squeaking of bed-springs and the rustling of sheets.

"I need to go to the bathroom."

"Okay, come in," Dennis said in a frustrated voice.

The only way to get to the bathroom was to walk past the bed, clear to the other side of the bedroom. Katherine glanced at her brother and his wife lying in the bed; she saw the sheepish look on their face. The couple lay very still, embarrassed at being caught, and by someone so young. Katherine quickly went to the bathroom and hustled out of the room.

Dennis let a few seconds pass then turned to hug his wife again. Alice quickly pulled away and sat up.

"Well, I don't like that a little bit!" Katherine heard her sister-in-law snap at her brother. Katherine lay back down on the couch, but she could hear Alice's displeasure.

"I'm going to have to put up with this for six week?" Alice complained.

"Alice, she's my sister; what am I supposed to do? I have to try to help her." Dennis pleaded with his irritated wife.

"Well, it better not be any more than six weeks. I'm not going to put up with her interrupting us all the time," Alice snorted. The bedroom went quiet so Katherine fell asleep.

The morning brought a little testiness from Alice. Dennis tried his best to smooth thing over; he even got the coffee started. As the morning wore on, Alice soften up a bit, she gave her husband a little kiss before she left to go to work at the drugstore. Dennis had arranged to take the day off work so he could make sure that Katherine was well situated before she had to stay alone.

The first week went pretty well; Katherine began to eat better and her stomach seemed to tolerate the extra food. Though she continued to talk about her and Dennis' time at their father's house, with Dennis holing his breath that she didn't slip and reveal their secret, and her continuous recollection that she almost died from pneumonia, Katherine slowly began to change the subject to more pleasant things. This allowed her discontent a therapeutic environment and she began to heal; she even began to put on a little weight. The doctor's orders had worked.

As Katherine's healing progressed, so did her desire for fun and excitement. She wanted to go to the beach. Dennis and Alice obliged, but short trips until she grew stronger, which she did day by day. Katherine wasn't thrilled about going in the water; however, she loved playing around on the beach and watching all of the people, particularly the young men in their stylish swimsuits. Dennis sat on the beach and watched Katherine walk to the edge of the ocean; she got just close enough to get her toes wet and then scurried back as a fury of waves chased her up the beach. A big wave chased her back to the blanked where Dennis and Alice sat.

"Alice, my work is going to have a picnic next month. Maybe we can go and take Katherine with us,' Dennis informed his wife. "It's going to be a hot dog roast at the boss' house on the beach. Doesn't that sound like fun?"

"Yes, that does sound like fun," Katherine jumped in; Alice couldn't help but give her a dirty look; the question was to her, not her sister-in-law.

"Sure, that does sound like fun; of course, we can go," Alice quickly interjected so that she was the one who gave the approval.

The exercise, which Katherine got on the beach, was very good for her strength and stamina, and the sunshine was wonderful for her mood and coloring. She no longer looked pale and pasty; even her auburn hair began to shine.

Alice tried very hard to cope with the living arrangements; it wasn't easy giving up their privacy. Katherine didn't help matters any either; now that she felt better she was able to plot ways to aggravate her sister-in-law; it was always easy to suddenly to have to go to the bathroom at just the right time; that is, the right time to irritate Alice. She loved seeing the disgusted look on her face as she meandered through the bedroom and back out again.

Katherine absolutely loved telling that part of the story to Carolyn and Judy, who sat attentively in the back seat of the Nash. The feeling that she got the best of Alice gave her great satisfaction. The fact that her brother let her come live with them gave Katherine the feeling she longed for, and still did; the feeling someone thought she was worth caring about.

"You know, they were newlyweds, and it was hard for them to have me stay there with them. Oooh, Alice hated that. When I had to walk through their bedroom to get to the bathroom, oooh, she got so upset." Katherine told her story with a gratifying grin on her face.

"Was she nice to you, mama?" Carolyn asked.

"Well, not very; and she gave Dennis a real hard time because of me being there. Sometimes at night I could hear them arguing about me," Katherine said as she drifted back to the sea side apartment.

One evening after dinner, a co-worker of Dennis' stopped over. He had an electrical problem and he wanted to ask Dennis for some advice; Tommy Hunter was younger than Dennis by four years, making him four years older than Katherine. He was a handsome Irishman, taller and more muscular than Dennis. He had the slightest brogue because he had come to the U.S. as a little boy; Katherine found it very charming. Alice had met Tommy before and both she and Dennis liked him. He was very conscientious and had a good head for the mechanics of heating and cooling. Katherine was quite taken with him; and he with her.

The following evening brought another knock at the front door. Katherine could see the shadow and she knew who it was. She ran to the door and let Tommy in.

Tommy used the excuse that he had another electrical question. That sufficed and for the time being no one was the wiser. Alice had baked a cake and they sat on the porch and had a piece with a glass of iced sweet tea. Most of the talk centered on the two men's work; every now and then Katherine and Tommy stole a glance at each other. Alice saw the flirting, but Dennis had his face buried in his cake; Dennis loved to eat. Tommy stayed a little while longer and then excused himself because it was getting late. Before bed, Dennis, Alice, and Katherine listened to a radio program, but Katherine had a hard time keeping her mind on what was going on; her thoughts were somewhere else. That night, while she lay on the couch, she went to sleep and dreamt about Tommy.

"I just realized something," Dennis said as he sat down at the breakfast table. "Tommy has been over every night this week,"

"Well, Dennis, are you just now noticing that?" Alice asked her husband, making him feel foolish for not noticing.

"Why is he coming over so much? Oh," Dennis asked, suddenly enlightened. "Is he interested in Katie?"

"Yes, Dennis, he is."

"And I'm interested in him too," Katherine jumped in.

Dennis took his time letting all of this new information sink in.

"I don't know about that, you're still very young."

"I'm not that young," Katherine protested.

"What do you think, Alice?" Dennis asked.

"Well, I don't see anything wrong with it as long as they behave themselves."

"Well, okay; but no getting serious. You'll be going home soon anyway," Dennis reminded his sister.

"Not soon enough," Alice remarked under her breath. Katherine heard her, but ignored the remark; she had Tommy on her mind.

The evening was warm and balmy; a gentle salt breeze tossed the palm branches. Tommy had come by to see if Katherine could go for a walk on the beach. Dennis was hesitant at first; he finally said okay. As they walked, Tommy reached down to take hold of Katherine's hand. They strolled on the sand until the sun dipped below the horizon. Dusk was very close to vanishing as a pale moon awaited to emerge and cast its hypnotic glow on the two lovebirds; they realized they'd better get back to the apartment; a good thing because Dennis was waiting at the door.

"It's a little late to be coming home, isn't it?"

"I'm sorry, Dennis, it's my fault. It won't happen again." Tommy was so sweet it was hard to be mad at him.

"Okay," Dennis said as Tommy slipped out the door.

"What's going on, Katie?" Dennis asked as Katherine floated around the room.

"He's so nice," Katherine swooned.

"He's also a lot older than you," Dennis snapped.

"He's not that old; besides, he's just being nice, that's all," Katherine said; she tried not to sound as interested as she really was. Alice stared at her; she understood the look in her eyes.

"Well, I don't want you staying out that late alone with him," Dennis ordered.

Katherine didn't even hear him; her head was too far in the clouds. She was totally consumed with thoughts of Tommy; and she tried not to think about having to go home.

Work at the shop was slow so Tommy only worked three days a week. Consequently, when Dennis and Alice left for work, Tommy rushed over to the apartment. The attention he showed Katherine had her head spinning and she loved it; it was also just the medicine she needed. So far, their relationship had only been mildly physical; simply holding hands, nothing more. Tommy had been a very respectful young man, given that Katherine was only sixteen and he was twenty; however, his desires were becoming stronger and his attentions more aggressive.

"Come on, Katie, let's sit over here on the couch." Tommy said as he led Katherine into the living room; he picked up calling her Katie from Dennis. Katherine noticed the change in his body language and it made her uneasy. He put his arm around her and pulled her close. She resisted just slightly, not because she didn't want to be close to him, but because she wasn't sure what she should do, or if she should do it. It wasn't that she hadn't seen a boy and girl together, she had flashes of Vesta romping with her boyfriends; however, she had already implanted in her mind that only bad girls did that kind of thing; now she was getting ready to do the same kind of thing. On the other hand, she didn't want to chase Tommy away.

He kissed her gently on the cheek at first, and then moved slowly to her lips; that made Katherine snicker.

"Tommy," she giggled.

"I want to kiss you. Don't you like it?" Tommy whispered in her ear.

"Yes," she shyly replied, "but I'm scared."

"Don't be scared. I won't hurt you," he whispered between puckered lips.

He kissed her again. He moved from her lips, to her cheeks, to her neck and back again. Katherine was stiff with uneasiness. She tried to relax but petting was all new to her; she felt terribly anxious. Tommy got more and more aggressive, and the kisses got more and more fervent. His hands began to explore more of Katherine as his excitement grew; she began to pull away.

"Tommy, stop, you're going to fast," Katherine yelled between the kisses. She pushed him away and this time, to his credit, he stopped.

"I'm sorry, Tommy," Katherine whispered.

"That's okay, Katie, you don't have to be sorry. You're just inexperienced, that's all. It's okay," he said trying to cope with his arousal.

Tommy sat for a few minutes waiting for his hot young body to cool off. He was a good Irish bloke and he wasn't going to force Katherine to do anything she wasn't ready to do. Besides, he actually had more on his mind than kissing; he thought this would be a good time to plant a seed.

"You know, Katie, my mother was married at sixteen."

"She was?" Katherine replied, but that didn't really surprise her because she knew of some girls that had gotten married at sixteen.

"How old was your father?"

"He was about my age." Tommy watched closely for her reaction.

"Really?" Katherine responded.

"Yea," he said as he played with her long hair.

Tommy was ready to get more specific when she jumped up from the couch and screamed.

"Oh my gosh! I've got to start dinner. Alice will be home soon." She pulled at Tommy to get up.

"Come on, you'd better go. I don't know what s she would say if she found you here. I don't think she would like it. I *know* she wouldn't like it. You'd better leave now." Katherine pushed him toward the door.

"Okay, okay, but give me a kiss first," he said as he pulled her close one more time.

This time Katherine didn't pull away. She placed a quick, confident kiss on Tommy's lips and pushed him out the door.

Chapter 23

Katherine quickly started to wash some vegetables for dinner. She replayed the whole episode with Tommy over and over. Something kept popping into her head as she worked; she heard Vesta's words, *you'll like it some day, you'll see.* Now she knew what her cousin had been talking about, she did like it; but, more than the kisses, she liked the fact that Tommy wanted her.

Just as she was about to slip a chicken into a pot of hot water, the screen door flew open. It frightened her so much that she dropped the chicken in the water, which made it splash and overflow onto the hot cook stove. The water sizzled as she screamed and jumped back. Dennis didn't even ask if she was okay.

"What was he doing here?" Dennis yelled at her.

"Dennis, you're early."

"Yes, I'm early; I just Tommy turn the corner. I said, what was he doing here?"

"He was just visiting. We weren't doing anything, just talking," Katherine shot back, startled to hear her brother raise his voice.

"I don't want him here during the day when you're alone. What's the matter with you? Don't you know what can happen if you're alone here with a man?" Dennis yelled in her face.

"Nothing happened. He's a nice boy," Katherine said as she tried to convince her brother nothing happened.

"He's not a boy, he's a man, and you're just a girl." Dennis paced the floor. "Don't you know how this looks to the neighbors? They're probably thinking God knows what went on in here." Dennis was just about out of control and it frightened Katherine.

"Dennis, nothing happened," Katherine told her brother, clearly upset.

As Katherine stepped in the light, Dennis could see that her cheeks and neck were red.

"What's all this?" Dennis yelled, pointing at her cheeks.

"What?" Katherine sniveled.

"Why are you all red? I know why. That's what happens when whiskers rub against skin. What was he doing to you?"

"Nothing Dennis; we were just hugging that's all."

"Hugging! It takes more than hugging to get that red," Dennis shouted.

"That's all we did, I swear it," Katherine sobbed.

Dennis was furious; he continued to pace the floor while he listened to his sister sniffling.

"Okay. We'll talk about this when Alice gets home," Dennis told her; he went outside to wait for his wife; he slammed the screen door behind him.

Katherine continued to fix dinner; she had never seen her brother so upset before. Alice came home to a terribly disturbed husband. She listened to what happened that afternoon and then tried to calm him down enough to have dinner. The threesome ate in silence, all the while stealing glances at each other. Alice could see a red and purple mark on Katherine's neck; of course she knew what it was. Dennis had missed it, and a good thing; he might have popped a blood vessel.

There were very few words spoken that evening, and after an early radio program, Dennis and Alice retired to their bedroom. Of course, right after they had gotten in the bed, Katherine had to go to the bathroom. She could feel their stare; she didn't care if she made them mad, they made her mad. She finished her business and plopped down on the couch; however, she didn't go to sleep.

"Dennis, what's the matter?" Katherine heard Alice ask her brother.

"What do you mean?" He replied.

"Why are you so upset just because Katherine has a boyfriend?"

"It's not that I mind if she has a boyfriend; she is very young and naïve; she doesn't know what can happen being alone with a man," Dennis shot back at his wife.

"How do you know she doesn't know?" Alice asked him in such a way that made him remember her experiences as a little girl.

He thought to himself *surly she doesn't remember any of that.* "I just know, that's all, Alice."

"Okay, but I don't understand why you are so upset just because she and Tommy like each other; and okay, so he gave her a little kiss." Alice sounded irritated. "You almost sound jealous."

"Jealous! Don't be ridiculous, Alice," Dennis said disgustedly. "I just don't want to see my sister get into any trouble, that's all." Dennis lay quiet for a few minutes. "Maybe I should send her home a little early."

Katherine sat up at hearing her brother's comment. "No," she mumbled. Katherine went to sleep hoping she could change her brother's mind.

At breakfast everyone was unusually quiet. Before Dennis left for work, he barked out some orders.

"Okay, Katie, you'd better not have Tommy over here today. If you do, you'll go home tomorrow." Out the door he flew; he even forgot to kiss Alice.

Katherine sat at the table picking at her eggs. Alice also got up to go; however, first she had her say.

"Katherine, you'd better listen to Dennis. You've got my husband very upset and I won't have it. Do you hear me?"

Katherine didn't answer and Alice went out the door. Meanwhile, Dennis looked for Tommy. When he found him, Dennis gave him a piece of his mind. Tommy apologized for sneaking around but not for being interested in Katherine. He implored Dennis he would never do anything to hurt Katie; he really liked her and he only had the best intentions for her. Eventually, Tommy's charm won and Dennis said he could see her, but not alone; that was enough for Tommy.

Alice got home with some bad news. "Well, I have to work Saturday. Someone is sick so I have to cover for them," she told Dennis disappointedly.

"That's too bad. We were looking forward to going to my boss' hot dog roast. Are you sure there's nobody else that can work Saturday?"

"Yes, I'm sure; I'm the only one available. I have no choice."

"Well, I really wanted to go." Dennis was clearly disappointed.

"Well, you're not going to go without me, are you?" Alice asked.

"No, no. I don't want to go without you. We just won't go," he reassured her.

Katherine heard what was being said and she started getting upset; she knew Tommy would be there and it was her plan to see him at the party.

"You mean we can't go to the beach party?" Katherine complained. Alice gave her a dirty look.

"No, Katie, we're not going to go without Alice and that's that," Dennis insisted.

Katherine pouted all night and the next few days. Saturday came and Alice was ready for work.

"What are you and Katherine going to do today?"

"Oh, I don't know, maybe I'll change the oil in the car; she can help me. I don't know, we'll do something," Dennis said indecisively.

That pleased Alice and she gave him a kiss goodbye.

"Come on, Dennis; let's go to the beach party," Katherine begged the minute Alice was out of site.

"Katie, I told you that we are not going."

"Come on, let's go anyway," Katherine begged.

"I told Alice we were not going."

"Come on, she won't know it. We'll be back before she gets home. Come on Dennis, I want to go," she pleaded with a whine in her voice. "We won't have to stay very long."

Dennis' daring spirit and yearning to have fun pulled at him and Katherine could see it. When she felt good, she had the same propensity for adventure as her brother; she knew if she kept at him she could make him break.

"Come on, Dennis, let's go to the party," Katherine implored.

"Okay, but only for a little while. We have to be back before Alice gets home."

"That's fine. I'll get ready." Katherine excitedly put on her swimsuit.

They arrived at the beach home of Dennis' boss just after noon. It was a hot, sunny afternoon and the sky was as blue as Katherine's eyes. Though Tommy was on the other side of the beach, he saw them arrive; he had been watching. Katherine's eyes scanned the crowd looking for her sweetheart. Their eyes locked.

"Where's Alice?" Dennis' boss asked.

"She had to work today. She usually doesn't have to work on Saturday, but she did today."

"And who is this lovely, young lady?" He asked as he took Katherine's hand in his.

"This is my sister, Katherine. She's been staying with us," Dennis explained.

"Well, welcome, Katherine," the boss said as he patted her hand, "now go and get something to eat. There's a lot of food."

Suddenly Tommy appeared. "Dennis, is it okay if I sit down here next to Katie?" he asked politely.

"Yes, its okay, Tommy," Dennis said a little perturbed that he made such a point of it.

Other workers sat down and talked, mostly shop; while they ate, the other wives stopped by and asked Dennis' about Alice's whereabouts.

The two lovebirds sat at the picnic table and watched the party-goers play beach games.

"Hey, you two; come on, we're going to play dodge ball," came a shout from the beach. Tommy jumped up ready to play. He took hold of Katherine's arm and tried to pull her up with him.

"Come on Katie. Let's go play," he urged. Her shyness made her pull back.

"Come on," he said playfully.

She finally gave in and they ran side by side toward the fun.

Katherine glowed in the sun; her laughter carried over the ocean breeze and her blue eyes danced as she watched the ball bounce around her; she finally felt alive.

"Hey, Katie, lets go for a walk," Tommy said. As he took her hand, Katherine glanced in Dennis' direction and saw he wasn't looking. The two lovebirds quickly ran off together.

Tommy spied an area partially hidden by a sand mound and some tall beach grass; he and Katherine ducked behind it. They fell down on the sand and embraced. Tommy started kissing her and she struggled to slow him down.

"Tommy, we have to be careful that Dennis doesn't catch us. He said he would send me home if he did," Katherine told her lover.

He continued to kiss her almost oblivious to what she said.

"Tommy," she said again more forcefully.

"I know, I heard you; we'll be careful," he said between the kisses.

Katherine could feel his whiskers rub against her cheek; she remembered it was the redness that gave them away in the first place. She pushed him away.

"Tommy, slow down."

"Okay, Katie. But I can't help myself when I'm with you. I want to be near you. Katie, I like you very much."

Katherine was smitten with him; he made her feel so good, so wanted.

"I like you too, Tommy," she said softly.

Tommy looked at Katie. It was the first time he had seen her in a swimsuit and now he could see the body that formed the curves underneath her clothes. She had put on a bit more weight and began to fill out in the areas that mattered. Katherine watched him study her. He looked at her straight, broad shoulders, not as bony as they first were. She saw his eyes followed her curves down to her tiny waist, which accentuated her ripening breast. His eyes continued downward and glided over her curvy hips, which smoothed out into perfectly shaped thighs, firm and tight. He placed his hand on her shoulder and ran it down her arm to her fingertips, where he placed a soft kiss. He began to breath heavy.

"Katie, what do you say we get married?"

That took the breath out of Katherine; she didn't answer right away.

"What do you think?" he asked again.

"Married?" Katherine gasped. "Tommy, I don't know. Married?"

"A lot of girls get married at your age. You're not too young, and I have a job. I can take care of us. What do you think your brother would say?" he asked, excited at the possibility of it actually happening.

"I think he will want to kill you, that's what," she said, half joking and half serious.

"I'll talk to him about it, okay? What do you say?" Tommy pressured.

Katherine wasn't sure what to say. She knew she liked Tommy a lot, but she didn't know about marriage. At the same time, the more Tommy talked about sixteen being an acceptable age to get married, the more she thought about it.

"Katherine, I'll work hard to provide for us; I'm a good man, I will never be cruel to you. We can have lots of children and they'll all have blue eyes, just like you," Tommy envisioned.

The thought of someone wanting to love her captured her wanting spirit; she sprang up and wrapped her arms around Tommy's neck. Katherine found herself deep in the mystique of this unfamiliar passion; her age was of no consequence in feeling the need for it, and the euphoria of getting it. She knew deep in her heart that she would always love Tommy for loving her.

Katherine and Tommy bounced out from behind the grass right into the path of Dennis.

"Where have you two been? I've been looking all over for you!" he demanded.

"We went for a walk, that's all," Katherine explained. Dennis was in a hurry so he accepted her explanation.

"Come on. We have to leave, Alice will be home soon."

Tommy made a gesture toward Dennis as if he wanted to say something, but Katherine pulled him back.

"What?" Tommy whispered.

"Not now," Katherine whispered back. Tommy sighed with impatience.

Dennis gathered up their things and left. Katherine was quiet on the ride home.

"Did you have a good time?" he asked.

"I had a great time. It was a wonderful afternoon. I hope we can do it again," she replied with more enthusiasm than Dennis expected.

"Did Tommy behave himself this time with you?"

"Of course he did. I really like him; he's wonderful." Katherine swooned.

"Katherine, you're too young to get serious, you're only sixteen."

"I know lots of girls that have a boyfriend at sixteen, some even get married," she informed him.

"I know, but you're not ready for that right now," Dennis said, not even remotely thinking that she might be serious. He passed if off as a young girl's infatuation.

They barely got things put away and settled down when Alice walked in.

"Hi, honey, you're early." Dennis said; he gave her a kiss on the cheek.

"Yea, he let me go early, we weren't very busy," Alice explained.

"Great," Dennis said; he hid a big sigh of relief that they left the party when they did.

Alice started dinner; she chatted with Dennis as he read the paper. The phone rang. "I'll get it, just stay there," Alice said as she walked past her husband to the phone stand.

"Well, hi, Corrine." Dennis recognized the name; he put the paper down in a panic.

Corrine was the wife of one of his coworkers, who happened to be at the party; Katherine noticed his concern.

"Yes, it was too bad; Maybe we can make the party next year," Alice said appreciating being missed. Suddenly there was silence.

"Oh? Well, yes they were just telling me about it," Alice replied; not letting on that Corrine was telling her something that she didn't already know.

She turned to look at Dennis, who sat guiltily with the paper in his lap. She stared at Katherine who could tell by the look on her face that she had just been made aware of their betrayal.

"Really? Well, I'm glad the party was such a success. It was so nice of the boss to invite everyone to his home and the beach," Alice said; she laid on the charm as thick as she could. No one would ever know she had been deceived.

"Thank you, Corrine. We'll be seeing you," Alice said sweetly. When she heard Corrine hang up she slammed the received down, nearly breaking the phone stand.

She stood her ground and glared at Dennis. He was frozen in his chair, as was Katherine, who was sitting on the couch.

"Now, Alice, I can explain." Dennis began to grovel.

"Oh, you think you can explain," she yelled as she slapped the newspaper out of his hands; it went flying across the room.

"How could you go after you told me you wouldn't?" Alice drilled her husband.

"How could you, Dennis? After you gave me a kiss and said that you wouldn't. Did *she* talk you into it?" Alice yelled; she stared at Katherine. "Did *she* talk you into going to the party without me?"

"Come on, honey, it really was no big deal and we only stayed a little while. We had nothing to do so I thought we would go for just a few hours." Dennis tried desperately to explain.

"That's not the point, Dennis, you lied to me," Alice screamed.

"I didn't mean to lie. I really didn't intend to go at first; I changed my mind. I didn't think it would hurt anything; Katherine was board and wanted to go." Katherine cringed as soon as he said that.

"Oh, *she* wanted to go. *She* wanted to go. So because *she* wanted to go, it was okay to break your promise to me?" Alice bellowed.

"No, it wasn't just her; I wanted to go too." Dennis attempted to accept some of the blame.

"Well, I've had enough of this shit!" Alice said, not buying Dennis' excuse. She angrily flew into the bedroom and slammed the door. Dennis and Katherine stared at each other.

"She's really mad, isn't she?" Katherine whispered to her brother.

He ran his hands through his thick curly hair.

"Yea, she's really mad."

He went outside and sat on the porch; he genuinely felt bad he had upset his wife.

"I guess we messed up," Katherine said; she sat down next to her brother.

"Yea, we did."

Dennis was tired and wanted to go to bed, however, he didn't know if he should go in the bedroom. He thought he would take his chances as he slowly turned the doorknob; to his surprise the door wasn't locked. He went in.

"Alice," he said softly, "I'm sorry. I shouldn't have agreed to go to the party. I'm real sorry."

Katherine strained to listen as she got ready for bed.

"I want her gone, soon!" Alice made sure she spoke loud enough for Katherine to hear.

Katherine lay on the couch loathing her sister-in-law. She finally found someone who truly cared for her, and now Alice was going to get in the way.

The following evening, Dennis and Alice arrived home to a meal cooked by Katherine. The atmosphere was much calmer; however, tension floated about.

"We're going to have company tonight," Dennis informed the two women.

"Who?" Alice demanded.

Katherine was about to cut the carrot cake, which she had baked for dessert, when a knock came at the door.

"I'll get it," Dennis said as he quickly jumped up.

"Hi, Tommy," Dennis said. Katherine's face lit up when she heard her brother.

"Hi," Tommy returned.

"Hi, Katie, Mrs. Williamson."

Alice always liked Tommy; she invited him to sit down and have some cake and ice cream with them; the diversion was welcomed.

"Thank you, I don't mind if I do," he said happily.

Katherine sliced the carrot cake and gave Tommy an extra large piece; she dropped a huge scoop of peach ice cream on the top. He noticed and he smiled at her. Dennis noticed too, but he wasn't amused; he still had some uncomfortable feelings about their relationship.

The four diners ate their carrot cake and peach ice cream.

"Katherine, Aunt Etta was right, you have become a good cook," Dennis complemented.

"I agree, Katie, this is wonderful," Tommy agreed.

"Thank you."

Everyone finished their dessert and the women began to clean up.

"Dennis, can I talk to you?" Tommy asked.

"Okay, Tommy. Let's go outside on the porch," Dennis suggested.

The two men went outside. As the screen door slammed behind them, Katherine bit her lip.

Chapter 24

"Married!" came a shout from the front porch. Katherine had been washing dishes and nearly dropped a plate when she heard the bellow.

"What's going on out there?" Alice said, she looked in Katherine's direction. She went to the front door and yelled through the screen.

"What's going on? What in the world are you yelling about, Dennis?"

He jumped up from his lawn chair and stomped into the apartment; Tommy followed.

"What's the matter?" Alice asked again.

"I'll tell you what's the matter," Dennis blurted out.

"Tommy thinks he and Katherine should get married, that's what! He just asked me for permission, and our blessing!"

"Did you know about this? Did you agree to marry him?" Dennis quizzed his sister; she began to get upset.

"Well?" He demanded.

Dennis stood in front of her waiting for an answer. She didn't respond right away; on the verge of crying, she finally answered her brother.

"Yes. We think it's a good idea."

"We? We? I don't think you know what to think about all this. I think he put the idea in your head," Dennis bellowed, "I can't believe this. Are you crazy? You are only sixteen!"

"A lot of girls get married at sixteen," Katherine yelled back.

Tommy could see how upset Katherine was and he didn't like it.

"Dennis, all this yelling is upsetting Katie," he said like a caring, potential fiancé, which really pissed off Dennis.

"Oh, you think this is upsetting Katie? You haven't seen anything yet!" Dennis shouted in Tommy's face, his light blue eyes had darkened to a fuming azure.

"Look, Dennis, can't we talk about this calmly?" Tommy begged; Dennis glared looked at him.

"Katherine and I love each other," Tommy insisted. "Besides, she's missed so much school; it would be hard for her to catch up. Sixteen isn't all that young to get married; a lot of girls get married at sixteen and I can support her just fine."

Dennis stared at Tommy and Katherine; Katherine knew what he was thinking, that she was too young to know about love; but he was wrong, she did know about love, and she knew she wanted it.

Dennis paced the room deep in thought. Katherine took his hesitation as a positive sign. Surly her brother was going to let her be happy; he was going to let her be with the man that loved her.

"No! You two don't know what you are doing! This would never work. Tommy, Katherine is too young. I just can't allow it," Dennis finally decided. Tommy and Katherine both rushed over to him in protest.

"Dennis, you're wrong. We do know what we are doing; it would work out just fine," Tommy continued to argue.

"Dennis, Tommy is right. We want to be together and it would work out, it would," Katherine pleaded.

Dennis had enough. He was exhausted listening to them beg.

"Tommy, perhaps you should go now. I don't want to talk about it any more," Dennis said; he was worn out.

Tommy was heartsick. He left the apartment with his head hung low and feeling empty at having to leave his sweetheart behind; a very sad picture indeed.

Katherine ran to the door and cried; she watched her first true love walk out of sight. She ran all the way to the bathroom and slammed the door.

Later that night, Katherine heard Dennis call Aunt Etta.

"Katherine is coming home."

Chapter 25

Dennis made arrangements with Uncle John to meet him along the highway in the small town of Tifton, Ga. on Saturday. He could have, he supposed, gone all the way, spent the night at Aunt Etta's, and gone home on Sunday. However, Katherine was in such a bad mood, so was Alice, that he decided to spare himself the agony of prolonging the whole mess; one of the few times he actually thought about himself. He had enough with the events of the last two months. He was tired of fighting with his wife, he was tired of fighting with his sister; he was tired of everything. Dennis was glad that his sister had grown healthier, and he was glad to help, but his part was done.

Katherine sat in the back seat and stared out the window. She felt wounded; it hurt so badly. All she could think about was how much Tommy cared about her and how wonderful it made her feel; and how everyone prevented her from being happy. Now her whole being ached with loneliness; she thought how unfair it was to drag her away from her love, her shinning Knight. She knew she was going to be miserable back in Chattanooga.

"There's Ruby's Diner," Alice pointed. "I don't see them yet."

"We can get out and stretch," Dennis suggested as he parked.

"I don't want to get out," Katherine crabbed.

"Fine," Dennis shot back; he and Alice got out.

Uncle John wasn't far away, about a half hour. He and Aunt Etta had decided to make the trip together; Etta was eager to see Katherine. June didn't feel well so she decided to stay home.

Finally, John pulled off the highway into Ruby's parking lot. Uncle John and Aunt Etta could see Dennis and Alice standing out beside the car. Aunt Etta felt

- 146 -

excitement build in her as she got closer and closer. For two months she had worried like a mother wondering if her child was okay.

Katherine finally got out as Uncle John's car came to a halt. Aunt Etta jumped out and ran over to Katherine. Katherine ran to her as well; they met in a vigorous embrace. Dennis and Alice looked at each other just waiting for the bomb to drop. As Katherine and Aunt Etta pulled away from the embrace, Aunt Etta could see her niece had started to cry.

"Why, Katherine, what's the matter?" Aunt Etta asked very concerned. Dennis took a deep breath and started to walk toward them. After a few moments to collect his thoughts, he proceeded to tell Aunt Etta and Uncle John why Katherine was coming home early. As they listened intently, they were caught off guard by the actual reason; never the less, interested in the details. Of course, Aunt Etta was stunned.

"Married! Why Katherine, you're too young to get married. What ever made you think about doing such a thing?" Etta questioned.

Katherine buried her head in her aunt's chest. "He said he loved me, Auntie," Katherine sobbed.

Katherine's comment struck Etta like someone stabbed her in the heart. The pain was so sharp she nearly grabbed her chest. Etta felt her niece's pain; she knew love was all Katherine ever wanted; that in her tender sixteen years, her actions had all been geared toward getting the love she so desperately ached for. Although Etta couldn't believe Katherine actually thought about getting married, she could believe Katherine was drawn to the person offering her the rapture of love; Etta absolutely understood.

At the same time, she was disappointed to find this state of affairs. Etta had hoped Katherine's emotions, along with her body, would be healthier; it was one of the reasons she decided to send Katherine to Florida in the first place. She looked at Uncle John; although he said nothing, she could see in his eyes he felt the same way, they shook their head's in disenchantment.

"Come on, Katherine, let's go home. All of your friends are asking about you and want to know when you will be home," Etta said; she hugged her niece and walked her toward the car. "It will be okay, you'll see, honey."

The newlyweds road home in silence; the hot southern breeze blew against them through the opened car windows, acting as foreplay, hoping to put the flame of passion back into the chilled lovers. Dennis got a glimpse of what it would be like to lose the love of his sweetheart. When he made the decision to take his sister home, he also made the decision that Alice would definitely and absolutely, now and forever, come first. He would never again let his sister get in the way of their relationship, or marriage.

Aunt Etta, Uncle John, and Katherine had a tough journey home. Katherine bitched and complained all the way. She bitched about her sister-in-law and complained about how snotty she was. She bitched about the sleeping arrangements, and the cooking and cleaning arrangements; she complained about the bathroom situation, and how Alice got mad when her brother stuck up for her. Finally, and mostly, she bitched about how Dennis kept her from being happy with Tommy.

Her mood changed when she talked about Tommy. Aunt Etta could tell she was genuinely hurt at the loss of what she considered the love she deserved. Aunt Etta let her talk, complain, and bitch; she let Katherine get it all out of her system. By the time Katherine finished, they pulled into their driveway in Chattanooga. Both Aunt Etta and Uncle John breathed a sigh that radiated *thank God*.

They piled into the house weary from the trip; Aunt June wanted to know all the particulars. Her red hair nearly stood on end when Aunt Etta delivered the bombshell.

"Married!" she screeched. "What in the world has gotten into that girl?"

"June, not now," Uncle John groaned.

"I told you, Ettie, I told you," Aunt June scolded. "I told you she was getting out of control. You have to stop spoiling her! You have to!" June continued to fuss in her high pitched voice.

Katherine ran to the bedroom and slammed the door.

Chapter 26

▼

Katherine talked about Tommy all summer, which kept her stomach in turmoil. Fortunately, her yearning for him became less and less passionate as time went by; soon it was time for school to start, which presented another problem.

"Miss Tomas, Katherine; please sit down," the school counselor said.

"First of all, how is Katherine doing? We know she had some serious health problems at the end of the school year," he recalled as he looked at Katherine.

"She's doing just fine," Etta said; Katherine shook her head in agreement.

"That's good. However, the school feels that it would be a good idea for Katherine to repeat the tenth grade. She missed so many days throughout the year, and then the entire last month. It would be in her best interest to repeat," he explained.

"I understand; if you think it is the best thing for her then okay," Etta agreed.

"Katherine, do you understand?" the counselor asked.

"Yes," she replied; the counselor was surprised there was no opposition.

Katherine started the school year relatively healthy. Though her bad nerves still wreaked havoc with her stomach, her maturation allowed her to focus on new interests, which fueled some character changes.

"Aunt Etta, why does Aunt June call me wild?" Katherine wondered. "I'm not wild."

"I know you're now wild, honey; but, you have to focus on doing your homework instead of going off with your friends all the time. It's important; you know that," Aunt Etta said. "And, your report card says that you talk too much in class. What about that?"

"I don't talk that much. The teacher is just being stupid," Katherine replied.

"Katherine," Aunt Etta scolded.

"Tomorrow after school, Aline Narcissus and I are going to stop by Vern's for ice cream, okay?"

"Okay," Aunt Etta said. "But come home right afterwards to do your homework."

The store was actually an old Inn, which was remodeled into a grocery store. Katherine loved the atmosphere; it had a very romantic feeling, and she loved romance. Katherine liked the rout iron light fixtures and hardware left over from the inn; she also liked the wooden floors and the sound they made when walked upon.

There were four tables with chairs set up for the ice cream parlor area, which were also made of rout iron. The seats of the chairs were padded with red and white striped fabric and Katherine loved sitting on them. The whole ambiance awakened a new emotion in her; she couldn't explain it, perhaps it was independence, maybe the privilege of freedom, or the excitement of new places; all she knew was that she liked it.

As the two girls entered through the beautiful wooden doors, they heard the familiar bell ding-a-ling, and heard the wonderful mellow sound as they walked across the wooden floor; they sat down in the sweet little chairs. However, something was different that day; there was a new clerk at the counter.

"Who is he?" Katherine breathlessly asked her friend.

"Why, Katherine, that's Donald, you know him," she whispered and she proceeded to refresh Katherine's memory.

His name was Donald Weber. He was a couple of years older than Katherine and had already graduated. He was from a good family in town and a most likable guy; the kind of young man every mother wanted their daughter to marry.

"He's cute," Katherine giggled.

Donald was a very attractive young man with classic Spanish features, which he got from his mother. He had a head full of black, curly hair and matching black eyes that could dance when he was happy, or shoot flames when he was angry. He had a wonderful mouth, rather big with a wide smile, which revealed lots of pearly white teeth. Donald was tall, at least 6 foot; his wide shoulders and chest were developed from playing football in high school, and throwing stock around in the store. He always rolled up his shirt sleeves just far enough to reveal huge biceps, which seemed to want to rip the sleeves when they were flexed. Donald had such a welcoming demeanor that he made everyone feel comfortable in his presence.

"Don't you remember; Donald's father owns the Feed & Grain Store outside of town? Aline Narcissus asked.

"Well, I guess so," Katherine replied.

"Donald's Uncle Vern owns this store. He's uncle needed help because he is sick, so Donald said he would help out until he started college."

The girls finished their ice cream; as they left, they directed a good-bye wave at Donald.

"What are you thinking about, Katherine, Donald?" Aline Narcissus teased as they walked home.

"I was just thinking it was pretty nice of Donald to help his family," Katherine said; she was impressed with his devotion.

"I know," Aline said. "Everyone thought it was awfully nice of him to do that. In fact, my mom said every mother in town would give their eye teeth to have their daughter marry him."

Both girls giggled, imagining they could possibly be that girl. Katherine couldn't get him off her mind.

"I never saw Donald in there before, Vern was always there," Katherine said puzzled she hadn't seen him, or noticed him before.

"Well, I guess he was always in the back doing the ordering and taking deliveries; I hear tell Vern has taken a turn for the worse; so now, Donald has to do it all."

"Oh," Katherine said thoughtfully.

"I sure hope Donald doesn't get stuck in that old store instead of going to college," Aline Narcissus said.

Katherine hardly heard her because Donald, and his curly dark hair, flashed through her mind.

Now that Katherine knew all about Donald, she was determined to stop by the store as much as possible, with or without Aline Narcissus, and whether or not she had money for a banana split. She just wanted to be around Donald.

It was quite a job for Donald to handle both areas; it kept him busy running between the ice cream customers and the folks buying groceries. Even if he got behind, his personality was so charming that no one complained; they simply waited their turn with the women enjoying his magnetic good looks, and the men talking to him about his college plans. Everyone loved Donald.

As Katherine and Donald became better acquainted, he developed a cute little way with her; after he finished a rush of customers he winked at her; every time he did that it gave her goose bumps. There was no mistaken it, Katherine was head over heels for Donald.

"Katherine, you're in an awfully good mood these days," Aunt Etta noticed.

"I guess so."

"What's going on?" her aunt asked.

"Do you know Donald Weber?"

"Yes, I know who he is," Aunt Etta said.

"He is so dreamy," Katherine swooned. That was all Etta needed to hear; she knew Katherine was in love.

"So, that's why you stop for ice cream every day after school?" Aunt Etta smiled at seeing her niece in such a good mood. It had been a long time.

"Yes, and I like banana splits," Katherine confessed.

"Well, I hear that Donald Weber is a very nice young man."

"Yes, he's wonderful," Katherine said as she nearly floated away.

"Don't forget to do your homework," Aunt Etta yelled out.

Throughout the summer, Dennis called to see how his sister was doing and to talk to her. Katherine refused to talk to him.

"Katherine, come to the phone. Dennis wants to talk to you," Aunt Etta encouraged. Katherine pantomimed, "no." Even though she was over Tommy, she wasn't over her brother and sister-in-law betraying her; she didn't forgive easily.

Katherine was preoccupied with getting to know Donald better. Time strengthened their friendship and soon it seemed they were always together. People talked about whether they were lovers or just friends; Katherine and Donald provided a lot of fodder for the gossipers; at the same time, it was undeniably obvious that the two got along very well.

Katherine started the 11th grade much the same way as the year before, stopping in to see Donald and getting a banana split almost every day. When it was slow in the store, Donald sat down at the table with Katherine.

"How do you eat all of those banana splits and never gain an ounce?" Donald teased.

"Just lucky, I guess," Katherine said as she shrugged her shoulders and smiled.

Her friend, Aline Narcissus, wasn't so lucky; she had started gaining weight so she didn't stop as much any more.

There were enough slow times for Katherine and Donald to have some intimate conversations. He was a great listener and a compassionate companion; Katherine felt comfortable to delve deep into her past with him. Nobody had been as privy to her innermost feelings as Donald. She allowed him to look into her blue eyes as she revealed her tortured past; she permitted him access to her clear, blue pools, with all her many hurts and scars laying at the bottom, clearly visible. Her caring for him deepened.

As Donald talked, Katherine wondered how warm it would feel to be wrapped in his arms. Sometimes she barely heard what he said because she was lost in a romantic moment in her ivory tower, with her present knight.

"Donald, would you like to come over for dinner tonight?"

"Sure, I'll be there," Donald answered. Katherine couldn't wait.

"Donald, I heard tell there were some robberies going on around here. You make sure you are very careful when you close up and leave the store. You don't want anything to happen. You know you can't be too careful," Aunt June warned.

"Do you keep a gun in the store?" Uncle John asked to the women's surprise.

"Well, actually yes, Uncle Vern has a shotgun under the counter," Donald told him.

"Is it loaded?" Uncle John asked.

"I don't really know, I never checked."

"Well, maybe you should," John advised.

Donald shook his head in agreement, indicating he also thought that was a good idea.

June continued to explain her reasons for caution.

"These days, you know, with so many people out of work, with the depression making things so hard, some people will do anything to get some money. It's true some men can't even buy a loaf of bread for his family; they think they have no other choice but to rob and steal. They get so distraught they do things they wouldn't ordinarily do. Yes, you can't be too careful you know, Donald," she cautioned again.

Donald agreed times were hard and caution was necessary, but he didn't feel the same alarm Aunt June. Nevertheless, he said he would heed the warning and Katherine was happy to change the subject; the thought of violence and guns made her uneasy.

The balmy nights of October in Tennessee found Katherine and Blue sitting on the porch swing on the nights that he stayed for dinner. Aunt June always got pissed off if he and Katherine got outside before her and Uncle John.

"They're always out there on that swing, Ettie. How long do they plan to be out there? I can't even sit on my own swing." Katherine and Donald heard June complain. They chuckled.

The holidays were fast approaching; Katherine loved the holidays. On an exceptionally cool November day, just a couple of days before Thanksgiving,

Katherine ran into the store to get warm before continuing home, and to see Donald.

"What you doing?" she asked.

"Getting the supplies ready for the holidays," Donald replied.

Katherine stood at the counter where he worked on his stock list; she watched him mark the items he wanted to order. Gradually, she began talking, and gradually the subject began to get deeper; soon she was revealing her most vulnerable secrets.

"You know, Donald, I'm his only daughter; you'd think he would have stuck up for me. He has four boys and only one daughter, but he never tried to stop her, not once," Katherine confessed.

Donald felt her pain; he didn't understand why her father hadn't tried to stop the abuse. He could see blue pools swell up in her eyes and suddenly burst forth causing tears to roll down her cheeks.

"Oh, come on, Katie," that was the first time he called her Katie. "Don't cry. That's all in the past; you've got to let it go," Donald said tenderly. She did try to change the subject but she couldn't; she just had to ask him the question that gnawed at her.

"Well, if you had a daughter that was being beat, you'd stop it, wouldn't you?"

Donald listened very intently, truly wanting to know what she was now comfortable telling him; he felt privileged. He always knew there was more behind those pretty, blue eyes, he could see it; but he was surprised just how much lay deeper still.

Just as he was about to answer her, the door flew opened; the bell above the jam rang wildly, and the door slammed shut leaving Emory Akers, a foreboding figure, standing in the doorway. He was a nasty lowlife who spent his time irritating everyone in town. He was tall, skinny, and dirty and he had lost his job when the old mill closed. Ever since then, his bitterness at being unable to provide for his family made him bad-tempered.

"What do you want, Emory?" Donald asked nicely, but sternly.

Emory didn't answer; he just gave Donald a dirty look. Both Katherine and Donald felt uncomfortable while Emory walked around and looked at the goods in the store. Even though Donald always felt uneasy when Emory came in, he remained patient, never condescending to him or asking him to leave. Donald's goodness always offered a certain amount of respect to Emory; he actually felt empathy for Emory's predicament, which he had seen happen to so many others. Emory walked around a little while longer and left without a word.

"I'm glad he is gone," Katherine said with great relief. "I don't like him, he scares me."

"Oh, I don't think he would do anything; he's just a broken down man, like so many these days," Donald philosophized, trying to put Katherine at ease.

"Well, I still don't like him. He's scary and he smells." Katherine turned up her nose.

"I'd better get home; I have homework." Katherine waved at Donald; he winked and waved back.

Katherine forgot about the depressing subject she and Donald had been talking about before they were interrupted; she forgot about nasty old Emory. She skipped home and thought about what she was going to get Donald for Christmas.

Chapter 27

When Katherine got home, Aunt Etta and Aunt June were fixing dinner while Uncle John read the evening paper. Katharine proceeded to tell everyone about her and Donald's encounter with Emory Akers. Aunt Etta and Uncle John cautioned Katherine to stay away from him; they knew how unstable he was; Aunt June screeched from the kitchen.

"He's the devil, that's all. He's the devil."

"June, for heaven's sake; he's not the devil. He's just a broken man," Uncle John scolded his wife.

"Well, I think he's the devil," she shot back at him. Uncle John just shook his head.

"Katherine, you be careful around him, do you hear me?" Aunt Etta warned.

"I will. I don't like him anyway and I told Donald that. He knows I don't like him," Katherine agreed as everyone sat down to dinner.

"I have some news; your oldest brother has a new girlfriend," Aunt Etta announced.

"Really, Ray has a girlfriend?" Katherine asked with excitement. She never liked his first wife anyway, so she was interested in the new woman.

"Yes, Raymond called me before you got home. Her name is Josephine; he sounds very happy," Aunt Etta explained.

"I sure hope she is nicer than MaryJo. She was such a b.... ." Katherine nearly slipped.

Aunt Etta stopped from putting a bite in her mouth and Aunt June nearly dropped her fork; Uncle John simply stared at her.

"Katherine, we don't talk that way," her aunt scolded.

Aunt Etta could read Aunt June's mind, "See, I told you that she was getting wild!"

Katherine didn't say anything; she simply started picking at her food. She didn't like being called down; it was something that was very hard for her to deal with. Aunt Etta tried to lighten things up again.

"Well, maybe we will get to meet Josephine soon."

"I bet Dennis will be happy to find out Raymond has found someone else," Aunt June said.

"I bet he will. He hasn't called lately. Maybe I'll call him and see how things are with him and Alice, and let him know about Raymond."

Katherine didn't say anything; she continued to pout about being scolded. However, the mention of Dennis made her think about Tommy. He was kind and gentle, just like Donald. However, while Tommy had been an escape; her relationship with Donald was real. While she picked at her mashed potatoes, she contemplated whether or not to tell Donald about Tommy. She thought perhaps she would after the holidays.

One wintry day after the New Year, Katherine walked home as usual; she planned to stop by the store to see Donald. It was the day she was going to tell him about her time in Florida.

As Katherine approached Vern's, she could see a crowd of people around the doorway.

"Huh, I wonder what's going on," she muttered. As she neared the door, she could see the CLOSED sign in the window.

"Why is the store closed?" She asked one of the bystanders.

She quickly scanned the group and could see the sad looks on everyone's face, some were even crying. *How odd* she thought.

"Where's Donald?"

"Katherine, you'd better go home now. Your aunt can tell you about what happened," someone spoke up from the crowd.

"What are you talking about? What happened?" Katherine insisted.

She began to feel uneasy. Something was not right, but what? She hurried home. As she hustled along, the only explanation she could come up with was that Vern must have died. That was the only logical answer. He had been sick so it wasn't unreasonable to think he must have died.

She ran up the front steps and burst through the front door. There she saw Aunt Etta and Aunt June standing near the dinning room wringing their hands. Katherine ran over to them.

"What happened at the store? Did Vern die or something?" She shouted, not even considering anything else.

Aunt Etta and Aunt June didn't say anything. Katherine began to breathe hard; she sensed that her assumption was not right. The look of panic started to show on Katherine's face so her aunt finally spoke.

"Katherine, come sit down by me," Aunt Etta said; she led her over to the dinning table.

"Now listen. There was a terrible accident at the store today," Aunt Etta said softly; she took Katherine's hands in hers.

Katherine looked at her. When Aunt Etta looked up to meet her niece's eyes, Katherine could see the tears welling up ready to burst forth; she froze. Aunt Etta had a hard time getting the words out; Aunt June didn't help when she ran into the kitchen crying.

"What, Aunt Etta? What is it? It was Vern, right?"

Then it hit her; Katherine turned white as a ghost. Her eyes got big and her mouth contorted as she forced out the unbearable words.

"Did something happen to Donald?" Katherine said in a guttural scream. Aunt Etta shook her head yes.

"What?" Katherine asked, barely able to make her throat work.

Aunt Etta still could not say the words as the tears streamed down her cheeks. Katherine stared at her aunt encouraging her to tell her the awful news.

"Katherine, honey, Donald was shot today in a robbery."

Katherine was stunned. Her mind raced. She heard what her aunt said, but it couldn't be true. "Shot? Is he going to be okay?"

Aunt Etta took her handkerchief out of her pocket and wiped her eyes.

"No, honey, he's not going to be okay," Aunt Etta said in a whisper. "He died."

Katherine didn't move. She went blank; the room went dark; she felt all alone in a weird, cold, void space. A squeeze of her hand brought her back to a place where she didn't want to be; back to the anguish of a cruel and heartless reality.

"No, it can't be true. It can't be," she sobbed.

Aunt Etta held her niece as tightly as she could, hoping to take some of the hurt away.

"Who did it?" Katherine asked through her tears.

"Emory Akers."

"I hate him! I hate him!" Katherine bellowed. Aunt Etta held Katherine for several hours.

The next few days were very hard for the whole town; when news spread that Emory Akers was found dead from suicide, it only added to the injustice of the whole tragedy. It wasn't that anyone felt the loss of Emory, except of course his family, perhaps they didn't either, but his suicide prevented Donald's family and friends from getting the closure they needed by knowing someone paid for his death.

Katherine barely moved from the sofa, where she sat and stared at the curio with all the pretty ribbons. Katherine's solemnity worried Aunt Etta.

In the months that followed, folks began to heal in the normal fashion; Katherine did not. Once again, her instability had to deal with a devastating loss; the elusive hold she had on her nerves slipped away.

Everyone, the neighbors, the teachers and the friends knew how Donald's death devastated Katherine; they were all willing to be gentle with her, but they were kept in the dark about the latest turn her condition took. Sadly, Katherine's depression sprouted panic attacks. This was all new territory for Aunt Etta and she found it quite unnerving. The manifestation of Katherine's attacks made it appear she was smothering, even having a heart attack, which scared her aunt half to death.

Aunt Etta got up to get the coffee on to perk while John sat at the table and patiently waited for a cup. Katherine lay in the bed rubbing her stomach.

"Etta, I think you should get her to a doctor," Uncle John advised.

"I will, John. I know you're right." She confided in him. "I just wish Katherine could get her nerves under control. It hurts me so much to see her this way; I don't know how to help."

"Etta, you're doing the best that you can; you're being there for her, you're kind, patient, and understanding. That's all you, or any of us, can do," he comforted. "You know, Etta, seeing what Katherine is going through is just like watching May. She has inherited the same imbalance her mother had. Don't you see it?"

Katherine listened; however, her inward trembling prevented her from fully relating to her own mother's condition. She cried, but she didn't know why.

"I think you should take her to a doctor," Uncle John advised again.

"Yes, I will. I'll call the doctor today."

Aunt Etta made an appointment with their family doctor; she took the day off work and took Katherine out of school. The doctor's office was across town so they set out to catch the bus. As they waited, Aunt Etta noticed Katherine's growing anxiety. Her breathing began to get more rapid the longer they waited.

"Katherine, what's the matter?" Aunt Etta asked, very concerned. Katherine looked down the street and saw the bus coming.

"I don't want to get on the bus," she said, more anxious than her aunt had ever seen before.

"Well, Katherine, we can't walk. The office is too far," Etta explained. "Come on honey, it will be okay. I'm here with you. Just try to relax."

Katherine took some deep breaths and tried very hard to relax, but it was easier said than done; and only she knew that. The bus pulled up to the curb and the doors opened. Katherine froze; she looked in at the bus driver. Etta took hold of her arm and gave a gentle tug.

"Come on, honey, let's go."

Though hesitant, Katherine got on the bus. During the entire trip across town she fidgeted, panted, sweated, and couldn't wait until the bus got to where they were going; she wanted off. Etta watched her niece; she made metal notes about her actions as new symptoms rapidly revealed themselves.

"Miss Tomas," the doctor said after the initial examination, "Katherine is a very nervous person; I can see that she is prone to panic attacks. However, there isn't a lot I can do to help her. I could prescribe some drugs; however, she's so young, I hate to do that at this point. I could arrange some electroshock treatments, but I'd rather not; I don't think she is bad enough for that."

"Doctor, you can see the nervous state she's in," Aunt Etta said as she looked at her frantic niece. "She can barely breathe."

"Yes, I can see that; its part of the anxiety associated with the panic attacks."

"She needs something to calm her down. She needs some help," Aunt Etta pleaded.

"I understand your concern, Miss Tomas. However, I don't want to introduce her to psychological drugs and treatments at this point; I don't want her to get lost in the quagmire of vague mental imbalances; I don't want her to end up in a mental institution, like so many others," the doctor warned.

"I wouldn't like that either. What can I do to help her?" Aunt Etta was clearly distressed at not knowing what to do for her niece.

"Take her home; be understanding and patient. Reassure her that the panic attacks will pass. Give it a little time. That's the best advice I can give you."

Katherine and Aunt Etta left the office; they were disappointed that a more substantial treatment wasn't offered.

Katherine rode home in silence; she thought of nothing else except trying to take a deep breath.

Chapter 28

Katherine sat in the front seat of the brakeless Nash and stared out the window. She remembered how uncomfortable it was when she got a panic attack and unable to fill her lungs with the precious air they needed. She had experienced countless attacks since that first frightening one; as she watched the road going north, she restrained herself from feeling that same horrible feeling. So many things troubled her; any one of them could have set her off. Usually an attack was beyond her control; luckily for everyone, she was able to hold back.

Miles had finally stopped at a small restaurant. The kids settled down with a full stomach and went to sleep. Linda was contented with having taken a full bottle of fresh milk and was ready to drift off. In fact, Miles was getting sleepy himself; since it was dusk, he decided to pull over at a rest stop and take a nap. The weather was quite cool since they were a good distance north of the Mason Dixon Line; Katherine had Miles get some blankets out of the trunk to cover up the girls.

Before long everyone was asleep except Katherine. She simply couldn't leave the past long enough to allow her mind to relax and let her body give in to much needed rest.

Katherine sat quietly and looked out into the darkness; so many things ran through her mind. She remembered when Aunt Etta was so kind and gentle with her. Katherine recalled how her aunt walked up and down the street for hours with her because she couldn't get on the bus or streetcar. Katherine couldn't forget that her aunt gave up hours upon hours helping her talk out an anxiety or panic attack. She wondered who would help her way up North. Miles had been understanding when they were first married; however, now he was easily irritated; he had gotten, in his words, fed up with the whole mess.

Her thoughts wandered back to Tommy and Donald. She wondered how different her life would have been if she had been allowed to marry Tommy. He was so kind and attentive; perhaps he would have been more faithful than Miles. But Miles was kind and attentive too, at first. If Donald had lived, would she have actually married him? He was so funny and smart; he would have been a good provider. But Miles was funny too, and he always had a job and provided for her and the children.

Dwelling on what might have been only made her melancholy, which didn't help her to cope with what was happening now; in addition, the uncertainty of the future bothered her. She was a woman who liked having plans. Miles' spontaneity always irked her; she very seldom found it exciting or romantic. She twitched as she mumbled, "where in the hell did Herbert end up with all their furniture."

Katherine puffed on her cigarette as she stared out into the darkness. At one short time in her life she was happy and at ease. That time, not so far back, felt like many lifetimes ago. Katherine searched the rising stars for Pegasus, which carried her back to her senior year in high school.

Aunt Etta kept Katherine involved in activities, spent endless time with her, and talked for hours; for the most part, it worked. Katherine grew and matured and her personality began to exhibit a wonderful sense of humor. She began to finally make some good friends and she seemed very happy.

One particularly good friendship was with her cousin, Erlene, Uncle Terah's daughter. She and Erlene had not been around each other very much as youngsters; the timing was never right with Katherine moving around so much. However, the girls had gotten re-acquainted and they liked each other. Actually it was Erlene who wanted to get better acquainted with Katherine, rather than the other way around. To Erlene, Katherine was worldly; she had seen other places and had enjoyed a couple of boyfriends. Though Katherine had been somewhat sheltered in her life, it was nothing compared to Erlene.

Erlene was the only child of Terah and Marles and her parent's world revolved around her. Because of all of her difficulty getting pregnant, Marles never had another child. Needless to say, Erlene was pampered and protected; she was treated like a fine, china teacup, which fit her dainty, delicate persona to a tee. For Erlene, living in her mollycoddled world made Katherine seem like a sophisticated women; but to Erlene's parents, a wild woman.

Erlene enjoyed visiting with Katherine so much her parents couldn't say no and family visits gradually turned into overnights pajama parties for the girls. The first time Erlene stayed overnight at Etta's, her parents interrogated Etta endlessly about what she would allow them to do.

"Terah, yes I will watch them. Katherine is not wild. I don't know why you keep saying that. She may be a little spirited, but she is not wild!" Etta reprimanded her brother as they made plans over the phone. Katherine listened, irked that her uncle thought of her as wild.

"Don't worry, Terah. The girls will have a good time; just don't worry."

Katherine enjoyed going to school dances and parties; sometimes Erlene's parents let her go, but *only* to dances they chaperoned, and *never* parties! Terah and Marles continued their strictness and tried to limit Erlene's time with Katherine; they still thought she was too undisciplined for their daughter.

"Katherine, Erlene is here," Aunt Etta called out.

"Great," Katherine replied as she ran toward her cousin.

The girls couldn't wait for the adults to go to bed. They wanted to get on with their pajama party.

"Katherine, did you have a boyfriend in Florida?" Erlene asked.

"Yes, his name was Tommy. Dennis didn't like it. He sent me right home when we got too serious," Katherine explained.

"Did Tommy kiss you?" Erlene asked.

"Yes."

"Did it feel good?" Erlene whispered.

"Yes. His lips were warm and soft; and it tickled when he kissed my neck." Katherine giggled.

"Oh, Katherine, you're so sophisticated," Erlene sighed. "I don't know why my father thinks you're so wild; I think he's wrong; you're experienced, that's all."

Katherine tried to ignore her cousin's gauche remarks.

"You know, Erlene, boys like to touch and kiss. I guess if you want them to stay your boyfriend, you have to let them," Katherine explained; her thoughts went back to another cousin who first taught Katherine that lesson. Katherine avoided telling Erlene about Vesta's fate; however, Katherine did add one more warning.

"Just don't let them go too far."

The girls stayed up for hours talking and giggling, but Erlene mostly listened and stored the information. This was a new world for her, and she wanted in.

"Daddy, Katherine is on the phone. She wants to know if I can go the amusement park with her," Erlene yelled. Katherine heard her on the other end.

"Please, please," Erlene begged.

Katherine waited impatiently for an answer.

"Katherine, he said okay; but just for a few hours." Erlene was so excited she could barely get the words out.

"Great, see you later."

Aunt Etta dropped the girls off at the entrance. "Now be back here at 4:00."

"We will," Katherine called back as they ran into the park.

"Hi, Katherine," a voice came from behind the girls; Katherine turned around.

"Hi, Billy," Katherine returned. "This is my cousin, Erlene." Billy nodded at her.

"This is my friend, Norbert," Billy introduced, "but everybody calls him Bert."

"Do you want to walk around together for a while?" Billy flirted.

"Sure," Katherine answered shyly. The girl's bashfulness made them blush but Erlene felt something she had never felt before, and it felt good.

Aunt Etta picked the girls up and they went home full of giggles and infatuations.

"So, you girls had a good time?" Aunt Etta asked.

"We had a great time!" Erlene emphasized *great*. The girls giggled on the phone for days afterwards.

"Katherine, come sit down, I want to talk to you," Aunt Etta told Katherine a few weeks after the visit to the amusement park.

"Terah tells me Erlene has been talking a lot about a boy named Bert. Do you know him?"

"Yea, I know him. He seems okay. I don't know him very well, but he's always nice when he's around me. Why?" Katherine replied, not too concerned.

"Well, Terah and Marles don't know anything about him. They don't know anything about his family or what his dad does for a living. They want to make sure he is a good boy," Etta explained.

"He seems like a good boy," Katherine replied, "I really don't see him that much at school. He runs with other kids."

"Well, maybe you could discourage Erlene from being interested in him," Etta suggested.

"Okay, I will," Katherine agreed.

The next time the two girls were together, Katherine asked Erlene about her and Bert. Erlene giggled and proceeded to tell Katherine everything. In a whisper, she confessed.

"I've been calling him. He can't call me because my dad won't allow it; so, I call him. He's so dreamy," Earlene swooned.

"Erlene, I don't think you should do that," Katherine scolded.

"He wants me to meet him somewhere, alone," Erlene confessed.

"Don't do that, Erlene. Don't do that!"

Chapter 29

▼

"Let's go sit on the swing," Aunt Etta said to Katherine one evening. "We haven't talked for a long time."

Katherine willingly agreed; the swing had always been a source of comfort for her.

"Are you still thinking about going to business school?"

"Yes, I think I would like that. I did well in typing and shorthand class; my teacher suggested that I go," Katherine explained.

"Well, I think that is a good idea too; but, we have to figure out where we can get the money," Etta said sounding concerned. All was quiet for a few minutes.

"I was thinking about asking Raymond if he could possibly pay back the money he borrowed from your inheritance. That would probably be enough to pay for the tuition," Etta offered as a solution.

"I was just going to suggest the same thing. You read my mind."

"I'll call him later," Etta said.

"Do you think he is going to marry Josephine?" Katherine asked.

"Yes, I think so. They seem pretty serious. I like her; I hope he marries her," Etta said.

"I like her too," Katherine replied, "a whole lot better that Mary Jo. Maybe they will have some kids. I would like to be an aunt some day," Katherine said.

"Oh, you will be some day, honey; you'll see."

"I wonder if Dennis and Alice are going to have kids," Katherine speculated.

"I think they will. The last time I talked to him he said they would like to have a family. In fact, he seemed a little anxious about it. Sometimes it takes a while.

They'll have one sooner or later," Etta reassured Katherine. Both women sat quiet again.

"Raymond really should pay back my money. Mom left if for me. He should pay it back. That's all I have since I don't have a father that cares enough about me to help. I'm his only daughter. You'd think he would want to help me," Katherine reflected. "Lillian probably won't let him. He never stopped her from beating me. He never did a thing!" Katherine whimpered.

"Katherine, now you have to let that go. It's in the past and Sam will have to answer for that come judgment day. You have to move on now. You're young and you have your whole life ahead of you. That's what you have to focus on," Etta said as lovingly and wise as possible.

Katherine didn't say anything, she didn't agree or disagree, she just pouted, and threw in a couple of sniffles.

"What is going on with Erlene? It doesn't seem like you two have seen much of each other lately," Aunt Etta questioned; she wanted to change the subject.

"I don't know. She's awfully quiet these days. The last few times I've asked her to go somewhere she said she had something else to do. I think she talks to Bert a lot," Katherine said.

"I didn't think Terah and Marles liked him," Aunt Etta said.

"I know but I think she talks to him anyway."

"Well, what kind of graduation dress do you want?" Aunt Etta said as she changed the subject once more.

"I know it has to be white, but I thought I could have a blue sash around the waist," Katherine said, interested in the subject.

"That sounds pretty. We'll go see Aunt Lilly at the shop. Do you want to ask Erlene if she wants Lilly to make her dress too?"

"No, her mother is going to make her dress. She told me that," Katherine informed her aunt.

"Oh, okay. I'll have to call Marles and see what style she is going to make and what material she is going to use," Etta said, again trying to add some excitement to the whole conversation; it worked.

Etta and Katherine went over to Marles' house to talk about the dresses. The four women had a good time talking about their ideas for style, fabric, and accessories. Marles thought Katherine's idea about a blue sash was wonderful and asked Erlene if she would like a colored sash. Apparently she didn't hear her mother and Marles asked again.

"Erlene, would you like a colored sash, I think that sounds lovely," Marles asked her daughter. Erlene didn't answer.

"Erlene, did you hear me?"

"Sorry, mom, I guess not," Erlene said, embarrassed she wasn't paying attention.

"I don't know where your head has been these days. You always seem to be somewhere else," Marles said.

Etta and Katherine looked at Erlene and then at each other. They knew where her head had been, but they didn't say anything to Marles.

"I asked if you would like a sash on your dress too?"

"Yes, I guess so," Erlene answered, very uninterested.

"Okay then, come over here and let me measure your waist."

Erlene protested. "That's okay; we can do it later, can't we?"

"What's wrong now?" her mother asked.

"I don't feel like it."

"Nonsense; come over here," Marles ordered.

Erlene stomped over to her mother clearly protesting all the way. Marles held the measuring tape tight around Erlene's waist; she took a double take indicating her daughter's waist was larger than when she last made her any clothes. Erlene went stiff. As soon as her mother recorded the measurement, Erlene quickly sat down hoping nothing would be said; it wasn't.

Graduation had arrived; the dresses were done, the caps and gowns were ready, and everything should have been just wonderful for Katherine and Erlene; however, when Erlene arrived at the football field to line up for the procession, Katherine noticed she looked pale.

"What's wrong, Erlene?" Katherine inquired.

"I don't feel good. I must have the flue or something," Erlene replied; she looked like she was going to vomit.

"Are you going to be able to get through graduation?" Katherine whispered.

"I don't know. I'll try," she answered. The girls took their place in line; Katherine celebrated the graduating class of 1938.

"Katherine, was Erlene okay? She didn't look good," Aunt Etta asked.

"She said she didn't feel good. She nearly threw up," Katherine told her aunt.

"Really? That's too bad," Aunt Etta said. "By the way, which boy is Bert?" Katherine pointed to him. "He's a handsome young man," Aunt Etta observed.

"Where are Erlene and her parents?"

"They already left; Erlene was going to get sick again," Katherine told Aunt Etta. The two women exchanged looks. They could read each other's thoughts.

Katherine was so glad school was out; now she turned her attentions toward business school. She kept pestering her aunt to call Raymond about repaying her inheritance. Finally, Etta made the call.

"But, Raymond, the money would really help Katherine right now. She could go to business school and get a good job," Aunt Etta explained. "I know times are hard, but their hard for me too."

Katherine didn't get a good feeling from the one sided conversation she heard.

"Okay, Raymond, I understand," Aunt Etta surrendered; she hung up.

"What did he say?" Katherine inquired.

"He said he and Josie want to get married and that he needs what money his has to set up a house." Aunt Etta was clearly disappointed.

"That's not right. The money was supposed to be for me; for my education. He should pay it back," Katherine complained.

"I know, but times are hard now. He said he would try," Aunt Etta said, she tried to justify Raymond's actions; it didn't work for his disgruntled sister.

"We'll get the money, don't you worry, honey," Etta reassured her.

Aunt Etta refigured her budget to allow money for Katherine's education. Alas, her check didn't leave enough money to pay the entire tuition. Katherine and her aunt fretted for weeks.

"You know, Etta, I was thinking," Uncle John suggested one evening at dinner. "You have that apartment upstairs. Why don't you fix it up and rent it out? The money you get from that would help put Katherine through school. I could even help with some of the work." Aunt Etta thought for a few minutes.

"You know, John, that's not a bad idea. I think that would work out fine, but I haven't been up there in years; I don't even know what needs to be done."

"Well, let's go up and see," he encouraged.

"Yes, let's go," Katherine interjected.

Aunt Etta, Aunt June, Uncle John and Katherine started up the stairs. The open stairway ran up the side of the house, which made it nice to have a separate entrance; it offered privacy for the family and the renter. The foursome proceeded up the old creaky stairs, which were in surprisingly good shape. Uncle John figured nothing needed to be done to them. He pushed opened the door and everyone went in. They quickly looked around; aside from needing a good cleaning it was in good condition.

"John, I think you're right. This would be a perfect way to make some extra money," Aunt Etta said with excitement. "The only problem is that there is no bathroom up here. I suppose the boarder can use a slush pot for his bathroom needs; but, to wash up he'll have to come in the house."

"Well, I don't like that idea," Aunt June said in a huff. "What if you rent to someone like Emory?"

"June," her husband scolded.

"June, I'll be very careful who I rent to. I think I need to give this a try," Aunt Etta decided.

"Great!" Katherine hollered. "I can help you clean it up."

While the search was on for a boarder, Aunt Etta and Aunt June cleaned the apartment; Uncle John worked on a few repairs and painted the dingy walls. Katherine helped some, but mostly found excuses so she could be with her friends. However, one afternoon, Katherine and Aunt Etta worked hard at washing the curtains and bedding.

"Where has Erlene been? I haven't seen her in a while," Aunt Etta asked.

"I haven't seen her either. Every time I call, her mother tells me she's not home."

"I'll have to give Terah a call," Aunt Etta planned. She and Katherine took a break from the cleaning to have a glass of iced tea.

"I'll get it," Katherine yelled as she ran for the phone.

"Ettie, Ettie," came through the earpiece in a nearly unintelligible shriek. Katherine handed the phone to Aunt Etta.

"I think its Aunt Marles," Katherine said, clearly shaken.

"Marles, is that you?"

Katherine and Aunt June could see the look on Aunt Etta's face. She was obviously stunned.

"What's wrong, Ettie?" Aunt June demanded.

"Yes, of course, we'll be right there," Aunt Etta replied; her hand quivered as she hung up.

"What's wrong?" Katherine asked. Aunt Etta sat down before she fell down.

"That was County Hospital. Erlene was brought in about an hour ago," Aunt Etta replied, "she passed away a few minutes ago."

"Oh, no," Katherine gasped.

"Terah and Marles are so distraught the nurse asked if the family could come to be with them."

"Ettie, what happened?" Aunt June grabbed a chair for support.

"I don't know," Aunt Etta replied, still unable to believe it.

Uncle John arrived home just after the phone call and the family headed to the hospital. Katherine hurried into her cousin's room.

"It's your fault. It's your fault. You're wild. You're wild," Marles' voice echoed throughout the hospital halls.

Terah held his wife back from lunging at a shocked Katherine; however, it was obvious by the look on his face that he thought the same thing. Uncle John stepped up and confronted his brother-in-law.

"Here, here, Terah. What's going on?" John demanded.

Terah tried to answer Uncle John as tears of sorrow rolled down his cheeks; he wiped his running nose with the back of his hand as he spoke through his sobs.

"My daughter is dead. My little girl was killed by a butcher," Terah screamed.

"That boy got her pregnant. He took her to a butcher to get an abortion in a dirty alley somewhere!" With saying it out loud, Terah collapsed in a near by chair.

Katherine slipped back into a corner of the room, shaken by how her aunt had attacked her. The shock of what killed Erlene finally sunk in and she could feel the tears coming. Katherine couldn't believe that her aunt and uncle blamed her for Erlene's death; it was incomprehensible. With one blink of her blue eyes, Katherine's face became wet with a steady stream of sadness.

"It's her fault. She's too wild. She made Erlene wild. If she hadn't introduced her to that boy, we'd still have our daughter," Marles sobbed.

"Marles," Aunt Etta said with firmness in her voice.

"That's not fair to say about Katherine. This isn't her fault. She didn't cause this to happen."

"Yes she did! She was a bad influence. Erlene wouldn't have gone out with that boy if it hadn't been for her," Marles shouted as she pointed her finger at Katherine.

"Etta, why don't you take Katherine out of the room? We'll stay here and try to help Terah and Marles with some arrangements, or what ever they need. Okay?" Uncle John suggested.

Aunt Etta agreed; she and Katherine went out of the room. They found their way to the lobby and sat down. Katherine laid her head in Etta's lap and cried. Aunt Etta patted her head and tried to comfort her.

"It wasn't my fault. It wasn't. I kept telling her to be careful with him," Katherine cried. "She never told me she was expecting. I didn't know it."

"You're right, honey, it wasn't your fault."

"I'm not wild," Katherine sobbed.

"I know you're not wild, Katherine. Terah and Marles are distraught, they're just lashing out at anyone they can; they have to blame someone," Etta said softly.

The next few days were torture for the Tomas family. Terah was torn apart thinking about his little girl in some dirty room, lying on a dirty table, with dirty sheets. The image of a dirty, skuzzy quack spreading his daughter's untainted legs, putting dirty instruments up inside her young, uncontaminated vagina, and ripping at her tender female organs was almost more than he could stand. He tortured himself even more as he thought about how Bert soiled Erlene, putting his hard, obviously experienced, penis inside his little girl, breaking the innocence meant only for her husband. Terah wanted to get his hands on Bert for causing his little girl to be in the situation in the first place; however, the family knew Terah would kill Bert if he got a hold of him. Marles never stopped crying; the poor woman, and her marriage, was never the same.

Katherine lay awake in bed staring at the ceiling. She went over and over the last few months trying to figure out why the family thought she was so wild; why they thought she was to blame for Erlene being with a boy. Her stomach began to hurt. Katherine went to sleep mumbling, "It wasn't my fault."

Katherine sat in the front seat of the old Nash looking up at the stars. She had told Miles the story about Erlene's death; however, she never told them she was blamed for it. It hurt so badly that she could not even utter the words to anyone; she was afraid if she did, it would be true. Katherine had planned to take those unspeakable accusations to her grave.

Chapter 30

"Come on, Katherine, you can help me plan Raymond's wedding," Aunt Etta encouraged her niece, trying hard to keep her from falling into a nervous episode.

Katherine loved the festivities of a party and this one enabled her to get her mind off the terrible events of the summer.

"Are Dennis and Alice coming for the wedding?" Katherine asked.

"Of course," Aunt Etta replied.

"That's good, I'm anxious to see him." Katherine had all but forgiven him for sending her home early. "I'm can't wait to tell him about my plans to go to business school."

Dennis and Alice got into town a couple of days before the wedding and went straight to Dennis' cousin's house. Aunt Etta simply didn't have enough room; plus, Alice liked Jimmy and Clara Yates.

Dennis visited his aunt and sister while Alice stayed at the Yates's; that was jut fine with Katherine.

"Let's sit on the swing," Katherine called out. Sitting, and simply talking, had become one of Katherine's favorite pastimes; it also had become very therapeutic.

Dennis sat on the swing, silent at first, listening to the rhythm of the squeaky chain.

"You know, Dennis, it wasn't my fault Erlene got mixed up with that boy. It wasn't." Katherine had continuously defended herself since the funeral; she had persistently agonized over the guilt thrown at her.

"I know, Katherine." Dennis patted her leg. "I know." He changed the subject. "I'm glad that Ray found someone as nice as Josephine."

"Me too, I like her. She's very nice to me," Katherine said with the inflection on *she*, which insinuated there was someone in the family who wasn't very nice to her. Dennis caught her meaning, but chose to ignore it.

"I hope they have some children," Katherine said excitedly.

"Oh, they probably will," Dennis said; he stared off across the yard, obviously lost in thought.

Katherine wanted desperately to ask her brother if he and Alice were going to have children; however, she refrained.

Dennis had finally told Alice about the pain he sometimes felt in his scrotum; they figured he had been injured in his motorcycle accident. Many times he cursed his love of the machine. Although he knew Alice loved him very much, he could see the disappointment in her eyes. She wanted children so badly. Often times he felt inadequate as her husband, which grew into a deep appreciation that she loved him anyway. In fact, he became so deeply appreciative that he doted over her almost to the point of making people sick, especially Katherine.

"I can't wait to start business school in the fall."

"That's great. It will be good for you," Dennis said; he tried to show sincere interest in what she said; however, the mention of school brought up another sore subject.

"You know, Dennis, Raymond wouldn't pay back my inheritance. I needed that money to pay for my schooling, but he wouldn't pay it back," Katherine complained.

"Well, Katie, just try to focus on your business courses. It seems Aunt Etta has worked things out with the boarder and all; try to focus on that," Dennis said, hoping by some sort of osmosis his positive attitude would flow into his sister.

As they swung, the new boarder walked past them and slipped up the stairs.

"Is that him?" Dennis asked.

"Yes, that's him," Katherine answered.

"How are things going?"

"So far things have been okay. He keeps to himself; he never comes in the house. I think he's weird."

"Well, don't ever let him in the house if you are alone," Dennis warned; he didn't like the feeling he had.

"I won't," Katherine agreed emphatically.

The two were silent for a few minutes.

"Have you seen Tommy lately?" Dennis was surprised she asked about him.

"No, he got a job at a different company. I haven't seen him in a long time," Dennis replied. Just then, Clara drove up with Alice sitting next to her in the front seat. As soon as Katherine caught a glimpse of her sister-in-law, she hopped off the swing and made an excuse to go in the house. Dennis let her go.

Ray's wedding was delightful and Katherine had a wonderful time. She managed to stay in a good mood and she forgot about Raymond owing her money. Katherine clung to her new sister-in-law; they got along famously; and Josephine promised some babies for the family.

It was time to start business school; Katherine was excited and enthusiastic. She went faithfully every day and gave it all she had. The first few weeks were focused on review, giving the students a chance to get reacquainted with the typewriter keys; most of the young women had already taken some of the same courses in high school. After the review period was finished, the instructor started accelerating the class, which put pressure on the students. Katherine felt stressed as she concentrated on her typing speed.

There were thirty young women in her class and her desk was right in the middle of the throng of Underwood typewriters, which were arranged in neat rows. The women on both sides of her sat very straight in their seats; they were flawlessly groomed, very serious, and perfectly poised for entering the business world. Katherine felt out of place in the middle of these prim, precise, future executive secretaries; she hated them all.

"I don't know, Aunt Etta, it's hard," Katherine told her aunt.

"How is your speed, Katharine?"

"Actually, it's fine; I'm one of the fastest," she bragged.

"Good. You'll do just fine." Aunt Etta encouraged her to keep trying.

Katherine tried to focus and keep her speed steady; however, all she could hear was the tap, tap, tapping of the typewriter keys resonating all around her. The harder she tried to concentrate on her own typing, the louder the tapping got. Each day got harder and her hands began to quiver. As Katherine glanced at the hands of the women next to her, she could see they were steady and quick, which only made her more nervous.

The same thing began to happen when she worked on her shorthand. Although Katherine was one of the fastest at taking dictation, trying to remember the characters that made up the shorthand alphabet intensified her nervousness.

"Aunt Etta, I don't think I can do this." Katherine's quivering voice validated her concern.

"Katherine, you wanted to go to business school for so long. Do you think you can try a little longer?" Aunt Etta asked.

"I don't know; I guess so," Katherine replied with a whimper.

However, after two short months the pressure was too much for Katherine; her attempt to have a career in the business world gave way to a nervous breakdown.

Once again, Etta walked up and down the streets with her niece as she tried to help her work her way out of this collapse.

Another visit was paid to the doctor; again he prescribed only love and patience. Katherine had to find enough strength from her own resolve to get through the darkness she now felt; she had to have enough will to *want* to find her way out of this place that made life so damn hard.

Chapter 31

Katherine brooded around her aunt's house with the memory of the Underwood's tapping ringing in her ears. Even though it was a short two months out of her life, she talked about it as if it were years; to her, it felt that way. Her desire to do well and have a business career gave her a sense of purpose and worth; her failure was crushing. To her fragile psyche, it was simply one more reason to demonstrate her unworthiness; it ate away at her morale, and her stomach.

Toward the summer of her twentieth year, Katherine deepened her relationship with Hazel, a school friend. Unlike Erlene, Hazel was defiantly knowledgeable about boys, and many other things. She introduced Katherine to smoking, drinking, and dancing, of which she like two, smoking and dancing.

Hazel always had a lot of friends around and Katherine like the excitement. Of all the people that hung around Hazel, most were boys; some were boyfriends, some just friends, and one was her cousin, Miles. He teased and flirted with Katherine all the time; and even though she rejected his attentions, she secretly enjoyed his interest in her. It felt good to have a man show her attention again.

"Katherine, you've been over to Hazel's almost every night. What do you do over there?" Aunt Etta asked.

"We just talk and listen to the hit parade; that's all," Katherine told her aunt she left out the part about boys being there.

"You've been staying out very late," Aunt Etta mentioned.

"I know, but we're not doing anything bad." She knew her aunt didn't like her keeping those late hours; nobody in the house liked it.

"Ettie, as long as Katherine lives in your house, she should respect your rules. If you want her to come in earlier, then tell her to. If you don't, she'll just keep running wild," Aunt June lectured her sister; Katherine listened from the bedroom.

"June, Katherine is not wild, she is a good girl. She knows right from wrong. She is twenty years old," Etta replied, showing steadfast support for her niece.

It was two o'clock in the morning when Katherine quietly slipped up the front steps. To her surprise, the boarder slipped up the outside steps at the same time; knowing that he was lurking in the shadows unnerved her.

"I wonder where he's been," she whispered. In the dim glow of the porch light, their eyes met in a quick glance before they both stepped out of sight of each other.

"He's weird," Katherine mumbled.

Katherine had developed into a lovely young lady. She was on the thin side but still proportioned nicely with curvy hips and noticeably ample breasts. Her long auburn hair was a stark contract to her bright blue eyes, and she had taken to wearing light pink lipstick. Between her coloring and her figure, she turned the heads of many young men, and the boarder was one of them; he stole a glance whenever he got the chance.

Katherine tried to be as quiet as possible when she snuck in late; the household wasn't use to noise in the night so everyone heard her moving around in the wee hours of the morning.

Katherine undressed in the dark and slipped into bed being as quiet as possible. She moved ever so slowly as she pulled the blanket up over her legs. Aunt Etta didn't stir so Katherine thought that she had been successful at sneaking in; she relaxed in the quiet darkness.

"Katherine, do I smell smoke?" Etta softly inquired. Katherine was shocked at the question.

"Oh, it's nothing; the people I was with were smoking. I'm sure that is what you smell," Katherine lied. She wanted to believe that her aunt accepted her answer; however, she had her doubts.

In the mean time, Katherine honed her cooking skills, and enjoyed sharing them.

"Let's have Raymond and Josephine over for dinner," Katherine suggested.

"That's a good idea," Aunt Etta agreed. Katherine planned the menu.

"Katherine, you have become a wonderful cook," Uncle John said as he stuffed meatloaf in his mouth.

"I agree," Josephine spoke up.

"Katherine, would you like to go shopping with me tomorrow?" Josephine asked.

"I would love to," Katherine answered excitedly. She and Josephine had become good friends; Katherine dearly loved her. Their relationship even made Katherine forget about her brother's debt.

"Are we going to look for baby clothes?" Katherine asked, jokingly.

"No, no," Josephine chuckled, "not yet." Everyone else chuckled, except Raymond; he was obviously irritated.

"Katherine, you have a since of humor just like your mother," Aunt Etta said.

"I do?" she asked. That was the best thing anyone could say to Katherine; the memory of her mother was of a perfect woman, and any good comparisons between the two made her feel very special. Actually, it was true; both May and Katherine, when their nerves were under control, were fun-loving and jovial women. Now that Katherine was experiencing a stable period, her cheerful, funny personality shown through.

At the same time, her head was filled with thoughts of romance. Katherine had finally succumbed to Miles' affections and they had started dating exclusively.

"Katherine it's a little soon to be talking about marriage, isn't it?" Aunt Etta asked.

"I suppose; but let's do it anyway."

"Okay," Aunt Etta laughed, "we can talk about it."

Katherine spent hours upon hours on the swing with her aunt; they talked about wedding dresses, wedding cake and where the wedding could take place. They had great fun with their fantasy plans; and strengthened a special bond. Unfortunately, not all family members were enamored with Katherine's boyfriend.

"Well, what do we know about Miles? We haven't met his family. Does he go to church? Does he have a job? We need to know these things," Aunt June demanded at dinner.

"Aunt June, Miles is a very nice man. He is a mechanic and he is very good at it. He works very hard." Katherine defended her sweetheart.

"I'm sure he is a nice person, but you hardly know him. You've only been going out with him for a few weeks. I think you should slow down, that's all."

"I know what I am doing, Aunt June."

Katherine was happy and in love. The summer days were starting to get hot and so was Miles.

"Stop it, Miles. You can't do that. You're going too far," Katherine said as she wrestled with her aroused boyfriend. "I told you I won't do that unless we're married."

"Katherine, you're driving me crazy. I want you," Miles said as he tried to kiss Katherine's neck. Miles was a very passionate man. Whether he realized it or not, or liked it or not, he inherited his father's driving sexuality.

Katherine's resistance began to irritate Miles. She knew it, but she simply couldn't give in; it would make her as cheap as her cousin, Vesta, and the other whores her aunts talked about. However, she didn't want to lose Miles. Her quandary made her smoke more.

Miles always parked in front of the iron gate when he took Katherine home. After a few good night kisses, he would watch her bounce up the steps. Sometimes, to her dismay, he pulled away in a rush, squealing the tires of his brother-in-law's car; at two o'clock in the morning, that was not appreciated. Katherine bit her lip and Miles grinned from ear to ear.

One particular night Katherine didn't go in the house right away. She wanted a cigarette. She sat down on the top step and lit up. As she drew in on the cigarette, she thought she saw something out of the corner of her eye; there was an orange glow that matched the glow on the end of her cigarette. After a few minutes, she realized the boarder was sitting on his stairway about the same level as her. Even though she was a bit uneasy, an unexpected feeling of acceptance came over her. He was the one person who knew her for exactly what she was; he knew that she snuck in late, that she and her and her boyfriend petted in the car when he brought her home, and that she liked to smoke, really liked to smoke. He was the one person she didn't have to hide anything from; she didn't have to pretend around him. Katherine sat on the step and finished her cigarette.

It was a warn night; a gentle, balmy breeze blew the cigarette smoke back into her face. She knew it would be uncomfortably warm in the house, so she stayed outside a little longer. As she slowly smoked her cigarette, she began to evaluate her life thus far; she still had trouble putting her demons to rest. They kept rearing their ugly heads at her. She wanted to put them down, but she didn't know how. The more she wanted them silent, the more energy they seemed to gain; it was as if they fed off her every effort; *how cruel they were* Katherine thought. Why wouldn't they just leave her alone so she could move on and have a happy life?

She had a boyfriend that loved her. She enjoyed the periods when she felt comfortable and happy; but it took so damn much work. She sat on the stoop puffing away on her cigarette hoping that if she did marry Miles, he would be as understanding and patient as her aunt; that he would be as accepting as the boarder. After all, these demons were just as much a part of her as her eyes or her hair; to love her was to accept the demons; to love her was to learn to live with them too.

Katherine sighed deeply. These thoughts made her jittery; a long drag on the cigarette calmed her nerves. She began to realize a cigarette was about the only thing that calmed her nerves. It was the only thing that helped her handle the quivering inside of her, or at least, made it bearable.

Katherine took her time with the cigarette; the boarder lit another one. Her mind wandered back to her father's house. As if by some powerful force pushing her, she started saying to herself, "why didn't Dad stop her, why? I'm his only daughter, why didn't he love me enough to stop her." It hurt so badly.

Katherine blew out a full mouth of smoke; she looked up at the night sky. She thought fondly about Tommy and Donald as the stars peeked through the dissipating smoke. However, bad memories always seemed to creep in and overshadow the good ones. She still had not gotten over Erlene's death, and being blamed for it.

Katherine could feel her insides start to quiver; a long hard drag on the cigarette filled her pneumonia scared lungs with blue-gray smoke. She closed her eyes and held the nicotine in for a few seconds, allowing it time to numb the depressing memory; she blew hard and forced the remainder of the memory out along with the swirling smoke, which floated and disappeared high above her head; and far away from her heart. She was happy to discover just how much this simple little roll of tobacco helped her get over the humps; she wished she had discovered it a long time ago.

Katherine started to light another cigarette when she decided not to; she wasn't ready to go in the house yet, though. She knew the boarder was still there; he lit what she thought must have been his third cigarette. She wasn't keeping tack of how much he smoked, just keeping track of him; she knew enough to be careful. Katherine had always been physically careful; the recklessness she saved for her passions.

Katherine finally decided to go in the house. She had visited long enough with her albatross'. She turned in the direction of the boarder and stared. As if she thought perhaps she could reach him telepathically, she mentally spoke, "okay mister, here I am, you see me as I really am, not perfect, but not bad, unprotected by my Father, but loved by several other men, without a Business School degree, but not stupid, enjoy kissing my boyfriend, but not a whore. What do you think?" Then she turned and ran up the stairs.

She didn't see him node with approval.

Chapter 32

▼

"Come on baby, I want you," Miles whispered as he tugged at Katherine's clothes.

"No, Miles, it's not right. We're not married," Katherine protested, pushing his hands away for the hem of her skirt.

"Well then, let's get married." Miles tried to cope with his arousal.

Katherine was momentarily stunned. Even though she had thought about marriage, this was the first time Miles had mentioned it; and, in the form of a proposal.

"What?" she asked.

"Let's get married, now!"

Usually Miles was much more playful; however, at that moment he was intense and determined to find a way to get Katherine into bed.

"What do you mean, now?" She asked perplexed; she held his hands back from fondling her breasts.

"I mean this weekend; let's get married this weekend!"

Katherine was quiet; this caught her completely off guard. "You mean elope?" she shouted, her blue eyes wide with amazement.

"Yea, let's elope. That way we won't have to wait for wedding plans or worry about all of the arrangements; and it's cheaper," Miles reasoned. Katharine knew he meant that he wouldn't have to wait any longer for sex.

For a brief moment Katherine thought about the big wedding she had always dreamed about, the one she had planned with her aunt. She and Aunt Etta had spent many hours talking about that very subject, and Aunt Etta had been so excited at the thought of being able to give her a beautiful wedding. They had become very close while making those plans.

Katherine stared out the car window and bit at her lip. Did a big wedding really matter to her; would it really matter to her aunt? She looked at Miles and saw a man in misery from wanting to be with her, *with her*, she thought; she felt all sorts of things, proud, grateful, fulfilled, but most of all, loved.

She smiled; her blue eyes sparkled. "Okay."

She released his wanting fingers and they embraced harder and more passionately then ever before. Katherine began to cry with happiness. This was what she had been waiting for, someone to deliver her from her bad memories, her darkness, and her suffering. She felt a huge weight lift off her heart, allowing her the bliss of pure joy. Finally, she was loved.

After a passionate interlude of kissing, hugging as official fiancés, Katherine started asking all sorts of questions of her new husband-to-be.

"Where are we going to go to get married? Where do we get a marriage license? Who will be our witnesses?"

"Slow down. Slow down," Miles chuckled.

Katherine tried to settle herself down. Her excitement was genuine. She didn't know what to focus on first.

"We'll go to the Justice of the Peace in Rossville. But, we'll have to go on Friday; he won't be there on Saturday," Miles told her.

"Friday? Tomorrow?" she shouted.

"Yea, tomorrow. I'll take off work and then we'll have the weekend for our honeymoon," Miles said, *and to spend in bed making up for weeks and weeks of excruciating restraint*, Miles thought to himself.

The plan was set; Katherine didn't sleep a wink that night. She tried not to toss and turn; she didn't want to wake her aunt; it was all she could do to keep from blurting out the whole plot.

"Katherine, I'm leaving for work. Do you want up?" Aunt Etta asked.

"No, I want to sleep a little longer," Katherine mumbled; she didn't want her aunt to see her excitement.

"Katherine, I'm going to the market, do you want to go?" Aunt June called out.

"No, I don't feel like it today," Katherine answered from the bedroom.

When she was alone, she dressed in one of her best dresses, a light blue jersey with white swirls all over it. She stood in front of the mirror and prepared herself for her groom. She combed her hair back off of her forehead and secured it with some hair clips. She put on her lipstick, which had gradually gotten to be a darker pink; all that was left was her hat. It was a small, navy blue disk with a bit of light netting, which could be pulled over her eyes.

Katherine stepped back from the mirror and took a look. She turned this way and that as she inspected the dress. This was her wedding day; however, her reflection did not match the picture in her dreams.

"Oh, well; I don't need a big wedding," Katherine said to Snowball; she was quick to settle for reality.

Katherine waited anxiously; her stomach quivered. It wasn't the quiver of a nervous attack; it was a delightful quiver. In fact, she thought that getting married would take away all of the bad feelings inside her. Katherine had always thought if she could simply be happy, all her problems would go away; she counted on it.

While she waited, she began to think about what her aunt was going to say. She knew her aunt was excited about the possibility of giving her a big wedding, and Aunt Etta never complained that it would cost too much; it was something she wanted to do.

"Well, she'll understand," Katherine mumbled as she stared out the front window.

Snowball jumped up on the arm of the chair; Katherine patted her head. Just then Miles drove up and Katherine flew out the front door; she left the cat mystified by her sudden departure.

The boarded walked down the side stairway; Katherine noticed that he watched her jump into the front seat with Miles'.

"Who's that?" Miles asked.

"The boarder."

"Do you think he will tell your aunt?" Miles asked.

"No, he doesn't talk to the family anyway." A fleeting moment allowed Katherine to realize that the boarder knew one more secret.

The lovers drove the short distance to Rossville; they arrived at the City Hall and filled out the application for a marriage license. After they waited their turn, they were called into the Justice of the Peace's office. A stout, portly man sat at his desk and smiled at them.

"So, you want to get married, do you?" he grinned.

Miles and Katherine looked at each other and smiled; they looked back at the J.P. and shook their heads yes.

"Okay then, let's go into the next room."

The Justice of the Peace led them into a room used just for that purpose. The room had what might be called an altar, which had white pillars on either side with ferns sitting on them; behind the pillars was a back drop with palm trees painted on it. Miles, Katherine and the Justice stepped up to the altar, a clerk was the witness.

Katherine was nervous and excited; Miles was anxious. While the J.P. got situated and found his place in the wedding ceremony book, Katherine looked at Miles. She saw a young, handsome man with playful eyes who was willing to take her as his wife. That moment was the first time she realized she love him. It all happened so fast, she hadn't had time to think about whether she loved him or not. But now, she realized that she did love him. Miles gave her a wink.

The J.P. started the ceremony and each one repeated their vows; then he asked for the rings. Miles pulled out a wedding ring and handed it to the Justice of the Peace. Katherine was embarrassed that she didn't have a ring for him; it didn't matter to Miles.

Miles placed the ring on Katherine's finger; she could see the diamond sparkle through her teary eyes. It was a tiny diamond with a tiny sparkle, but to her, it represented the brilliance of her future with her new husband.

"I now pronounce you husband and wife," the Justice concluded. Miles held her tight and placed a huge kiss her lips.

"Now wait right there. I'll take your picture." The J.P. seemed genuinely happy for them. They got situated and the light bulb popped with a flash.

"The picture will come in the mail in a few weeks." The Justice showed them to the door.

It was done. No relatives to hug and get good wishes from; no flowers, no wedding cake, no gifts, no dancing, no toasts; no one to share their happy moment.

Whether it was the impulse of youth, or recklessness of desperation, Katherine was a married woman.

"Do you want to get something to eat before we go back home?" Miles asked his new bride.

"Okay," Katherine answered; she took hold of Miles' hand. At last, she was truly happy.

Chapter 33

Katherine and Miles walked up the front steps of Aunt Etta's house, it was dusk by the time they ate and got back to Chattanooga. Aunt Etta rushed to the door when she saw them.

"Katherine, where in the world have you been?" Aunt Etta gasped. "Nobody knew where you were. I was so worried."

Katherine looked at her aunt with a sheepish grin on her face. Katherine wanted to blurt out the news, but the words wouldn't come. She took a few seconds to get up the nerve; she tried again. This time her excitement won over her nervousness.

"Aunt Etta, Miles and I have some news," Katherine squealed. She could see her aunt take in a breath.

"We got married!" Katherine held out her hand to reveal her wedding ring.

Aunt Etta's mouth dropped open and her eyes began to bulge with tears. Her stare was focused on Katherine's finger; it gradually moved up to her eyes. She couldn't speak.

"Married? When?" Aunt June yelled.

"We went to Georgia, to the Justice of the Peace today."

"Justice of the Peace!" Aunt Etta gasped; she had to sit down. Aunt June helped her to the sofa; Katherine followed.

"Aunt Etta, I thought you'd be happy for me. This is what I want," Katherine said; she tried to justify what she had done.

Uncle John stood up and walked over to Miles. Uncle John was a tall man. He wasn't fat, but he had a lot of meat on his bones. He looked at Miles with glaring eyes; Miles could feel his disapproval.

"What's the meaning of you two kids running off like this?"

"We're not kids. We are both 21," Miles defended.

"Can you support your new wife?" Uncle John asked like an angry, concerned father.

Yes, sir, I can support Katherine. I'm working. We'll be able to manage."

"Where are you two going to live?" Uncle John continued to interrogate.

"Well, for a while we'll say at my sister's house, just until we can find an apartment that we can afford," Miles explained.

Katherine looked at her new husband; she was proud that he stuck up for them; that he was confident and mature in Uncle John's attack. It made her feel grown up. However, that was a fleeting moment of confidence as Aunt Etta sat on the couch and cried; Katherine began to feel incredibly guilty.

"Aunt Etta, don't cry," Katherine begged. "I'm happy. We'll be just fine."

Etta looked up at her niece wanting so badly to be happy for her; that was all she every wanted for her niece.

"I am happy for you, honey," she whispered in Katherine's ear. "I just wish I could have been there to see you get married, that's all."

Etta tried to sound sincere; however, the shock was devastating. The disappointment of being left out was smothering. *Married*, Etta thought, *how can Katherine be married?* She looked at her niece unable to see her as a married woman. Yes, she was 21 and plenty old enough to be married, *but married!*

Though the atmosphere was tense, the newly weds stayed a while longer hoping to change the mood; however, it simply wasn't going to happen that evening.

"Let's get going, Katherine." Miles nudged his new wife; Katherine obeyed.

"We'll come by tomorrow so I can get my things; we'll visit some more, okay?" Katherine hugged her aunt.

"Sure, honey, we'll see you tomorrow, and congratulations you two," Etta choked out, as if acting on impulse; she gave Miles a reluctant hug too.

Miles and Katherine got in the car and headed to his sister's.

"Oh boy," Miles grumbled, "if that's the way your family reacted, I wonder what mine is going to do." Katherine started to cry.

"Come on, honey, don't cry. Everything will work out."

"I hurt my aunt. I didn't think she would be that upset," Katherine blubbered. "I thought she would be happy for me. That makes me feel terrible."

"Oh, she'll get over it, you'll see. Give her a few days," Miles assured her.

Katherine tried to dry her eyes. She wanted to feel happy; it was her wedding day. She fanned her face as she tried to take away the redness of her eyes, and push her guilt to the backside of her conscience. Katherine scooted close to Miles and put her head on his shoulder. She was sure his shoulder would always be there for her to lean on when she needed it. It felt perfect.

They sped closer to Lulabell's house and closer to their wedding night. As Katherine calmed down, Miles got more anxious. He hadn't told his sister he was coming home a married man, or bringing his bride home to live in her house. He hoped she would understand.

"You're married!" Lula shouted. "What made you do such a thing, slipping off like that without telling anyone?"

"Well, we didn't want to wait; and besides, we didn't have the money for a big wedding. It would have been a hardship for everyone," Miles explained to his sister.

Bunn, Lula's husband, didn't say much and soon went about his business; he didn't see any reason to be so shocked, people get married all the time. But Lula was stunned.

"You've only been dating six weeks. That's not very long," Lula preached; she was able to say what Aunt Etta and Aunt June had been thinking.

"I know it hasn't been very long, but we are in love and we wanted to be married," Miles defended all over again.

Well, where do you expect to stay?" Lula demanded. Miles paused as if surprised by her question.

"Well, I thought we could stay here until we find a place."

"Here?" Lula shouted.

"Yea, here."

Lula looked at her husband for his reaction. He shook his shoulders, "oh well, what are you going to do?"

Without saying yes or no, she went on to something else, keeping the couple hanging for a while.

"Why did you do this without better plans, Miles?" his sister demanded; she was irritated and it showed.

"It's done and that is that," Miles said; he wanted to put an end to it.

The room was uncomfortably silent for a few minutes; Katherine stood slightly behind Miles waiting for the decision.

"Okay, okay." Lula tried to settle down.

She took a few minutes and then hugged them both and congratulated them. She wasn't particularly happy about the situation, but she told them they could stay for a while.

"Welcome to the family, Katherine, honey." Lula hugged her new sister-in-law.

"Thank you, Lula," Katherine said, relieved all the surprises were over.

Miles' brothers, Herbert, Larry, Harry, and Lula's kids all gathered around in excitement. Finally, Katherine had a celebration on her wedding day. She talked and laughed; however, behind all the gaiety, she missed her aunt celebrating with her.

Though Aunt Etta tried with all her might to find a way to be happy for Katherine, she felt a consuming sadness. She couldn't help but feel Katherine had neglectfully forsaken her. How was she going to find a way to forgive her? Her niece, who had been like a daughter to her, had broken her heart once again; this time, the pain was nearly unbearable. She went to bed early and held a handkerchief to catch the tears.

While Etta tossed and turned in her bed, Miles enjoyed the pleasure of Katherine lying in his bed; he wasted no time collecting his husbandly rights. Though she was clumsy and shy, she was more embarrassed knowing the rest of the family knew just what they were doing.

"Miles, they can hear us, I know they can," Katherine whispered.

"No they can't," he tried to assure her; at the same time, he began to react to her hesitation.

"Maybe we should wait," she resisted.

"Katherine," Miles said firmly; then he settled down. "Honey, this is our wedding night, I'll be quiet; just relax, it will be okay." Miles was not rough but he was eager; plus, he wasn't about to wait any longer. Katherine finally gave in to his desires. Soon her body welcomed Miles and she became oblivious to the family on the other side of the bedroom door. That night she became the women she had always dreamed about.

Katherine's inexperience kept her from knowing that Miles had impressive stamina; she didn't know enough to appreciate that he could go longer than most men. All she knew was that was what her new husband wanted, so she engaged the best way she knew how; she submitted until he climaxed; she never did.

The newlyweds visited Aunt Etta the next day. Katherine could see the sadness on her face. That was all she needed, one more thing to make her feel guilty and inadequate; however, she had no one to blame but herself, and she didn't like it.

"So, you two are going to stay at Miles' sister's house for a while?" Aunt Etta quizzed as she served dinner.

"Yes, she said we could stay there until we find a place we can afford," Miles answered.

"That's very nice of your sister, Miles, how many children does she have?"

"She has four kids; and my three brothers live there too," Miles informed her.

Katherine saw the surprised look on her aunt's face. Katherine didn't like a lot of people around; she liked her privacy, her own little domain; Aunt Etta knew that.

"Well, that's a house full, isn't it?"

"Never a dull moment," Miles chuckled.

"We won't be there that long anyway, so it will be fine," Katherine assured her aunt, a bit *too* much.

"Actually, Larry, my brother just under me, is going to move out very soon. He is going to get married," Miles explained.

"Oh, who is he going to marry?" Aunt June asked, as if she thought she might somehow know her.

"Nadean Hatfield."

"Hatfield!" Aunt June shouted, causing everyone to look at her. "Is she part of the …," she stopped herself.

With a nod of Miles' head, everyone knew that, indeed, she was part of that clan. Katherine saw Aunt June roll her eyes. The Tomas family was a religious and reserve group of people, even the men; they steered clear of rough talk and coarse people. It worried Aunt Etta that Katherine was going off to live in a world filled with influences that might lead her astray.

"I suspect Herbert will move out soon too. He's nineteen," Miles said quite nonchalantly; he was comfortable with his new family. "Harry, my youngest brother, is still very young. Lula has raised him like her own son since Mother died; so, of course, he will stay with her."

Aunt Etta, Aunt June, and Uncle John listened attentively; they were taken in by Miles' mild and easy demeanor. They liked him.

After the kitchen was cleaned up, Miles nudged Katherine.

"Let's get going."

"Aunt Etta, we have to get going. Miles has to get up early for work," Katherine announced. "I'm going to pack up the rest of my stuff."

"Okay, honey. I'll help you."

They went into what used to be *their* bedroom; Etta pushed the door shut. They sat down on the bed and embraced; they tightened their hold on the other and began to cry.

"I'm sorry I hurt you, Aunt Etta," Katherine sobbed. Etta refrained from saying *that's okay*, because it wasn't.

"I wanted to share your wedding day with you, Katherine. Why did you slip off like that?"

"We thought it would be the best thing to do. It was easier and cheaper, that's all," Katherine tried to justify.

"You've only been dating six weeks, Katherine. Are you sure he's the right one? Are you sure you love him?" Etta questioned.

"Yes, auntie, I do love him. I am very happy."

Etta looked deep into Katherine's blue eyes; she desperately sought to find happiness behind her pain.

"Okay, honey. Then I'm happy for you." Etta gave her niece another hug.

Katherine and Miles went back to their temporary, hectic home. It didn't take more than a few days of noise and chaos for Katherine to decide the arrangements were not going to work; however, for the time being, she kept it to herself.

Katherine liked Lula and Bun, they were very nice; in fact, all of Miles' relatives were nice people, which made things easier to handle.

"Lula, let me help you with dinner. That's the least I can do to repay you for letting us stay here," Katherine offered.

"Okay, Lord knows I can use the help," Lula laughed.

Dinnertime was pandemonium; however, it didn't bother the Snider's. Lula got everyone seated and paid little attention to the noise; Bun watched Katherine's hips sway back and forth as she carried food from the kitchen to the dinner table. Lula was so busy with the kids, and Miles was so busy talking to his brothers, neither one noticed; however, Katherine did.

In the privacy of their bedroom, Katherine began to complain.

"I know it's crowded, Katherine, but what can we do right now?" Miles tried to settle down his restless wife.

"I don't know, but I want to move as soon as possible," Katherine whined, "It's just too cramped."

Miles patted her arm then proceeded to push her over so he could get on top.

"Miles, I think they can hear us," Katherine complained again; she looked at the closed bedroom door.

"No they can't," he moaned, clearly miserable.

"Just listen to this squeaky, old bed."

"I don't hear anything," Miles answered; he was already too far aroused to care if the bed squeaked or not. While Miles performed, Katherine was oblivious to his grunts and groans; she wasn't lost in a wild, romantic fantasy; she was lost in concocting a plan to get out of Lula's house.

Chapter 34

▼

"Look, Miles, the Michigan state line is only twenty miles away," Katherine exclaimed with excitement.

She wasn't excited about getting close to Michigan; she was excited about being able to get out of the car, and staying out.

I can't wait to see the house," Katherine exclaimed. Miles nervously grinned at her.

"I'm cold," Carolyn complained.

April in the North was not always warm and the spring of 1950 was exceptionally cold.

"Miles, won't the heater work even a little bit?" Katherine grumbled as she wrapped her arms around her shoulders and shivered. "I thought Larry said the weather was nice in April up here."

"Well, I guess you can't always be sure," Miles rationalized.

"That's great; one brother doesn't know what he's talking about, and the other brother is lost with every piece of our furniture," Katherine bitched.

"Herbert better get there when we do; we're going to need the coal," Katherine warned. Miles had packed two large garbage cans filled with coal just in case they needed it; it looked like they were going to need it.

"He makes me so damn mad," Katherine said, plenty loud enough for the girls to hear. Miles ignored her comment.

"Look, mama," Judy shouted as she looked out the window, "a wedding."

Judy pointed to a church with a crowd in the churchyard; right in the middle of all the people stood the beautiful bride in her elegant white gown. Carolyn and Judy were mesmerized; they stared in silence. Katherine strained her neck to see;

the sight carried her back to the wedding she didn't have. After a few minutes of staring, she turned back around and situated herself. She was very still, as if she wasn't even there; for all practical purposes, she wasn't.

"I really disappointed my aunt. It nearly killed her when your dad and I slipped off to get married; she was in bed for a week. She wanted so much to give me a nice wedding."

However, if wasn't a new revelation; everyone had heard the story many, many times, and everyone let it pass, except Katherine. Miles hoped she would change the subject, but the girls were curious, and board.

"Where did you and Daddy live, mama?" her sweet little voice quizzed.

That was all Katherine needed to prompt her memory; she was back to the comfort of the blue haze and the warmth of the Smoky Mountains.

"Well, at first we stayed at Lula's, your dad's sister. She was very nice to let us stay there, but it was just too crowded. We had to find another place."

What Katherine didn't say was all the noise and chaos drove her crazy. She had gotten an idea after about three days at Lula's, and she wanted to talk to her aunt about it. Every time Katherine called to talk to her, Aunt June told her Aunt Etta was in bed.

"What's the matter?" Katherine asked. Aunt June wanted so much to blurt out in Katherine's ear that she nearly killed her aunt by slipping off the way she did. It was hard for Aunt June to refrain, but she did it, at least for the time being.

Katherine was worried; she wanted to go see her aunt; however, she had to wait for Miles to get home from work. She waited impatiently; at the same time, it gave her time to prepare the presentation of her plan.

Finally, Katherine got her aunt on the phone. "Aunt Etta, have you been sick?"

"Honey, I haven't felt very well for the last few days, but I'm better now," Etta said. She didn't tell Katherine the real reason.

"Can Miles and I come over tonight?"

"Of course you can; in fact, come for dinner," Etta invited.

"Okay, see you later."

On the way over to Aunt Etta's, Katherine talked to Miles about her plan to move out of Lula's house. He was all for moving out because he didn't like the cramped quarters either; at the same time, he was skeptical about her plan.

Katherine and Miles arrived at Aunt Etta's and everyone exchanged greetings and niceties. Aunt Etta felt better and there was little evidence of her depression; however, Aunt June knew better and she itched for the right opportunity to let loose with her feelings. For the time being, everyone was jolly and they had a wonderful evening together. During dessert Aunt Etta gave the newlyweds some good news.

"Well, you two, we would like to do something for you. We would like to give you a reception here at the house, just mainly for relatives. Would you like that?" Etta asked in a very jovial way.

Katherine was very pleasantly surprised. "Why Aunt Etta, that would be wonderful. Don't you think so, Miles?" she asked her husband.

"Yea, I think that would be fine. That's very nice of you to do that for us. Thanks," Miles told his new family with a smile; his sparkling eyes were clearly pleased with the acceptance of his new in-laws.

As they ate their dessert, Katherine planed how to bring up her idea; she waited for the right time. After dinner, the women cleared the table. Katherine scraped the leftovers into the garbage can on the back porch; Aunt June joined her. Katherine didn't think much about her aunt being there, simply that she had some garbage to throw away too. Aunt June waited a couple of seconds; she then moved in closer, up against Katherine's back.

"You know, Katherine, you nearly killed your aunt by not letting her give you a nice wedding. She was in bed for a week pining over it," Aunt June whispered in her ear.

Katherine quickly turned around and stared at her bold aunt. Her aunt's words stunned her. "What?"

"You heard me."

At that moment Aunt Etta called out to the porch. "Are you out there, Katherine?"

"Yea, I'll be right there," Katherine shouted back.

Aunt June turned in a huff and went back in the house. She felt much better having gotten things off her chest; she had a satisfying smile on her face.

Katherine stayed out on the porch a little while longer; she had to collect herself. She had to get prepared to present her plan; however, she had a hard time concentrating after the slap in the face Aunt June had just given her. She needed a cigarette; she needed something to calm her. A cigarette would do the trick, but she knew she couldn't have one until after she left; she still hadn't smoked in front of her aunt.

Feeling bad that she disappointed her aunt slowly turned into being mad at Aunt June for upsetting *her*, for ruining *her* evening, for making *her* feel guilty. "Aunt June should have just kept her big mouth shut," Katherine thought out loud. She couldn't present her plan to Aunt Etta in a bad mood; she had to be positive and upbeat. This was going to take some control, some restraint, and some good acting. Katherine dried her eyes, lifted up her chin, and joined everyone in the living room.

Miles motioned for her to sit by him and he put his arm around her. He was very affectionate; everyone shyly overlooked his open expression. The group sat in the living room ready for some after dinner conversation.

"How is everything going at Miles' sister's house?" Aunt Etta began.

What a perfect lead in Katherine thought.

"Well, actually, things are a bit crowded. She has a house full; Miles and I don't have much privacy," Katherine explained. Everyone stared at her with the hint of a smirk; they weren't surprised.

"Actually, Aunt Etta, I've been thinking." She and Miles squirmed in their seats.

"What do you think about us moving into the upstairs apartment?" Katherine blurted out. Etta was quiet for a few seconds.

"Well, I don't know Katherine. What about the boarder? He's been here for a while and he hasn't been any trouble."

"I think it would be perfect for us," Katherine suggested excitedly.

"Well, I guess I could ask him to leave," Etta slowly surmised.

Aunt June stared at her sister with disgust that once again she was going to give in to Katherine.

"Do you think that would be okay, Aunt Etta?" Katherine asked again.

Aunt Etta had been happy with the boarder. He wasn't any trouble; he didn't use the main house except on occasion, he was quiet, he didn't bring guests home, and the money helped. Actually, she didn't really want to ask him to leave.

"Katherine, are you sure you want to move into that apartment? With no bathroom up there, it could get pretty inconvenient," Etta reminded her.

Katherine had already convinced herself that she wanted the apartment; nothing was going to discourage her.

"I think we'll be able to manage just fine, don't you Miles?"

Miles shook his head in agreement. He had been raised on a poor farm; pee pots and slush buckets didn't bother him.

"We can use the bathroom in the main house when we want too; I know it will work out fine," Katherine insisted.

As an adult, Katherine had never used a pee pot or slush bucket; she was being very naive and Aunt Etta knew it; however, there was no telling her *no*.

"Well, yes, it will be okay, I guess. I'll talk to him tomorrow." Aunt Etta sounded reluctant.

"Etta, do you want me to have a word with him?" Miles asked like a concerned son-in-law.

"That is nice of you to offer, Miles; but, I think I'd better do it," she explained. "I think I should give him a two week notice so he can find another place."

"Why does he need a two week notice?" Katherine crabbed.

"Katherine, I can't just throw him out on the street; that wouldn't be a very nice thing to do."

"I don't want to wait two weeks." Katherine pouted.

"We can manage for two weeks, honey." Miles attempted to calm her down. "We can give the fellow a chance to find another apartment."

"But why does he need two weeks?"

"Katherine, I'm going to give him two weeks; now that's enough." Aunt Etta was gentle, but firm, for the first time in Katherine's life.

Katherine didn't know if she could take two more weeks at Lula's. Her impatience showed on her tightened face.

Chapter 35

The next two weeks felt like an eternity for Katherine. One thing that helped to break up the misery was the reception Aunt Etta gave her and Miles. What a wonderful celebration; it made Katherine very happy. She got to show off her new husband; Raymond came with Josephine, Dennis came with Alice, all of her aunts, uncles and cousins were there; Terah didn't come; that was okay. Katherine felt fulfilled, she felt satisfied; she was ready to start a new chapter in her life. At that point she felt strong.

Josephine was thrilled for Katherine; Raymond didn't say much. Dennis was very excited for his sister; Alice didn't say much either. Dennis sincerely hoped his sister would be happy; he felt she certainly deserved it. He hoped Miles could give her a good life. Alice said her niceties to Katherine, but secretly she looked down on Miles. To her he was poor, uneducated, and low class; she planned on having only limited contact with him. On the other hand, Dennis respected him as his sister's husband; he had no problem being around him; that was Dennis' way.

The large crowd was in a festive mood; of course, family gossip swirled around the room; Katherine listened intently, which was unfortunate.

"Can you imagine, Katherine slipping off like that," Aunt Jimmie whispered to one of her sisters.

"What a terrible shame, Erlene dying that way. That butcher must have cut her all to pieces during the abortion. It wouldn't have happened if Katherine hadn't introduced her to that boy," Aunt Ila softy gossiped. That comment made Katherine sad.

"Ettie sure is going to miss Katherine. I suppose she'll always be an old maid now," Lilly assumed. Katherine didn't like it when the relatives called her dear aunt an old maid; mainly, because she caused it to happen.

Katherine wanted to say something to all of the Tomas women; however, she knew it would be useless. Their Dutch tenacity could not be challenged. All the sisters, the quiet ones, the loud ones, and the troubled ones were a bunch of tough broads, of which she was one.

After hearing all the whispers, Katherine needed a cigarette. She decided to sneak outside for a few drags. She didn't want to go on the side of the house where the boarder's staircase was; she didn't want to accidentally run into him, so she ducked in between the houses on the other side. Alone in her private little world she drew in and blew out slowly. It felt good, so good. After a few more puffs, she turned to go back into the house. To her surprise, she found herself staring right into the eyes of the evicted boarder. He glared at her. At one time he had been on her side; he had defended her; he had accepted her. But now, he found himself on the wrong end of her agenda and his needs were unimportant to her.

"So, you're throwing me out, missy?" he whispered in the dark; his foul breath hit Katherine in the face. She tried to run up the steps, but he stepped in front of her. The danger of the situation eluded her for the moment and she defended her actions.

"My husband and I need that apartment more than you do; besides, you can find another place to go," Katherine said rather condescendingly.

"Yea, where might that be, down by the trestle?" he smarted back.

Katherine turned away; she wasn't about to think that his needs took precedence over hers.

"Yes, you can stay there until you find something else," Katherine rationalized in her spoiled way.

She appreciated his acceptance at one time, but now there was nothing more he could do for her, except leave. She ran up the steps as quickly as she could to avoid any more of the boarder's prying eyes and judgmental remarks.

Katherine took a deep breath and melded right back in with the guest; no one was the wiser. Etta smelled smoke but she didn't say anything.

It was a nice party and Katherine was happy. She couldn't wait to move into the apartment the following week; then, everything would be perfect.

The day came for them to leave Lula's house. They packed up their things. Bun watched Katherine's hips sway back and forth while she carried bundles of clothes out to the car. He was going to miss her; more precisely, he was going to miss looking at her ass.

"Lula, thank you for letting us stay here," Katherine said as she hugged her sister-in-law.

"Don't be strangers, you here," Lula said, and she meant it.

Katherine's first night in the apartment was glorious; for the first time, she really felt married. She didn't have to worry that someone was going to hear their bed squeaking during their love making, or hear Miles' deep voice grunting and moaning; it was heavenly. However, it wasn't so heavenly was when she had to go to the bathroom early in the morning.

"Just go in the pot," Miles suggested.

"I don't want to go in that pot." Katherine turned up her nose.

Miles turned over in the bed while Katherine slipped on her robe, ran down the staircase, around to the back of the house, across the back porch, through the kitchen and finally to the bathroom. No one was up in the main house, but they heard her just the same. Aunt Etta and Aunt June wondered how long this would last. It didn't last long.

"You need to start looking for a better job, Miles. We need a different apartment," she grumbled.

"Katherine, we've only been here two months. You had the renter kicked out so we could move in. You want to move already?" Miles was a little irritated.

"Yes, I want to move. I don't like the bathroom situation. It's too inconvenient."

Miles gave in. "Okay. I've been looking anyway."

While Miles looked for a better job, he continued to work long hours at the garage, which caused him to get home late most nights. Katherine stayed in the main house and talked to her aunts while Miles was gone.

"I wonder what Miles is doing so late," Katherine complained to Aunt Etta.

"Oh, honey, he's working, you know that. Stop talking like that," her aunt scolded. She didn't like seeing Katherine's jealous tendencies, especially since there was no basis for them.

"Oh, Katherine, you got some mail today," Aunt June said as she handed Katherine a large envelope.

"Let me see." Katherine excitedly ripped open the sealed flap and pulled out their wedding picture. She squealed as she peered at her and Miles and the most unusual background.

"Why, it looks like you got married in paradise," Aunt Etta chuckled. "Look at the palm trees in the background. It's a beautiful picture, Katherine. You and Miles look so happy."

Katherine beamed with pride. She turned the picture over and saw June 21, 1940, her wedding date, written in pencil on the back. She mouthed, "June 21," as if to etch that date in her mind forever as her wedding anniversary.

One day Miles knocked off work early because he heard that the Sava Company, a machine shop, was going to hire approximately one hundred workers. There was a mad rush of desperate men, all in need of a good job; Miles got in line early. As he waited with the fellows, all hoping for a chance at a better life, Miles thought this job would be perfect. They could get a larger apartment and really be on their own, and his wife would be a lot happier.

"Miles, here's a letter from Sava," Katherine said as she handed the envelope to him.

Miles' eyes opened wide. "Good News, I got hired!" Miles yelled.

Katherine gave her husband a hug. "Now we can get our own place."

Katherine was the happiest she had been in her life. Miles was jolly and showed her a lot of attention, especially sexual attention, which she managed to handle. He made her feel very desirable, which was wonderful for her self-esteem. In addition, when Katherine felt good, she loved to laugh.

Katherine never thought she could feel this tranquil; it almost felt strange. It was a harmony that she wasn't used to. In an odd way, she actually felt like something was missing. Surly she liked the wonderful life she now had; surly she liked peacefulness her marriage gave her; so what made her feel this way? At times, when she was alone in the afternoon, she had to shake off the edginess that came over her. She didn't understand it; she tried to disregard it with a cigarette.

"Isn't this great," Katherine told Miles as they toured a little house for rent in town.

"Yea, this is nice; and we can afford it," Miles agreed. Katherine hugged her husband. Everything had worked out just as she had planned.

Moving day came and the family helped the new couple get settled.

"Oh, I'm gonna be sick," Katherine moaned as she left the box of unwrapped dishes and ran to the bathroom.

"Katherine." Miles ran after her. He got there just in time to see her vomit in the toilet.

"What's the matter? Do you have the flu?"

"I don't think that is the problem," Katherine said as she wiped her mouth. "I think I should go see Dr. Polk."

The news spread through the family like wild fire; Katherine was going to have a baby. Aunt Etta was delighted; it felt as though she were expecting an actual grandchild.

However, not everyone was that happy; Raymond was quite miffed. While he was actually happy his sister was going to have a baby, he looked at his wife and wondered why she couldn't get pregnant. After all, they had been married a lot longer than Katherine and Miles. He and Josephine were not practicing any birth control, so what was the problem? Ray began to get disenchanted with his marriage. The fact that he had a wonderful, beautiful and kind wife didn't matter; he wanted a family. His chauvinism never allowed him to consider the fact it just might be his fault. His only concern was that he had been unfortunate enough to marry two unfruitful women.

And Alice, well she was green with envy for days. While a new baby in the family was always a joyous occasion, why did it have to be Katherine, instead of her? She was pissed. Though Dennis was very happy for his sister, he could see the discontent on his wife's face; it hurt him. Alice hated that Katherine had one up on her, simply hated it.

On the other hand, Katherine loved it. Finally she was able to rise above both of her brothers and produce an offspring for the May Tomas side of the family. That felt good. Again, everything was going right for Katherine.

In November she gave birth to a beautiful, strawberry blond, little girl, which they named Carolyn Ann, the apple of her daddy's eye. Katherine, though thin and sometimes puny from her poor eating habits, could be surprisingly strong when she needed to be, and she made it through childbirth just fine. She stayed in bed for the normal ten days and Aunt Etta came over to help her until she gained her strength. Aunt Etta was thrilled; this little baby made all her sacrifices worth while. All the bad times, and all the sad times, melted away in the blue eyes of this baby girl.

Before long, Katherine was up and around feeling fine; however, Miles was on edge.

"You know Katherine, the war in Europe just might spread to include America," Miles told his nervous wife.

"Well, you won't have to go, will you? You're married and you have a child. Aren't you safe from being drafted?"

"I don't think anyone is safe. But, I should be okay, at least for a while."

Since the war did not involve the United States yet, Katherine refused to even consider that Miles might have to go. However, on that fateful night of December 9, 1941, Katherine sat in her chair holding her month old baby; she was stunned when President Roosevelt interrupted the radio broadcast with the horrible news about Pearl Harbor being bombed by Japan on December 7; now she had to consider it, Miles just might be called to duty.

The broadcast came on late, 10:00 p.m.; Miles had just walked in the door. He had been at the bar where some of the men were talking about the president addressing the nation because something horrible had happened in Hawaii. He raced home to hear the news with his wife. When he saw the panic on her face, he rushed over and sat down near her and the baby; they listened to President Roosevelt together.

"… Powerful and resourceful gangsters have banded together to make war upon the whole human race. Their challenge has now been flung at the United States of America. The Japanese have treacherously violated the longstanding peace between us. Many American soldiers and sailors have been killed by enemy action. American ships have been sunk; American airplanes have been destroyed…."

Miles and Katherine looked at each other in disbelief. Miles was pale; Katherine's eyes bulged with tears.

"… We are now in this war. We are all in it; all the way. Every single man, woman and child is a partner in the most tremendous undertaking of our American history. We must share together the bad news and the good news, the defeats and the victories, the changing fortunes of war …"

"My God, Miles! We're in the war! Will you have to go? Are you going to get drafted?" Katherine screeched. Miles' head spun. He didn't know the answer to that question.

"I don't know, Katherine," Miles responded. He hushed his wife so they could listen to the rest of the broadcast.

By the time President Roosevelt signed off on that ominous night, Katherine's peaceful, harmonious world ceased to exist. She was nearly hysterical at the thought that Miles might have to go in the Army and leave her all alone. He tried to calm her down by telling her they would just have to wait and see; nothing was certain yet.

The world reeled throughout December and Miles stayed late at the bars as rumors about the draft flew. Before long, information was released.

"Okay, Katherine, this is what I have found out. My classification is Class III; that means I am deferred because of dependency and hardship; however, all deferments are temporary; the government will draw from deferred classes when more soldiers are needed," Miles explained as calmly as possible.

"You can't go and leave me alone. How will I manage?" Katherine cried.

"You'll have to manage just like everyone else. I don't know what else to tell you." The quivering in Katherine's stomach was back, in full force.

"Hello," Katherine said as she answered her phone, which rang off the hook, like everyone else's.

"Good, I want to see you too," Katherine answered.

"That was Dennis; he and Alice are coming to see us. He said he wants to see the baby."

Miles, Katherine, Dennis, and Alice hugged and sat close to each other as they discussed what current information had been reported. The looming war allowed the four to enjoy a calming closeness before it pulled them apart. After an exhausting conversation about all of the news, Dennis broke from the overpowering gloom.

"Now, let me hold my little niece," he said as he took the baby from Katherine's arms.

"She's beautiful, sis." Dennis held Carolyn tight.

He gave the baby a long hug and Katherine could see his blue eyes starting to water; she knew why; however, there was another reason.

"Well, you know that I'll probably be drafted. I'm classified 1A, available for service," Dennis announced. "So, I've decided to enlist in the Navy."

"What?" Katherine screamed.

"Now, sis, calm down. Like I said, I'm going to get drafted anyway," Dennis explained.

"I know, but why don't you wait until then. Maybe it will be over before you get called," Katherine augured.

"We're going to be in this for a long time. Anyway, I've made my decision."

Katherine cried, so did Alice. The thought that their world was going to be torn apart cast a daunting sadness around the room. As if by some strange phenomenon, it took a war to put Alice and Katherine in the same mindset.

"What about Raymond? Have you talked to him?"

"Yes, he doesn't think that he'll get drafted because of his age; and I don't think he is going to enlist. He's going to see what happens," Dennis explained.

"Dennis, that's a damn courageous thing you are doing; good luck." Miles shook his brother-in-law's hand. He thought that was a manly thing to do. He started asking Dennis questions about it, which was a big mistake; Katherine freaked out.

"Miles, you're not thinking about enlisting are you?" she screamed. "I don't want you to go. I don't want to be alone. No, you can't enlist," she bawled hysterically.

"Settle down, settle down. No, I'm not going to enlist. Katherine, settle down!" Miles gave Katherine a hug and tried to calm her. He was sorry he mentioned it.

"I need some cigarettes. I'll be right back." Miles abruptly rushed out the door.

"Katherine, you've got to settle down; everyone is on edge right now," Dennis said in his claming way. "Let's talk about something else."

Alice took little Carolyn Ann in her arms and played patty-cake. Time passed and Katherine got antsy.

"I wonder where he is." Katherine paced from window to window.

"Oh, he'll be back soon," Dennis told her. Miles wasn't back and Katherine continued to fret.

"He should be back by now. I hope he didn't go to the bar. He'll be there all night," she said with a worried look on her face. "Where is he?"

Dennis didn't know what to say; in addition, he didn't like what he saw. He hadn't seen his sister in such a paranoid, mistrustful state before; at the same time, he wondered if her suspicions were founded. He hadn't heard that Miles was laying out at the bars. Her comments surprised him.

"Oh, come on, sis. He'll be back soon. You're just being silly. Miles isn't doing anything that he shouldn't."

Just as Dennis spoke, Miles burst through the door. Katherine breathed a huge sign of relief; at the same time, she lit in on him.

"Where the hell were you?" she demanded. Miles ignored her sharpness but Dennis was taken aback.

"I ran into a guy from work. We were talking, that's all," Miles explained, ignoring her bitchy tone. He went over to make goo-goo eyes at his daughter.

"Why did you have to stay away so long? We have company."

Dennis and Alice threw a questioning glance at each other as Katherine continued to pick at her husband.

"Well, we'd better go now," Dennis announced. Katherine was too annoyed to care.

Months of uncertainty went by; though she became a devoted mother, her moodiness grew. Aunt Etta came over to visit Katherine and the baby; they were having a most pleasant talk until some bad news came up.

"Katherine, you'll hear this soon enough, so I might as well tell you."

"What is it?" Katherine asked, very concerned.

"Raymond is divorcing Josephine." Aunt Etta was clearly dismayed.

Katherine looked up from feeding Carolyn and stared at her aunt. "What!" she exclaimed.

"Yes, he told me the other day," Aunt Etta continued.

"Why?" Katherine quizzed.

"Well," Aunt Etta paused, "he simply got disenchanted with Josephine because she wasn't giving him any children. He wants a family."

Katherine could tell there was more.

"And," Aunt Etta hated to say the rest. "I guess he got involved with a woman at his company. I hear she has promised to give him as many children as he wants." Aunt Etta was disgusted with Raymond's unfaithfulness.

"What an awful thing to do to poor Josephine. Raymond should be ashamed of himself," Katherine admonished her brother. She loved Josephine, they had gotten very close. Katherine was distressed with this news. Now she had one more reason to resent her oldest brother.

"I know, everyone feels that way; but, we are going to have to accept his new wife. After all, he is family," Aunt Etta said, being the understanding person that she was. Katherine gave a disgusted gesture and went on feeding Carolyn.

"What's going on with Dennis and Alice?" Katherine asked her aunt.

"Well, he called the other day and said he will be leaving for basic training soon. In the mean time, they are going to keep Alice's niece for a little while. You know, Clovis' girl, Shirley."

"Oh yea, what's the matter? Is he getting another divorce?" Katherine asked.

"Yes," Aunt Etta replied.

"What does that make, about the fifth one?" Katherine remembered the stories her brother told her about Clovis.

"Something like that. Anyway, he took off for a while and left Shirley with them."

Katherine simply shook her head. "He's really messed up. But, it's nice of Dennis to take Shirley in," Katherine admitted.

"So, how are you doing, Katherine?" Aunt Etta asked as lovingly as a mother.

"I'm so nervous that Miles might get drafted. I can't stand it," she whimpered.

"Well, Katherine, he has no control over that. If he has to go, you'll just have to manage, that's all. You have family to help," her aunt assured her.

"I know." Katherine heard Aunt Etta's words, but they didn't help to calm her. Nothing helped. She was sure she couldn't handle it. She didn't want to even think about handling it.

Etta went home before Miles got home from work so she didn't get to hear his news.

"I just talked to Herbert. He's enlisting in the Navy too. He'll probably be at the same camp as Dennis. How about that?" Miles said excitedly.

"Well, he's single. He has no family to take care of," Katherine snapped; she wasn't impressed with Herbert's decision.

"Well, I think there's something decent about enlisting," Miles boasted. He flopped down on the couch and read the paper.

Katherine's stomach was in knots.

Chapter 36

"Miles, will you get the phone?" Katherine yelled; she held Carolyn in one arm while she stirred a pot to beans.

The phone continued to ring. She yelled again; since he didn't answer it, she figured he must be outside and couldn't hear her yelling at him.

"Hello," she said hurriedly. There was silence, then a voice.

"Kat, is that you?" came the familiar voice on the other end.

Katherine was stunned; she was motionless. There was only one person that called her Kat so instinctively; her mind raced to place what she heard on the other end of the line. She hadn't heard that voice in ten years; now, all of a sudden her ears rang with a voice that made her quiver; the voice that was still unforgiven.

"Kat!" She heard again. Katherine was almost afraid to acknowledge that she was indeed, Kat.

"Kat, this is your daddy, are you there?"

Finally she shook her head back to awareness.

"Dad?" She slowly queried.

"Hey, Kat, how are you?" Sam sounded genuinely excited to talk to his daughter again.

Katherine did not feel the same excitement. The shock made her leery of why he was calling, and how he even knew where she was. She wasn't very welcoming.

"How did you get my number?" She quizzed.

"Well, Lil saw the birth announcement in the paper and then we called the information operator. Actually, she saw your wedding announcement too; when she saw the birth announcement, we wanted to call and see how you were doing," Sam told her.

"Oh." Katherine was unable to say anything else.

"So, you had a little girl?"

Katherine was tense. Why was he calling? After all these years, why was he interested now? *Does he think I have forgotten everything? Does he think I have forgiven him?* All these thoughts and feelings raced through her head like a car racing around a dirt track, kicking up dirt and clouding her mind. She stumbled for a response.

"I'm surprised you're calling after so long," Katherine finally answered.

Even if she wanted to feel excited, it simply wasn't happening. Excitement was the last thing she felt.

"I know, Kat, it's been a long time. I was hoping we could let the past go and get to know each other again. Lil and I would really like to see you, your husband, and your little girl. I'd like to see my granddaughter." Sam's confidence at being welcomed irritated Katherine.

Lil and him, Katherine thought with a sneer on her face. There he was, still putting Lil first; and he dared to call Carolyn his granddaughter.

"Well, I don't know. I didn't leave on such good terms, you know." Katherine reminded him.

"I know, Kat, but can't we put that behind us and start over? I really would like to get reacquainted," Sam almost begged.

Katherine was still in shock; making a decision right then was out of the question.

"Dad, I don't know about that. I'm going to have to think about it. You call me out of the blue after ten years, I don't know," Katherine tried to explain without coming out and saying what she really wanted to say; that he allowed his wife to abuse her, that he never stuck up for her; and then, he never called or visited her, even when she was near death; she started to quiver inside.

"Well, okay, Kat. We can take it slow. But I really want to see you," Sam implored; they finally hung up with the agreement that Sam could call again.

Katherine was barely able to continue with dinner. This was the last thing she wanted to deal with; she had enough to think about with the war and the possibility that Miles might have to leave her all alone. Why did he have to call now and get her all upset? Why did he expect that she could forget what happened? Her shock turned to being pissed at his boldness.

"Was that the phone?" Miles called to his wife; he could see she was pale "What's the matter?"

"Guess who just called me after ten years!" Katherine challenged him.

"Who?"

"My father!" She shot her response like a speeding bullet.

Miles had heard about Katherine's hard time at her father's house. Lord knows she always reverted back to that time whenever she got upset. However, Miles had given it very little thought.

"Well, what did he want?"

"He wants to come over and see us; he wants to meet you and Carolyn!" She nearly shouted. Miles thought for a few seconds.

"Okay. I guess that would be okay."

"Okay?" hollered Katherine. "What do you mean, okay?"

Miles was shocked at her ferocity. He had seen her upset before, but she was down right enraged.

"Well, what's wrong with your dad coming over? At least he wants to see you. That's good, isn't it?" Miles tried to reason with her.

She didn't answer him; she was visibly shaking. Miles walked over and gave her a squeezed.

"Come on, baby, its okay," he reassured her, nuzzling her ear. "It's a good thing that your dad wants to get back with you. Maybe it will help you get past all those bad memories you have," Miles said ever so sweetly; he kissed her neck.

"I don't know, Miles. He never stopped her from beating me. I don't know if I can get past it," Katherine said in a calmer voice.

The next few days were torture for Katherine. She was consumed with the battle raging inside her. Should she forgive and forget and let her father back into her life, along with her evil stepmother? Should she shut him out and continue the hate that tortured her soul? The tug-a-war pulled her apart. She was sure that if she got through the next few weeks, it would be a miracle.

However, Katherine got through the next few weeks despite her stomach aches. She had decided to let her dad come over and the arranged day had arrived. She was a nervous wreck; plus, she still hadn't told her aunt; she was ashamed to tell her.

Katherine continued to question her own motives. She knew she still resented her father; at the same time, the thought of having his affection was irresistibly potent, like a drug she wanted so fervently and had been so long without; she had to go through with it.

"Now, Katherine, calm down. It will be okay." Miles tried to calm his wife.

"I don't know if I want to see him."

"Come on, it will be fine," Miles said again, wrapping his arms around her.

The doorbell rang; Katherine froze. She looked at Miles and Miles looked at her. He started toward the door while Katherine held back. Miles opened the door to see a tall, thin, good-looking man with a brown felt hat, horn-rimmed glasses, and a big smile. The woman beside him was short and nicely dressed with a brown felt hat of her own, but hers had a bow on the right side. Miles' first impression was that this was a nice, friendly couple. He got no vibes that they were the evil pair he had heard about. The men shook hands and Miles invited them in. Katherine had picked up the baby so she wouldn't be free to accept a hug, she didn't want a hug from either one, yet.

"Kat, let me look at you."

He eyed his grown daughter up and down, his blue eyes sparkled. It was obvious he was happy to see Katherine. He wanted to hug her but he clearly understood her body language; he refrained.

"You look wonderful, gal; let me see that baby girl." Sam boasted like a proud grandpa.

Katherine couldn't believe she actually handed her baby over to him. That was a mistake because that allowed Lillian to grab her and give her a hug. Katherine couldn't believe this was the same lady who used to give her a slap across the face; and now, she let this woman, whom she hated, touch her. Katherine was befuddled by her own actions.

"Why, Katherine, you have grown into a beautiful woman. It's so good to see you again after all this time." Lillian sounded surprisingly sincere.

Lillian fussed over the baby. She took Carolyn from Sam as she talked baby talk to the infant. The whole scene was surreal.

Once they got all of the baby talk out of their systems, Sam and Lillian asked Miles and Katherine about their lives. After that was summarized, there were concerns about the war and finally what Miles did for a living. Miles told Sam about the small factory where he worked, but his real love was something else.

"And what is that?" Sam asked.

"I'm really a mechanic at heart." Miles replied, "The automobile is my first interest."

Sam's blue eye's lit up again. "Mine too!" he exclaimed. "Old Henry Ford really knew what he was doing when he invented that machine. It has changed the world."

From that moment on, Miles and Sam were buddies. The rest of the evening the two men conversed about the automobile, the gasoline engine, and the trends for the future. Even if Katherine didn't want to see her father again, she wouldn't have gotten any support from Miles. He liked Sam. He saw the man, and the father, that Katherine had been denied.

While the men talked, Katherine entertained Lillian. Thank God the baby was a diversion. Katherine didn't know what to say to this woman for which she had only contempt for so long. Now, here she was being nice to her and letting her hold her baby. This two people weren't even the same two she had in her memory. It was like meeting new neighbors or something. The whole evening was bizarre and Katherine was exhausted.

"Katherine, you look tired," Sam said.

"Yes, I am."

"I know this has been a lot for one evening. We should get going," Sam announced. "Can we come again?"

"I guess so," Katherine said instinctively; she was too tired to resist. Sam and Lillian departed leaving Katherine in a stupor as to what really happened that evening.

"I like your dad, he's nice," Miles said; Katherine didn't answer.

"And Lillian's not so bad," Miles admitted. Katherine started to get defensive.

"Yea, well they weren't like that when I lived with them. She was mean to me. She beat me and he never lifted a hand to stop her. She wasn't so sweet then," Katherine informed Miles; her stomach hurt.

Katherine didn't sleep very much that night; her battles kept her tossing and turning until morning.

After a few more visits, Katherine became comfortable with having her father back in her life. While her demons continued to lurk just over her shoulder, she was able to hold them back with the happiness at receiving her father's affection. She didn't know if forgiveness would ever come; however, for now, she enjoyed the attention.

She had to tell someone, someone in the family; at the same time, she wasn't ready to tell her aunt; not yet. In fact, along with the anxiety she felt about accepting her father, she also had terrible guilt feelings where Aunt Etta was concerned. She literally spent years complaining to her aunt about the mistreatment she received at her dad's house; now, she was going to rekindle a relationship with him; more guilt to add to her already ladened stomach.

However, this was an event that had to be told to someone; she wrote to Dennis.

Chapter 37

The next eight months were hard on a nervous nation and a panicky Katherine. Between worrying about Miles having to go in the army, and dealing with her dad's reemergence, she began to have more nervous problems and panic attacks. Added to her problem was the fact that Dennis told Etta, through a letter, that Sam was back in her life; the guilt was smothering.

Katherine's psychological well-being continued to evolve, but not for the better. It seemed she had to deal with an emotional crisis continuously ever since she could remember; it began to feel like the norm. Despite what brought on the calamity, Katherine continually questioned her worth, and doubt the sincerity of others; she had become quite a paradox of emotions; Miles experienced, for the first time, the extent of his wife's neurosis.

Miles tried to understand when he saw the fear in her eyes. He felt as though he had plunged deep into a pair of blue pools with infinite bottoms, and he was right. Little did Miles know just how deep and dark those blue pools flowed. It confused him. It was something he didn't understand; sadly, nor did Katherine. She didn't want to have panic attacks, they scared her, and she had no idea why she had them. All she knew was when she had one she needed someone to reassure her that she would be okay; her husband tried.

"I can't help it, Miles, I can't help it," Katherine whined; she wrung her hands.

"What do you want me to do?" he asked as gently as he knew how.

"When Aunt Etta took me to the doctor, he suggested walking and talking about something else."

"Okay, let's go." Away they went with Carolyn in the baby carriage.

"I'm shaking; I can't help it," Katherine whimpered. My throat feels like it is going to close up."

"Katherine, change the subject. You have to talk about something else; you have to get your mind on something else," Miles gently lectured. Four miles later, Katherine had calmed down.

Despite the war worry and her nervous spells, Katherine was contented in her marriage. She loved Miles very much and she loved her little girl. Miles did indeed help his wife get her mind on something else; by autumn she was pregnant again.

"Hi, sis," Dennis hollered through the receiver.

"Hi, Dennis. Where are you?"

"I'm at home with Alice. I'm on a weekend pass; I get shipped out next week," he explained.

"Where are you getting sent?" Katherine asked.

"I'm getting sent to the south Pacific; maybe the Philippians."

"Oh," Katherine said, she didn't know where the Philippians were.

"I have some news," Katherine said.

"Yea, what?"

"I'm going to have another baby," she announced.

"That's great," Dennis said. Katherine heard him yell to his wife, "hey, Alice, Katherine is going to have another baby."

"Well isn't that just peachy," Katherine heard Alice snap at Dennis. She would have been mad except for the little smirk on her face; two up on her sister-in-law.

"Congratulations, sis, how are you feeling?"

"Pretty good so far," Katherine answered. "Do you and Alice still have Shirley with you?"

"Yea, Alice's brother comes around every once in a while for a visit; every times he comes by he has a new wife. He never mentions wanting to take his daughter; it's not a good environment for the little girl anyway; she's better off with Alice," Dennis confided in his sister.

"Have you talked to Raymond?" Katherine asked.

"Yes, he couldn't get engaged to Polly fast enough when she assured him that she would give the Williamson family a lot of babies," Dennis chuckled.

"Well, you be careful, Dennis, and write me when you have a chance," Katherine told her brother.

"Okay. Good-bye."

Raymond's fiancée, Polly D'Luca, was a striking woman. She was tall and thin and was always dressed to the nines. She had a creamy complexion with back hair and eyes, a beautiful combination of her English mother and Italian father. She worked in the corporate offices of the Crystal Company, the restaurant chain which Raymond had worked for since he left the bank; and the restaurant that he had borrowed Katherine's money to buy. He had eventually grown his business to owning three restaurants, which caused him to interact with Polly. Raymond was struck by her beauty, her elegance, and her sophistication. He loved to watch her glide across the room. He always felt he deserved a classy woman, and Polly was it. Even though she seemed to have an air about her, she was friendly and easy to like.

At the wedding reception, Katherine had to admit that Polly was nice and she was going to be okay as a sister-in-law; at the same time, she missed Josephine terribly. It was going to take a while to forgive Raymond for leaving her.

"If I have to hear Polly say one more time that she is going to give Raymond Williamson lots of children, I'm going to get sick," Katherine complained to Aunt June. "On the other hand, she's better than Alice." Aunt June smiled; she knew what Katherine was talking about.

Actually, Alice liked Polly too. In fact, she felt that finally there was another woman in the family that she could relate to; finally, there was someone with the same panache as her. Alice couldn't be happier about the union.

Of course, all of the men at the reception talked about the war, enlistees, draftees, rations and such. Katherine listened nervously.

"Well, I probably won't get drafted because of my age," Raymond boasted.

"That's not very nice of Raymond to brag about not having to go to war. What about all the young men that might have to go? What about Miles?" Katherine complained to her aunts.

"You're sure trying to keep your husband out of the Army," one of Raymond's friends teased Katherine when he saw that she was pregnant. "Just keep having those babies and they'll never take Miles."

The crowd laughed. Katherine didn't like his brashness; she was modest and she didn't like that kind of talk. She made a face at him.

Katherine's pregnancy went fine and she had the baby just as naturally as she did the first one, another little girl, Julia Katherine; Miles wanted a boy.

Curiously, Katherine's nervous problems never interfered with her caring for her children. She always made sure that they were well fed, dry, and watched over with an over protective eye. No one could ever accuse her of being neglectful; that became one of her biggest sources of pride.

The nation went about its business of adjusting to a new order, and so did Katherine and Miles. There was no doubt about high stress levels; Katherine was certainly aware of it. She worried day and night that she was gong to be left alone yet one more time. The angst was almost unbearable and it affected her psyche more than she was aware of. To tell her not to worry was useless; she didn't know how not to worry. Her dread took on a life of its own and Miles very seldom saw his happy wife anymore.

Her anxiety developed into a foreboding fear and Miles found himself trying desperately to deal with her panic attacks. He continued to be confused with his wife's contradictions; she could be funny and happy; she could be bitchy and nagging, she could be nervous and in a state of panic; and it all could be triggered by a mere word or action from him, which made him have to handle her like fine china; it began to bother him. Katherine found herself alone most evenings because Miles stopped at the bar until late into the night, until after she was asleep.

His behavior only made Katherine worse. It made her bitchier, but Miles didn't seem to understand his contribution to her moods. One thing that really pissed him off was she started using sex as a ploy to get him to do what she wanted. No more was she the submissive young woman that he married; that goaded him. They were like two lovers gone astray, unable to reach the other; the more she bitched at him the more he stayed out; the more he stayed out the more she bitched. They were lost in a vicious circle.

Even so, they struggled through their discontent and managed to keep their little family together; they fought, then they made up, over and over again. They were back and forth all the time; it became the nature of their relationship.

"Miles, are we going to the revival meeting tonight?" Katherine asked.

"I don't know, I hate the thought of sitting under that hot tent for hours," Miles complained. While they lived in the apartment, Aunt Etta pretty much insisted that they go to church with her. Miles had no objection; in fact, he enjoyed getting involved, which is when he agreed to drive the church bus. However, he had lost interest a long time ago.

"I told Aunt Etta we would be there. I hate to disappoint her," Katherine explained.

"Well, I guess we'll go," Miles grumbled.

Katherine dressed the girls and packed some snacks and prepared several baby bottles; she knew they would be at the meeting all afternoon and into the evening.

To everyone who knew her, Katherine appeared to be a devoted Christian. Her life had revolved around the church while she lived with her aunt. However, somewhere along the way, Katherine lost her conviction. The way she saw it,

God hadn't helped her thus far; perhaps, she felt she wasn't worthy of God's help. So, in her times of need, it wasn't faith that she turned too; but only she, and God, knew that.

"Katherine, what's the matter," Aunt Etta asked when Miles got up to help with the offering, "you look troubled?"

"I don't know, Aunt Etta, Miles is so different now. He stays out late; I know he drinks, I can smell it," Katherine confided. "All we do is argue; it's not good."

"You're awfully thin, Katherine, are you eating?" her aunt asked.

"My stomach hurts, food makes me sick," Katherine answered; she fanned herself in the sweltering heat under the tent. "I'm so worried that Miles might get drafted."

"Well, Katherine, there is nothing you can do about it if he does," Aunt Etta firmly told her niece. "You'll have to manage like everyone else."

"I know," Katherine agreed; she was quiet for a while. "Miles is going to give up driving the church bus. He says he doesn't want to do it anymore."

"Why not?"

"I don't know; probably because he is out late on Saturday night and he doesn't want to get up early on Sunday. He's changed."

"Well, honey, why don't you talk to the pastor? Maybe that will help," Aunt Etta advised. Katherine mentioned it to Miles; he wouldn't hear of it.

Before long, Miles stopped going to church altogether. He was more interested in getting together with some new friends; one couple in particular, Ralph and Carmen Ward. Miles worked with Ralph at the factory and they quickly became buddies. Before long, the couple was coming over on Saturday evening to visit; eventually they started playing cards, pinochle or hearts.

Though it was a different life style for Katherine, it helped break up the monotony of their stress filled life; furthermore, Ralph and Carmen were fun to be around. Ralph was a large guy, not bad looking; he was nice, but had the factory roughness in his language and attitudes. Carmen was beautiful; she had a fantastic figure and she wore tight sweaters that showed off her bosom; plus, she had the sweetest giggle. Miles talked to Carmen a lot. Katherine fought back her pangs of jealousy, which was not easy for her. She knew Miles was friendly with everybody; that was his way; at the same time, it was hard to ignore. Even so, the two couples had fun together and Katherine didn't want to put a damper on the few good times that they had.

"Katherine, Ralph and Carmen are coming over tonight," Miles announced when he got home from work.

"Again? They were just here last week."

"Well, they had a good time. They want to come back," Miles explained.

"Okay," Katherine returned. "We don't have any beer; are you going to go get some?"

"Yes, I'll go to the store; I'll be right back." Miles rushed out the door. Katherine detected an unusual amount of excitement from her husband.

The two couples had played cards for a few hours and everyone was ready for a break.

"I'll get some snacks," Katherine said as she excused herself.

"I'll go drain the lizard," Ralph said, hurriedly; everyone laughed except Katherine; she turned up her nose.

Katherine started back into the living room when she stopped short. She saw Carmen and Miles shoulder-to-shoulder whispering in each other's ear. She couldn't believe her eyes. She blinked to make sure she had seen clearly as she stared at the two surreptitious flirts.

Katherine had accused Miles many times of fooling around, but she never had any concrete evidence. Katherine stood motionless as she realized her worst fears were quite possibly true; in that instant she felt stupid.

She wanted to burst into the room and start yelling. She didn't. Despite what she saw, she held out for any rationalization that she could. Katherine told herself Miles was simply flirting; that didn't mean he was sleeping with her. She cleared the anger that stuck in her throat and went back into the living room. She quickly got back to the table and sat the bowl of peanuts down. Katherine was a very proud woman; to confront Miles and Carmen right there in her home, and in front of Ralph, was not going to happen.

"What are you two talking about?" She asked, more serious than before.

"Nothing," Miles said, as he straitened up.

Carmen avoided looking at her. Just then Ralph entered the room roaring with a big idea he got while sitting on the commode. Miles and Carmen were relieved the subject had been changed; however, Katherine glanced at Miles, just to let him know that she saw them.

The couples went back to playing cards and Katherine suspiciously eyed them for the rest of the evening. She had feelings she had never had before. She had dealt with Miles staying out late at the bars and she had seen him flirt before; however, this was different. She saw her husband giggling and touching a woman that was definitely more than two friends getting together to play cards.

Between the bellowing from Ralph, the giggling from Carmen, and the bull shitting from Miles, Katherine couldn't concentrate anymore; she had a headache. Besides, she felt some shuffling under the table.

"What in the world is going on under there," Katherine complained. She snuck a quick peek.

"Katherine, you're awfully quiet, what's wrong?" Carmen asked.

"I'm just tired, that's all," she lied; irritated that Carmen would act so innocent.

"Well, why don't we call it a night?" Ralph announced. The card game broke up and the brassy couple left.

"What the hell were you doing?" Katherine yelled the minute the Wards left. "What do you have to say for yourself? Right here in our home; do you think I'm stupid? God, Miles!"

"Oh, come on, we were just fooling around, Katherine; calm down," Miles said as he tried to play down the incident.

"Don't tell me to calm down. I know what I saw. You and Carmen were playing footsies under the table. What the hell!" Katherine screamed.

"I said calm down. It was nothing, we were just fooling around," Miles responded, attempting two thwart an argument.

"What are you doing fooling around with another woman? I won't have that going on in my home," Katherine yelled; her blue eyes filled up with tears.

Miles and Katherine went to bed without touching. She laid awake most of the night thinking, crying, and wondering what happened to the happiness she once had; what happened to the man she loved. She felt betrayed. She wanted to close her eyes and go to sleep; she wanted to wake up in the morning with the evening being a bad dream. She was crushed.

Chapter 38

"Come on, Katherine, let us take Carolyn for the weekend," Lillian begged.

"I don't know, Lillian, let me think about it," Katherine responded.

Katherine couldn't believe how their relationship had developed; it was almost beyond her comprehension. Sam and Lillian were very nice to the kids, they bought them clothes and toys, which was a big help, and the girls loved being with them. Katherine had become comfortable letting her children go with their newly acquainted grandparents, and it did alleviate some of the stress she felt with the troubles her and Miles were having. However, it was still a strange situation.

Many times, during a nervous episode, Katherine reverted to her childhood and complained about her father letting her stepmother beat her. In a complete reversal of behavior, she turned around and let her children go home with that very woman. It was as if her strained psyche created two different women; the dark, unexplored parts of Katherine's brain created multiple personalities for another person.

Katherine never forgave the father that neglected her, but she accepted the father that now showed her love; he too was allowed to exist as a duel entity. Katherine allowed the separation of the evil Sam and Lillian and the good Sam and Lillian and they each lived in separate parts of her mind, a very confusing situation for Miles, Aunt Etta, and the rest of the family. However, they saw her managing so they did not confront the ambiguity.

The war in Europe was no fiercer than the one raging in Miles and Katherine's home. Things were getting worse as far as Miles laying out at night. His brothers tried to talk to him; they tried to tell him what he was doing was wrong. Lula even tried to talk to him; however, Miles continued his carousing; he continued to neglect his wife; he even started neglecting his work.

"Mrs. Mangrum, is Miles' there?" Katherine heard when she answered the phone.

"No, he left for work this morning. Isn't he there?"

"No, he didn't come in today," the boss told her. Katherine didn't know what to tell him.

"Well, he isn't here right now," she said with embarrassment.

"Okay, tell him he'd better be in tomorrow if he wants to keep his job."

Katherine was furious; then she was worried, and then suspicious. Where was Miles; what was he doing? One thing she knew was that he couldn't lie about going to work anymore.

"Where the hell were you today? Your boss called here looking for you." Katherine attacked Miles the minute he walked in the door. He was shocked that his wife knew about his shenanigans; he had to think fast.

"I went to the bar to talk about the war, that's all," Miles said.

"You don't miss work to do that; we need the money. Besides, you do that every night at the bar," Katherine complained; she wanted to believe him, but she didn't.

"What do I smell? Is that perfume?" Katherine continued to interrogate Miles.

There's always women in the bar; that's nothing," Miles explained; Katherine didn't' believe that either, and Miles knew it.

Miles' laying out only added to their vicious circle; the calls from work caused more bitching and nagging from his wife, which only made Miles pissed off at his boss, which made him stay away from both.

After four years of marriage, Katherine found herself thriving on her unhappiness. She smoked a lot. Dennis sent her cigarettes from wherever he was stationed; the soldiers were rationed a carton per month; Dennis never picked up the habit.

Katherine sat for hours and stared out the window. What went wrong? She was unable to even perceive that her insatiable need for attention was too much for Miles; it was simply too tall of an order for him to fill. He was a happy-go-lucky fellow. Katherine's seriousness was a downer for him, and he didn't like it. He wanted his laughing, fun-loving wife back; since it didn't seem like she was coming back, he found a lighthearted atmosphere elsewhere.

The saddest part of their dilemma was that they truly loved each other; they were each other's first true love, each other's soul mate. Unfortunately they simply couldn't find a way to reach each other any more. Miles drank away his bewilderment; Katherine cared for her children and smoked her way through her abandonment.

The family saw what was happening to this young couple. Both sides were concerned and wanted to help, but how? Obviously, somebody had an idea.

One afternoon while Miles was at work, or perhaps not, Katherine heard a knock at the door. She was surprised to be confronted by two strange men.

"Can I help you?" Katherine asked through the locked screen door.

"Mrs. Mangrum?" One of the men asked.

"Yes."

"Can we come in and talk to you?" The same man asked very gently and unthreateningly.

"What about?" Katherine was suspiciously.

"Can we come in?" The man asked again.

Katherine wasn't about to let strange men in the house.

"What do you want to talk about?" she demanded.

The men finally accepted that she wasn't going to let them in so they decided to have their conversation there in the doorway.

"Well, Mrs. Mangrum, we understand that you are having some problems with your husband. We would like to help."

Katherine was confused. What were they talking about? How did they know about her and Miles' problems?

"What do you mean?"

The men looked at each other and realized they were going to have to spell it out for her.

"Well, it has come to our attention that your husband has been, shall we say, not acting like a good husband should act. We think we can help him come to his senses. You see, Mrs. Mangrum, we are from an organization that wants to help white men act like good Christian men," they explained.

They weren't spelling it out well enough for Katherine. She didn't know what they meant. *An organization, white men, what were they getting at*, she thought.

"The KKK," one of the men whispered through the screen.

That remark made Katherine open her eyes wide with recognition. Yes, she had heard her family talk about that organization, but they didn't have anything to do with it, or at least she didn't think so.

"Who sent you?" She demanded.

"Well, that doesn't matter. We're simply here to help."

"What do you mean? How can you help?" She asked, wanting more information.

The men fidgeted as they got up the nerve to offer their proposal.

"Well, sometimes a man just needs a little shaken up to get himself straightened out. You know, shock him back onto the straight and narrow path. We'll snatch him when he leaves work and we'll tar and feather him for you. That should make him think twice about running around," the man explained with a silly, sinister smile on his face

The other man had the same smile, like they couldn't wait to get started.

Katherine was stunned. She didn't know what to say to these two morons. They actually expected her to give the okay to tar and feather Miles. Hordes of thoughts rushed through her mind.

"You want to tar and feather Miles?" Katherine exclaimed, her blue eyes trapped in confusion and shock.

"Yes. We find is a very effective cure for an unfaithful husband. We think it is important to keep the white, Christian families together," the man said, sounding perfectly convinced that what they proposed was acceptable and moral. Katherine shook her head.

"No, I can't let you do that! I just can't!"

"Who sent you?" She sternly asked again. But the men were not about to tell.

"Who wanted me to do this?" Katherine persisted.

"Well, we were approached to do this, but we said we had to have the wife's permission to go through with it. So, here we are," one of the men explained, not really answering the question.

Again Katherine shook her head in condemnation.

"No, I won't give my permission," Katherine said firmly enough that the two men knew that she wasn't going to change her mind.

"Well, Mrs. Mangrum, we're only trying to help. If you change your mind, we'll come back," the man said sounding disappointed that he wasn't going to get to do the dastardly deed. Truly disappointed, they turned and walked away.

Katherine stood in the doorway watching the two members in good standing walk away. She went back into the kitchen and sat down at the table.

"What in the hell just happened? The KKK? What in the hell did they have to do with domestic troubles? What in the hell did they have to do with us?" Katherine was baffled

She knew a little about that organization and what they felt their calling entailed, which she did not think was right; she never condoned any person being hurt or treated unfairly. As it was, she paid very little attention to other people's lives and problems, mainly because she was consumed with her own.

However, she had no idea the KKK involved themselves in the domestic problems of white people, or black for that matter. The thing that bothered her the most was wondering *who* ordered this contract. Was it someone from church; surly there were members of that group who were part of the congregation, and that knew what was going on between her and Miles. Did it come from her sister-in-law, Gladys; surly her family had the right connections. Perhaps it was Ralph; maybe he was tired of Miles screwing his wife. She concluded that she probably would never know who it was.

Now, Katherine had to decide whether to tell Miles, or not. She thought perhaps telling him would make him think twice about running around; knowing someone out there was willing to hurt him might make him stop. At the same time, she thought telling him might send him into a rage and start accusing everyone, especially family. She was in a quandary; she lit another cigarette.

Katherine sat in the old Nash seat, now very hard and uncomfortable, looking at Miles, thinking whether it would have made a difference if she had let the clan tar and feather him. Maybe he wouldn't have continued to run around if she had given the okay. She had tucked that strange offer away in her file of unspeakables; Miles was never the wiser. Thoughtfully, she gazed at her husband. She remembered the months following that visit and how she thought someone, somewhere must have gotten to him; he had been exceptionally good for a while. At the time, she was glad she had not allowed him to be tarred and feathered; unfortunately, his good behavior was short lived.

All was quiet in the car; the kids were asleep and she and Miles had taken a break from conversation, good or bad, which allowed Katherine's mind to drift back again.

While Katherine cooked dinner, she saw the mail truck pull up to the mailbox and drop some white envelopes inside; the mailman slid up the red flag. She was in no particular hurry because they got very little important mail, other than war related news; she had become somewhat comfortable with Miles' status. She finished pealing potatoes before she went to fetch it.

It was a beautiful spring day and she took her time walking to the mailbox. The gentle breeze softly tossed her hair off her shoulders and playfully swirled her skirt up above her knees. It felt good; she stood a few minutes enjoying the day. Katherine saw her neighbor looking out her window and mumbled, "What is she looking at?"

Katherine grabbed a hand full of letters and started back to the house. As she flipped through the letters, she stopped dead in her tracks. She was unable to take a breath; her hands started to shake. She stared at a letter from the United States Draft Board.

Katherine stood in the kitchen holding the potentially life-altering letter. She wanted desperately to know what was inside, but she didn't have the nerve to open it. She went over and over in her mind what she would do if it announced that Miles was getting drafted; how could she manage being alone with two little girls. She lit another cigarette and blew the smoke toward the window; the breeze coming in made the smoke swirl and drift high above her head, taking with it the last shreds of hope.

"He can't go, he can't leave me," she said to herself as she stared at the letter lying on the table.

Her entire body began to shake; soon her stomach was in knots. She couldn't bear the thought of being left alone again, it terrified her. Even though she wouldn't actually be alone, she had her family and her two little girls, she even had her in-laws, they couldn't fill the void. Conversely, the very raison d'être for her fear was not being left by family; it was the painful, continuous, reoccurrence of being left by the one she loved, her Knight.

Katherine picked up the letter with her quivering hands.

Chapter 39

Katherine spent days crying, sometimes hysterically; she actually had to go bed. Miles called on Aunt Etta and Lula to help with the kids.

The letter from the United States Draft Board did indeed inform Miles that he had been drafted; he had 30 days to report to Camp Claiborne in Louisiana.

There was so much to do, so much to get in order. August was going to be hell! It was hot, nearly sweltering; Carolyn was in her terrible two's, Judy was just barely a year old, and Katherine was out of control. Miles almost couldn't wait for his check-in date.

After a few days, Katherine was able to get out of bed; at the same time, she went over and over in her mind how she was going to manage being alone, not to mention the financial hardship. Of course, she knew G.I.'s got a monthly check, and that Miles would send her money; she also knew it wasn't very much. Katherine already realized she couldn't afford the house they presently rented.

"Where are you going to be sent?" Katherine blubbered.

"I don't know, Katherine. I'll have to wait and see," Miles explained. "But, it will probably be over seas." Miles' explanation sent Katherine into a frenzy.

She knew Dennis got sent to the Philippians, and that the Army sent Larry to Germany, and Herbert to England; and young Harry, a sailor, got sent to Hawaii; she didn't need Miles to remind her that he would be sent over seas too.

Miles tried to be patient with his distraught wife; she acted terrible, simply terrible! Aunt Etta and Lula tried in vein to settle her down. Katherine got to the point of making everyone afraid that she was going to have a complete nervous breakdown.

However, just before Miles could take no more, just before Aunt Etta called the doctor, just before the last piece of straw had been lopped up on the camel's back, a miraculous turn around happened. Like a spoiled child that finally realized the tantrums were not working, Katherine started behaving herself. She hadn't stopped crying all together, but it was obvious she accepted the inevitable; a surprising strength emerged.

A few days before Miles had to leave for basic training, he and Aunt Etta were finally able to breathe a sigh of relief. He was able to shove off knowing Katherine would be okay to manage the kids, and herself.

"I asked Bunn if he could drive us to the train station," Miles informed Katherine. "He said okay."

"Is Lula coming too?" Katherine asked.

"Probably." Miles packed his last pair of socks.

Katherine stood in the train station lobby and stared at all of the young men; some were husbands and some were sons. It was obvious that they wee anxious as they milled around and hugged their wives and mothers. At the same time, there seemed to be a carnival atmosphere. She didn't understand that; she felt only sadness.

Katherine pulled out a cigarette and lit it. She looked at the package and thought about Dennis and how far the pack of cigarettes had traveled to get to her. She knew Miles wouldn't be sending her cigarettes, he needed them for himself. She didn't care if he sent anything or not; that wouldn't make things any easier. It came time for the final boarding call. Miles had to go. Katherine clung to him. She wrapped her arms around his neck and squeezed. At that point it didn't matter what kind of problems they had in the past; it didn't matter how many women he had run around with; it didn't matter how many nights he laid out; all that mattered was that he was leaving her. She cried in his ear and made his cheek wet with her tears.

"Come on, Katherine, I have to go," Miles whispered, he tried to pull her loose from his neck.

"It will be okay, you'll see. Time will go fast. You have the girls to tend to; before you know it, I'll be home." He tried desperately to calm her fears.

Despite all of their recent troubles, Miles felt for his wife. He felt bad she was so distraught, so scared. He felt bad she was having such a hard time; he began to feel the love he had first felt for her. He did love her; despite all of the difficult times they had lately, he loved her. He leaned forward and kissed her, at first a gentle kiss, which slowly turned into a long, passionate expression of his love; it was going to have to last through six weeks of basic training. He gave his girls a hug too.

"I get a leave after boot camp; we can see each other then." Miles reassured her as the conductor yelled, "all aboard." He turned and ran toward the train.

He jumped up on the step and gave one last wave goodbye before he disappeared inside the iron giant, which would carry him away to uncertainty.

The little family group stayed until the train pulled out of sight, then Bunn wrapped his arm around Katherine's shoulder and walked her back to the car.

"Time will go fast, you'll see. You're going to manage just like all the other wives who have been left behind."

"You know, Katherine," Lula said, "there is talk about the war being over soon; if Miles does have to go over seas, maybe he won't be gone that long." Lula's attempt to calm her down didn't help much.

The car sped along on the gravel road, which was just as bumpy as Katherine's life had been. She stared out the window while she listened to the car radio. The station played *I'll Walk Alone*, which couldn't have been any more poignant. That was exactly how she felt; she had to go it alone, for now anyway. She listened to *Till you're walking beside me, I'll walk alone* as tears rolled down her cheeks; Lula handed Katherine a handkerchief while she wiped away her own tears.

They arrived back at the house and Bunn told Lula he would walk Katherine up to the door. Once again, he put his arm around her quivering shoulders.

"Now, Katherine," Bunn started, "Lula and I are not far away if you need anything."

Katherine's teary eyes met his; she shook her head acknowledging that she knew it. She started to turn and go in the house when Bunn pulled her toward him to give her one more reassuring hug. He wrapped his arms around her tiny waist and pulled her close to his chest. Their cheeks met and he could feel her trembling. Her vulnerability excited him.

"Things are going to be fine," Bunn told Katherine; his final hug lasted much too long.

Chapter 40

▼

Katherine looked for a cheaper place to live, which was the start of a life long habit of moving approximately every two years. Quite resourcefully, Katherine made an arrangement with a girl friend, Rosie; she agreed to watch Rosie's children while she worked; in return, Rosie gave Katherine free rent. Although the quarters were very cramped, it worked out nicely for the two women.

In addition, Katherine helped with the food when she got money from Miles; plus, she took in ironing to make a little extra. Aunt Etta was delighted with Katherine's responsible attitude; she was pleased that Katherine exhibited a certain amount of bravery not seen before. In the past, Katherine had only shown fear and frailty. This side of Katherine was a welcome surprise; Aunt Etta was proud of her.

Despite Katherine's difficult times, she always bounced back with a will to survive. Her puniness, bad nerves and panic attacks always gave way to a colossal will to endure. She came by this strength quite naturally. Her ancestors had the spirit of adventure and a strong will to carry on, even in the hardest of times. On her mother's side, the Tomas' ventured across the ocean from Holland and made their way to North Carolina, and then on to Tennessee, which was unsettled by Europeans at that time. Equally, on her father's side, the Williamson's made the same trek, crossing the big water from England; they also settled in Tennessee. Both sides of her family played a large part in settling Wood Station; it took a lot of courage and strength, and a keen sense of adventure to put down roots in an area inhabited only by Indians and wild animals; but that was the stock she came from.

Miles was right; the six weeks had gone by quickly and he had a weekend leave before being sent to Ft. Maxey in Texas, and then on to Europe. Miles had kept in constant touch with Katherine, mostly with letters, which helped her tremendously. Miles had asked her if she would come down to the base for a visit before he went to Texas. To his surprise, she said that she would. She was so excited at the thought of seeing her husband that she was willing to bury her fear of venturing out alone. Katherine even decided to take the girls with her.

"Katherine, you and the girls aren't going down there by yourselves, are you?" Aunt Etta exclaimed. "I don't know if you should do that!"

"Oh, Aunt Etta, we'll be okay. We'll take the Greyhound Bus; it will be fine." Actually, Katherine felt anxious about the trip; however, she wasn't going to let her aunt know that.

"I don't know, Katherine, it's is a long trip to Louisiana. Are you sure it's a good idea?" Etta was concerned about Katherine's emotional health; what if she had a problem so far away from home.

"Yes, Aunt Etta, it's a good idea; besides, I want to see Miles while I can. It might be the only chance before he gets shipped over seas."

"Okay, but let me keep the girls. It's too much to take two little girls on the bus," Aunt Etta begged.

"We'll be just fine; besides, Miles wants to see the girls."

Katherine contradicted everything Aunt Etta said; she finally gave up her appeal. Aunt Etta had become accustomed to Katherine's determination to get her way.

"Okay, but let me give you a little traveling money."

"Thank you, auntie, that's very nice of you." Katherine gave her aunt a hug.

Katherine and the girls got on the bus; they made their way to the back where there was more room. Everyone watched this nice looking woman with two little girls, one three years old and the other one a year and a half, struggle down the narrow isle; they were impressed she had the courage to travel with such young children, and without a man.

The girls jumped up on the seat; Katherine sat down on the aisle seat trapping Carol and Judy on the inside, preventing them from getting away from her. All three were excited. Katherine looked around the bus; she was amazed to see that a large number of passengers were soldiers. She found that comforting.

The bus engine revved up and they were off on an adventure. Katherine figured it would take about ten hours to get to the base, so she settled back for the long ride. As the hours went by, the passengers began to talk to each other. To her surprise, the soldiers were all very nice to her and the girls; it was like everyone was tuned in to the same emotional state, and all were sensitive to it. Women were going to visit their husbands, children were going to see their dad's, soldiers were leaving their loved ones and going back to their bases; collectively, everyone tried to ease everyone else's loneliness. Katherine felt relaxed with the group of people.

As the hours went by, Carolyn decided to entertain the troops. One of the top songs on the hit parade was *Don't Fence Me In*, which she had heard on the radio. She began to sing at the top of her lungs. *"Oh give me land, lots of land, under starring skies above, don't fence me in,"* sounded through the bus. The soldiers were enchanted by this strawberry blonde, freckled faced little girl. It was almost magical how she made the soldiers smile and feel temporarily free of their uncertain future.

"Carolyn, hush now, you're disturbing the passengers," Katherine said as she tried to hush her.

"No, don't make her stop," one of the soldiers protested. "We like it; she sings like a little angel." The diversion was consoling and the trip to Louisiana seemed much shorter.

Carolyn singing and the soldiers being so nice, was one of Katherine's fondest memories, and remained so throughout her life. It was a story she loved telling and she smiled as she sat in the front seat of the old Nash traveling deeper and deeper into the North Country.

Katherine remembered that visit fondly; Miles had been affectionate and attentive to her and the girls; for one day, all of the bad times had vanished and everything was good.

Katherine and the girls jumped off the bus into the arms of a lonely soldier.

"Daddy, daddy," the little voices rang out. Miles hugged his girls and gave Katherine a kiss.

They spent the night at a very small, dirty motel not far from the base, which Katherine was willing to over look in order to be with her husband. When the girls went to sleep, of course Miles wanted sex.

"Miles, the girls will hear us. We can't do this with them in the same room," Katherine protested.

"Katherine, come on; we haven't seen each other in six weeks. I want you, now," Miles insisted. He had been so busy with basic training he hadn't even had time to go out and fool around; he was horny.

Katherine's modesty made her object, almost causing a serious scene right there in the motel; however, she didn't want to wake the girls. Miles' persistence won out.

"All right, but we have to be quiet." She was embarrassed to the point of turning off all of the lights; she quickly jumped into bed to undress under the covers.

Miles quickly stripped down to his underwear and jumped into the bed beside her.

Katherine was very quiet during sex, she always was, but she had to keep shushing Miles.

"The girls will hear you, Miles. Be quiet," Katherine whispered.

If he heard her, he didn't acknowledge it. He kept moaning and rocking the bed until he was satisfied. Katherine never knew if the girls heard or not.

It was a short visit and the trip back home was long and lonely. Their one day together had been so nice that she had renewed hope for when Miles got out of the service; however, that was two years away; what a gloomy thought. At the same time, her new hope made things bearable for the next few months.

Miles finally got his orders. The war in Europe was indeed coming to an end; at the same time, the U.S. Army was going to stay in Germany to help rebuild the infrastructure of the country. That was Miles' assignment. He had proven himself worthy of being a mechanic, so he was assigned to the motor pool. He couldn't have been happier about that. He wouldn't be shot at and he got to do what he loved; as far as he was concerned, that was the perfect way to be in the Army.

Miles got another leave before he shipped out to Germany. Katherine wanted to visit him again before he left. This time Miles protested, along with Aunt Etta.

"Katherine, Texas is a long way for you to come by yourself. I don't know if that is a good idea," Miles said, sounding concerned.

"I'll be okay. I made it to Louisiana, didn't I?" she boasted.

"Yes, but Texas is a lot farther."

"I can do it. I want to come and see you before you leave for Germany," Katherine insisted; she wouldn't take no for an answer. The only thing that pacified Miles was that she promised not to bring the girls.

Again Katherine was excited about seeing her husband; away she sped on the train. The rhythmic rattle of the train against the tracks brought back memories of when she and her mother and brother spent so much time traveling on the rails. The sound soothed and relaxed her. It felt good.

The long trip to Texas gave Katherine a lot of time to think. She had felt so hopeful with the last visit; she still felt encouraged things just might work out for them. She made a conscious decision she would forgive Miles his indiscretions and try to look ahead. After all, she never really knew if Miles had slept with other women, or if he simply did a lot of flirting. He may have been inconsiderate about staying out late and not thinking about her feelings; he may have been stupid about his carousing around, but that didn't make him an adulterer; she tried every way she could to rationalize his behavior and forgive him.

Miles met her at the train station. They embraced and kissed, not quite as passionately as the last time they were together, but Katherine paid no attention to that; she simply thought he was in a hurry to get back to his apartment. He had told her about sharing the rent with a fellow soldier and that it was much better than the barracks. She was anxious to see it.

"Who's car is this?" Katherine asked.

"It' my buddies; the one I share the place with."

"Oh, it's nice," Katherine observed.

They drove up to the apartment; she could see Miles had been right, it was very nice. They walked up to the door with Katherine hanging onto Miles' arm. It felt so good to touch him, to be close to him. The hot Texas sun shone down on her and made her dark hair shine; the desert breeze played with the hem of her dress. Katherine never minded the heat so she paid it no attention to it. The rays bounced off the sand and reflected in her eyes, making them seem a much lighter blue; she looked beautiful.

He opened the door for her and they stepped in. To her surprise, there was a woman in the room standing in front of a big fireplace. She took one look at Miles and Katherine and took off running to one of the bedrooms.

"Who was that?" Katherine asked, surprised to see someone else there. "What's wrong with her?"

"Oh, that's my buddy's girlfriend. She's crying because he is being sent to Germany too. That's all," Miles explained; he glanced in the direction of the woman's bedroom.

He did his best to make his wife comfortable; before long, he and Katherine sat down to dinner with the roommate and his girlfriend, who cried to whole time.

Katherine couldn't put a finger on it, but Miles seemed edgy, a little distant. He squirmed a lot in his chair; he tried to hide the glances he cast toward his buddy's girlfriend. Katherine naively thought the woman's carrying on was getting on his nerves. Katherine told the couple about her and Miles' two beautiful little girls, which made the girlfriend cry even more; finally it was time for bed.

To Katherine, it appeared the couple was stalling, trying to keep her and Miles from going to bed; she rationalized they were simply lonely. Finally, she insisted that she was tired and wanted to go to bed. As they made their way toward the bedroom, Miles glanced back at his buddy's girlfriend.

"What was wrong with that woman?" Katherine asked. "I've never seen anyone carry on like that. Is she really that upset?"

"Yes, she's having a hard time."

"Well, so am I, but I'm not acting like that. She's nuts."

Katherine crawled into bed very willing to make love to her husband. This time she had no children to worry about waking up. It was only her and her sweetheart.

She and Miles made love; however, his eagerness had cooled considerably. What he offered was fine with her, because many times he was too aggressive, but this time she noticed a difference; she didn't say anything and she slept good.

"What! You want me to go home today?" Katherine asked in astonishment. "I just got here!"

"I know, but I just got called to do extra duty for the next two days. You'll be sitting here all by yourself. You might as well go home," Miles explained.

"Well, you'll be home at night, won't you? We can see each other then."

"Sometimes it's very late, and then I'm tired," Miles said. "I think it's best if you go back home."

It was such a fast trip for such a long way to come, a one day turn around and she was back on the train heading home trying to figure out what happened. Something didn't add up; she thought Miles hurried her off a bit too fast. Then again, she was simply glad to see her husband and she enjoyed the adventure of the journey.

Katherine laid her head back on the seat and felt the sway of the coach car as it rode along the rickety tracks. It was soothing as she thought about the two nice visits she had with her husband. She was even more convinced they could work things out when he got back from Germany. Every time she saw him, she felt the love she first felt for him. She felt renewed and optimistic about their future. Even her stomach felt at ease.

Shortly after the visit to Texas, Katherine got a letter from Miles telling her where he would be stationed and an address where she could write to him. The conclusion of his stateside orders made her feel isolated. Even though he had been gone, he was still in the U.S.; she could still get to him. Now, he was really going to be gone. She was depressed for weeks after receiving that letter.

The family was good to her; Sam and Lillian helped with the children, Aunt Etta had she and the girls over for dinner regularly, and Lula called often; so did Bunn.

Chapter 41

The women left behind to fend for their families, to fill the jobs, and basically keep the country going, were forced to find a strength they might never have known they possessed if it hadn't been for WWII; Katherine was one of those women.

However, she got lonely and sad, but so did everyone else. Her, and the other war wives, cried to the sad songs, sobbed at the sad movies, and sent their husbands letters with tear stains on them.

In return, Katherine was thrilled every time she saw a letter in the mailbox from Germany. It was quite an adventure reading the censored pages. Unfolding a letter from Germany was like unfolding paper doll cutouts; the proof readers snipped out parts of the letters when the soldiers inadvertently mentioned something that was supposed to be secure, like their position or how long they would be in a certain spot; classified things. However, the readers always managed to leave the parts of Miles' letters where he described what kind of gifts he had bought her; she read about a fine German made wristwatch, nice dressmaking shears, and a gold necklace. Katherine couldn't wait to receive these things. It made her feel special that he thought about her, and bought her gifts; it added voracity to her dream, to her fantasy. Katherine managed to put aside the memory of the unfaithful Miles and thought about the devoted husband; it was her survival technique, and it worked.

She also enjoyed getting letters from Dennis and her brothers-in-law; she always shared the information with the rest of the family, particularly Lula and Bunn, since all four of Lula's brothers were now over seas.

One afternoon Katherine answered a knock at the front door. She was surprised to find Bunn standing there without Lula.

"Hi, Bunn," Katherine greeted, "What are you doing here?"

Bunn gave some excuse about the shop having to shut down because of a machine malfunction; he quickly changed the subject.

"Where's Lula?" Katherine asked.

"She's at home," Bunn said, as he more or less pushed his way past Katherine and into the apartment.

"Just thought I would stop by to see what you've heard from Miles," Bunn said, looking around the apartment, as if trying to see if anyone was there besides the children.

"Well, I got a letter just the other day. It's in here." Katherine started toward the kitchen with every intention of showing it to him; he followed her.

She reached up in the cupboard where she kept the letters; she turned around to find Bunn so close that their bodies were practically touching. It startled her.

"Bunn, what are you doing?" She struggled to move away from him. He didn't budge as he held her in place.

"Bunn, stop it," Katherine said; she pushed against his chest. "What do you think you are doing?" Bunn didn't move; instead, he started to snicker.

"Come on, Katherine. Miles is away and Lula's busy getting fat," Bunn said. Lula was pregnant with their fifth child, which Bunn was furious about. "Why don't we spend some time with each other?" His breathing had become heavy; he was obviously aroused.

"What's the matter with you?" Katherine shouted. "I don't do those kinds of things. I'm not going to fool around on Miles."

This time she was able to free herself from his trap. She scurried away from him; he could see the curves of her hips through her cotton skirt and he couldn't help himself. Her hips had excited him from the first time that he laid eyes on them; he grabbed her arm and pulled her close to him.

"Oh, you're not that goodie, goodie. I know you would like some attention," he mocked her.

"I'm not that kind of person, Bunn. I wouldn't do that to Miles or Lula. You should be ashamed of yourself," Katherine scolded as she pulled away. That made Bunn mad; he started toward her again; this time not so playful; he was irritated.

"I know you would like a man." Bunn pushed Katherine on top of the kitchen table and slip himself between her legs.

Katherine fought to break free; she dug her nails into his arm. He jumped back.

"You bitch, that hurt."

"Go home, Bunn," Katherine shouted; this time the girls ran into the room. Bunn saw them, and saw the determined look on Katherine's face; he finally decided he wasn't going to get what he came after. Before he flew out the door, he gave Katherine an evil look.

"You'd better keep your mouth shut, bitch!" He warned as he stormed out.

Katherine was shaken. She poured a cup of coffee and sat down at the kitchen table; she lit a cigarette. Things weren't hard enough, now she had to deal with her brother-in-law's indiscretion. Again, she had to decide if she was going to keep yet another secret from her husband.

"Damn it," she whispered.

She knew Miles was very close to his sister, and looked up to Bunn; Miles always figured he owed him. After all, he let Lula take in all of her brothers when their mother died; that couldn't have been easy for him. Miles felt beholding to Bunn. "But, damn it, Bunn was in the wrong," Katherine muttered

Unfortunately, Katherine was privy to the ugly side of the opposite sex; her father had met Lillian through adultery, she suspected her husband of committing adultery; and now, it was obvious that her brother-in-law was an adulterer. Her trust in men sorely waned.

She took a long drag on her cigarette and decided she wouldn't tell Miles or Lula, unless it was absolutely necessary. However, she decided that she wouldn't go over to Lula's as much anymore.

By the time she finished her second cigarette, she had calmed down some; however, she was still angry; she couldn't understand adultery. As many problems as she had, as difficult as she could be, adultery never entered her mind; being unfaithful was not part of her makeup, and nothing hurt her worse than being a victim of adultery.

"That asshole, Bunn, why did he have to go and do that," she mumbled as she put out her cigarette.

"Mama, what did Uncle Bunn, want?" Carolyn's little voice asked.

"Oh, nothing really, Carolyn," Katherine said, trying not to upset her children.

She kept the rest of the comment to herself; *he was just being an asshole.*

Rosie got home and the two women started dinner; Katherine didn't tell Rosie about Bunn.

"Katherine, why don't we go dancing tonight? I can get a babysitter," she suggested.

"I don't know, Rosie, I don't feel that good," Katherine said, still upset.

"Come on, Glenn Miller is going to be at the Casino tonight."

Katherine loved Glen Miller; plus, she loved to dance, and the music of the big bands carried her away from all of her worries.

"Okay, maybe it's a good idea," Katherine finally agreed.

"Hello, ladies," a man said as he approached Katherine and Rosie; they figured he was deferred from the service for one reason or another.

"Hello," Rosie answered.

"Care to dance?"

"Sure." Rosie jumped up from her chair.

The couple came back to the table as another man joined them. The conversation got around to talking about the Army USO clubs.

"Oh, I'm sure your husband has learned to dance," one of the men laughed as Katherine brought up the subject, "and a whole lot more!"

Katherine didn't like that. "What do you mean?"

"Oh, lady, I hear those German gals are something else. They've taught our soldiers a lot of things, and I don't mean the new dance steps," he laughed again.

"Oh, stop that now, you two. Don't upset Katherine," Rosie scolded. One of the men asked Katherine to dance; she did, but her mind wasn't on the Fox Trot; she felt a suspicion that she hadn't felt in a long time.

Miles and the other soldiers did indeed go to the USO clubs. Miles started out innocently enough. He learned to dance by pairing off with the service women who attended the clubs; however, as he became more familiar with his immediate surroundings, and the Germans customs, he began to venture away from the base and into the local bars. He wasn't the only one; many young soldiers found their way into the cities, which were near their army bases. The German bars had plenty of women, single, and war widowed; all simply looking for a little company. The noisiness of der biergartens was loud enough to block out the sounds of war; even though the bombs had ceased dropping, there were still tanks moving around, and plenty of ethnic and political epithets being shouted out. At the same time, the high-pitched giggles of der fräuleins helped block out the voice of the soldiers' consciences as they learned what der fräuleins had to teach.

"Uncle John, I read in the paper that Miles' company will dock in New York Harbor in December," Katherine excitedly told her uncle.

It had been nearly two years since Miles went into the Army. His stint was nearly over.

"That's good news, Katherine; when will he pull into Chattanooga?"

"I don't know yet. I'll have to wait for his letter to come."

Katherine couldn't wait until he was back in America. She couldn't go to New York, but that was okay. The anticipation was so great she actually felt like a new bride again; they were going to get to start over.

"When he gets in, can you drive me to the train station?" Katherine asked Uncle John.

"Sure, but I thought you normally ask Bunn to take you."

"I do, but I don't want to ask him this time."

"Okay, just let me know," Uncle John answered.

Katherine paced nervously as she waited for the train to pull in. The time went slowly; she chattered at her uncle the whole time.

Finally, the train came into sight. A jubilant roar went up from the crowd. All the lonely wives and children cheered; all of the anxious mothers and fathers cried, and all the friends and near by people waved and jumped up and down; the hero's were home.

Katherine caught a glimpse of Miles waving from the window; when the train stopped she followed his trek to the doorway. He jumped down from the steps and Katherine jumped into his arms. They embraced and kissed wildly. By then, Uncle John and the girls had caught up.

"Daddy, daddy." The girls jumped into his arms.

"Hey, girls, how are you?" Miles squeezed them with genuine affection.

Miles put the girls down and shook Uncle John's hand.

"Welcome back, Miles."

"Thanks, John."

As the excitement began to diminish, everyone headed toward their cars. Miles threw his duffle bag over his shoulder; he was ready to go home. Katherine stared at the bag; she couldn't help but wonder what the watch and gold necklace looked like.

CHAPTER 42

▼

"Where's the watch you told me about," Katherine asked excitedly, "and the necklace."

Miles searched his duffle bag. "I don't know what happened; they must have fallen out of my bags when I went through customs," Miles offered as an explanation.

"Look again," Katherine coaxed.

"I'm looking; I don't see them. But I do have the dressmaker's shears I told you about." Miles handed Katherine two pair of the biggest scissors she had ever seen.

The scissors sufficed, but she was clearly disappointed about not receiving the promised gifts; however, she let it go; she was just happy to have her husband home.

Of course, the first thing they did was find a place of their own. The arrangement at Rosie's was simply too invasive; Miles was not about to put up with that. They found a small house just outside of town, which happened to be a few doors from one of Katherine's aunts, Aunt Lilly, nosy Aunt Lilly.

The first few months were heavenly.

"Man, that's good; I dreamt about this carrot cake for two years," Miles swooned. Carolyn and Judy sat on his knee as he spent hours telling his wife and daughters about Germany and all his adventures. It left little time to argue, and before Katherine knew it, she was pregnant again. The baby was due in March of '49; Miles was so hoping for a boy this time.

It seemed everyone was going to have a baby; Larry's wife was pregnant with their third child, Herbert's wife was pregnant with their only child, Harry had not impregnated anyone since he had discovered his true persuasion in Hawaii, and dozens of their friends were going to have babies; the baby boom was in full swing. Unfortunately, the one person who wanted a baby more anyone else, Alice, was still not pregnant.

Dennis had been stationed in the South Pacific; while there he contracted some sort of tropical disease. The family never knew the name of it, only that it made all of his curly hair fall out. When his hair grew back, it grew in straight as a poker. Whether the doctors had actually told Dennis this bit of information or not, Alice relayed to the family that the tropical disease had made him sterile. She had to have a tangible reason why she was unable to get pregnant; she couldn't bare the humiliation of admitting that she couldn't conceive, or that her husband had some sort of problem. Dennis' condition, being war related, made it somehow less stigmatic; so the reason now and forever for Alice never having a baby was the tropical disease.

Polly, Raymond's wife, despite all of her boasting and promises, had still not given the Williamson family even one baby; now Katherine had three up on her brothers.

The country was getting back to normal and so were Katherine and Miles; unfortunately the excitement of being reunited wore off. Miles began to get board; he wanted what der fräuleins had taught him. Just like the song from the Great War, *How 'Ya Gonna Keep 'Em Down on the Farm After They've Seen Paree*; well Miles saw Weisbaten and he wasn't satisfied with the farm anymore.

"Miles, you can't get on top of me; it might hurt the baby," Katherine complained. That was the door he had been waiting to open.

"Okay, Katherine, I don't have to get on top, we can do something else." He began to slowly move down Katherine's body.

He raised her nightgown and gently kissed her breasts; he then moved down toward her stomach. He stuck his tongue in her belly button, which made her twitch.

"What are you doing, Miles?"

Miles didn't answer. He slowly started to take her panties off; he bent down and kissed the lower part of her stomach. Even though it was dark, Katherine could feel herself blush.

"What are you doing?"

Katherine was totally uneducated in sex, other than the mercenary position or on her side, as was Miles before he went into the service.

He moved farther down and kissed her tuft as he tried to spread her legs apart. He had a good teacher in Germany and he had learned very artfully how to please his partner; he wanted a chance to demonstrate.

"Miles, what are you doing?" Katherine yelled; she pushed his head away from between her legs. "I don't like that; stop it!"

"Why not give it a try? Maybe you'll change your mind," Miles coaxed.

"Where did you learn to do that?" Almost from the moment the question left her lips, she knew the answer. She remembered the man in the dance hall who talked about the German women. "Did you learn that in Germany?"

Miles didn't answer right away. He wasn't exactly embarrassed, more like uncomfortable. "Yes, I did, and I learned a lot more; and I'd like to teach you."

"I don't want to learn that, it's nasty. No!" Katherine insisted. She was upset; this wasn't the man that left her two years ago. He was different; he was worldly.

Miles was uncomfortable; he was excited and Katherine wasn't going to let him take care of it. Now that she was upset, he figured it wasn't a good time to explain how she could help him get satisfied; he was angry that she didn't cooperate.

Katherine lay next to him with her body stiff and her mind bewildered. Of all the problems she thought they might have, this certainly wasn't one of them. She knew Miles loved sex and required a lot of it, but it threw her off guard to argue about having sex a different way. What he wanted she saw as vulgar and dirty; she didn't want to do it. She wondered how angry he might get if she kept protesting; she wondered if he would get it from someone else.

In the coming months Katherine's fears came true. Miles started laying out after work again. It was hard enough for her to handle that stress and worry, but her nosy aunt made matters worse.

"Katherine, when are you going to put your foot down and tell Miles to straighten up?"

"Aunt Lilly, I'll take care of it; you don't have to worry." Katherine tried to be polite; it was difficult.

During that time, Katherine befriended a lady, Lil Walling; she lived just over the hill. Her husband, Jean, worked at the factory with Miles. Lil constantly visited Katherine; she talked, drank coffee and butted-in. Her personality was annoying, but Katherine needed the company. Lil took Jean to work so she had the car during the day, which allowed the ladies to go shopping together. Every time they took off, Aunt Lilly had her head stuck out the front door. Katherine would be home only a few minutes when her aunt wanted to know where they went and what they bought. Katherine didn't like it; she never got used to the constant meddling. Her business was her own and she didn't like prying questions, which was why her and Lil's relationship was curious. At the same time, and to her credit, Lil was always there for Katherine.

"Aunt Lilly, I'm ready to have the baby and I can't find Miles. Can you go get Lil for me?"

"Okay, honey. We'll be back as soon as we can." Aunt Lilly had to walk to Lil's house, which was a good distance over hilly terrine. Twenty minutes later, the two ladies pulled into Katherine's driveway.

"Where's Miles?" Lil asked when she arrived.

"I don't know where the hell he is. He makes me so damn mad," Katherine grunted between contractions.

"Well, let's go. Let me help you in the car."

"Aunt Lily, can you stay with the kids?"

"Of course; and, when Miles gets home, I'll send him to the hospital, but not before I give him a peace of my mind."

Katherine didn't object; he deserved it.

Miles bounced into Katherine's room. "Well, do we have that boy?"

Katherine gave him a dirty look. "Where were you?"

Miles didn't answer that question. "Do we have a boy?"

Katherine didn't look at him; she knew he wasn't going to be happy.

"We have another girl," she finally said.

"Another girl?" Miles tried not to show his disappointment. "What do you want to name her?"

"Linda," Katherine said, "Linda Faye." Miles shook his head in agreement.

"Where were you?" Katherine asked again, as if she didn't know.

"I stopped off at the bar with some buddies, that's all."

"You knew my time was close; you should have stayed around. I had to tell everyone that I didn't know where you were."

"Katherine, don't start anything. I don't want to hear it."

Katherine tried to be happy about her new baby girl; however, her husband's bad behavior overshadowed the blessed event. Miles tried to be happy too; however, he was so disillusioned with his marriage, and another baby girl, that he too missed the wonder of the miracle.

Katherine stayed her expected ten days in the hospital. She had a lot of time to think. She began to entertain some thoughts that had been put in her head, mostly by Lil. She didn't want to be a divorced woman, but it seemed she just might end up that way. The days passed by with her thinking how she would manage with three little girls if she were divorced. The thought frightened her; at the same time, she felt she couldn't handle Miles' continued laying out and running around with other women any longer. She even had the naiveté to think that maybe filing for divorce would scare him into being good. She wondered if she should take the chance.

She looked down at her baby girl. Linda had plump cheeks but she was a small baby; all of Katherine's babies had been small. As she looked at Linda, she thought this little girl would not get a chance to know her father if she left him. Katherine felt sad.

With the fate of her marriage on rocky ground, Katherine went home in a solemn mood; Aunt Etta was concerned.

"Katherine, I can't tell you what to do; I also know you can't go on like this." Etta was clearly distressed with her niece's predicament. "But, honey, being divorced with three children would be awfully hard."

"I know, Aunt Etta, but I can't handle knowing that he's out at the bar all night doing God knows what," Katherine cried. "I don't know what to do."

Aunt Etta hugged her niece; it was obvious that her heart ached.

"I can't take it anymore. I can't take his running around, it hurts so badly," Katherine sobbed.

Etta didn't know what to say. She hated to see her niece hurting this way. "Well Katherine, I know you have to do something, but take your time, don't make any decisions that you'll regret."

Katherine wiped her eyes and shook her head in agreement.

Katherine took her aunts advice and thought about it for a while; during that time, Miles continued to lay out. Their arguments became loud and fierce. One blow-out argument was the last straw.

"By the way, I didn't lose the watch and gold necklace; I gave them to my two German girlfriends," Miles taunted. At that point, he didn't care if he hurt his wife.

"You mean the two whores that taught you those nasty things?"

"Yea, and they were good at it; they knew how to please a man. They weren't finicky, or a bashful, little mouse; they were real women."

Katherine's ears burned as his hurtful words made their way to her brain; her head throbbed with his painful confession. She wanted to lash out at him and hurt him as badly as he just hurt her.

"I think you should know something about your precious Bunn. When you were gone protecting the country, he came by the house and made a pass at me; and it happened more than once."

That made Miles furious. "You're just making that up, you bitch. Bunn wouldn't to that to my sister or me. You're lying." That was the first time he called her a bitch; it wouldn't be the last.

"I'm not lying. You think Bunn is such a great guy; huh, he couldn't wait for you to go to Germany," Katherine yelled back. "He even complained about your sister being fat when she was pregnant."

"You don't what you're talking about," Miles shot back.

"I know what I'm talking about; I know Bunn would have slept with me if I had said okay." Katherine rubbed it in as hard as she could.

"You're lying, you bitch," Miles said again. "I don't know if I even want to be around you anymore."

"Well, maybe I'll just kill myself. Then you won't have to be around me."

"You're too mean to die."

The wounds they inflicted on each other were painful and deep. Miles took off to the bar while Katherine had to pull herself together and put the kids to bed. After they were asleep, she sat at the kitchen table and had a cigarette. Though Miles hadn't laid a hand on her, she felt beat up; every inch of her body hurt, her soul was bruised. In between drags, she cried.

She wrestled with the hurt for days. Love didn't turn out the way she had dreamed it would. She agonized; and she smoked.

Katherine made her decision; on a warn summer day she got a babysitter, caught the bus and went to town. She didn't tell anyone about her trip to Rossville. How she was able to sneak away from Aunt Lily and Lil she'll never know, but she managed to get there and back in perfect secrecy. Another thing she would never know was how she was able to catch a bus, go to town, and find a lawyer all by herself, and without the company of her phobias.

The few years, which she had been on her own during the war, brought out a hidden strength in Katherine; a strength that clearly stemmed from the pure instinct of survival; a strength that turns terror into determination.

Katherine sat on the bus in a daze. It wasn't a happy a trip, like when she took the girls to Louisiana to see their dad; this was a sad trip. The first few miles she sat in silence; she was heartbroken. She looked out the window and watched the buildings go by; but, saw nothing. As she neared the city, her sadness turned to anger when she thought about the betrayal of her husband. Her strength was in her anger; however, as she sat on the bus, a new, stronger feeling began to grow; she felt bitter, far too bitter for a young woman. Life had not fulfilled its promise of happiness; it had not been fair; love had not been there for her. The strength she found in her anger gave her the bravery to forge ahead into the city to find her vengeance

In Katherine's mind, she had done nothing to contribute to her and Miles' bad behavior. She had been a good wife, gave her husband sex, her kind of sex, kept a clean house, cooked good meals, and took care of the children. She was right; she did do all those things perfectly. She had no clue as to what she may have done wrong, she thought nothing; she didn't know what drove him into the arms of other women. She simply didn't understand why he couldn't be the perfect knight that she placed in her ivory tower.

Katherine refused to accept any contribution to her and Miles' troubles. She was sure it did not always take two. All she thought about was what Miles had done wrong, and how she wanted to get through to him that she couldn't take any more; she *wouldn't* take anymore. Katherine was determined to give Miles a big surprise.

Katherine saw her husband pull up into the driveway. She didn't know whether he had been served or not. The lawyer hadn't said when it would happen; he simply said it was standard practice to catch the person off guard.

Miles rushed into the house and hurried over to Katherine. She could see he was excited and sweating; she held her breath.

"Honey, why did you do this? Why do you want a divorce?" Miles asked with sincerity. He was truly baffled. Katherine got what she wanted; she got his attention.

"Why did you have them come to my work? That was embarrassing," Miles asked; she could tell he was irritated about that, and she didn't blame him.

"The constable shoved the papers into my hands right in front of all the workers. Everyone stared at me."

"I didn't tell the lawyer to have you served at your job. No, I didn't tell him to do that. I didn't even know they would go to someone's work place," Katherine vehemently explained.

Miles still appeared to be in shock. "How did you get this arranged? Did someone help you? Did Uncle John help you?"

"No, he didn't help me. I went to town all by myself."

Miles was obviously impressed. However, he let that go and put his arms around Katherine; he gave her a little kiss on the cheek. "Honey, why did you do this? I don't want a divorce."

"Miles, I've had enough. I can't take it anymore. I can't take you running around any more," Katherine admitted.

"Honey, I don't run around. I just stop at the bar to talk to the guys, that's all." Miles insisted on his fidelity.

"Miles, you come home with lipstick on your collar; and I know it isn't mine. How stupid to you think I am?"

"I told you, there's nothing going on, maybe just a little flirting, but that's all."

Katherine knew better. She resented the fact that he expected her to believe he was just hanging out with his buddies. She resented the fact that he thought she was so foolish as to believe him.

The next few weeks Miles behaved himself, but he knew something was going to have to change if their marriage was going to survive. That's when he started seriously listening to his brother Larry, who had migrated north to get a job at the auto factory. Miles knew if they stayed in the south he would lose his family; he saw moving north as the only way to keep them together.

When Miles was good, he was very, very good; and he was good for the next few months. Katherine began to soften. She loved him this way; it made her realize that she still loved him and wanted her family to stay together, which was her first priority.

Another need, and perhaps more influential, was making it work with Miles. Katherine had no power, no good judgment and no résistance if she thought she was going to get the love she longed for; the love she so desperately needed. With Miles acting like he was going to straighten up, with him showing her the attention she desired she was willing to keep trying. Miles' powers of persuasion were potent and Katherine gave in. She dropped the divorce charges and took him back.

Chapter 43

Katherine hoped with all her might this journey north would lead her to a renewed life and better marriage. She hoped the change of scenery and location, and the change of job and people would cool Miles' impulses. She lit a cigarette as she admitted to herself that she had some doubts. However, she wanted it so badly that she was willing to take the chance.

It was going to be difficult not having family around to help, though. Aunt Etta, her dad, and Lillian had been such a big help with the children, she couldn't imagine being without them.

Katherine looked over at Miles. She could tell he was getting tired. The girls started cheering because they had just crossed the Michigan State Line.

"How much longer?" Katherine asked.

"Not much farther now. About an hour and a half," Miles answered. The girls cheered again. Katherine looked out the windows. Miles knew who she was looking for. Katherine looked at Miles; her eyes were ready to shoot blue, hot flames at him.

"I hope Herbert gets here soon. We're going to need that coal." Katherine wrapped her arms around herself with a shiver.

"He'll be here." Miles could only hope that his brother wasn't too far behind.

"Where did you say Larry and Gladys found a place to live?" Katherine asked.

"It's called Warren," Miles replied, "I guess it's about an hour from where we're going to be."

"That's a long ways away; I thought they were going to be closer."

Katherine wasn't all that upset about not being close to Gladys, she didn't particularly care for her anyway. She didn't think Gladys was a good housekeeper, or that she kept the kids up the way she should; after all, Katherine had been trained by the best. Gladys, being raised in a very different environment, was a very brash woman, which Katherine found uncomfortable. At the same time, Gladys was better than no family.

Looking around at the strange landscape and flat ground made Katherine terribly homesick. She saw no mountains, no blue haze hanging anywhere; no sharp curves or winding roads, nothing that resembled the south. She only saw flat land, straight roads, and farm after farm; cold gray clouds welcomed her in her new northern home; certainly not the greeting she expected. Katherine knew there was a lot of water around Michigan, and she expected to see some; however, they weren't in the right area to see it. Actually, they were not far from Lake Erie but Katherine didn't know that, and she hadn't taken the time to look at any maps or geography books to learn about her new home. She had no interest in anything outside of her emotional stability and the state of her affairs. Matters pertaining to her survival became her primary focus; anything else was just a nuisance and held no importance in her realm of existence; it simply took up space in her brain that was reserved for her problems.

As Katherine looked around at this uninteresting land, she suddenly missed her aunt. Aunt Etta and Katherine had cried at their last visit and Aunt June had bawled. Sam and Lillian were very distressed because they were losing their only grandchildren; Stanley and Sonny were not married yet. Aunt Etta understood the reason behind Miles wanting to move; she knew the jobs were better up north, and of course, the pay was a lot better; however, she also knew that folks can't run away from their troubles.

"Katherine, wherever you go, you take your problems with you," Aunt Etta said in all her astute wisdom.

Katherine didn't want to hear that. She hoped their problems stayed back in Tennessee, left behind in their abandoned attic.

Katherine was so tired of riding in the car. She couldn't wait for the next hour to be over. Though she hadn't prayed in a very long time, that was exactly what she did. She prayed that her aunt would not be right; she prayed their troubles would not be hanging on the bumper eagerly waiting to rush in their new home ahead of them, letting them get all settled and comfy before making their presence known.

Katherine tried hard to think of their move as not running away, but as trying to make a new start. Her only reason for agreeing to the move was to try to keep her family together. She couldn't be a failure, she just couldn't. She had to succeed at this one thing; it simply had to work.

Chapter 44

"Katherine, are you sure this is the best move for you and Miles; it's so far away," Dennis said with mixed emotions. He understood about going where the money was, after all, he went to Florida for a better job and more money. However, he knew his sister; the thought of her being so far away from family, and with the problems her and Miles had, made him nervous.

"I know, Dennis, but Miles wants to go, and I want to keep my family together. I don't think I have much choice. Miles says the opportunities are much better there, and he already has a job lined up." Katherine tried to convince herself as much as her brother. "Besides, you can come and visit us up north."

"Yes, we'll come see you," Dennis reassured her.

Dennis had done quite well in the heating and cooling business since he got out of the service. In fact, he was looking into buying his own business. Alice had become active in their community; she had joined some social groups like the Garden Club, Ladies Literary, and women's groups in their church. She still had a snooty air about her; however, she was very well respected as one of the sophisticated ladies in their community.

Katherine always thought Alice looked down on her, and she was right; that *frosted her ass*, one of Katherine's favorite expressions. Katherine knew where Alice came from, a much lower station than the Williamson's; so, for Alice to act like she was above her, well that *frosted her ass*. Katherine wasn't going to miss Alice, but she was going to sorely miss Dennis.

Raymond and Polly had moved to Knoxville for his job; he and Katherine had conversed very little since then. Raymond had been a business owner for some time now, and with Polly's good job, they were living very comfortably.

Katherine still held a lot of bitterness toward her oldest brother. She thought since he was doing so well financially, he could have paid her back the money he borrowed; heaven knows she could use it now. Her bitterness continued to fester; in addition, more than the money, she kept a raw restlessness in her soul about Raymond's lack of affection toward her.

Katherine had continued a very good relationship with Lula, despite the secret; she was going to miss her. Lula had seen her brother and sister-in-law struggle through their relationship for almost ten years. She knew Miles had inherited their dad's sexual appetite and that it caused a huge strain on their marriage. She had also seen how difficult Katherine could be too, which agitated Miles' carefree spirit. They were a sad pair; so much in love but so unable to love each other. Often times Lula's heart ached just as much as Aunt Etta's for these two struggling souls. So, in the end, Lula was all for this move if it was going to help.

Katherine hadn't said anything to Miles, or anyone; however, in the back of her mind she felt comforted with the thought that if things didn't work out for them in Michigan, she would move back to Tennessee; that was her secret plan.

"I've got to get these brakes fixed as soon as I can. I don't know where the money is going to come from, but they've got to get fixed," Miles told Katherine.

"I'm still upset that neither one of my brother's offered to help us. They both have enough money; they could have spared a little." Katherine said; he lip quivered with disappointment.

"We'll be fine. As soon as I start the job, we'll manage." Miles tried to settle her down.

"I know Alice wouldn't let Dennis give us any money; I just know it."

"Katherine, stop it. You don't need to be getting all upset about that now," Miles scolded; she ignored his warning.

"She never wanted Dennis to do anything for me." Katherine pouted.

Miles changed the subject. "It won't be long now, girls." Carolyn and Judy cheered again. They drove past an auto plant and an airport.

"Is this the airport that we're going to live near?" Katherine asked, curiously.

"No, this is the smaller airport, mostly for cargo, which is close to the plant that I will be hauling for; see right over there." Miles pointed in the direction of the auto plant.

"We have just a few more miles to go to get to the big airport."

Katherine looked around and thought the area was ugly. April in Michigan was indeed ugly, nothing like April in Tennessee. The trees were only just starting to bud, the grass was still brown, and the spring flowers were not yet in bloom. How dreadful everything looked to her. As they drove through this bare, brown land, she longed to be in Tennessee. Carolyn and Judy had their noses pressed against the car window as they started to see large airplanes roar overhead. They had never been that close to such large planes; they squealed with wonder. As they neared the main hub of the airport, they could see the air traffic control tower sticking up in the middle of miles of flatness, a strange sight to them. They didn't realize the road was so close to the runway; a landing plane was so low that they all ducked inside the car certain its wheels were going to roll right across the roof. Katherine's screams were barely heard over the loud roar of the plane engines. She was genuinely scared.

"God, Miles, that almost hit us," she shouted. Even though he was a little shaken himself, he chuckled, "no it didn't. There was at least a few inches between us."

The ride past the airport was a bit unnerving but the displaced family trekked on toward their final destination. They hadn't traveled very far past the runway when Miles turned off the main road onto a dirt road; the change of direction displayed an assortment of small, weathered, gray houses sitting in rows. Katherine was astonished at the lack of color; it was as if she viewed the scene only in black and white; mostly gray.

"This isn't where we're going to live, is it?"

Miles shifted in his seat and sighed. "Yea, this is it."

"God, Miles," Katherine said with her nose wrinkled. "Which house is it?"

"Its right over there," Miles said; he nodded to the right as he pulled up in front of one of the dingy houses.

Katherine, and even the girls, sat quietly and stared at their new home. The house was very close to being a shack. It was dirty gray, and surrounded by dull, brown, partially frozen dirt. It was all Katherine could do to keep from bursting into tears. In all her dreams, Miles couldn't have found a place this bad. He saw the look on her face, which he expected. He knew she was used to better; he had hoped to find something better; however, he simply couldn't afford anything else, at least not until he got going in his job.

Katherine hated to, but she got out of the car; the girls followed. She simply couldn't imagine that this was going to be her home. As she stepped up on the uneven cement porch, a huge, four-engine, prop plane roared down shaking everything in sight; it seemed as though it barely missed their roof before it touched down on the runway right across the street. After she stood up from ducking out of the way, she looked at Miles in disbelief. In the south, Katherine was used to living a solid, middle class life; she had to be brought to Michigan to live like a hillbilly.

Miles unlocked the door and they went in. The inside was just as dingy as the outside; Katherine saw that she had a lot of cleaning to do. But first things first, it was cold and Herbert had not arrived with the coal.

The girls began to whine: they were cold. "Just settle down girls, Uncle Herbert will be here soon." Miles tried to believe what he said.

Katherine walked from room to room, which didn't take very long considering there were only two small bedrooms, a small living room, a very small kitchen and a tiny bathroom. Despite her forlorn feeling, she arranged the rooms in her mind while getting herself ready to set up housekeeping for her family. What else was she going to do; her inherit survival instincts kicked in. This was where they were going to be, for now any way, so she had to adjust. She was glad her aunt wasn't there to see where she ended up. She felt like crying.

"Miles, is this the best you could fine?"

"Yea, with what I had to work with. Plus, a lot of places wouldn't take kids."

Katherine went about her exploration. Finally, everyone was cold so they all got back in the car. Katherine stared at the road; she waited for a glimpse of the U-haul. As the minutes ticked away, she got more ticked off with Herbert. She figured he was sitting in some bar that he simply couldn't pass up.

Katherine closed her eyes and thought about the warmth of the mountains she left behind, the warmth of the blue smokiness, which had reached out to wrap around her, comforting her, tugging at her. At that moment she wished with all her heart she was back in those familiar mountains. For a brief moment, she wished she had left Miles and let him come to Michigan alone. However, it was too late; this was where she had to make a home for her family.

Finally, a welcomed dot appeared on the horizon of the long, blacktop road. The family perked up and fidgeted with excitement.

"Is it him?" Katherine guardedly asked, not wanting to be disappointed.

"It looks like it."

"Thank God," Katherine sighed. She didn't wake the girls yet, just in case it wasn't him.

It was Herbert and his asinine friend; Miles got out of the car so his brother could see where to turn in. What a welcoming sight. The old, rickety truck held a tangible piece of home, something familiar to touch, something to hold close. Standing among these cold, gray surroundings felt inhospitable and unwelcoming; a place they shouldn't be.

Herbert jumped down from the big truck and walked over to Miles and Katherine. He looked around.

"God, Miles, couldn't you find something better than this?"

Miles looked at his wife and back at his brother, whom he could have busted in the mouth at that very moment. Katherine stared at her husband: she felt satisfied that her opinion had just been validated.

"This will have to do for now," Miles replied. "Let's get to work."

"Okay, let's get this stuff unloaded," Herbert barked at his friend.

Katherine walked around to the back of the truck as Herbert opened the heavy door. She could smell the beer on his breath; she wasn't surprised. As he opened the doors of the truck, a black cloud of dust puffed out.

"Oh, no!" Katherine yelled.

"What?" Miles hurried to the back of the truck.

"The can with the coal in it tipped over. There's coal dust all over everything," Katherine said disgustedly. "God, what a mess."

Miles walked away and lit a cigarette. "What else can go wrong?" All he had to do was wait a few more minutes to have his question answered.

"Oh, no!" Katherine yelled again.

"Now what?" Miles moaned.

"Look, the big mirror to the dresser is broken in a million damn pieces," Katherine bellowed.

Even though it was a nice piece of furniture, Miles didn't see it as a major problem; they could get another mirror. However, Katherine didn't agree with that. She was very fond of the large mirror.

"It's not worth making a fuss over, Katherine. We've got more important things to worry about. We've got to get all of this stuff unloaded. I don't want to hear any more about the damn mirror."

Katherine didn't let up. "The dresser is ruined now. I'll never be able to match it. Herbert must have been driving like a bat out of hell to cause this mess."

Miles gave her a dirty look and started moving furniture.

"We need a fire started, Miles. The kids are cold."

"I know."

As the men unloaded each piece of furniture, they hap-hazardly wiped off the coal dust. It was going to take a lot more cleaning than that to get the black, smeared sediment totally cleaned off. It was going to be a terrible job. "God, look at that mess," Katherine complained.

Katherine watched the furniture being unloaded and directed each piece to its proper place. She waited for the next item; when she saw the piece, it sent her reeling back to her southern home. Herbert held her hope chest, the one her mother had left to her; the one she had retrieved from Lillian's custody; it was one of her most prized possessions. It still held the now infamous embroidered table cloth, other doilies, and one of her first dolls; a baby doll with a porcelain head and a beautiful hand painted face. Some of her most peaceful times were when she showed her daughters the contents of her hope chest, particularly the doll. She directed Herbert to put the hope chest in her and Miles' bedroom.

All of the furniture was finally unloaded; after a rest and a few more beers, Herbert and his friend left to go back to Tennessee. Katherine didn't care how many bars they stopped at on the way back, they had already done their damage.

Katherine's first night in her northern home was cold and damp. Miles had a hard time keeping the coal fire going; he stoked the coals while Katherine nagged over his shoulder.

After days of cleaning, and wiping coal dust away, Katherine got around to taking a peek inside her hope chest. To her horror, she made a heartbreaking discovery.

"Oh, no," came a squeal from the bedroom.

"Now what?" Miles yelled.

"Look at what your brother did. My doll's head is broken in a million pieces!"

"Oh, well, it's just a doll."

"It's not just a doll; I loved that doll," Katherine whimpered as she stared at the porcelain pieces. She had kept the doll tucked away all these years, certain that the chest was the safest place for it; sadly, the chest couldn't protect the doll from the clumsy idiots who had been assigned as its guardian. Katherine was even angrier at Miles' attitude.

"Do you want me to pick the pieces out of there and throw them away?" Miles offered.

"No, just leave them there," Katherine snapped; she couldn't bear to throw them away. She left the broken pieces lying on her mother's embroidered tablecloth.

The chilly spring turned into a warm summer and the relocated family worked hard at adjusting. Miles had started his job at the car hauling company and the girls were thrilled when he brought his big hauler home over night. It amazed them to see the cars sitting high in the air. At the same time, it was tough on Katherine; Miles was gone a lot, sometimes late into the night, and sometimes over night. She was lonely in this strange place. Katherine sent Aunt Etta a letter asking her to come for a visit.

Katherine was not merely lonely, she was nervous; she was afraid to go to bed alone.

"I have an idea, Miles suggested. "Why don't you drink a beer before you go to bed? It will make you drowsy and able to go to sleep faster."

"I don't like the taste of beer," Katherine gagged.

"Well, I can't help it when I have a late shift. My boss isn't going to change my hours just because my wife can't go to bed without me, Katherine. You're going to have to manage; just give it a try."

Katherine wasn't thrilled about the idea, but the next scary night compelled her to pop the cap on her first bottle of beer. Miles was right; it made her relax and go to sleep rather fast, and the taste wasn't as bad as she remembered; she quickly got used to it.

Katherine had set up housekeeping rather quickly; however, the place was in dire need of being painted, inside and out; unfortunately, Miles' job didn't allow him much time. When he did have the time, as usual, he spent at least half of it in the local bar. Miles' head was thick; the fact that he was simply giving his wife a good reason to bitch at him simply didn't get through. The weary pair was on the cusp of their intimate, destructive circle.

Time allowed Miles and Katherine to get acquainted with their neighbors; some were nice. Some respected Miles for being a veteran and over looked the fact the he was from the south, while some were crude, unwelcoming northerners who teased them about being hillbillies. Katherine didn't understand that attitude. She had been raised in the city; she didn't know anyone personally that had their washing machine on their front porch, like the Yankees teased about; her relatives all had their appliances inside the house. She did not see herself as the hillbilly she was being called. She decided very quickly that she didn't like the north.

Katherine's loneliness prompted her to search for something that would allow her a familiar comfort.

"Look girls, I got a cat?" Katherine told her daughters; she remembered the security Snowball had given her.

"I think I'll call her White Mama. What do you think?"

"Yea," the girls squealed. White Mama was a long-haired, white Persian. It was beautiful and Katherine did indeed find comfort having the cat close to her. It felt like a friend from home.

"Let's go see Larry and Gladys this weekend," Miles told Katherine; she turned up her nose.

"Every time we go, you and Larry head to the nearest bar. You don't even stay around to visit."

"I won't let him stay very long this time," Miles assured her; she didn't believe him.

Larry had drunk to the point of becoming an alcoholic and Katherine didn't like Miles being around him that much. At the same time, she couldn't stop Miles from visiting his brother.

"I wonder where they are," Katherine complained to Gladys; she began to pace.

"I expect they'll be back soon, Katherine," Gladys assured her. "We're going down to Chattanooga next weekend. Why don't you guys come down too?"

"I don't know about Miles' schedule. I'll have to ask him. He doesn't seem to want to go home much," Katherine explained. "He seems satisfied with staying here."

"I like visiting my family," Gladys explained. "I like going back every few months; Larry likes it too."

"I would like to visit my aunt. I wrote her and asked if she would visit us up here. I haven't heard back from her," Katherine told her sister-in-law.

"I finally got some news from Harry," Gladys said.

"Oh?"

"He's going to move to Michigan."

"Why?" Katherine asked.

"When he was in the Navy, he made a good friend; his name is Jerry. His mother lives here and Jerry lives with her. They have a spare bedroom and they offered it to Harry."

"That's good news." Katherine liked Harry; she was happy that he was going to be close. "What's his friend's last name?"

"Pepper."

"Does Harry have a girlfriend yet?"

"No, Katherine, he's never going to have a girlfriend," Gladys grinned. He's homosexual."

Katherine blinked. "Oh? He is? Is Jerry his boyfriend?"

"No, Jerry is just a friend."

"Oh. Well, if that's what Harry is comfortable with, it doesn't matter to me. I'm just glad he is going to be in Michigan." Katherine didn't understand Harry's life style; nor did she judge him.

Katherine got some more good news. Not far from where they lived the government planned to build some nice, two story, duplex houses, which would first be available to veterans, and at a lower cost. Miles thought with what he earned they could easily afford to move. The thought of getting out of the loud, dirty, dingy airport homes thrilled Katherine; the only drawback was that the homes wouldn't be ready until the following year. At the same time, that gave her something to look forward to.

In the mean time, Katherine and the family worked their way through the many differences between the north and south; the first one being Halloween. While in the South, the tradition centered on a town celebration; in the North, the children dressed up in their costumes and went from house to house to collect candy. Katherine found this strange, dangerous, and a lot less social. She wasn't about to send the girls out by themselves; she was far too protective to allow that, so she went from house to house with them. After walking around the small neighborhood, the girls sat down in the middle of their living room and dumped all their candy out in front of them. They were excited as they rummaged through the goodies.

"Mama, do you want a piece of candy?"

"No." Katherine didn't feel good, she was sick to her stomach.

The end of October could be cold in Michigan. After the long, hot summer, Katherine had to adjust to the drastic temperature change. She didn't like that either; and by mid November, she was throwing up.

"Miles, I'm going to have to go to a doctor. I think I'm pregnant."

"I don't know where there's a doctor's office close by." Miles pondered. "I'll look around tomorrow. Hey, maybe it will be a boy this time."

While coping with her sick stomach, Katherine prepared for Thanksgiving, which was also celebrated very differently in the north.

"Now, honey, you've got to cook a turkey," Katherine's neighbor insisted.

"I've never cooked a turkey; we always had ham at home."

"Ham! Well, that won't do here; you've got to cook a turkey. I'll show you how," her neighbor offered.

Katherine followed the neighbor's instructions and prepared a turkey with all the trimmings; however, the old stove was not reliable.

"Look at this thing. I've burnt the hell out of it," Katherine cried. Her heightened hormones were obviously out of control.

"Don't worry about it." Miles tried to calm her down. "We have all the other stuff to eat. It's okay."

Before Christmas, Katherine visited a local doctor and got her approximate due date, which was mid June. Miles still held out hope for a boy.

"I have some good news, Katherine," Miles announced. "The housing project will be ready this spring."

"Great! We can move in before the baby is born."

"Yep, it looks that way."

Alas, the airport homes were not going to release the anxious family with only the memory of the eardrum-breaking airplane engines, they weren't going to be that kind.

"I can't find White Mama. Have you seen her?" Katherine asked around the neighborhood. Nobody had seen the cat. A few days later, Katherine found White Mama lying on the front porch, lifeless and stiff. Someone had found the dead cat and laid it on their porch. The only thing Katherine and Miles could figure out was that somehow the cat got into the neighbor's rat poison. Katherine had gotten the cat for comfort and it ended up causing her more heartache. She had to find a way to thwart her reoccurring pain. She told herself she would never get another cat; and she never did.

The sorrow of losing the cat was softened by the excitement of moving to a newer and cleaner neighborhood. The houses were big and spacious and Katherine loved the large kitchen, which came equipped with a stove and refrigerator. A door led from the kitchen into a good size living room with a big picture window, which looked out at a large back yard, with grass instead of dirt. A wooden staircase led up to three bedrooms, a bathroom, and a linen closet. They didn't even have this much room in the south; the whole family was thrilled.

"Mama, this is like a palace," Judy squealed. Katherine shook her head in agreement; finally things were looking up.

Miles and Katherine were proud of their new home. They had Larry, Gladys, Harry, Jerry, and Mrs. Pepper over to share in their delight. Katherine was drawn to Jerry and his mother. As the months went by, a very endearing friendship grew between her and Mrs. Pepper; Katherine had someone she could truly talk to.

Mrs. Pepper was a short, plumb woman who had a lot of the same qualities as Aunt Etta. She was kind, even-tempered, and very sweet to Katherine and the girls. Every time she visited, along with Harry, she brought the girls a little gift; Katherine grew to adore her. Harry was young enough to become very much like a son to Mrs. Pepper, which made Jerry and his mother feel like family. When Katherine talked about Mrs. Pepper, she could have been talking about their favorite aunt.

Miles brought home a crib and highchair; he got them put together for what he hoped would be his son. Katherine's time was near; she was ready to be free of her big bell, while Miles was anxious to get back to having sex. Katherine had no trouble carry her babies; she took any awkwardness or discomfort in her stride; that was part of her fortitude.

Katherine lay in the delivery room, only slightly drugged, listening to her doctor yell instructions at her. She didn't particularly like this doctor, but his office had been the closest to their house. He was a coarse man, almost vulgar, nothing like the southern doctors who were proper and respected a woman's modesty. He was a large man, not fat, just large. He had red hair and lots of freckles, which Katherine focused on in between her contractions. She didn't like his bedside manner; however, he was there to help her deliver her forth child; she trusted him with that task.

Miles lingered in the waiting room as he anticipated of the doctor's announcement about his newborn son. He paced the floor as he smoked and made light chitchat with the other waiting fathers. Suddenly the doctor appeared in the doorway.

"It's all over, Mr. Mangrum," the doctor said with a matter of fact look on his face, like he was adding another baby to his long list of deliveries.

Miles stood anxiously waiting to hear the magic word. The doctor toyed with him; he paused a few seconds before giving him the news.

"It's a girl!"

"Another girl?" Miles groaned.

"Yep, another girl; baby and mother are fine. You can see them in a few minutes."

Miles stood motionless with the cigarette burning between his fingers. He had never felt a disappointment this great. He had really expected a boy. He sat down on the couch next to a perplexed expectant father and finished his cigarette.

Chapter 45

Medical practices had changed since Katherine's last baby; she was home in five days instead of the ten-day stay she had been used to with her other babies.

"I made arrangements with Aunt Etta; she is going to come and stay with you for a week," Miles informed his surprised wife.

"Aunt Etta is coming? That's wonderful!" Katherine was thrilled. "How is she going to get here?"

"I made arrangements."

"What arrangements?" Katherine insisted.

"Well, she was afraid to come upon the bus alone, so I got someone to come with her."

"Who?"

Miles hesitated. "Sam and Lillian."

"What? Aunt Etta agreed to come up with dad and Lillian?" Katherine practically yelled. "I can't believe it."

"Yea, she said it would be okay," Miles answered; he was surprise too, but grateful for her cooperation.

Katherine lay in her hospital bed; she tried to feel excited about her aunt coming to help; however, she felt a gnawing guilt about expecting Aunt Etta to swallow her pride. To Aunt Etta's credit, her Christian values allowed her to put Katherine's needs above her own; while she could have wallowed in the muck of the past, she didn't. Sam and Lillian were equally positive; the three had a pleasant ride north. They arrived the day after Katherine got home from the hospital and tears were shed for a variety of reasons. Katherine was so happy to see her aunt; she couldn't help but break down as she laid her head on Aunt Etta's shoulder. Aunt Etta cried as she kissed her niece and cuddled the new baby. Katherine was still wet eyed when she hugged her dad and stepmother. Having her family with her was a comfort beyond words; and words were not necessary.

"Katherine, this is a beautiful house. I'm so happy you were able to get this," Aunt Etta complimented.

"Thanks, we are very happy. It's so much better than the other one." Katherine was so thankful that her aunt and dad hadn't seen their dingy, run down, airport home.

Miles had been on his new job for just over a year and he was making decent money, decent enough to buy one of those new fangled inventions that had the world reeling, a television set. It was a popular table model with a 10" screen set in a dark walnut cabinet. After all the niceties were paid to the baby, and a few minutes to catch up on family gossip, the three sets of visiting eyes turned toward the T.V.; for all intense purposes, they never left it. Aunt Etta, Sam and Lillian did not have a television set yet, so they were mesmerized beyond words. There wasn't a large program selection in 1951, but what ever was on was good enough for them. Sam thought he had seen everything with the invention of the automobile, but this was a true marvel.

It was a comical scene; Katherine tried to get some rest, but she had to get up and tend to the baby anyway. Aunt Etta, Sam, and Lil couldn't hear the cries of the baby over the volume on the television; they wouldn't even get up during the commercials, which were just as entertaining. Katherine didn't get the help she needed, or expected; she was ticked off. However, in the contradictions of life, most of the help, though somewhat preoccupied, came from Lillian. She helped with Barbara Jean more often than Aunt Etta or Sam; she even took on the supper duties while the comedic pair sat clued to the television set and watched a most uncharacteristic program, at least for Aunt Etta, Saturday night boxing.

"Hit him," resounded from an elderly, southern voice as Aunt Etta threw air punches.

"Hit him," Sam yelled. "Ouch, that's a low blow,"

It was humorous to watch Sam, a calm passive man, and Aunt Etta, a prudish, church choir member, relate on such a barbaric level. However, Katherine saw nothing funny about it.

Katherine still had not smoked in front of her aunt. Since she couldn't get anyone to tend to the baby as often as she wanted, she had to sneak out to the coal bin with Barbara held close to her with one hand, and a cigarette in the other, just to get a few drags. She was pissed as she shot disgusted looks at the back of their heads. They never even noticed when she left the room.

As Katherine stood shivering in the coal bin, she stared at her dad. The irony of the situation finally hit her. How could she have expected her aunt to be cordial to Sam and Lillian with all that had happened? She felt ashamed. Her mood turned to annoyance at herself for allowing her dad and Lillian back into her life. Even though she had been able to have an amicable relationship with them, every once in a while her resentment worked its way to the surface. She suddenly realized that she wanted to ask Sam about what went on at his house, why he let his wife abuse her. She was tired of the pretence that she forgot about it; she decided she would confront him; but not now.

"They might as well go home. They're not helping me. All they do is watch that damn T.V," Katherine complained to her husband. "Look at that; they're not paying any attention to me or the baby. They're no help."

"Tell them you need more help." Miles was disgusted with her complaints.

"There's no point. They'll be leaving in a few days." Katherine was disgusted.

"That's just a well; then things can get back to normal," Miles fussed. Katherine knew what he meant by normal; he wanted sex.

Katherine was concerned about getting pregnant again, which she did not want to happen; four was enough and she wasn't going to try any more for a boy.

Katherine didn't want to bother with the rhythm method, it was to nerve racking, and Miles refused to wear a condom; that left only one solution, a vasectomy, a fairly new procedure in 1951. Katherine managed to talk Miles into the procedure, which was a miracle by any stretch of the imagination. While they consulted with the doctor about the procedure, Katherine attempted to squelch more than just the possibility of getting pregnant.

"Doctor, is there anything you can do about Miles? He can't get enough sex," Katherine complained. "Can't you give him something for that?"

Miles was stunned; he stared at Katherine, surprised that his modest wife had the nerve to bring up such a subject. The doctor noticed Miles' surprise.

"Yes, there are some medications that will help with that problem," the doctor replied. "Miles, are you willing to give it a try?"

Needless to day, Miles was still stunned.

"I guess so," Miles replied like a trapped animal; there wasn't anything else he could say.

"Good." The doctor went to the medicine cabinet. "Here are some pills, Miles. They won't take away all of your sex drive, just cool it a bit."

Katherine smiled with satisfaction.

Miles didn't talk to Katherine all the way home; as soon as they got in the back door Miles threw the bottle of pills in the trash can.

"You must be crazy if you think I'm going to take those pills. I'll have the vasectomy, but I'll be damned if I'm going to take those pills," Miles screamed at his wife.

"You told the doctor that you would give it a try," Katherine yelled back.

"Forget it!" Miles hurried out the back door.

Katherine's feeling of empowerment was very short lived, and her attempt only widened the crack in their crumbling relationship.

Miles tried to relax; his scrotum ached.

"I'll get the door, just stay there," Katherine called out.

"Hi, Jim."

"Hi, how is Miles doing?" their landlord asked.

"Pretty good. Come on in; he's in the living room."

"Hey, Miles, how are you doing?"

"It hurts like hell."

Jim laughed. "I bet it does."

"What's up?" Miles asked. It was obvious Jim wanted to say something.

"I hate to tell you guys this, but, I'm going to have to ask you to move."

"Move? Why?" Katherine gasped.

"My brother is moving to Michigan from Tennessee. He needs a place to stay."

"Well, what about us?" Katherine interrupted.

"I'm sorry, but I told him he can rent this place."

"What are we supposed to do?" Katherine was close to being irate.

"I'll ask around. Maybe someone knows about another duplex for rent." The landlord appeared to genuinely feel bad about the predicament he put them in. "I'll be in touch." He left Katherine and Miles in a stupor.

"Well, if that don't beat all." Katherine was disgusted. "What are we going to do now?"

"We'll think about it later." Miles felt too bad to think about it right then.

Luckily, there was a duplex for rent just a few streets away. Miles was able to get a deposit down and their landlord pushed to have them out in just a few short weeks, which they managed to do thanks to Katherine's incredible organization and astute perseverance. When she had something to do, she got it done, damn the obstacles.

The new duplex was just as nice as the first one; however, the landlord was very different; quite intimidating. The girls thought he looked like the evil landlord from the Fago commercials; he was tall and dark, with a black goatee, a long black overcoat, and black top hat; the top hat was in their imagination. They saw him as the wicked man that tied the pretty damsel to the railroad tracks until he got his way, or until the shinny, spotless admirer on a big white horse rescued her. They ran and hid when ever he came to collect the rent. Katherine hoped they could stay in this house for a long time; she needed to feel rooted.

The New Year came in with Katherine getting news that yet another southerner was making the move north to take advantage of the auto jobs. Her busybody friends, Lil and Jean were on their way up. Even though Katherine got irritated with Lil and her big mouth, at least it was someone from home to visit with. Miles never developed a close buddy relationship with Lil's husband; Jean had three boys, a painful reminder of what he didn't have.

However, the visits that Katherine looked forward to the most were from Harry, Jerry, and Mrs. Pepper. Sometimes Mrs. Pepper came out by herself during the day and took Katherine shopping; as soon as the visit was over, Katherine immediately looked forward to the next one. She needed those visits; they were therapeutic; they helped with her loneliness, since she never knew when Miles would be home, or what color of lipstick would be on his collar.

Katherine spent many hours sitting in her rocking chair, her favorite kind of chair; she smoked and pondered why she could not find happiness, why things had turned out like they had, what was so wrong with her that she couldn't possess happiness; her resentment smothered her.

She couldn't help herself from reliving the turbulent times with her father and stepmother, those times far outweighed the more recent good times; she couldn't forgive herself for disappointing her aunt twice. Katherine resented Raymond, for taking her money, and she simply couldn't understand why Dennis could love a woman like Alice. Everyone else had been able to move on with life and let the past rest; however, for Katherine, it was still very much alive, and eating away at her. There was hardly ever a smile to light up her blue eyes anymore. Her sense of humor had dulled and her laughter was hardly ever heard. Her heartbreaking resentment toward her husband for rekindling his adulteress ways was the straw that left her spirit broken. As much as she wanted to find the way out of her dark tunnel of hopelessness, she felt herself stuck in the mire of her misery. She slipped farther away from where the light of happiness shown just out of her reach; her quivering stomach ache from self-pity.

At night, her one beer turned into two while she waited for Miles. More often than not, she meandered up the wooden staircase and went to bed by herself.

Chapter 46

"Well, why don't you file for divorce like you did before," Miles screamed.

"I'm not going to file. If you want to leave, you file," Katherine screamed back.

"Maybe I will," he shouted.

"Where are you going; off to see one of your girlfriends?" Katherine watched as Miles put on his coat.

"It won't be the first time," Miles confessed.

"What do you mean?" Katherine shouldn't have asked.

"That women in Texas; she wasn't my buddy's girlfriend. She was mine."

"So, that's why she was so upset."

"That's right; she was crying because you broke up our little love nest."

Katherine felt one more piece of her heart crumble; at that point there was very little left, but even the crushed pieces ached with dejection.

"Then why did you have me come out to see you in the first place?" Katherine demanded.

"You weren't taking no for an answer; I felt trapped."

Though Miles never abused his wife physically, his words left deep bruises just the same.

"I might as well just kill myself." Katherine repeated her threat more often now.

Miles knew she was just talking; he knew she would never have the nerve to hurt herself, besides she was too afraid of dying to make it happen; however, he repeated his hurtful goad.

"You're too mean to die."

Katherine fled to the other room just to get away from him. Her attempt to get sympathetic love didn't work; it only made it hurt more.

Katherine spent the evening in her rocking chair, alone.

"How stupid could I be?" She scolded her self for being so naïve about the crying woman in Texas. "All those years had been full of lies." Her lip quivered.

Katherine complained to Miles' brothers about his laying out; they tried to talk to him, they tried to convince him to stay home with his family and be faithful to his wife. He more or less told them to back off.

New Year's Eve, 1952, found Katherine and the girls waiting for Miles to get home, which he did; however, just before the children's bedtime. He didn't say anything to Katherine, he simply ran up the wooden staircase; the squeaks sounded much louder than normal. In no time at all, he ran back down all dressed up in his wedding suit and smelling of Old Spice. Katherine was practically speechless, but she managed one question.

"Where are you going?"

"Out!" Miles whooshed out the door just as fast as he had come in.

Katherine held Barbara in her rocking chair; she was stunned that he pulled such a stunt; that he left his family all alone on New Year's Eve; that he left her all alone with four little girls on the most romantic night of the year. And worse, who had he dressed up for? She began to cry.

"Mama, what's wrong? Where did daddy go?"

"I don't know," Katherine answered her little girls; however, she had a pretty good idea.

The silence was broken by a knock at the door. To Katherine's surprise, Harry and Jerry stood in front of her; they came to wish her and Miles a happy new year.

"Where's Miles?" Harry asked.

"Hell if I know. He rushed in here about an hour ago, got all dressed up and left."

"Where did he go?"

"Probably to the bar," Katherine answered; she fought back the tears.

Harry was disgusted with his brother. "I'll call Larry and get him out here. We'll try to find Miles."

Larry wasn't thrilled about leaving his family on New Year's Eve; however, he agreed to do it if it would help his oldest brother come to his senses.

The three men tried to get some idea from Katherine where to look for Miles. She mentioned the few bars that she knew about. The brothers and Jerry were like the Three Musketeers, determined and steadfast, as they set out on their quest to bring Katherine's knight back to her, unscathed from the evils of the night. She rocked Barbara and hoped they would be triumphant; at the same time, she didn't allow herself to admit that forcing Miles to come home would not make him want to be there.

Katherine put the girls to bed and sought refuge in her rocker; she smoked, drank her beer; she watched Guy Lombardo as the hours ticked away and brought in another uncertain year. Her wish for the New Year appeared to be out of reach; however, her fear for the New Year, one of being alone and far from her home in the south, was dangerously close.

Katherine still didn't consider the north her home; she felt an indescribable homesickness for the mountains, for the blue smokiness, and most of all, for her family. In the lonely North, the only family she had to cling to consist of her four daughters; they were all she had.

As Katherine listened to Lombardo's band play *Auld Lang Syne* by herself, she hoped the trio would be successful in their mission of finding her misguided knight. As she dozed in her rocker, she was awakened by a pound on the door. The trio entered the house feeling defeated and ashamed. It wasn't the fairytale ending they had hoped for.

"We found him; you were right, he was in a bar in town," Harry regrettably told Katherine.

"Was he with someone?"

"Katherine, I don't want to go into all that."

"I want to know, Harry. Was he with another woman?" Katherine insisted.

"Yes."

"Did he introduce you?" Katherine began to get angry.

"Yes, he said her name was Emma." Harry's answer stunned Katherine.

"Emma! God, that is my first name. I hate that name."

"Do you know her?" Larry asked his sister-in-law.

"No. I don't know her. Did Miles say where he met her?" Katherine needed details. She felt that if she could get some details, she could get some kind of control.

"No, he didn't say. We just tried to get him to leave."

"Is he coming home?" Katherine continued.

"No. He was mad that we were there. He said he'd come home when he was good and ready."

"Katherine, we're real sorry that we couldn't get him to leave," Jerry said.

"We tried to talk some sense into him; he was too drunk to listen," Larry said. "We'll talk to him next week."

Harry was mad. "Miles should be ashamed of himself; leaving a wife and four little girls like this. He should get himself home where he belongs."

"Well, thanks for coming out. I appreciate your help," Katherine told the men as she walked them to the door. "Goodnight."

The three men left to go home having failed in their mission. They left Katherine all alone to contemplate what happened on that disastrous New Year's Eve, the night that changed everything. She was never going to be able to listen to Auld Lang Syne again without crying.

Miles never came back home to live with his family after that night. He occasionally popped in to get some clothes; sometimes he'd leave Katherine some money for groceries and be gone again. He paid no regard as to how she was going to get to the store; he made no arrangements to help her care for the children. He more or less forgot about the family he dragged away from their roots; he left his girls exposed and vulnerable with a terrified caretaker to step in to assume the role he so cowardly deserted.

Miles brothers were good to Katherine and the girls at first. They took turns coming out to take her shopping and sometimes brought her food; Harry and the Pepper's came more often than Larry. Katherine walked the two miles to a store when no one came to help. Again, her instinct as a mother caring for her young kicked in; domestically she managed, though stressful; however, the toll on her psyche was extreme. Wondering why Miles left her and the girls ate away at her and kept her on the edge of managing. However, something died that New Year's Eve. Katherine never again made a carrot cake. The feeling of warmth and comfort the cake provided was gone forever.

Katherine needed extra money; she pondered what to do. She drew strength from her war days and decided to take in ironing. She laid the white shirt on the kitchen table and sprinkled it with water. She rolled it into a log and placed it in her laundry basket; this continued until all the clothes had been moistened; the next three hours were spent ironing and thinking.

"There you are." Katherine handed a bundle of shirts and pants to one of her customers who had just stopped by.

"How are you doing, Katherine?" The woman was concerned.

"I guess okay, but I'm having some trouble with my teeth," Katherine grimaced, rubbing her jaw.

"You'd better get to the dentist. There's a good one uptown. Why don't you go see him?"

Before Katherine could protest, the woman opened her pocketbook. "Here." She pushed a few extra bucks in Katherine's hand.

"Thank you," Katherine returned. She finished her ironing as she acknowledged that there are still a few good people around.

Uptown was not very far away and Katherine was able to walk to the dentist's office rather quickly.

"Well, Mrs. Mangrum, I have some bad news; you have gum disease. And worse, it's in the advanced stages," the dentist explained.

"Can you do give me some kind of treatment?" Katherine sounded worried.

"Unfortunately, there isn't very much that can be done to help correct the problem." The dentist wrote on her chart. "I recommend we pull all your teeth."

"Pull all my teeth!" Katherine shouted. "What do you mean? You want to pull all my teeth? How will I eat?"

"Now don't worry, we can have false teeth made for you," the dentist continued. "It's the best way to handle this problem; it's really quite common these days."

"How much will it cost to pull my teeth?" Katherine got down to business.

"I can do that rather inexpensively; we can make arrangements for payment."

Katherine went home to think about it for a while; in the mean time, her gums became more and more inflamed. She knew she had to do something, but having all of her teeth pulled seemed so drastic. After months of enduring the pain, the bleeding, and the foul taste in her mouth, she did it; she let the dentist pull all of her teeth.

She was miserable as she tried to care for her four little girls; her entire mouth ached. However, she blocked out the pain. Between her cigarettes and nightly beer, Katherine got through the ordeal. Several days later, her gums started to heal and the throbbing subsided. Every time she looked in the mirror she wondered how in the world she was going to pay for her new teeth.

She swallowed her pride. "Hi, Dennis."

"Hey, sis."

"I need to talk to you about a problem. I had to have all my teeth pulled because of gum disease, and I don't have enough money to get false teeth. I can get both plates for a hundred dollars. I was wondering if you could lend me the money."

Dennis was silent for a few minutes. "Katherine, I don't know. Things are tight right now. I don't think I'll be able to help."

Dennis' words stabbed at Katherine's heart. "Well, could you ask Raymond; maybe he could send a little bit? Anything would help," Katherine begged.

"I'll call him." Dennis didn't tell Katherine, but he knew what Ray's answer would be.

Katherine never got a call back from her brothers; she decided to let it go; just the way they had let her go.

With no teeth in her head, Katherine's gums sunk in and made her look a lot older than she was; plus, she had to learn to chew food without the help of molars. Eventually, her gums toughened up and she managed; however, she hated her reflection.

As the end of the year drew near, and she had successfully struggled through the pain and adjustment of being alone, a knock came at the door.

A strange man stood in front of her. "Are you Katherine Mangrum?"

"Yes."

"You are hereby served," he announced as he shoved an envelope full of papers into her hand and ran back to his car.

She looked at the return address, *Emil Johnston, Attorney At Law*. With her mind reeling, she took the onion skin papers out of the envelope and quickly scanned the first page: *Robert Miles Mangrum vs. Emma Katherine Mangrum*. He had done it; he had filed for a divorce. Katherine began to quiver; she was shocked. She went over to her rocker and sat down to read the entire petition. She read it at least ten times before she could put the papers down; she was heartbroken.

She sat in her chair and let the cigarette burn between her fingers; she stared into space. She cried. What was she going to do? She was all alone with four little girls, no car, no job, no money, no family, no close friends, nothing. She was overwhelmed with fear; she was flooded with thoughts of how to carry on, how to provide for her daughters and herself.

She was sickened by the hurt that oozed from her shattered heart. The only man she had really loved had slipped away and she didn't understand why. She didn't know why he fell out of love with her; she didn't know how he could leave his children. Her fingers trembled as she looked once more at the papers that were going to dissolve her dream of happiness, the papers that would crumble her ivory tower.

After a few days, she was able to get herself out of her rocking chair and face her situation.

"You know honey, you should get your own lawyer and counter sue the bastard," a divorced neighbor advised.

"I don't have any money to get a lawyer."

"Oh, honey, let me tell you; since the bastard filed for the divorce, he has to pay for his layer, and yours," the neighbor informed her.

"Oh?" Katherine was clearly interested in being educated on the subject.

"You get a lawyer and counter-sue his ass," the jilted neighbor demanded.

With that information, Katherine found the courage to locate an attorney within walking distance of her house; she made an appointment. Her introverted nature was no match for her determination to get what was legally hers, what she rightfully had coming to her and her girls. Her pain and humiliation of being abandoned turned to anger; fierce, undaunted anger. She was going to make sure Miles paid.

The plaque on the building read *Harvey Valentine, Attorney At Law*. This was all so new to her; she nervously went in. After the awkward introductions, she began to relay her life's story to the lawyer. He asked for all of the pertinent information, like how long they had been married, the ages of the children, where her husband worked and so forth. When he got into the money situation, he was appalled when she told him what little money Miles gave her to take care of four children. When he heard the story surrounding her lack of teeth, he was further appalled.

After the attorney got a good overview of Katherine's situation, he was impressed with this young woman's determination to care for her girls; at the same time, he was sickened by their father's lack of caring. During all his years as a divorce attorney, Katherine's case was one of the most disgusting. Harvey Valentine became Katherine's supporter and defender.

Katherine sat in the big leather chair while Mr. Valentine placed a call to Emil Johnston.

"Mr. Johnston, I have a thirty-four year old woman sitting in front of me without a tooth in her head. We will not sign any divorce papers until your client, Mr. Mangrum, pays for her to get a set of false teeth. Is that clear?" The attorney demanded. "Furthermore, Mr. Mangrum should be ashamed of himself for leaving his wife and children in such a state. We will not sign until this is taken care of."

Katherine stared at her attorney. Her eyes became moist as she realized that she finally had someone in her corner.

"Well, that is taken care of. You will get some teeth. Mr. Mangrum will not get his divorce until you get some teeth!" Mr. Valentine's red face made Katherine believe every word.

Miles was furious when he found out he had to pay for Katherine's set of false teeth; however, he had no choice if he wanted to be with Em; Miles' nickname for her.

Miles got the money together and Katherine got her new teeth, an upper and lower plate. She had a hard time getting used to them, but they were worth it.

Katherine's youthful looks returned; she always looked a good ten years younger than her actual age. Her new teeth improved her appearance so much she was more attractive than before.

"Mommy, you look pretty," Judy complemented her mother.

Though Katherine's new teeth took away her self-consciousness, they didn't do anything for her loneliness.

Every few months the lawyer contacted Katherine to see if she was ready to sign the divorce papers. She always came up with a reason to hold off, either she couldn't get to the office, or she would not agree to the terms, always something. Periodically, Miles stopped by to give Katherine a little money.

"Why won't you sign the divorce papers?"

With daggers darting from her crushed, blue eyes she responded." Why should I; so you can marry that woman? What about your family here?"

"I don't want to get into it any more, just sign the damn papers," Miles yelled.

This was the scene every time he stopped by. However, the one thing, which was most disturbing to Katherine, was that Miles showed no remorse about leaving his children; she could count on one hand the amount of times he had held Barbara since her birth. She knew men fell out of love with their wives, but falling out of love with their children was beyond her understanding, she hated him for that the most.

Not only had Katherine lost Miles; she also lost Harry, Jerry and Mrs. Pepper. She missed the visits; she missed Mrs. Pepper, her confidant and her friend. Her loneliness was stifling; the *only ones* she had to cling to, *the only ones* there for her in the God-forsaken north were her daughters.

"Honey, why don't you move back down here," Aunt Etta suggested.

"Aunt Etta, I can't take the children out of the state. In order to collect child support, I have to stay here," Katherine explained. "What did Dennis and Alice say about me getting a divorce?"

"They feel bad for you, honey."

Katherine knew better than that, especially about Alice. She was sure her sister-in-law looked down on her because of the divorce; Katherine was ashamed of it herself. At the same time, she grumbled that Alice had no place criticizing her because her own brother had been married and divorced, by that time, about twelve times. Katherine angrily thought to herself, *she'd better not say anything to me.* However, Katherine still felt a certain amount of disgrace; she felt a sense of failure for not having a successful marriage, something Alice did manage to have; of course, that was because Dennis allowed her to rule the roost.

Katherine's humiliation grew as the rest of the family found out. Her dad made it worse.

"Katherine, Lillian and I have an offer for you?"

Katherine listened intently. For an instant she felt optimistic that he was going to send her some money.

"Let us have Carolyn; we can finish raising her. That would take some pressure off you; it would give you one less mouth to feed."

Katherine was shocked into silence. She couldn't believe they wanted her to give up one of her children. She knew they favored Carolyn, their first grandchild, but this offer appalled her.

"What! No!" She exclaimed. "I can't give up one of my children. Are you crazy, dad?"

"But, Katherine, you can't support four children. Let us take Carolyn; we'll be good to her. She won't want for anything." Sam continued his argument.

I could never do that, never!"

"We're just trying to help," Lillian said as she grabbed the phone from Sam.

"Lillian, I'm not going to give up one of my children. Things may be tough, but we'll manage." Katherine hung up; she was offended, terribly offended. She decided right then that she would show them; she would show them all.

The family could have helped Katherine with her money woes; it would have been the loving thing to do; particularly, since most of the family members were financially comfortable. However, not one person offered monetary help for Katherine and her girls.

Katherine found it hard to understand why most of her relatives shunned her after they found out she was going to be a divorcee, at least it seemed that way; it was a time when she needed family more than ever. At the same time, she understood why her aunt didn't come up, she didn't have a husband to drive her the long distance; however, there was nothing stopping her brothers. She needed family support so desperately; she was left wondering why no one wanted to see her, much less, help her.

Another new year slipped in while Katherine found ways to stall signing the divorce papers. Miles was more and more agitated with every visit; he tried continually to coax her into signing. Katherine became more and more stubborn, wanting him to suffer for leaving her. She wanted him to be as miserable her.

Katherine's lawyer paid her a visit at the house." It's inevitable, Mrs. Mangrum; you might as well sign the papers," he encouraged her. "Holding out is not going to change things, I assure you."

The finality of signing was too scary for her to even think about. If she didn't sign, she was still connected to Miles; part of her very being still had a lifeline connected to the man she fell in love with. She couldn't bear to break it. She couldn't bear to sever the hope that everything would change and he would come back to her.

She got a letter for her attorney; he asked her to meet him at his office as soon as possible.

CHAPTER 47

▼

"Mrs. Mangrum, I am advising you to sign the divorce papers and get it over with. Mr. Johnston and I have worked out the details. If you simply sign, and don't contest, it will be done and over with. You can get on with your life," the attorney pleaded with Katherine.

"Life? What life do I have to get on with? I'm all alone in the north with no money, no job, and no husband?"

"You need to sign the papers." The attorney was frustrated.

"I don't know if I can do that yet, Mr. Valentine," Katherine stalled.

"I want you to seriously think about it," he pleaded again as he rubbed his head.

"Well, I'll think about it," she told her lawyer; and she did just that, she thought about it.

In fact, she thought about it the rest of the year and into to next. Finally, early in March, 1955, she signed the papers making the first cut in the lifeline she feared losing. A court date was placed on the docket for Miles, the plaintiff, to appear; if it was not contested, the defendant did not have to attend, which saved Katherine from a scary trip downtown among the maze of skyscrapers. However, the agony of not knowing what was going on was stifling for her. She always wanted to know every detail of every part of what was going on; it was the only thing that gave her even the slightest sense of control.

It was a good thing Katherine wasn't in court the day that Miles' lawyer read the charge against her, EXTREME MEMTAL CRUELTY. It was good that she wasn't there to have her dirty laundry exposed to everyone in the courtroom. Since there was no contest to the divorce, no witness was needed; the charges were read and presumed to be true by everyone in attendance, an unfair assumption.

The lawyer presented his final argument. He explained how Katherine caused Miles mental anguish; how her constant arguing and nagging, and her constant accusations caused him extreme suffering. He explained how Katherine denied Miles his husbandly rights, in the Biblical sense; that she had even hit him on occasion.

Of course, Mr. Johnston didn't tell the judge anything about his client's adulteress ways, or that he neglected his wife and daughters. Many of the reasons for Katherine's nagging were conveniently left out. Miles wasn't going to confess to the Judge that perhaps Katherine withheld his husbandly rights because she was turned off when he came home with lipstick on his collar, or smelled of some other woman's perfume.

Katherine's faults were publicized and proclaimed by the condescending tribunal. The atmosphere was that of a group of male elders, arrogant with power; shamefully, they pounced on a defenseless lioness who had only tried to protect herself and her young pride.

However, since there was no one there to contest the petition, and since it had been filed so long ago, the judge had no reason to prolong the proceedings. His gavel slammed down on the big, cherry wood pulpit. "Divorce granted!"

Katherine knew the day Miles was to go to court; she had gotten a notice in the mail. As she sat in her rocker and smoked, she knew that when 5:00 arrived, and the court closed for the day, the second cut in her lifeline to Miles would be made, leaving only one piece to sever.

A week later the mailman delivered a copy of the granted divorce decree; the filing date was stamped in big, bold, black ink, as if mocking her, shouting to her that Miles finally got what he wanted. She read, and re-read, the particulars. He was to pay her $1.00 dower, the property settlement, and $9.00 per child per week, making it $144.00 per month for child support for four children; that amount was to provide them with food, clothes, doctors appointments, medicine, school supplies, and making a decent home for them. Katherine got no alimony; a shameful settlement.

She read on to the next paragraph; *neither party can re-marry for six months from the date the papers were filed.* At least Miles had to wait still longer before he could become someone else's husband; that last little bit of hassle for him pleased her. Katherine finished reading the divorce papers; as she sat in her rocker, she stared into space and let the tears roll down her cheeks. With all her misfortunes, she never in a million years saw this happening to her. Life had played a damn dirty trick on her and she wasn't about to forgive it for making her life so damn hard.

Katherine tried to carry on in spite of her depression; the little family of five women endured life without a male head of household, a stigma in those days. Miles' child support payments were erratic, which only added to her stress and bitterness. She continued to iron for people and did some babysitting.

Even though Katherine could stretch a dollar better than anyone, there simply wasn't enough to go around; the rent payments became hard to come up with. The tall, dark, scary landlord stopped by to collect.

"I'm sorry, but I don't have the whole amount. Can I give you the rest as soon as I get my ironing money?" Katherine asked him, scared to death that he would throw them out on the street.

"Now, not so fast," the landlord said; he invited himself in and sat at the kitchen table to talk things over with her. The older girls were in school, but Barbara went and hid.

"Can I get you the rest of the money in a few weeks?" Katherine begged.

The landlord paused while he scanned the rooms in his view. He didn't want to kick her out with four kids; he really wasn't as mean as he looked; however, he was strictly business. Nevertheless, he offered a compromise.

"Well, Mrs. Mangrum, do you have anything that you can sell in order to come up with the money, or perhaps that I could accept in lieu of the balance," he negotiated.

Katherine was surprised at his suggestion; at the same time, she had to keep her home. She and the children had nowhere else to go. She thought about what she had. She looked in the living room and mumbled, "No, I can't let the T.V. go' it's our only entertainment. She thought about the upstairs and what might be of any value up there. Then it hit her, *the hope chest.*

The beautiful hope chest, which was her mother's, which she had wanted to pass down to one of her daughters, which held the only link to her past, was the only thing of value; perhaps the landlord would accept that. She made the offer.

"Well, let's have a look."

Katherine led the landlord upstairs to evaluate the piece.

"That's a mighty fine piece of furniture. It's in very good condition, I don't see any scratches," the landlord said as he stroked his goatee. "Yes, I'll accept it."

"Thank you," Katherine felt a wave of relief pass through her body. "Do you want to come back and get it another day?"

"No, I can take it right now," he answered. "I can wait until you clean out your belongings. I'll wait downstairs."

Katherine nodded in agreement. She bent down and started to take her precious treasurers out of the beautiful box. She reached inside and took hold of her mother's embroidered tablecloth. She lifted out the rest of the linens and stacked them on top of her dresser. She couldn't stop the tears that rolled down her cheeks as she picked up the body of her baby doll. Barbara toddled into the room.

"Baby," Barbara shouted as she looked inside the opened chest.

She started to reach in and grab some of the broken porcelain.

"No, Barbara, you might cut yourself." Katherine pulled her little hands away.

Katherine continued to collect the sharp pieces; she felt as broken as her doll head. She wanted to sit down on the bed and cry her eyes out; however, she didn't have time; she had to complete the transaction.

Her hope chest had been exactly that, a source of hope. She had gathered some treasurers throughout her childhood and placed in them the chest with the hope of a happy marriage some day. She had carted the chest north with the hope of a new beginning for her troubled marriage; ironically, the chest still gave her hope, hope that she could get through the month and somehow be able to have the next rent payment.

Katherine shut the lid down and ran her hands over the top; she felt the smooth finish as she thought about all the hours she and her girls spent going through the items while she told them a fantastic story about each one. The girls loved the adventure; it created at closeness between mother and daughters; it was also tangible evidence of their mother's tumultuous past; it gave validity to her repeated stories.

Katherine took one last look inside the chest just to be sure it was empty. He eye caught a glimpse of something black in the corners of the box. She touched it with her finger and realized it was coal dust. Torrents of memories crashed in on her with the force of flood waters. The sight of the dust took her back to when she and Miles moved to Michigan with the hope of a new life. The hope she had been filled with was never realized; in fact, nothing good had come from moving north. She stared into the empty chest, her eyes filled up again. Katherine shut the lid and sniffed up her tears.

"Okay, I'm finished cleaning it out. You can come and get it," Katherine shouted as she wiped her nose.

The landlord ran up the steps; he had the audacity to ask her to help him take it downstairs. It was very heavy; she was barely able to assist him in getting it down the narrow, wooden staircase. He grumbled not to scratch it; he knew the true value. He knew it was worth far more than the credit she got toward her rent. Finally, they got the chest in the trunk of his car and he started to get in the driver's side. Katherine stopped him.

"Can I get a receipt stating that my rent is paid in full for this month?" Katherine's request was totally out of character for her timid personality.

Her boldness was evidence of the emerging *bitc*h necessary to survive in a man's world; plus, she wasn't in a good mood.

The landlord stopped and stared at her. Though he was a bit put out that she asked, he was impressed with her business sense. He gave her a receipt.

He left and Katherine went upstairs to straighten up. She angrily stuffed the tablecloth, and the other items, in her linen closet; she abruptly gathered up the doll body and broken head pieces and took them downstairs; with an angry hand she threw them in the garbage.

The welfare of her children was her priority now, and she accepted that; so, she wiped her eyes, smoked a cigarette, and started dinner knowing she had a month to come up with the next rent payment.

The same knowledgeable neighbor, who told her about getting a lawyer, continued to teach Katherine the ways of a single mother's survival.

"You know, honey, you can apply to A.D.C. for help."

"What's that?"

"Aide to Dependent Children. If you get approved, you'll get a monthly check and some food staples, such as cheese, flour, rice and powdered milk. It's not much, but it sure helps." The neighbor encouraged Katherine to make a claim.

Though Katherine hated to be in such a degrading situation, she had no choice but to apply; she was granted the help. The fact she had to live, in her opinion, like a poor person offended her terribly. She had never lived that way and she hated it. However, her resolve accepted the help and conceded that A.D.C. would be strictly temporary.

Katherine had kept a cordial relationship with her past landlords, having the same home State in common.

"Katherine, we have a very nice friend, Charlie. He's up here from Tennessee and we thought you and he might hit it off."

"Oh, I don't know about that. I'm not ready to go out with anyone yet. Besides, the divorce isn't even final yet. Technically, I'm still married," Katherine explained.

"Oh, come on, Katherine. Both of you are lonely; it would be okay to go out together. You two could go out to the bar with us," the landlord's wife suggested.

"I'll think about it."

As Katherine thought about it, she got acquainted with Charlie at the landlord's house. To her extreme surprise, she felt very comfortable around him. He was tall, skinny, and very funny. He made her feel relaxed inside, something she hadn't felt in a long time; his sense of humor brought back a welcomed smile. A twinkle in her blue eyes was seen again; she had a very good time with him.

"Katherine, would you like to go dancing tonight?" Charlie asked.

"Okay, I think I would like that." Dancing was one of her most favorite things in the world. When Katherine danced, she was able to let go of all her pain and resentment; she flowed around the dance floor light and free of her burdensome baggage. As Charlie twirled her around the floor, he looked into her beautiful blue eyes; to his credit, he recognized that she got the respite she needed.

"What do you say we do this again next week?" Charlie asked as he took Katherine home.

"I'd like that, Charlie."

Charlie knew a lot about her situation from the landlords, and once he and Katherine became friends, she filled him in on the rest of the story. Katherine tended to talk too much about her personal life to other people, but that was her way and Charlie seemed to understand. That appeared to be his best attribute, he understood her.

Katherine had no thoughts of getting married again, at least not yet. At the same time, she enjoyed Charlie's company; they began to build a relationship. She was doing something she hadn't done in a very long time, she was having fun.

"You're in a good mood today, Katherine," Charlie said.

"Yes, I got some good news. Remember when I told you that I applied for a job at the Kroger Store?"

"Yes."

"Well, I got it. I start next week." Katherine was so excited she could hardly contain herself; Charlie chuckled at her exuberance. "It's only part time; but, that's okay. What I'll make there, plus A.D.C., things will be a lot easier."

"I'm happy for you, Katherine. Having the job will take a lot of worry of you," Charlie said as he hugged her. His kindness was good medicine.

Katherine didn't have the money to get a car, so most of the time she walked to work. Her friend, Evelyn, who also worked at the store, picked her up when their schedules coordinated, but that was only sometimes. Katherine trekked through the rain, snow, and cold; her determination kept her going. She had begun to move on. Though she had moments of sadness, Katherine managed to feel encouraged with her job and her new boyfriend.

Happiness just might be possible.

Chapter 48

It was a cold November day; Katherine had not able to get a ride to work so she started walking. She paid no attention to the cold; she was focused on the hollowness inside of her. The third and final piece of the lifeline to her beloved knight had been severed. The stipulated six-month waiting period for her and Miles had come to an end. If she hadn't loved him so much, it wouldn't have hurt so badly. Now, the only connection she had left was the four daughters they had together; Katherine knew she would never have the same feelings toward any other man that she felt for the father of her children.

The following week was tough as Katherine fought through pangs depression; sweet Charlie stayed with her every step of the way. Now that the waiting period was over, Charlie felt as liberated as Miles.

"Katherine, why don't we get married?"

Katherine was shocked. She had no idea Charlie had gotten that serious. He could see the surprise on her face; he asked again.

"What do you say?"

"Charlie, I don't think I'm ready to get married again," Katherine tried to explain.

"Why not?"

She didn't have an answer. She didn't know why herself. She tried to change the subject. However, Charlie wasn't ready to let it go.

"Well, why don't you think about it, Katherine? I think it would be a good thing; good for you, me, and your daughters."

"I just don't think I can make that decision right now, Charlie. It's still too soon." Obviously, Katherine's wounds had not healed.

"Okay, we can wait for a while." Charles succumbed and squeezed her shoulder.

Charlie was a good, decent, and gentle guy; exactly what Katherine needed. He was taller and thinner than Miles; however, he also had some of the same qualities. He was jolly, he laughed a lot, and when he smiled, his eyes danced. Katherine liked that. At the same time, what Miles lacked in his attention to her, Charlie made up for it ten fold. He was able to ignore Katherine's nagging ways; he knew underneath all of that exasperating façade, lay a troubled, hurt, scared woman; one that simply needed some tender loving care,; some understanding. One major, and perhaps the best, difference between Charlie and Miles was that Charlie's personality lent itself nicely to being hen-pecked; he would be perfect.

Katherine thought about Charlie's proposal for the next few weeks; she was bewildered.

"I don't know what to do," Katherine told the landlord's wife as they drank coffee together.

"What's the matter, Katherine?" she asked.

"Charlie has asked me to marry him."

"That's wonderful," her friend said excitedly.

"I don't know," Katherine hesitated.

"Why not, Katherine? Charlie is a great guy; I think it would be a good thing for both of you. You two have a lot in common; I know he would be good to you and your children."

"I know he would be good to us; I don't doubt that for a minute," Katherine agreed. "I just think I need a little more time."

"He's a good guy, Katherine."

"I know; I like him a lot," Katherine said shyly.

Katherine and Charlie strengthened their relationship; the girls became comfortable with him and the future looked as bright as Katherine blue eyes. She hadn't felt this optimistic in many years.

"Well, Katherine, have you decided if you want to marry Charlie?" her friend asked when they met for their normal coffee klatch.

"I've thought about it a lot. He's a good man, and we get along great."

"Well, why are you hesitating?"

"I don't know; I'm having a hard time making the decision."

"You're not concerned about the situation with his wife, are you?" her friend asked.

Katherine nearly dropped her coffee cup.

"Wife? He's married?" she screamed.

"Oh my God, Katherine; I thought you knew," the landlord's wife gasped. "Let me explained, please, let me explain," she quickly said. Katherine jumped up from her chair.

"Wait, Katherine, wait; now listen. Charlie's wife, Marilyn, is in a mental institution in Clarkston; she has been there for years and she'll probably never get out. Charlie has lived alone all these years. You are the first woman he has been serious about since his wife got committed. Charlie is a good man, Katherine; he doesn't want to be alone anymore." Her friend defended Charlie's actions.

Katherine's head spun. She couldn't believe her ears. *Married, mental institution*, what in the hell was going on.

"Katherine, I know Charlie loves you; you two are perfect for each other. He talks about you all the time. I know he wouldn't do anything to hurt you. I'm sure he was going to tell you, he was probably waiting for the right time."

Katherine's shock turned to anger.

"I can't believe this; I can't believe he didn't tell me. How can I trust him if he keeps a secret like this? What else hasn't he told me?" Katherine grabbed her cigarettes and rushed out the door.

Katherine was appalled that Charlie actually did what Miles had done, ran around with another woman. Only this time, she was the other woman; he had made her the other woman. Katherine was furious!

"When was he going to tell me that he was married?" she mumbled to herself. She couldn't believe he hadn't said anything from the start. Simply because his wife was in a mental institution, did that give him the right to run around? She searched her soul for the answer. "NO!" she shouted; her brain burned from his betrayal.

When Katherine saw Charlie again she let him have it.

"Charlie, how could you not tell me, especially since things were getting serious with us," she lectured, "I'm not going to be involved in any plan where you divorce your defenseless wife so we can live happily ever after. That's not right."

Charlie sat powerless while Katherine unloaded her conscience; Charlie tried desperately to explain.

"Katherine, I was going to tell you; I tried many times, but it never seemed to be the right time. I'm so sorry." He pleaded for her understanding.

Katherine listened to Charlie; however, she couldn't get past the part where she unknowingly helped him become an adulterer.

"Charlie, how could you. I trusted you." Katherine sobbed.

"Katherine, I'm so sorry. I love you; I want to marry you."

"No, Charlie, I can't marry you." Katherine was devastated.

"Katherine, I didn't mean to hurt you. I was afraid you wouldn't give me a chance if I told you; I didn't want to scare you away. I know I waited too long and I'm so sorry. Let's talk about it. I'll explain everything," Charlie begged.

Katherine thought about Charlie's explanation. It wasn't good enough. It was still fresh in her mind that another man had not been truthful with her. She repeated her answer.

"No, Charlie, I don't think it will work." Katherine's sadness turned to anger.

Pitifully, Charlie hung his head and cried like a baby; he was so ashamed. He had fallen so deeply in love with Katherine he couldn't bear the fact he had lost her because of his deceit. Katherine had never seen a man cry as much as Charlie cried that day; however, she was so angry with him that his tears did little to soften her heart; she was brutally unforgiving.

Her anger kept her from crying in front of him; yet, when he left, and she was alone, the tears flowed. She couldn't believe this sweet, gentle, loving man had done this to her. Just when she had started to feel strong and confident, just when she was starting to feel worthy of being loved again, he renewed her mistrust in men. Damn him!

Katherine missed Charlie terribly. Questions and doubts swirled through her mind like a whirlwind, first one way than the other; first, she thought she had done the right thing, then, she thought that maybe she should have heard him out. As much as she thought about it, as much as she enjoyed being with him, she simply couldn't get the image of his wife laying in some dark, scary institution all by herself; and worse, that he planned to abandon her. It wasn't his wife's fault that she got sick; Charlie promised to love her in sickness and in health; but he was getting ready to break his vows, just like Miles.

Though, when the thoughts of Charlie's wife spun out of her head, Katherine saw a young, vital, affectionate man who was lonely and who had a lot of love to give; a man who longed to be loved. Was it right for him to spend the rest of his life alone? Was it wrong of him to want to be with someone? Katherine went back and forth for days weighing all the questions; she tormented herself with thoughts of whether her and Charlie's relationship was honorable. As mush as she missed him, as much as she enjoyed his company, she made her decision; no, it wasn't!

Katherine was told that Charlie went back to Tennessee; she never heard from him again.

Chapter 49

Katherine brooded for months; again she chastised life for leaving her forsaken; at the same time, some old problems began to resurface. However, she was convinced this was different.

"Okay, Mrs. Mangrum, what seems to be the problem?" her doctor asked.

"There's something making me choke, doctor. Without warning, my throat closes up and I can't breath," Katherine explained. "There must be something in there blocking off my airway."

"Let's have a look." The doctor depressed Katherine's tongue and peered down her throat. "I don't see anything to be concerned about. Why don't you give it some time? If it still bothers you, come back and see me."

Katherine went home discouraged at not getting any satisfaction. She knew there was something wrong.

After a second visit, the doctor became concerned about the possibly of a tumor in the throat or on the thyroid gland.

"The only way we can be sure is to take a look while you are asleep," he told her, which would require a two day stay in the hospital.

The thought of having her throat cut on frightened Katherine terribly; her throat was one of the most sensitive parts of her body and she didn't like having it messed with; on the other hand, something had to be done. That was only one of the problems though; how was she going to get to and from the hospital, what about the girls, and could she get the time off work? All of these concerns caused her throat to feel even tighter, and made her smoke way too much.

First things first; she asked her boss if she could get two days off work, which he granted without pay. Next, she had to get a ride to and from the hospital. It wasn't very far away, about a mile. It was a small hospital and Katherine wasn't thrilled about going there; however, she had no choice. At the moment, she had to work around convenience, and that hospital was the most convenient.

"Evelyn, I have to go in the hospital for a few days; could you take me and pick me up?"

"What's the problem?"

Katherine proceeded to tell Evelyn the details.

"Yes, I'm sure I can make arrangements," Evelyn said; she was a good friend.

Now, the big problem; who could she get to take care of the girls for two days?

Her first thought, and rightfully so, was that their dad could help out; he could take care of his children while she had surgery. However, the thought that Emma would have contact with her girls irked her to no end. On the other hand, she needed help; she was desperate. As much as she hated to, as awkward as it felt, she had to call Miles. While she worked things out in her mind, she realized she didn't have Miles' phone number. What was she going to do? The only thing she could do was call Larry; he would know how to get in touch with his brother.

Since Katherine had to give up her phone when Miles left, she walked a few blocks to a public phone.

Having to place the call to Larry was painful; it brought back so many memories; but, worse than that, having to call Miles was just plain excruciating.

"Hello," answered a feminine voice.

It gave Katherine pause to actually hear Emma's voice. It was all she could do to keep her composure.

"Can I talk to Miles?" Katherine ordered; the hairs on the back of her neck stood on end.

There was silence on the other end of the line. Katherine had never called Miles, but Emma deduced it was her; she was suspicious. Reluctantly, Emma called Miles to the phone.

"Hello."

It was odd, but Miles had been able to forget his family and their needs easier than any man should. There was mistrust in his voice rather than concern that his children might need something.

"Miles, I'm going to have to have surgery and I need help with the girls."

"What kind of surgery?" Miles asked.

"There is something in my throat; maybe a tumor the doctor said. I'm having a problem with choking," Katherine explained. "I need someone to watch the girls for two days. Can you take them?"

Miles didn't answer; he was preoccupied. The mention of her throat made him remember the problems she had every since he had known her.

"Are you sure you should let the doctor cut on your throat? Did you tell him that you've always had a problem with your throat?" It was odd for Katherine to hear any sort of concern from him.

"The doctor thinks there might be something causing the problem," Katherine explained.

"Katherine, I'd be careful." Miles' doubt irritated Katharine. She hoped the doctor's found something, just to prove to him that it wasn't all in her head.

"Well, can you watch the girls?"

There was silence. Katherine was annoyed with his hesitation.

"Well, let me get back to you."

Katherine could feel her body heat up; she was mad. He couldn't even agree to help with his own children. Damn him! She figured he was going to have to get permission from his new wife. Disgusted, Katherine slammed the phone down and lit a cigarette; she burned as hot as the tobacco.

A few days later, Miles stopped by. He had the audacity to tell her what he could do to help.

"We can take Carolyn and Judy for two days."

He didn't tell her Emma really didn't want to take care of any of them, but the two little ones were out of the question; she wasn't going to be anyone's babysitter.

"Carolyn and Judy? What about Linda and Barbara? What am I going to do with them?" Katherine raised her voice with worried concern.

"Well," Miles continued, "I mentioned it to Harry and he said Mrs. Pepper offered to stay with Linda and Barbara."

As pissed as Katherine was, that wonderful news allowed her to calm down. The fact that the Linda and Barb would be taken care of by her once good friend was a welcomed relief; plus, she would get to visit with the one person, whom she missed so desperately.

"Okay," Katherine said, relieved.

She gave Miles the dates so he could make arrangements; she asked him to let Mrs. Pepper know. He said he would and their awkward conversation was over.

Katherine dreaded the thought that Emma, Katherine never referred to her as the girls' stepmother, would get to have any contact with her daughters at all. Her brain stung; it was as if jealous honeybees hit every sensory ending and left their poison to fester. She hated her situation; at the same time, she had no choice. It had to be this way. She lit a cigarette to dull the pain.

The day came for Miles to pick up the girls; thank goodness he came alone. Katherine wasn't in the mood to deal with seeing *that woman*. She looked at Miles, he looked good. His sandy hair was neatly combed, as it always was. He had gotten false teeth too, his real teeth were crooked; the new teeth made him very handsome.

Katherine felt a familiar pull at her heart. As much as she hated him, a love for him still smoldered deep inside her; he was her soul mate and the void burned. As much as she had tried for the past several years, she hadn't been able to smother that flame. For a brief moment, she felt some tears run down the back of her throat; she didn't want to cry, not here, not now.

Katherine handed Miles one suitcase containing both of the girls' clothes, and they were off. She sat down at the kitchen table and had a smoke; she was glad that encounter was over. While she waited for Mrs. Pepper and Evelyn, she slipped into her abyss of self pity; she missed her life, and the man that was in it for so long. It wasn't fair that she had to struggle this much; it wasn't fair that she had to be so lonely; it wasn't fair that Emma had Miles instead of her. It just wasn't fair.

"Hi, Katherine, are you ready to go," Evelyn asked.

"Not yet; Mrs. Pepper isn't here yet."

"How are you doing?"

"Okay, I guess. Miles just left with the girls. He still makes me so damn mad. He only sees the girls because he has to," Katherine complained to her friend.

"Katherine, you don't need to be thinking about that now. You don't need to be all upset when you get to the hospital; you're nervous enough as it is," Evelyn advised while Katherine puffed away on her cigarette.

Evelyn was happily married to Ken, who had just been diagnosed in the beginning stages of lung cancer. Katherine liked Ken; he was a nice guy.

Evelyn tried to get Katherine out of her blue mood. "Katherine, we have a friend that we'd like you to meet."

"I'm not interested in a man! I don't want to get into another mess."

"I know, I know; but I can assure you that John is not married. In fact, he is a widower. Actually, he is going to be released form the Tuberculosis Institution very soon. He is almost cured," Evelyn explained.

"He's sick! I don't want to get involved with someone that's sick!" Katherine turned up her nose. "Tuberculosis? That's bad."

"It's bad during the contagious stage; but John is not contagious anymore."

"Evelyn, I don't want to talk about it right now," Katherine said as she saw Mrs. Pepper drive up in the driveway.

Introductions were made and Katherine gave Mrs. Pepper a big hug.

"I've missed you so much," Katherine whispered in her ear.

"I've missed you too, dear."

Katherine hated to leave; she wanted to stay and absorb the connection she so sorely missed. Sadly, she had to go. Katherine hugged her two little girls.

Evelyn pulled up in front of a two-story, red brick building. Katherine scanned the front façade and spied the corner stone, 1849. She could tell it was a very old building by the style and shape of the windows. There was fancy wrought iron work along the sides of the steps and porch, and tall wrought iron fencing, which encircled a courtyard on both sides of the building. There were a number of huge shade trees on the property, which protected the hospital from the sun; at the same time, made it look dark, mysterious, and full of shadows. It was very early in the morning; perhaps that was why it looked a bit ominous. She spied a gray, stone slab above the door; the name was carved in Roman letters: CARTER HOSPITAL. She wasn't so sure she wanted to go in there.

"Well, are you ready, Katherine?" Evelyn asked.

Katherine took a deep breath. "Yea, I guess so."

They walked up the front steps and through a very large, old, wooden door, which was arched at the top and squeaked as it closed. While standing at the receptionist's desk, Katherine looked around. She could see that everything looked clean with fairly new paint. The smell wasn't too bad, just a little musty with a little antiseptic mixed in. The nurses and orderlies, who were scurrying around, looked neat and proper. She supposed everything was okay.

"Well, Katherine, I guess I'll go now. Call me when you're ready to come home, okay?" Evelyn hugged Katherine good-by.

"Okay, Evelyn; thanks for your help."

Katherine stood all alone in this strange building with strange doctors and nurses; no relatives around to comfort her, no one around to reassure her, no one around to give her a kiss and say they loved her; she had to be strong and courageous all by herself.

Though she was nervous, she was convinced the surgery was needed. After she was placed on the cold, stainless steal operating table, her thoughts focused on what the doctors might find. She was anxious.

The gas mask was placed over her nose; a few minutes later she felt relaxed, which was indeed rare for her; she never felt relaxed. The next few seconds relieved her of all her worries and burdens; the weight of the world floated around the room above her head; finally, a deep peaceful sleep.

Katherine struggled to open her eyes as she heard the hustle and bustle of nurses scurrying around the room taking blood pressures, temperatures, and pulses; she heard the nurses yelling at a number of patients laying all around the room, "Come on, it's time to wake up." Could I be in recovery already she thought; it fells like I just went to sleep. As the minutes passed, Katherine became more and more awake; suddenly she was awake enough to know that her throat hurt.

"Don't try to talk, honey," one of the nurses said as she passed by.

Katherine obeyed; it hurt too much anyway.

An hour passed and the anesthesia had just about worn off; Katherine started to get impatient. She didn't like lying in a room full of people she didn't know; she felt vulnerable with everyone staring at her. She wanted to go to her room.

Katherine attempted to whisper to one of the passing nurses.

"I said, don't talk. We'll get you to your room as soon as we can," a hurried nurse said more sternly than Katherine liked.

Katherine lay on the gurney and pouted that she didn't get moved as fast as she wanted to; plus, having to take her teeth out made her extremely irritable. She kept her hand over her mouth to hide her sunken cavity while she watched the other patients get attended to.

Finally, and not a moment too soon, Katherine was rolled up to her room on the second floor.

"Where's the doctor?" Katherine whispered.

"He'll be in soon; you'll have to be patient and wait," the nurse instructed.

Katherine had no choice but to wait; however, patiently was not how she was going to do it. Her eyes remained fixed on the door; she waited for the doctor to walk through and deliver the results. The longer it took, the more nervous she got. The delay convinced her there was something terribly wrong. He throat hurt. She closed her eyes and rubbed the sides of her neck. Her eyes popped opened as she heard the doorknob turn.

A strange doctor appeared in the doorway. He wasn't the doctor who had done her surgery. This wasn't good.

"Hello, Mrs. Mangrum. I'm Doctor Plummer; I assisted Dr. Carter, with your operation." Katherine was surprise Dr. Carter didn't come in, but she let it go.

"What did you find?" She whispered.

"Well, good news, Mrs. Mangrum. There was nothing seriously wrong. We removed a few small nodules; everything else looked good," he told her while he looked at her chart.

"Was that causing my choking?" Katherine murmured.

"I doubt it, they weren't that big." The doctor approached her with concern on his face. "Sometimes choking or tightness in the throat can be caused from something else."

Katherine became concerned with what the doctor was going to say. She braced herself.

"Do you have problems with your nerves?" Dr. Plummer asked.

Katherine didn't like his train of thought; she didn't necessarily think that was pertinent; however, she finally confessed.

"I had some problems when I was young."

The doctor shook his head indicating that he understood the root of her problem.

"Well, now that you know your throat is okay, maybe you can calm down. I know you have had some personal problems, which understandably can affect your nerves. I'll prescribe some nerve pills; you can pick up the prescription when you leave," the doctor said reassuringly; he left the room.

Katherine was relieved there was nothing seriously wrong with her throat; at the same time, she refused to admit that her nerves brought on her throat problem. It would have been so much more convenient for him to tell her he had fixed everything, that it was physical, not neurological. Now she had to go home knowing she was the one who had to fix it; she was going to have to take care of the problem. That was easier said than done; she felt exhausted.

Katherine called her friend. "Evelyn, I'm ready to come home."

"I'll be right there."

Katherine waited anxiously; she was disgusted with the doctors and the hospital.

"Well, did they fine anything?" Evelyn asked.

"Not really. They removed a few nodules, but that's all."

"Well, is everything else okay?"

Katherine mumbled something as she reviewed her list of post-op instructions and medications.

"The doctor gave me a prescription for some damn nerve pills. He thinks that is the problem," Katherine complained softly, her throat still hurt. "I'm not taking any damn nerve pills. I don't think the doctor knows what he's doing."

"Katherine, you'd better listen to him; he's only trying to help you."

Katherine shook her head; she had already decided that she was not going to take the pills. She didn't like taking medicine; more than that, she wasn't going to admit that she needed nerve pills.

Katherine got home and whispered to Mrs. Pepper. "Thank you for watching the girls. I wish we could talk longer, but my throat hurts."

Mrs. Pepper could see Katherine was in pain. "I know, Katherine. I don't want you to even try to talk. I'll call you in a few days." Katherine hoped that she would.

Miles brought Carolyn and Judy over after they got home from school. He didn't walk them to the door. He didn't check to see if Katherine was okay; he didn't check to see if Linda and Barb were okay either; he simply drove away.

Katherine tended to her girls with a horrendous ache in her throat. As sensitive as she was to pain, she was able to work through it enough to take care of her children. She tried to relax in her rocker after she put the girls to bed. Katherine reviewed her discharge papers; she threw away the nerve pill prescription.

Chapter 50

A difficult year had gone by as Katherine struggled to work and provide for her girls; she argued with the Friend of the Court about Miles not paying child support. At the same time, she fought with her nerves as she wrestled with an annoying pain in her lower right side.

"Katherine, why are you holding your side?" Evelyn asked.

"I've been having a terrible ache right here," Katherine said; she pointed to her right side.

"Maybe you should go to the doctor."

"Oh, I don't know, I'll see if it goes away." Katherine favored her side as she went about her job.

"You know what I heard, Katherine?" Evelyn said quietly.

"What?"

"There might be a new Kroger Store opening up in town," Evelyn whispered excitedly. "I was just thinking; if some of our employees transfer to that store, you might be able to get one of their full-time positions."

"Really? That is good news."

Katherine was hopeful; a full time job would mean less struggling; and she could get off of A.D.C. for good. However, the pain in her side reoccupied her thoughts as it grew more and more intense; finally she went to see a new doctor.

"Lie down of the table," Dr. Haney instructed. He proceeded to press on her abdomen.

"Does this hurt?"

"No."

"How about here?"

"Ouch," Katherine yelled. "Yes, that hurts."

"Well, Mrs. Mangrum, your appendix is inflamed and enlarged." He was emphatic. "It's going to have to come out."

"I need surgery?" Katherine asked with a shrill in her voice. She didn't like the idea of more surgery.

"Yes, and right away."

"I can't do that right now; I have to make arrangements. I have to find someone to watch my four girls."

"Well, you'd better do it soon. It's dangerous to wait," the doctor scolded. "If it bursts, you won't be around to make arrangements."

"How long will I have to be in the hospital?"

"At least four days," the doctor answered.

"Four days? I don't know if I can get someone for four days."

"That's not my problem, Mrs. Mangrum. My problem is getting your appendix out, and soon."

Another surgery presented a great deal of problems for Katherine; she had to make all the same arrangements as before. The constant traumas fed Katherine's narcissism. With no one around to help, with no one to lean on, and no one to sooth her troubled soul, her self-pity deepened.

Katherine wanted to tell Aunt Etta about her predicament; however, there was no time for a letter. She headed for the phone booth.

"Hi, Aunt Etta."

"Hello, Katherine; how are you?"

"Not very good. I'm going to have to have surgery. My appendix is badly inflamed. Do you think you could come up to help me with the girls?"

"Oh, Katherine, I don't think I could come right now," Aunt Etta explained.

"Oh." Katherine was clearly disappointed. "I wonder if Dennis could help out."

"Well, you'll have to get in touch with him. Have you checked with your dad?"

"No, not yet; but, I can't wait too long. The doctor said it has to be done right away."

"You call your dad and I'll call Dennis," Aunt Etta planned. "How should I get in touch with you?"

"I'll call you back in the morning, okay?" The women said their good-bys and Katherine fished for more change.

"Hi, dad."

"Kat, how are you?"

"Dad, I have to have surgery. My appendix is badly inflamed; I have to have it out right away. Could you and Lillian come up and help me with the girls?" Katherine heard silence on the other end.

"Well, Kat, I don't think we can make the trip right now. Have you asked your aunt?"

"Yes, she can't come up either."

"How about Dennis?"

"I'm waiting to hear from him. Aunt Etta is going to call him."

"Well, I sorry we can't help; but let me know how everything goes, okay?"

"Sure." After a little more conversation, Katherine hung up. She knew that if Dennis said no, there was only one place to turn; however, she decided to wait until she heard from her aunt.

The next morning Katherine trekked to the phone booth; her side ached. The public phone was inside a three-sided, wooden structure with benches along the back side. The little edifice would easily accommodate four people. Katherine sat down on the bench and waited for her side to ease before she called Aunt Etta.

"Hi, did you get in touch with Dennis?" Katherine asked her aunt.

"Yes. He said he can't leave work right now."

"Okay; well, I'll have to figure out something. I'll talk to you later."

Katherine hung up; she dreaded the thought of calling Miles; then again, he should be willing to help with his children. Having no other recourse, she placed the call. The whole telephone conversation was almost a carbon copy of her first call for help. Katherine and Emma hissed at each other, and Miles said he would get back to her. She was left at his mercy, which irked her.

Katherine was surprised when she saw Miles walk up the sidewalk; he stood at the door.

"Katherine, I won't be able to watch the girls this time," Miles informed her.

"Why?" Katherine demanded.

"I just can't. I have something else going on."

"What?" she challenged. "Won't *she* let you take care of your own children?"

"Katherine, don't start anything."

"I have to have emergency surgery; my appendix is about to burst, Miles. I need help," Katherine pleaded.

"Well, I have another suggestion." Miles fidgeted in the doorway. "Larry and Gladys have offered to keep the girls while you're in the hospital."

"Larry and Gladys will keep all four?"

"Yes, they said they would," Miles repeated.

"That's very nice of them; I don't know why you can't help."

Miles gave her a look and turned to leave. "Call them when you have the date."

Katherine slammed the door; he made her so damn mad.

Actually, Katherine had hoped Mrs. Pepper would come and stay again, but she didn't hear from her; in fact, she never heard from her again. Katherine pined terribly for her old friend.

The plans were made and the day came for Larry and Gladys to come and pick up their nieces. Katherine fretted about Gladys' messy house, but she knew the girls would be okay; she had no choice anyway. She assumed the girls had her courage and fortitude, which they did.

Since her last surgery, a new hospital had been built on the other side of town; Dr. Haney was licensed at the new facility. Even though it was a little farther to go, Katherine liked the fact that she didn't have to go back to Carter Hospital. The thought of its age and gloomy structure still unnerved her. The new hospital was much more welcoming.

Again, Evelyn took Katherine to the hospital on the morning of the operation.

"Good luck, Katherine. Call me when you get in a room."

"Thanks, Evelyn."

Katherine sat in pre-op all alone. Again, there was nobody to hold her hand or to tell her that she would be fine. All of her encouragement was left up to her own resilience. The lack of concern from her relatives was hard for her to understand. She was sure Dennis didn't come because Alice wouldn't let him.

Katherine was prepped and laid on the familiar operating table. She had to remove her dentures, which she hated.

"Why is it so cold in here," she asked the anesthesiologist who worked to get his station ready.

"We keep it cold in order to slow down the patient's blood flow," he told her; she didn't think that was a good enough reason.

"I'm freezing," she complained some more. "Can I get another blanket?"

The anesthesiologist placed the ether mask over her mouth and nose, perhaps a couple of minutes sooner than necessary.

After her stomach was smeared with an antiseptic, the surgeon took his scalpel and sliced Katherine from her bellybutton to her pubic line; not the normal appendix incision. Dr. Haney had told the surgeon to check out a few more areas of concern. He somehow neglected to tell Katherine about his suspicions, and that he had ordered exploratory surgery.

After the surgeon cut through the abdominal wall and the organs were exposed, he started his exploration.

"Well, let's see here," the doctor said rather cool and calm; he moved some organs out of the way so he could get his hands in farther.

"Okay, I see the appendix; that looks nasty," he said as he got a good hold on the little strip of tissue and snipped. After a few stitches and a quick inspection, the doctor tossed the diseased organ in a stainless steel tray, which the nurse quickly discarded.

"Okay, now let's have a look around," he said as he turned his attention back to Katherine's opened abdomen.

"Look at these ovaries," the surgeon said to the rest of the surgery team. He moved some parts around so he could get a better look; his nose wrinkled under his surgical mask.

"This doesn't look good," he announced.

The doctor could see that Katherine's ovaries were festooned with cysts and beginning to shrivel; however, he did not think the cysts were malignant.

"Did she sign a consent form to remove anything besides the appendix?" the surgeon asked one of the nurses. She fumbled through the papers.

"No, I don't see one."

Since there was no husband to ask, in fact, there was no one to ask, the doctor had to make a judgment call.

"Well, I guess I'll leave them. She probably won't be able to get pregnant again, though. Everything else looks good. Close her up."

The doctor thought everything looked fine, including the stomach; however, he couldn't tell just by looking that it was far from okay. Every quivering nerve ending was still in place to cause Katherine a great deal of pain.

Katherine woke up in the recovery room. She fussed to go back to her room so she could put her teeth back in her mouth. The nurses in the post-op room let her fret as they went about their duties. Finally, the orderly came to roll her up to the third floor.

"Don't look at me; I don't have my teeth in," she mumbled through cupped hands, which covered her mouth.

She drifted in and out while the anesthesia continued to wear off; every time she opened her eyes she had a pleasant surprise. She could see that her room was painted blue. She liked that; blue made her feel good. She always felt happier around blue. With a slight smile on her face, she had a few hours of peaceful rest. Finally, the surgeon appeared.

"Mrs. Mangrum, I'm Dr. Pujara," the doctor announced with an Eastern Indian accent.

Dr. Haney, an Arab, also had an accent, but Dr. Pujara's accent was much thicker.

"Who are you?" Katherine snapped.

"I am the doctor that did your surgery."

"Where's my doctor?" Katherine snapped.

"Your doctor is not a surgeon. When he has a patient who needs surgery, he acquires the services of a surgeon."

"What?"

"I said your doctor is not a surgeon. He has to call a surgeon when his patient needs surgery."

Dr. Pujara's explanation was barely audible to Katherine's ears; she always had trouble with accents. She wrinkled her nose as she tried to register his words. Whether she understood every word or not, she got the gist of what he was saying.

"Why didn't he tell me that he wouldn't be doing the surgery?"

The doctor didn't know how to respond. He had never been confronted so boldly by a patient before. He decided to move on to the surgery report.

"Let me explain the results of your surgery." The doctor wanted to get her mind on something else. "Your appendix was quite inflamed, so I removed it. Actually, you were very lucky it didn't burst. In addition, your ovaries are in pretty bad shape; they are full of cysts and shriveling up. However, I did not suspect any cancer so I saw no reason to take them out," the doctor explained.

"What about my ovaries?"

The doctor spoke very slowly. "They are shriveled up, but I didn't remove them."

"Will that cause me any problem?" Katherine asked, still irked at his accent.

"The only way it should affect you is that you will probably go through an early change of life. You weren't planning on any more children, were you?"

"Heaven's no!" Katherine nearly shouted; she wanted to say more, but she didn't.

The doctor failed to explain that the organs probably were not producing the vital hormones needed for good health, and no hormone replacement was prescribed. The fine-tuning those particular hormones provide the body were now sorely absent; the long-term effect on Katherine's well being had begun.

The lonely hours in the hospital gave Katherine too much time to think. Tears rolled down the sides of her face and wet her pillow. She was lonely, she missed the blue mist of the mountains, she missed her aunt and she missed home.

The hospital stay was completed and Evelyn came to take Katherine home.

"What did they find?" Evelyn asked.

"Well, the doctor said my appendix was about to burst so he took it out; he said that my ovaries were full and cysts and shriveled up but he left them in."

"Oh." Evelyn could tell that Katherine wasn't in a good mood so she didn't pursue the subject.

"So, what is going on at work? Is the new store opened?" Katherine asked.

"There's no word yet," Evelyn told her. "Listen, Katherine, while you're off work, why don't you let me introduce you to our friend, John?"

"Evelyn, I'm not interested right now."

Katherine got her four girls home and that made her feel better. Having them close and knowing they were okay always made her feel better; that was the only part of her life where she felt she had any control.

She heard the horror stories from her daughters' stay at their aunt's house. They proceeded to recall how they had to sleep on the floor, which gave them a better view of the mice running across the room a night; they told about how they got to jump on the beds, which she did not allow, and how Barb got gum stuck in her hair, which explained the missing clump on the side of her head. Katherine rolled her eyes for she expected as much; however, she let the whole episode pass rather quickly; she knew what a big favor Gladys had done for her.

Katherine went to see Dr. Haney for her post-op check-up and to get the release to return to work. As shy as Katherine was, she had developed an ability to confront dissatisfaction; and dissatisfied she was with Dr. Haney.

"Why didn't you tell me you weren't going to do the surgery? A strange doctor had to tell me that he cut me open," Katherine said; she stared at him right in the eyes.

The doctor made a quick excuse; he was offended at her abruptness. He explained the same thing Dr. Pujara had, which led to her next question.

"Why didn't you tell me you had ordered exploratory surgery?"

Her pointed glare unnerved the doctor. He too had never had a patient confront him so blatantly. He managed to explain; however, it did little to satisfy Katherine. She couldn't abide being deceived; it had happened too many times; she had become very intolerant of that particular trait. Katherine made a decision, when she was healed from her surgery, Dr. Haney was history.

Chapter 51

The news back at the grocery store was not good. All the transfers to the new store, and placements at the old, were finished. The only position left opened to Katherine was in the meat department at the new store. That wouldn't have been so bad, except the new store was farther away and there was no direct bus line to its location. Katherine was in a tough spot. Her friend, Evelyn, was also transferred to the new store, which was a good thing; however, Katherine couldn't depend on riding with her all the time. What would she do when their schedules clashed? In spite of the inconveniences, Katherine accepted the position; she was determined to give it a try.

"Katherine, what's wrong," Evelyn asked.

"My incision hurts." Katherine held her stomach and winced in pain.

"You probably came back to work too soon. You shouldn't be lifting those heavy meat trays yet," Evelyn scolded.

"I have to do my job. I don't think the others are going to do it for me," Katherine replied. "Besides, this cold really makes my hands hurt." She rubbed her arthritic knuckles.

"Hey, girls," one of the butchers yelled. "What do you think about this?"

Katherine and Evelyn turned around to see the group of meat cutters teasing them with rolls of hard salami. They held the sausage in such a way as to suggest their sexual prowess; Katherine made a face and blushed. She wasn't used to such crudeness; she didn't find it as funny as Evelyn, or the other female workers.

Katherine tried to do her job; unfortunately, the heavy lifting and the cold got the best of her.

"Come in, Katherine, what's on your mind?" The store manager motioned for her to sit down.

"I'm afraid I'm going to have to quit."

"Quit? Why?"

"I'm having a hard time lifting the heavy meat trays; and the cold is making my hands worse," she explained. "Is there another department I can transfer to? I could be a cashier."

"Not right now' I'm sorry." The manager was concerned. "Are you sure you want to give up this job? It's hard for a woman to get a good job like this; and it's not bad money. You might be able to transfer in the future."

"I know, but I just don't think I can handle the cold right now."

"I hate to lose you, Katherine. You're a very good worker; one of the best."

"Thank you, but I don't think I can hold out until something else opens up."

"Well, okay. Good luck." The manager was clearly disappointed.

Katherine hated to lose the added income; she detested the thought of reapplying for A.D.C. She tried not to think about it and did what she had to do.

At the same time, Evelyn continued with her matchmaking plans.

"Katherine, why don't you come over and have a few beers with me and Ken," Evelyn invited. "It's so hot; come on over and cool off."

To Carol and Judy's protest, Katherine made them watch the two younger girls as she walked over to her friend's house. She was unaware of Evelyn's plans and walked in on her well-plotted scheme. Katherine spied a tall, dark stranger who sat in one of the lawn chairs in the back yard. Before she could ask who he was, Evelyn started with the introductions.

"Katherine, this is our friend, John," Evelyn introduced. Katherine recognized the name and gave Evelyn a questioning look; even so, she greeted John politely.

The evening was spent talking, drinking, and smoking; John smoked but he didn't drink much. Katherine learned that John was a Frenchman, which prompted her to think *he must be a good lover; all Frenchmen are good lovers.*

John was a widower; his wife died from complications while giving birth to their third daughter. Katherine was surprised to hear that John let his wife's sister adopt the baby girl.

"Do you have the other two girls with you?" Katherine asked.

"Not right now," John explained. "Shortly after my wife died, I came down with tuberculosis and had to be hospitalized. I had to do something with the girls so I let a very good friend adopt my middle girl; my oldest, Jeanette, is in a foster home until I get out of the hospital."

Katherine was concerned. She had heard her aunts talk about T.B. her whole life; in fact, she remembered that her own mother was suspected of having the dreaded disease and was ostracized by her own sister.

"What do you mean, when you get well? Why are you here if you're not well?" Katherine asked.

"I guess I'd better explain," John chuckled. "Technically, I'm well; but, I still have to stay at the institution for a certain amount of time; sort of like a waiting period. Then, I will be released for good."

"Can you leave the institution any time you please?" Katherine asked; she wanted more information.

"I get one pass a week. Ken drove out and picked me up for the day."

Katherine shook her head with understanding. What she couldn't understand though, was how John had been able to give up his children. It struck a sensitive cord. She realized he couldn't take care of the children while he was sick, but to have them raised or adopted by someone else was beyond her comprehension.

"So, you are going to get your oldest daughter back when you are released, aren't you?" Katherine asked, finding it unimaginable that he wouldn't.

"Yes, of course; I always intended get my oldest daughter out of foster care when I got on my feet."

Katherine relaxed some at hearing his explanation. She was curious about the girls; but, for the time being, she held off asking any more questions. She turned her curiosity toward John's condition; she wanted to know about the institution and how much longer he had to stay there. Katherine wanted all the particulars; she was like that; she thrived on details.

The evening wore on as John and Katherine stole glances at each other. They were each unexpectedly attracted to the other.

John was tall and very thin due to the tuberculosis. He had black hair, obviously a descendent of France's ancient Roman invaders, and he had a long, narrow face. His mouth was rather small and his dark eyes sparkled when he smiled at Katherine. He liked her southern accent and he found her candid sense of humor amusing. If Katherine could manage to get her bad luck off of her mind, she could be quite entertaining in a group; that evening she kept John, Evelyn, and Ken laughing. John decided that he liked her.

One of the most drastic differences between John and the other men in Katherine's life was that he was Catholic. The vastness between a southern raised Methodist and a northern raised Catholic was very large indeed; however, Katherine chose not to dwell on that difference at the moment.

Evelyn noticed her two guests got along famously. She felt good about that. John had been terribly lonely since his wife died and Katherine had been lonely since her divorce; maybe these two could fill the void in each other's lives. Evelyn hoped so as the evening came to an end.

"Goodbye, Katherine." John looked right into her eyes.

Katherine felt something she hadn't felt in a long time. Her stomach turned over and her knees felt weak; she even felt a little flushed. These feelings surprised her. Katherine shyly returned the salutation and started home.

As she walked away, John paid little attention to Katherine's small waist and curvy hips. The sway of her dress against her butt did little to draw his eye or to put a twitch in his crotch; perhaps it was the medicine.

The couple of blocks home seemed shorter as girlish thoughts danced around in Katherine's head. It felt good to have a man pay her some attention. She couldn't help but fantasize a little; his Frenchness put a curious smile on her face. When she got home the girls noticed their mother was in an exceptionally good mood; she stayed that way for the next few weeks.

"Katherine," Evelyn called to her friend as she knocked on the door. "John called and asked if you could be at my house at 6:00 to take his phone call."

"Sure. Let me get the dished done and I'll be over."

Evelyn didn't mind being the go-between in order to help with her arrangement. However, after a path was worn between the houses, Evelyn got tired of the hassle; she offered a suggestion.

"Why don't you two go ahead and borrow my car. Katherine, you can go out to the hospital and visit, or pick John up and bring him back here; when you are ready, you can take him back to the hospital."

"Are you sure about that, Evelyn," Katherine asked.

"Yes, I'm sure. Plus, this way you two can have some privacy." Evelyn continued to play the matchmaker.

Katherine hadn't been driving all that long, Miles taught her when they got to Michigan, and she was still nervous; in addition, she felt anxious about driving someone else's car; however, she agreed to give it a try. She courageously set out on the rural, poorly marked roads, which led to the Northvale Institution.

The first few miles were still in the city so it was fine; it wasn't until she drove another few miles that the roads started to narrow and deep ditches appeared; she began to feel on edge. She kept a 10'o clock and 2'o clock death grip on the stirring wheel while she stayed well below the speed limit. The area was dark and desolate due to the abundance of trees, which shaded the whole area. The road actually cut through what was once a very dense woods; she felt vulnerable in its isolation. Katherine kept driving, focused on her destination; she hopped she would be there soon.

Katherine drove up good size hill, nothing like the mountains in Tennessee; however, for Michigan it was a good size hill. When she got to the top she could see a large building, which looked like a hospital; she hoped it was. Katherine was relieved that the area opened up to daylight and she could see that, indeed, it was the institution. Her next challenge was to find the right driveway, the right parking lot, and the right door. After asking for directions, she found her way into the lobby where John waited for her. Finally, she could relax.

John reached out to embrace Katherine and she accepted it. She actually expected a kiss but he didn't offer one. She knew he wasn't contagious anymore so she wasn't afraid if the intimacy. *Oh well,* she thought, *maybe he's embarrassed with public affection.*

"Did you have trouble finding the place?" John asked.

"No, but the dark, narrow roads were a little scary," she confessed.

"Yes, that's a lonely stretch of road. Well, I'm glad you made it okay. Come on; let's go up to my room." John took hold of her arm and led the way to the elevator.

Katherine was obviously tense. "Are all these people contagious?"

"No, of course not. This is a safe wing."

"Oh, okay."

"I have some good news," John announced as they rode up to his assigned floor.

"What?"

"I am going to be released in six months."

"That's good news, John."

"Katherine, this is my roommate, Bill."

"Hello." Katherine greeted the roommate as she sat down in an old, over stuffed chair, which was worn practically thread bare on the arms. The rest of the furniture was pretty badly beat up and the dingy green walls didn't do much to brighten up the surroundings

"These rooms are awfully dreary," Katherine complained.

"Well, they're better than the sick rooms," John informed her. Katherine felt bad for John; she felt bad that he had spent the last two years of his life in this gloomy place.

"Can we walk around a little bit?" Katherine asked. She didn't like the dismal atmosphere of the space.

"Sure, let's go this way." John led her to a brighter part of the hospital.

They spent their time together telling each other about their hopes and dreams for the future; before Katherine knew it, visiting hours were over.

"Can you come back next week?" John asked.

"If Evelyn lets me use her car, I can."

"Good." John placed a little kiss on her cheek.

Katherine found her way back to the car; she headed down the lonely, dark road that took her back to the city. She paid little attention to the solitude of the area; she daydreamed about John and their possible future together. She was concerned that he had no place to go when he got released from the hospital. Perhaps it was her mothering instinct, but something made her want to take care of him. She thought of possibilities to suggest the next time they were together. John's welfare became her mission.

Before she knew it she turned onto a lit road. Katherine exhaled with relief that she made it back okay.

Katherine handed Evelyn the car keys and told her a little bit about the visit. As she turned to walk home, Evelyn could see a little bounce in Katherine's step.

The girls began to get comfortable with the new arrangements; all except her oldest daughter.

"Why do you have to see him?"

"Carolyn, that's not fair. He's a nice man and he's good to me. God knows I need that."

"I don't like him!"

"You didn't like Charlie either. You're not going to like any man that isn't your dad," Katherine argued. "I should be able to be happy again."

Katherine continued to see John despite her daughter's displeasure. As the snowy roads of winter gradually gave way to the clear roads of spring, and then summer, the little family group spent time more together. Their relationship strengthened despite the differences.

During a late summer visit, Katherine and John went out to the courtyard to have a smoke. She noticed that John looked healthier; he had put on weight and his color was much better, not so pale.

"Katherine," John said; he hesitated a bit. "when I get released, why don't we get married?" He could see the surprise on her face. "We get along very well; so, why don't we make it permanent?"

"Married." Katherine obviously let the idea roll around in her head. "Okay, yes. Let's get married."

They embraced. Katherine expected a long, romantic kiss; however, John ended the embrace with a little peck on her lips. Despite the fact that neither one vowed their love for the other, Katherine was happy; she felt positive about the future; she had a man that cared about her.

It took Katherine no time at all to start her wedding plans. This time she didn't have just a few hours to think about it; she had as much time as she wanted. First, though, she needed a date; and she got one, December 7th. D-Day was going to be her new anniversary; she hoped it wasn't an omen. There were still a few problems to work out given John's unusual situation. He had to coordinate a release date with some place to stay; of course, there was the money problem, he didn't have any. He hadn't worked in two years; what money he had went to pay off his wife's funeral and other bills, and to help care for his oldest daughter. However, none of that mattered to Katherine; her only concern was to find a way to make love happen.

"I have an idea," John announced. "I'll call my sister, Cathy."

"Do you think she'll let you stay there until we get married?" Katherine asked.

"Yes, we've always gotten along, and I get along with Duke, her husband; I think she'll let me stay there."

Cathy and Duke were very nice people; they wanted to help John, especially since he had such a difficult couple of years; they agreed to his request.

John signed out on a day pass and Katherine picked him up feeling more excited than she had in years. John motioned for her to move over and he got in the drivers side. She didn't bother to ask if he had a current driver's license; she was simply glad he was going to drive. Away they went to enjoy the day that was designed especially for them. Katherine glanced over at John; she had an exhilarating hope for the future. No more lonely nights, no more fatherless children, no more money problems, that is, once he gets a job. She was anxious to write to her aunt and brothers.

The first stop for the lovebirds was at John's sister's house. Katherine liked Cathy and Duke, although she thought they were slightly mismatched. Cathy was short and very overweight, totally the opposite of her brother; Duke was tall, dark, thin, and very good-looking. Katherine liked looking at him, but wondered what he saw in fat Cathy. They were very pleasant and accepted Katherine as part of the family immediately.

Next, they made a short stop at John's parents' house; actually it was his father and stepmother. John's father, who was called French, was a gruff, old coot; he was unshaven with a potbelly that almost got in his way when he leaned over to release a drippy mixture of tobacco and saliva into his spittoon. Katherine turned up her nose when she saw that disgusting sight; she wasn't very discreet at showing her dislike. Bea, John's stepmother, was a short, petite woman, very frail looking, but tough from living with French. She was sweet to Katherine.

French and Bea seemed quite pleased with the news about the marriage. John's father offered his son a piece of advice as they were about to leave.

"Now, John, you make sure you are good to Katherine."

"I will, dad," John answered with a self-conscious smile.

Katherine decided she liked French. In fact, she liked everyone so far. She had gotten over her nervousness about meeting the family and she now felt at ease with all of her soon to be in-laws. She felt good.

Their next stop was at the jewelry store. With the money Duke had loaned John, he was able to buy Katherine a decent wedding ring; it had an 1/8 ct. diamond in the middle and a few diamond chips on the side, all set in 14 ct. gold. She didn't have any diamonds in her first wedding ring so she was absolutely thrilled with this ring.

Even though it was late in the day, the two lovers had one more stop; John had to get a suit. They stopped at a popular men's clothing store and John began to get measured for the special occasion. Katherine had a wonderful time; she loved all the planning. It made her feel important; it made her feel alive; it validated that she was worthy of the love. She was absolutely at her best while making plans to be happy.

Katherine didn't bother Evelyn with asking to borrow the car; she took the bus downtown to buy her wedding dress. By then, Katherine had become an independent and brave woman. She had honed in her courage; she loved it and she utilized it.

As she browsed through the racks of dresses, she finally found one that she thought was perfect. She headed for the fitting room. It was a beautiful, shirtwaist dress with a scooped neckline, and a tiny matching belt, which buckled in the front. It had a straight skirt, which hit her just below the knees. The dress had a coordinated lace jacket with three quarter length sleeves, which buttoned up over the sleeveless bodice. It was a great fit, and it was the most beautiful shade of heavenly blue; Katherine was on cloud nine. The saleslady even remarked how it matched her eyes.

"This is perfect!" Katherine said. "Can I have a swatch so I can have the shoes dyed to match?"

"Sure," the saleslady answered. "Here's a piece for the florist, too. What kind of flowers are you going to get?"

"Oh, that's easy; white carnations tipped in blue."

Her mind raced; she had a lot of lost happiness to catch up on and she was determined to capture it all. The anticipation kept her thoughts going over her checklist constantly, which made her smoke more.

Katherine sent a wedding invitation to everyone down south; to her extreme surprise, Dennis and Alice accepted. She was happy, but a little leery. She just hoped Alice behaved herself.

Chapter 52

As long as everyone stayed out of Katherine's way, things ran smoothly. The girls had already learned that; John would learn it very soon.

Dennis and Alice rolled into town two days before the wedding; all the neighbors were impressed with the Continental that sat in the driveway. Katherine beamed with excitement; she hadn't seen her brother in a long. Dennis was happy to see her too; their embrace reminded them of the closeness they missed. Dennis didn't tell Katherine, but he missed Miles; she couldn't tell anyone, but she missed him too. Katherine and Alice hugged; however, it was a show for Dennis' sake. Dennis knew it but he went along with the façade.

Katherine quickly caught her brother up on all that had happened; he knew most of it because of Katherine's letters to Aunt Etta; nevertheless, Katherine gave him a few more details. Alice didn't particularly care to hear about all of her sister-in-laws troubles; it was all too shoddy for her.

"I just don't know how any woman could handle being divorced; it's such a disgrace," Alice managed to murmur in-between Katherine's stories.

Dennis pretended not to hear it; however, Katherine did and she was irked. After all, Alice's own brother had been married and divorced a disgusting amount of times, according to Aunt Etta's letters. Katherine decided to let the remark slide; she wasn't going to be divorced much longer.

John arrived at Katherine's house in his recently purchased used car. While John stayed with his sister, he and Duke went car shopping; they found a fifty-dollar jalopy. True to Dennis' kind nature, he looked it over with John, which allowed a bond to form; Alice didn't bother with a look.

Katherine fixed a delicious dinner, she was still a good southern cook; the group got to know each other, including the girls reacquainting themselves with their aunt and uncle. Dennis was his normal jolly self; he respectfully talked to John as his soon to be brother-in-law. Alice was her high and mighty self with strategically placed comments about her community work, her social clubs, and her church work. Katherine kept her cool out of regard for her brother, but it wasn't easy; she couldn't help but cast a few dirty looks Alice's way.

That night Dennis and Alice slept in Katherine's bed. It was the southern way for travelers to stay with family, and Katherine would have it no other way, nor would Dennis. Even though Katherine's house was not of the same stature as Dennis', it was clean and they were comfortable.

Before drifting off to sleep in the cold north, Alice whispered to her husband.

"What do you think about John?"

Dennis was quiet for a few minutes. "He seems okay I guess."

"I don't like him," Alice whispered again.

"Why?"

"He's too dark. His eyes are shifty. And, not only is he a Yankee, but he's a Catholic!"

"We have to give him a chance, Alice," Dennis whispered back. "If he's going to be good to Katherine and the girls, that's all that matters."

"I don't like him. There's something creepy about him."

"Alice, don't talk like that. Let's try to have a good time for Katherine's sake," Dennis scolded his wife.

Alice didn't agree with her husband. "You'll see."

Katherine looked lovely in her blue dress; her eyes shown with anticipated happiness. This was a new beginning; things would be better for her and the girls. It just had to be; she deserved it, and she wouldn't apologize for feeling that way.

Katherine and John, because of their religious differences, decided on a local, Lutheran church; it was an amicable solution and Katherine liked the minister. It wasn't the big wedding she had always dreamed about, but at least it was bigger than her first wedding; and this time, she was being married in a church.

The smallness of the wedding didn't bother Katherine all that much; she had always been able to accept the current state of affairs if it got her what she wanted, and this was what she wanted.

Dinner at a nice restaurant celebrated the marriage and it was done. There was no honeymoon because there was no one to stay with the girls. Dennis and Alice didn't offer and they headed back down south right after the reception. The visit was short but Katherine appreciated the fact they came at all; at the same time, Raymond continued to hurt her feelings.

This wedding had been nothing like her first one, nor was the honeymoon. Katherine had prepared herself for a night of passion with her new husband. She and John had not been intimate; premarital sex was out of the question. Katherine had changed in many ways; however, that one scruple was impervious to a man's most passionate persuasion. Actually, John hadn't asked.

Katherine had purchased a beautiful, white, lacy negligé especially for her French groom. To her surprise, she didn't get the reaction she expected when she came out of the bathroom in her thin, see-through gown; John's interest was somewhat subdued. She slipped into bed and subtly pulled the lacy hem up to the top of her thigh; she scooted up next to her husband. John didn't turn to stroke her many curves or caress her hard nipples the way Miles had. He didn't even remove her negligé in order to consummate their union. He was quick and to the point; Katherine stared up at the ceiling amazed it was over almost as soon as it started. John turned on his side and went to sleep while his new bride tried to let go of the tingle that kept her wanting. Was she misled that Frenchmen were good lovers? Apparently so! Was she going to be okay with her cool lover? She was going to have to be okay with it. This time, Katherine wouldn't be able to use sex as a bargaining tool.

She rolled over and tried to put sex, or the lack of it, out of her mind. However, one thing she emphatically and unequivocally knew, John wasn't the lover that Miles was! She tried to ignore the fact that she longed for her first lover.

The newly formed family spent the next few months adjusting to the dynamics of the six personalities. It was going fairly well; as well as it could with two of the personalities being teenagers and one going through early menopause because of shriveled up ovaries.

Katherine answered a knock at the door. "Hello, Katherine; I understand congratulations are in order," her landlord offered.

"Thank you, and I have the rent right here," she announced.

"Well, I need to talk to you about that. I'm afraid I'm going to have to ask you to move." His announcement stunned Katherine.

"Why?" she demanded; she imagined him twisting his handlebar mustache.

"My sister and her family need a place to live. I can't turn down family; you understand," he said rather coldly; Katherine wondered if that was the real reason.

"Well, what are we going to do? We need a place too," Katherine barked.

"I've heard it on good authority that the duplex right across the street is going to be available." The landlord pointed to the unit.

"How do we get in touch with that owner?" Katherine asked, obviously irritated.

"Perhaps you can talk to the tenants on the other side," he said. "I can give you thirty days to move out."

Katherine made a face and paid her rent; she stared across the street. She was pissed. Things simply couldn't run smoothly for any length of time.

"What was that all about?" John asked.

"We have to move! The landlord just gave us thirty days to get out!"

"Okay, then we'll move." John's even-temper served to cool Katherine's excitable disposition.

The family moved into the duplex across the street and John started to look for a job right away; he felt good, his health was better and he wanted to get started on his new life with his new family. Things got better when he got called in for an interview at a factory near the river, which was quite a distance away. He was concerned about his fifty-dollar car lasting if he did get the job.

Katherine was happy and more relaxed than she had been in years. It helped that John got the job at the factory, and for the first time in a long time, Katherine felt positive about the future. She was no longer lonely; she had new relatives to fill the gaping hole left by Miles' relatives and the Peppers; John took her to new places, which sprouted a dormant interest in her, one that had been rooted when she journeyed with her mother so long ago. Katherine realized she loved to travel and see new places. It was also an activity that helped satisfy her inherent restlessness, which was undoubtedly left behind by her disconcerted mother.

"Do you think we can go down south for a visit," Katherine asked.

"I don't think so; this car isn't going to last much longer. It's smoking pretty badly," John informed Katherine. "But, I don't know how we can afford another one," John fretted. John had not been on the job long enough to qualify for a bank loan; they were in a quandary about what to do. Katherine got an idea.

"I'll write to Dennis. Maybe he will loan us the money," Katherine suggested.

She wasted no time getting a letter off to Florida; she felt Dennis would be willing to help her and her new husband; she knew they could afford it.

She got a reply to her request: *Dear Katherine, … we simply don't have the money right now.*

"They say they can't afford the money right now, yeh, right!" Katherine read aloud to John.

"With a Continental, and all the things Alice bragged about buying, it's only obvious they don't want to loan us the money."

Katherine was crushed; how hard up did she have to be in order for her family to help? One thing she knew for sure, she wasn't going to beg.

"I know why he won't do it; Alice won't let him, that bitch. I know that's the reason," Katherine criticized; she was on the verge of tears.

She got the feeling very quickly that Alice didn't like John. Some things don't have to be said, the gist rings out loud and clear. It was obvious that Dennis was henpecked; that irritated Katherine to no end. A curious thing, Katherine hated hen-pecked men, but she wanted to be able to hen-peck one; a paradox that always caused her problems, and perplexed her men.

"We'll manage, Katherine. I'll nurse the car along until we can get one."

Katherine pouted for a long time about Dennis not loaning them the money. She was disappointed in her brother, but mostly furious with her sister-in-law. That led her to crab about Raymond not paying back her inheritance; her face contorted with hate every time she spoke of it. John had a first hand encounter with his wife's enormous burdens. He had no idea just how low her mood could get. Just like Miles, John saw a woman, who's eyes sparkled when she smiled, turn into a bitter soul when she reverted to the past; he was perplexed. His first wife had been a beautiful, loving, motherly type, who never uttered a harsh word. Katherine was a totally different female and John didn't know what to do with her; he stirred clear of that side of his new wife.

Katherine and John began to explore other ways to get the money needed for a new car. They couldn't hit Duke up again; he had been generous beyond expectation. They came up empty handed; luckily, one day they complained to the right person.

"Man, I'm in big trouble," John said to their new landlord.

"What's the problem?"

"My car is about to die and I can't come up with the money to get another one. I don't know how I'm going to work." John was obviously worried.

The landlord took his time while he counted the cash John had given him.

"I tell you what I'll do. I'll loan you the money and you can pay me back along with your rent payments. Would that help you out?" The landlord liked John and Katherine; he trusted them.

"Yes, it would," John exclaimed.

"That's very nice of you," Katherine added. "Thank you."

John drove the newly purchased, used car into their driveway; he beamed from ear to ear. A car was very important to him, and this one was just a stepping stone toward getting his favorite, a Cadillac. John didn't like to work on cars like Miles; he simply liked to drive them. He took very good care of his automobiles; in fact, he babied them continuously, he washed and polished them weekly.

That wasn't the only thing John babied. His little Mexican Chihuahua named Chi Chi, a little, bug-eyed, yappy, black and brown, oversized rat looking thing, according to Katherine, received much of his attention. John sat every evening watching Bonanza, in color, with Chi Chi on his lap. It didn't take Katherine to long to figure out where John's affections lay. The car and the dog won out over the bedroom. She was peeved.

Even so, things were going well enough and Katherine and John decided to buy a house. They looked directly to the south side of the railroad tracks; a better kept and higher economic area. The duplexes had begun to run down as many undesirables moved in. Katherine was happy her new husband moved the family up the social ladder, where they always belonged. She left the project behind, along with many bad memories.

"Katherine, I think I'm ready to get Jeanette out of foster care," John announced one day. "Now that we are settled, I think it's time."

"I agree; she should come to live with us." Katherine and the girls always felt sorry for Jeanette, they often cried on the way home from visits with her.

However, having Jeanette come to live with them added one more female teenager to the household; the step-sisters trying to cope with each other, and a sometimes bitchy step-mother, changed the dynamics of the family. In addition, when ever there was a discipline problem with Jeanette, John always sided with his daughter, which irked Katherine. Her self-centeredness would not abide disregard for her feelings; Katherine wouldn't play second fiddle to anyone or anything. Consequently, after her step-daughter came to live in the home, things ran less smoothly; Katherine had one more obstacle as she vied for John's affections.

A lot of things kept Katherine ornery; the father of her children was still a splinter that she couldn't dig out.

"Mom, has dad called to say when he's coming to get me?" Linda asked.

"Not yet, but I'm sure he'll call soon." Miles saw the girls on their birthdays, and only on their birthdays, even though he had visitation rights every week. The three older girls were always agreeable to go with him; however, they came back home with stories about how unfriendly their dad's wife was to them.

Miles and Emma continued to live in the same town as Katherine and the girls. The broken family saw each other around town from time to time, which created very awkward moments; the pangs of loss and hurt were still felt by everyone. Katherine and Miles would go so far as to purposely dodge each other to avoid making eye contact. It seemed they couldn't bare even the slightest glimpse of what used to be.

Katherine was told that the hurt she felt would go away, but it never did. She stopped trying to make it go away and learned to side step it as she lived her life.

"I don't how your dad can ignore the needs of his children," Katherine grumbled to her girls. "It was bad enough that he deserted me, but I don't know how any man can desert his children. I'll never understand that."

Katherine's thoughts ravenously ate away at her heart. However, she shouldered the hurt for everyone and insisted that the girls go with their dad when he called. She was adamant that they got the time they deserved with him; the time she never got.

At the same time, sending the youngest, Barb, was a challenge; she didn't know her dad and she was afraid; their bond had never had a chance to form. However, Katherine made sure that her youngest daughter had her allotted time with her dad as well as the others; it was only fair. The two younger girls always went together; it eased Barb's angst; probably Miles' too.

If the truth be known, not only did the visits keep the children connected to their dad, they also kept Katherine connected to the man that would always have her heart, broken or not.

"So what did you guys do at your dad's?" Katherine asked the girls when they got home.

"Nothing really, mostly we watched T.V."

"Was *she* nice to you?" Katherine drilled.

"Not really, she wouldn't talk to us. She stayed in the other room."

"What does she look like?" Katherine continued.

"She's not very pretty," Linda answered, "not as pretty as you, mama."

"Oh," Katherine smiled. "I wonder what your dad saw in her in the first place." Katherine pondered. She gave the girls a little breather from her questions before she continued.

"Did your dad mention me?"

"He asked how you and John were doing."

"Oh? What did you say?" Katherine quizzed.

"That you were doing fine."

Katherine's actions didn't help her to get over her failed marriage; they only kept the embers hot, which charred her soul. The very oxygen that she breathed kept the flames of her lost love alive in her heart, in her stomach, in her very existence; sadly, the burn still hurt.

However, Katherine tried to move on with her new husband; she had an awfully hard time between the car, Jeanette, and especially Chi Chi.

"You have that damn dog in your lap again," Katherine complained. "I think you love that dog more than me."

"Katherine, knock it off. I like my dog; at least he doesn't bitch at me." John didn't shout; his passive personality kept him from yelling back at her. At the same time, his cool remarks hurt.

John watched his television while Katherine shot evil looks at him and the dog. She practically gagged as he stroked the black and brown, short hairs of the Chihuahua, and ignored her need for attention. She sat alone in her rocker every night; as she puffed away on her cigarette, her hatred of the dog and resentment of John grew.

Katherine was good at letting minor annoyances turn into big problems; besides the dog, the new neighbors, devout Catholics, got under her skin. To make matters worse, Jeanette got very close to the Catholic family, particularly their teenage daughter, Marie. Actually, Marie aided in Jeanette's adjustment; however, it goaded Katherine. Even so, the neighbors would have been a minor source of irritation for Katherine had not Claudia St. Antoine made one huge mistake at trying to make conversation.

"You know, you're nothing unless you're Catholic!"

Claudia might as well have declared holy war on Katherine; from that moment on, she was the enemy; in addition, John and Jeanette being Catholics only added fuel to Katherine's fire. There was always an augment just laying in wait on that subject.

In spite of all her fussing and complaining, Katherine lived more comfortably than she ever had. However, material things didn't fill her need for attention.

There was more that fueled her discontent; she missed the connection of someone with the same history. She wrestled with her inbred dislike of Yankees and Catholics; and more; she missed the love she had experienced early in her first marriage. Katherine began to get restless.

Chapter 53

Katherine rolled the chicken in flour and placed it in her mother's iron skillet. She shook the flour from her hands and hurried to answer the phone.

"Hello."

"Mrs. Mangrum?"

"Yes."

"There's been a terrible accident; your husband has been taken to the hospital," the man's voice excitedly relayed to her.

"What happened?" Katherine screeched.

It was obvious the man on the other end of the line did not want to tell her what happened over the phone. He hesitated for a few seconds.

"There was a malfunction with the sheet-metal press he worked on. You need to get to the hospital right away," the informant said in a rush.

Katherine was stunned; she had trouble comprehending what he was said.

"Is he okay?" she demanded.

"His hands were injured pretty badly and he was taken to the hospital. That's all I know," he answered back.

The man gave Katherine the directions to the hospital where the plant sent it's injured. She didn't know what to do. She was dazed. They didn't have a second car so she couldn't rush off to the hospital. Katherine turned off the chicken and sat down at the kitchen table to think. *Who should she call?* She finally decided; she called Cathy and Duke; they picked her up and went to the hospital together.

Katherine told her in-laws what she knew and they drove to the hospital practically in silence. Katherine was glad she wasn't alone; she was afraid to see what had happened to her husband; she was very squeamish about such things. They walked into John's hospital room and saw the doctor looking at his medical chart.

"Are you his wife?" the doctor asked looking at Katherine.

"Yes, and this is his sister and her husband."

Katherine stared at John lying motionless on the bed. She could see large, bulbous, white, gauze bandages at the ends of both arms.

"How is he?" she asked.

The doctor looked at John and then at his bandaged hands. Katherine didn't like his hesitation.

"Did anyone tell you what happened?" he asked.

"Just that his press malfunctioned," Katherine answered.

"Yes. It malfunctioned while he placed a piece sheet of metal inside; the press came down before he had a chance to pull his hands out. Apparently the safety stop didn't work; it was probably broken." The doctor showed his disgusted with the factory's carelessness.

"His hands were crushed."

"Does he still have his hands?" Katherine shrieked.

"Yes, his hands are still there; but, I'm afraid there was extreme damage." The doctor explained as gently as he could. "We see a lot of accidents like this. The factories are shockingly behind in installing proper safety stops. It's quite appalling."

Katherine stared in disbelief.

"How much damage was done," Duke asked the doctor.

The doctor picked up John's chart; he took another deep breath to prepare himself.

"On his left hand, we had to amputate the ring finger and the middle finger. On his right hand, only the ring finger was amputated. We were able to save the middle finger; however, he will not be able to bend it, the joints were too damaged; it will be stiff, but a least it is still there."

The doctor put the chart back on the end of the bed and excused himself; he left Katherine, Duke, and Cathy alone to digest what he had told them.

Cathy went over and hugged her sister-in-law; they cried together. Duke went over and hugged both women as John lay quiet and still, deep in a morphine induced sleep. While John slept, the trio headed for the lounge to have a smoke; a factory representative met them at the door.

"Which one of you is John's wife?"

"I am," Katherine answered; they continued on to the lounge as the representative introduced himself and established everyone's relationship to injured party.

"I want to offer my sympathy for what happened to John. It's terrible, just terrible."

Katherine was still in shock enough to accept his condolences; the anger hadn't set in yet. She was not prepared to ask about her husband's future at the factory or about his livelihood, which the factory may very well have just robbed him of; however, Duke was.

"What are you going to do for John?" Duke demanded. Their eyes met and the representative was speechless for a moment.

"Well, of course, we will pay for all of John's medical expenses; you don't have to worry about that at all."

"Will you have a job that John can do when he gets well?" Duke challenged. Katherine stared at the nervous man; her eyes bulged with tears. Desperation and fear rolled down her cheeks. They had just gotten on their feet. They had just bought a house and were able to buy new furniture. The family was succeeding; the girls were doing well; just as she got comfortable, wham, another blow. She was going to have to dig deep to find the strength for this one.

"We'll find something for him to do, I'm sure of it. Let's give him some time to heal, then we can talk about it," the representative said; he tried to sound reassuring.

"We'll find something that he can do." He patted Katherine's hand.

Duke gave a smirk and murmured, "Yea, we'll see." The company man ignored him.

Katherine finished her cigarette and wanted to go back in to see her husband. They stayed for a few more hours. John had roused up slightly, just enough to know she was there, and then went back to sleep. The doctor told them to come back in the morning.

Katherine reverted to her rocker and smoked well into the night. She rocked faster and smoked more as she re-ran the events of the day; she tried to figure out how she was going to help John with daily living, seeing that both hands were unusable. She worried about how they were going to handle living with no income. Sure, the factory was going to pay for the medical bills, but what about their other bills, what about food? With no check, what were they going to do?

"God, I don't want to have to apply for Welfare again," Katherine uttered. She smoked practically to the point of asphyxiation. She had to get to bed. Her mind needed a rest; so did her lungs.

John came home a week later with the bandages still on his hands and a little bag which contained the rings that had been sawed off of his mangles fingers. His gold wedding band and a ring he wore on his right hand, gold with a large, dark blue stone, jingled in the bag. The rings were never repaired.

Katherine tried to help her husband with his necessary activities like eating and dressing; however, she couldn't hide her disgust when she had to pull his penis out of his pants so he could urinate, or wipe his behind after a bowel movement. John didn't like it either; after all, it was a blow to his manhood having a repugnant woman fishing in his pants, and not very gently, grabbing his member, yanking it out and trying to aim it at the toilet bowl. He couldn't wait until he got the bandages reduced just enough so that his good fingers would be exposed; they would help with his most private functions.

"God!" Katherine snarled as she yanked away.

"Katherine, be careful, that hurts," John grumbled.

"God, this isn't the most pleasant thing to do, you know."

"Well, it's not as if I can help it," John grumbled back.

It wasn't easy for her to help John in that way, but she did it because it was something that she had to do; that she understood. However, there was one thing she didn't understand.

"Katherine, put Chi Chi in my lap," John instructed. Katherine bent down and grabbed the dog.

"You can't stand not having that dog in your lap, can you?" Katherine gripped as she tossed Chi Chi in John's lap, which caused John to jump and the dog to yelp. She was irked.

"Take it easy!"

A week later, the checkup at the doctor's office allowed John to leave with bandages only covering the damaged fingers; more accurately, the stubs. His good fingers were exposed to help with his personal care. Needless to say, Katherine was relieved about that; so was John.

However, while she relaxed about caring for John, another worry took its place.

"John, I don't know what we are going to do about all of these bills." Katherine was not one who could simply toss aside a late notice and figure it would *get paid when it got paid*. "Look, here is another late notice." She began to quiver in the stomach again; she pulled for her breath once more.

"Maybe I'll write to my dad. Maybe he can help us out."

"Katherine, why put yourself through that misery; you know what the answer will be," John reminded her. "We'll just have to work it out ourselves."

Katherine had sent word down south about their plight; however, no help came back. She received only words of encouragement and offers of prayers, nothing that counted, like money. Again, Katharine felt abandoned by her family.

"Look here, Katherine. This is an appointment with the factory attorney." John read from a letter. "We're to meet with him next week."

"John, we are prepared to offer you eight thousand dollars and a job for life; if you agree not to sue the company," the attorney explained.

"Eight thousand dollars? That's not very much; that won't last very long," Katherine argued.

"Well, that is all we are prepared to offer. But, I want you to consider the fact that John will have a job for life; that's nothing to sneeze at."

"What kind of job can you give me?" John asked.

"We can offer you the night watchman's job. It will be the midnight shift, 11:00 p.m. to 8:00 a.m., with an hour lunch break. It's not a bad deal. You should seriously consider the offer," the attorney suggested.

"Can we have a few minutes alone?" John asked.

"Sure."

"What do you think?" John asked his miffed wife.

"Midnights," Katherine snarled. "The cash settlement is not very much. But, I guess having a job is better than nothing. You might have a hard time finding something else with your hands all tore up."

The trauma John suffered, mentally as well as physically, prevented him from being able to even think about any other possibilities for his future.

"Okay, I guess I'll accept the offer." John called the attorney back into the room. "I'll take your offer and conditions."

"Good," the attorney said, "I think you are making a wise decision."

"We have another problem, though," John said before the lawyer got away.

"Yes?"

"I know that amount of money will not be enough to catch us up; our bills are way behind. Do you have any suggestions?"

"Well," the lawyer paused, "you can always file for bankruptcy. You do qualify for that action."

"What do you mean, qualify?" Katherine asked; legalities interested her.

"In order to qualify for bankruptcy, you must be working; technically, John is still working, he's simply on a medical leave."

Katherine listened intently; although she knew the legal action was going to be their only salvation, she didn't like it; it was degrading.

Precious time healed John's hands. The bandages had been removed to allow the air to get at the wounds. At first, Katherine couldn't look at the grotesqueness of her husband's hands, much less, let them touch her. However, just as time had healed the amputated stubs, it also enabled Katherine to become used to the disfigurement. She learned to ignore it.

Finally, John was ready to start his compensatory job as a night watchman. Katherine faithfully packed his lunch in a large, paper, grocery bag; she never forgot the chocolate covered, graham cracker cookies he liked so well, along with the newspaper and transistor radio. The large paper bag was a ploy to hide the newspaper and radio; after all, he was supposed to be watching the property. Needless to say, the nights were long and lonely; the extra items helped to pass the time.

The midnight shift kept Katherine on edge. "Be quiet; I don't want you to wake up John." Katherine scolded the girls continuously.

Everyone had to make the adjustment; with summer fast approaching, Katherine knew it would be a problem. The constant nagging at the children played on her nerves something terrible. Katherine's girls knew to stay out of their mother's way; however, sharp-tongued Jeanette gave her stepmother a run for her money, which only made things worse between Katherine and John.

The combination of many things, her high spirit, her anxiousness, her need for attention, and her need to feel loved, made Katherine feel like a bottle of fermented apple cider, ready to burst at the slightest provocation. Sometimes, though, the only thing that eased Katherine's tension was to burst. When she needed that release, and if no one provided it, she created her own provocation.

"You have to tell Jeanette to stop smarting off to me. I don't allow my girls to do it, so I won't take it from her," Katherine yelled at John.

"Try it ignore it; she's just a teenager." John appeared uninterested.

Katherine wouldn't be ignored; she pushed on John back, wanting him to turn around.

"Katherine, knock if off. It's not a big deal."

"It is a big deal; she thinks she can do anything she wants. She won't listen to anything I say. I'm not going to take that shit from her," Katherine shouted, now fully out of control.

It wasn't John's nature to argue and yell; he was a placid fellow. It made Katherine even more furious when she couldn't get a rise out of him.

"Listen to me, damn it; you never correct Jeanette. All you do is sit around with that damn dog on your lap and watch television." Katherine attempted to slap John. He saw her hand aimed at his face so he grabbed her by the wrists.

Katherine fought her way free as John tried to back away from her. She had reached a level of anger that she had never experienced before; she couldn't stop. She grabbed John's shirt and yanked with all her might. As they struggled, the shirt began to rip; in his own defense, John grabbed Katherine's arms and held her back. By the time Katherine's fuse had burned out, the shirt hung in tatters off John's shoulders.

During the ruckus, John never tried to hit Katherine; his only blow was that he didn't know how to sooth her troubled soul; he didn't understand her, and he wasn't so sure he wanted to try any more; his interest waned.

The realization that she hadn't found the happiness that she longed for only added to the bitterness that continued to grow. Once again, her frequent conversations revolved around the misfortunes of her childhood, and her first failed marriage, which she still had not gotten over. The entire family had heard the hard luck stories so many times they could repeat them in their sleep. She got the sympathy she sought from her daughters, but they couldn't give her what she really needed, the unconditional love from a man. The more she called out to John through her nagging, the more he pulled away. At the same time, her paradoxal personality was on the move.

"Let's go on a trip."

"Where do you want to go?" John asked.

"Let's go to Niagara Falls." The family packed their suitcases and away they went. The good thing about traveling with Katherine was that she enjoyed it so much it made her a pleasant companion.

However, returning home was like returning to the ring. The slamming of the car door was like the starting bell, and the fight resumed.

The pay cut John had to take left the family short of money, especially with five teenage girls.

"John, I was thinking; maybe I'll get a job."

"I don't know about that," John said back. He thought the wife should be at home with the kids.

"We need the money. There's nothing left after we pay the bills. We've got to have a little extra money," Katherine argued.

"Well, if you want too." He wasn't happy about it, but he didn't want to start any trouble; he let his wife have her way.

Katherine found a job at a fast food shop; she was immediately placed on a swing shift; however, she worked mostly days. The job made things rushed, but she managed. She always hurried home to make dinner for John before he left for work; she even fried him liver and onions, which everyone hated except John. True to Katherine's many ambiguities, she was dutiful wife.

Though the tension remained, they weren't ready to call it quits just yet. While Katherine's job kept her away from the house, the girls helped with the chores; the dysfunctional family pressed on.

However, Katherine began to feel uneasy; she couldn't put her finger on what was bothering her, but something didn't feel right. John seemed to be very distant, even less attentive than usual. The hot summer air around the house felt heavy with a secret.

Chapter 54

Katherine went to work every day; she came home and fixed dinner every night; all the while, she tried to catch any little bit of the enigma that floated around the house. She wanted to say something to the girls; she wanted to ask John something, but what? The uncertainty made her gut twist. Katherine went about her activities' she watched and listened.

Katherine felt put upon; after all, she had enough worries, she didn't need anything else. However, she allowed herself to ignore her wary feelings for the time being; Carolyn had an announcement.

"Mom, I'm going to get married; and I'm going to ask dad to walk me down the aisle."

"You're going to ask your dad?" Katherine challenge, "The dad that abandoned you?"

"Yes," Carol answered, confident she had every right to do so. Katherine was appalled. She didn't even think Miles had the right to be there, let alone have the distinction of giving the bride away; he hadn't earned the right; never the less, his daughter wasn't going to exclude him.

The wedding plans temporarily preoccupied Katherine's mind. There was so much to do to get ready to face her ex-in-laws, who were sure to be there. John stayed out of her way as she ranted and raved about past hurts, present disappointments, and the bitter sweetness of the occasion.

"I can't believe she's going to ask him," Katherine complained to John. "I just can't believe it."

"Well, you're going to have to cope, Katherine. You said she was always close to him. After all, he taught her to drive and took her to get her driver's license. Naturall, she would ask him," John told her.

"I still think it's terrible. He shouldn't have that privilege." Katherine pouted.

"Maybe it's that you're jealous."

"The hell I am; he wasn't there to help raise the girls; he didn't have to struggle to buy them food and clothes. I did it all by myself."

"And you did a good job; but, she loves her dad."

"Huh, she shouldn't," Katherine said under her breath.

Carolyn made a beautiful bride; her strawberry blonde hair was topped with a sparkling rhinestone tiara. Katherine was very proud of her oldest daughter; she always thought Carolyn was the prettiest. She tried to ignore the louse that walked down the aisle next to her.

Katherine had chosen a baby blue, sheath dress, low cut with a beautiful, Aurora Borealis, rhinestone necklace to accent the neckline. Her dark brown hair shown with a hint of auburn, and her flame red lips made a striking contrast to the light blue; she looked lovely. As she and the groom's mother lit their part of the unity candle, she hoped Miles and Emma got a good look, especially Miles.

The seating arrangements at the reception hall could have been decided by the Hatfield's and McCoy's. Miles' family sat on one side of the hall, with Katherine's on the other; it was very tense.

The band leader made an announcement.

"It's time for the bridal dance. Can I have the bride's parents on the dance floor?"

To Katherine's absolute horror, Miles and Emma rushed up to the middle of the floor.

"What the hell are they doing up there?" Katherine roared. "I'm supposed to be up there; I'm the mother of the bride."

"Let's go." John grabbed Katherine's arm in an attempt to pull her up on the dance floor. She pulled back.

"I'm not going up there with that bitch," Katherine snarled. "The announcer should have called for the mother of the bride. Someone should have told him to call up the bride's mother!" Katherine was livid.

"Come on, Katherine, we can go up too. Let's go," John coaxed.

"I'll be damned if I'm going up there now. I should have been announced." She was incensed beyond words. Despite everyone's attempts to push her onto the dance floor, she wouldn't stoop to being second string; her pride was fierce.

Katherine tried to determine who was at fault for not including her; she ultimately decided it was Miles and Emma. All she knew was that she missed the most important part of the wedding, her stoplight; she was crushed.

"I sure don't know what Miles sees in that homely woman," Katherine said to Evelyn as she eyeballed Emma from across the room. "And look at all of his relatives; they act like they arranged this whole wedding." Katherine made herself miserable with resentment.

It was difficult for Katherine on many levels. She liked some of Miles' relatives; not to be able to sit down and have a conversation about everyone back home was almost torture. It was all she could do to keep from staying in the bathroom and crying. However, she would never lower herself to do that. It was her goal to stay out in front of everyone; just so they all could see what they were missing.

In between conversations with John's family, Katherine stole glances at Miles. It should be her sitting on the other side of the hall; it should be her getting the attention as Mother of the Bride; it should be her dancing with Miles. Each glance in his direction cut away a piece of her heart, just like pieces of the wedding cake, which were cut away until nothing was left.

Katherine didn't notice that when she turned away, Miles stole glances at her.

"Katherine, can we talk a few minutes?" Lula said when she caught Katherine by herself.

"How are you, Lula?"

"Pretty good; but, I must tell you, the family misses you and the girls. Actually, we don't like Emma all that much."

"Oh," Katherine said with the slightest hint of a smile.

"Yes, she's not very pleasant. I don't know why Miles left his family for her," Lula said. "We never supported his decision to do that, Katherine."

Lula's revelation made Katherine feel better.

"I should have been up there for the bridal dance," Katherine snorted.

"I know; things got all messed up." Lula agreed. "Are things going okay with you and your new husband?"

"Yes, things are fine," Katherine lied.

"Well, I'm glad to here that. Katherine, you'll always be my sister-in-law." Lula whispered in her ear. The women embraced. Katherine never forgot Lula's kindness that night.

The next few months were tough. Carolyn and her new husband left for San Diego where he was stationed in the U. S. Marine Corp. She was going to miss her oldest daughter. Katherine had never been away from the girls for more than a few days at a time; now the embodiment of her very existence would no longer be in tact. It was as if her sustenance fed off the life forces of all four daughters; it was their existence that gave her life purpose. Katherine and her daughters made up five parts of the whole; one was leaving, taking with her part of what made Katherine feel complete. It was a void that would never be filled. Now she had a few more things to add to her repertoire of life's blows, *her crosses to bear*, as she referred to them; and she was in full voice.

With the stress of the wedding over, Katherine began, once again, to feel the stagnant secrecy that lingered over the house. She hadn't been able to put a finger on it until one day she walked into their bedroom at the wrong time.

"What are you doing?" Katherine gasped.

John didn't answer. He hurried to cover himself. She moved closer to him and asked again, "What are you doing?"

Katherine could see that his pants were unzipped and his penis lay exposed outside of his boxers. She stared at him for an answer.

"Well?"

John sat on the bed in front of the window. Katherine looked around; she finally discovered what John had been looking at. From where he sat he could see right into their next-door neighbor's bedroom window; the daughter's window. A disgusting thought entered Katherine's head.

"My God, John; you're playing with yourself while watching Marie undress?" Katherine screeched. John had not said anything thus far. He was red with embarrassment.

"Is that what you were doing?" Katherine took his silence to mean that indeed, that was what he was doing.

"How long have you been doing this?" Katherine demanded; she wanted answers. He grabbed a towel to clean himself up.

"I asked you how long have you been doing this?"

"Not that long," he finally answered.

"Why do you do that?" she asked with a snarl on her face.

"I don't know," John answered; he refused to look at her.

Suddenly everything made sense. Now she understood why John paid her little or no attention, why his physical interest had diminished to practically nothing. It all made sense!

"Who else have you watched undress?" Katherine interrogated. "You haven't watched my girls, have you?" Katherine was so aghast with disgust that she could hardly talk.

"No," John replied emphatically.

"Has it just been Marie?"

"Yes."

"Why her? Do you have a crush on her?"

"No; don't be silly." John wanted to change the subject; Katherine wasn't about to let it go.

"Then why do you do that while watching her?"

"I don't know." John couldn't explain his actions; that frustrated Katherine. "You're sure you haven't watched anyone else?"

"I told you I haven't."

Katherine wasn't so sure he was being truthful. She stormed out of the bedroom.

"Girls, come in here. I want to talk to you," Katherine yelled out as she lit a cigarette; she needed some help to calm down. She didn't know where to start; this was all new territory.

"Have you ever seen John staring at you? Has he ever peeked in your room while you were undressing?" Katherine yelled her questions while John coward in the corner.

"What? No, mom." Katherine's three daughters and Jeanette denied any knowledge of such activity. However, Katherine didn't like their nervousness. She hoped to God that they were telling the truth. Never the less, the flavor in the house was now bitter. Their manageable life had curdled with the sourness of perversion, an awful, acrid taste.

If Katherine hadn't concluded that she was disenchanted with this marriage before, she absolutely did now. How much more could her stressed psyche take; why was life doing this to her? What had she done to deserve all of this? Her mind raged with self-pity. It wasn't fair.

Life full of suspicion was too hard to cope with; after a difficult year of watching John's every move, and worrying herself sick at work, Katherine made a decision.

"I think we should separate."

"Katherine, I promise I will never do that again," John pleaded.

"I can't live like this, John."

"I don't want a separation; I promise I won't do that again. Let's not break up the family," John pleaded.

"No, I can't handle it any longer. I'm not comfortable when you're home alone with the girls. I want you to move out," Katherine ordered. Not only was she angry at John for being depraved, she was furious that he gave her one more cross to bear.

Over the following weeks, John could see there was no changing her mind. Reluctantly, he made arrangements to move; he didn't go far, however; just a few blocks away to a local motel. The small motel had a strip of eight rooms and a few one-room cabins with kitchenettes, which he and his daughter squeezed into. The smallness of the cabin was extremely uncomfortable for John, Jeanette, and Chi Chi; especially since there was a fourth occupant, his shame.

Katherine couldn't believe she was alone again. She expected this marriage to work. She sat in her empty living room and stared off into space; there was no one to tell her sad story too; there was no one to catch her falling tears. Katherine turned on her radio and lost herself in her favorite country music, the only music that understood her life; the lyrics to one of her favorite songs said it all, *Hello Walls*.

As hard as it was, Katherine kept her job, cared for her girls, and insisted that Judy go to her dad's for her upcoming birthday visit. Life carried on; she was bitter, but not broken.

Katherine's separation was going on three weeks when it was time for Judy to go to her dad's house. Judy always wanted to go; however, she purposefully stayed clear of Emma. Judy was gone most of that Saturday afternoon; close to suppertime she came bouncing up the front porch. She ran up to her mother with an announcement.

"Mom, there's someone here to see you."

"Who?" Katherine asked curiously.

Her first thought was that John had come over to try to talk her into getting back together.

"Come see," Judy said impatiently.

Katherine put down her dish towel and rushed to the front door. To her absolute astonishment there stood Miles; his figure filled the doorway. She was caught so off guard that her gasp left her practically breathless. Miles never walked the girls up to the door; he always dropped them off at the curb. She knew she should be cautious, and she was; but she couldn't help it, she was cautiously delighted to see him.

"What are you doing here?"

Her first thought, after she regained her composure, was he had to tell her something about their daughter.

"I just thought we could talk for a while; okay?" he answered.

Katherine paused, she was hesitant; finally, she motioned for him to come in. Miles took a quick look around and could see she was still a good housekeeper; he could smell the inviting aroma of a delicious dinner cooking, like the ones she used to cook for him. He sat down at the kitchen table, which is where all good southerners sit for a heart felt, personal conversation.

"Is everything okay? Did something happen with Judy?" Katherine asked.

"No, everything is fine." There was a stiff pause. "So, Judy tells me that you and John are separated," Miles blurted out.

His knowledge of the situation gave Katherine pause. Judy must have spilled the beans Katherine deduced. She thought for a minute; did she really want to talk about it with him?

"Yes, things haven't worked out."

"What's the problem?" Miles boldly asked. Katherine wasn't about to tell Miles what really pushed their relationship to its breaking point. Why was he so interested anyway? However, her urge to get the delicious attention she craved won out; she decided to talk.

"We just can't seem to get along anymore. We argue all the time and I'm getting tired of it. It's no way to live. He shows his damn dog more attention than he does me," she snarled.

Miles chuckled. He knew how much attention she required; he wasn't at all surprised. After a few moments of uncomfortable silence, Miles delivered a really big surprise.

"Well, Emma and I aren't doing very well either. Things don't seem to be working anymore."

"Oh?" Katherine inquired; she had a little smile lurking just behind her *sorry to hear that* look. As he proceeded to tell her about his marital wows, Katherine gazed at the grayish-blue eyes she knew so well. How wonderful it was they were right there in her kitchen, sitting at her table, letting her know what troubled them. She felt a wonderful pleasantness. Suddenly, she was able to forget all the pain and heartache he had put her through. She watched him as he took a drag on his cigarette.

"I don't know; there just isn't any spark left in our marriage." Miles continued to explain.

"Doesn't she have a son?" Katherine asked.

"Yes, but we never developed a good relationship. He never wanted to get close to me; and now, he's hardly ever around."

Katherine listened as she watched the kitchen light reflect off Miles' sandy blond hair. He still looked good. Her heart beat so fast that the extra blood rushed to her brain made her light headed; she heard Miles through a muffled blur. She tried to shake off the feeling; she wanted to make sure she heard every word he said so she could go over it a million times later.

"Well, I'd better go. I just thought I would stop in for a minute."

"Okay," Katherine replied. They walked to the front door together.

Katherine and Judy watched him go down the steps, get in his car, and drive away. They turned toward each other with a giddy grin on their face. They could read each other's mind.

"Mom, they might get a divorce," Judy whispered excitedly.

Katherine trembled like a schoolgirl who just caught a glimpse of the boy she had a crush on. She knew she had to get some control. This was crazy. They'd been divorced a long time; a lot of water had gone under the bridge, a lot of moving on had taken place.

"Judy, now just calm down. We don't know that for sure. We'll see what happens," Katherine gently scolded her daughter.

Shortly after that visit, Miles called regularly and began to visit frequently. Katherine and Miles weren't being very discreet and one day John stopped by the house before he went to work.

"What the hell was Bob doing over here?" Miles was called Bob by most Northerners.

"We were talking about the kids," Katherine fibbed; she was a good liar when she had to be.

"Are you sure about that? Have you forgotten how he left you alone with four little girls?" John taunted Katherine with her own grievances.

"No, I haven't forgotten. We were just talking about the kids," Katherine insisted.

However, John knew better than that, he wasn't stupid. Besides, he actually expected Katherine to take him back when she calmed down; now, Bob might get in the way. John didn't like.

"Where did you say Bob lives?" John asked Katherine before he left.

"On Cedar Street, why?"

"I just wondered; that all." John slammed his car door and squealed away.

Katherine began to relieve her first courtship. She was as enamored with Miles as she was eighteen years ago. Despite all the pain he caused her, she realized she still loved him. She was in a continuously good mood as she floated around the house on cloud nine. The girls, themselves, were overjoyed; they had always fantasized about having their father back; now it looked like their fantasy might be possible. It was a house full of dreams as the two renewed lovers continued to see each other; even talk about a possible reconciliation; and the girls egged them on.

"Miles, did John call you?" Katherine inquired.

"No, why?"

"He wanted to know where you lived; I thought he might have looked up your phone number."

"I haven't heard from him."

John tried in vain to get Katherine to change her mind about him and to trust his promises. He might as well have been talking to the walls; nothing or no one was going to get in the way of the return of her knight and reoccupation of her ivory tower. No one!

Emma was just as frustrated at having no luck in convincing Bob that he was making a big mistake. She tried to remind him of the problems that drove him into her arms in the first place. At the same time, Miles was sure things would be different this time. There was no getting through to him; he laughed at Emma's reference to the *seven year itch*.

Miles continued to see Katherine; he had already moved out of Emma's bed; he eventually moved out of her house. He moved into a motel, just like John; however, a safe distance apart. John had sent Jeannette to live with his sister; a motel wasn't a proper place for a teenage girl. She was more than willing to go just to get away from the madness.

John and Miles hung around Katherine like two hyenas in heat anxious for a ripe mate; one cocky because he knew he would be chosen; the other paced franticly, hopeful to have a chance.

Chapter 55

"Katherine, let's get married," Miles pleaded as he kissed her ear. She was euphoric having her lover back; however, she was cautious.

"What about the problems we had before?"

"What problems?" Miles moaned through his excitement.

"You don't remember? How about being gone all the time from working two jobs, and the running around with other women, and laying out at the bars?"

"I promise, honey, I won't do that anymore," Miles pleaded, "I promise."

"And, if we need more money, I can work." Katherine told him.

"Okay, that would be fine."

"Are you sure? You never wanted me to work before." Katherine reminded Miles of their many problems.

"It will be okay, I promise."

Miles kissed Katherine passionately. "Okay," she murmured, "let's get married."

All the pleas from their scorned spouses went unheard and Miles and Katherine looked for a divorce lawyer; they hoped to find one they could share. Katherine said she knew one.

Mr. Valentine's secretary buzzed him to say that his 1:00 appointment had arrived. He was more than surprised when Miles and Katherine walked in together, and appeared to be happy together.

"What's going on you two?"

Miles and Katherine smiled at each another not knowing who should talk first.

"We both want to file for a divorce," Katherine said sheepishly.

The attorney was obviously surprised. After all, he had handled the divorce for Katherine; he had been present when Miles admonish her in court; he knew all of the ugliness that had gone on.

"Well, what has changed?"

Katherine started. "John and I just don't get along anymore. We have nothing in common; she didn't give the most important reason. All he did was watch T.V. and play with his dog; he didn't pay any attention to me."

"Miles, what happened with you and your wife?"

Miles wasn't as willing to go into his and Emma's problems. "Our relationship fell apart. There wasn't any interest anymore."

"Well, why are you two here together?"

Katherine blushed. "We plan to get married when our divorces are final."

Mr. Valentine could see the sparkle in Katherine's blue eyes; not long ago there had been tears. He could see a big smile with beautiful white teeth; not long ago there wasn't a tooth in her head.

Mr. Valentine was apprehensive. He wasn't even sure he wanted to handle these divorces. He knew the track record of couples who tried to recapture the bliss they once had.

"Look, you two. Have you really thought about this? You know the problems that broke you up the first time are probably still there. Have you talked about those problems; have those issues been resolved?" Short of trying to be a psychologist, their lawyer attempted to be a marriage counselor, a therapist, and a friend. He didn't want to see them make another mistake.

"Wasn't there an issue about unfaithfulness? Weren't there issues about mental abuse on both sides? What has changed?" He insisted the couple acknowledge their problems. Miles and Katherine began to squirm in their big, leather chairs.

"Yes, we have talked about our problems; we think we can make it work. We want our family back together," Katherine defended.

"Miles?" the attorney questioned, wanting an answer from him.

"Yes, we want to give it another try. We want to be together."

"What about the children?"

"The girls are all for it. Their excited about having their father back," Katherine jumped in.

Mr. Valentine took his time deciding if he wanted to represent them; he wanted to make sure Miles and Katherine had actually thought it through; that they had honestly looked at their differences.

Actually, they had talked at length; Miles, particularly, promised to do better; he promised not to run around and not to work two jobs; Katherine chose to believe him. Katherine never promised to do less bitching, but Miles never asked her to. They were caught up in the memories of their early marriage and they longed to recapture those glorious days. During the time they were married to other people, they felt the absence of their soul mate. They were not going to let this opportunity pass them by; they were not going to let go.

"So, you're sure you want to do this?" The attorney clearly stalled to give them time to change their minds.

"Yes; we want to do it," Katherine and Miles said as they shook their heads in unison.

"Okay then; let's get things rolling." The lawyer buzzed his secretary to bring in the proper forms. Miles and Katherine gave their individual information and placed their signature on the document that would give them back their past.

"What's your fee?" Katherine asked; she was always efficient and to the point.

"I tell you what; since I'm handling both divorces, I can give you a little break. I'll even try to arrange to have both cases heard on the same day; that way I'll only have to make one trip downtown. How does that sound?"

"That sounds wonderful," they answered. Katherine and Miles were going to ask for the same court date anyway; they had their own agenda; so far, so good.

"Okay, I'll be in touch." The attorney saw the couple to the door.

Katherine and Miles were anxious to receive notification of their court date; it finally came. Unfortunately, an unexpected notice came along with it.

"Look at this! John is contesting the divorce, damn it," Katherine complained. "Look at yours, is Emma contesting?"

Miles opened his envelope. "Yes, she is. Shit!"

"Why are they doing that?" Katherine crabbed.

"Well, right off I'd say they are very pissed."

"That doesn't give them the right to mess things up for us."

"They're actually contesting the property settlement, Katherine; plus, to make it more of a hassle for us."

Katherine couldn't understand why they felt they had to challenge her and Miles' quest. "Well, that means we each need a witness."

They took the day off work and went downtown together. They had called Lil and Jean, their old friends from Tennessee, the ones they avoided but all of a sudden were their best friends, to help them out. Actually, Katherine had kept in touch with Lil; however, their friendship had become distant because Lil and John were not that fond of each other.

Lil and Jean were pleasantly surprised to hear about Katherine and Miles getting back together; they were glad to help. They rode downtown together and had a marvelous time reminiscing about mutual friends, childhood places and how they missed their glorious Tennessee. They all agreed on one thing; they never should have moved north.

They found their way to the right court room. Katherine located Mr. Valentine and sat down next to him at the plaintiff's table. She was captivated by this new experience.

"This room is big." Katherine gawked at the interior of the court; she was fascinated with the ambiance of the whole legal scene. It stimulated her intellect, which had never been used to its fullest capability; she hung on every word and action.

The opening remarks were offered and then Katherine was called to the stand. She was nervous; her heart pounded and her hands shook.

"Now just relax," Mr. Valentine whispered in her ear as she passed him.

She took a deep breath and tried.

After she was sworn in, the attorney asked Katherine about the factual information, like when she and John were married; how long they had been together; and so on. Then he asked her to describe the nature of their relationship. Prior to the hearing, Katherine's lawyer had told her to keep her answers short, just *yes* and *no* when possible; he had come to realize she didn't know when to stop talking once she got started on a subject. She always said more than she should.

"We simply didn't get along anymore; we argued all the time. He just sat in his chair and watched television," Katherine said disgustingly; she didn't bring up the *other* issue, which would have been the more justifiable cause.

Her lawyer gave a look, which she understood; it meant you've said enough.

"Was there any name calling?" her attorney asked.

"Yes, a lot," she answered; however, Katherine neglected to say that she did most of it.

"Was there any pushing or hitting?" the attorney asked.

"Yes." Again, Katherine avoided saying that she did most of that too.

"Would you say that you were ignored; emotionally neglected?"

"Yes," Katherine whimpered, and she was right about that.

"Would you say that you two simply could not get along as husband and wife even if you try to stay together?"

"Yes."

Her attorney told her he was finished and the judge told her to step down.

Lil was called to the stand to corroborate all of Katherine's statements, which she did.

It was John's turn.

"Can you describe the relationship between you and your wife?"

"She's right, we don't get along anymore. All she does is yell and complain."

"Anything else?"

"Yes, she threw me out of the house when all I wanted to do was try to work things out."

"Do you still want to work things out?" The lawyer continued to ask.

"Yes." John looked at Katherine. Her eyes shot daggers of blue steal right at his head; John winced as if he felt them.

"That's a bunch of bull-shit," Katherine whispered in her lawyer's ear. She could have saved herself a lot of blame if she had only told the real reason she left him. However, she was afraid she would have to explain why she stayed with him for almost year after she found out about his dirty little secret.

After a brief closing statement by both attorneys, Katherine's divorce was granted.

"That wasn't so bad, "Katherine whispered to her attorney. She took a deep breath and walked back to the gallery as Miles walked over to the plaintiff's table. The judge took a double take but didn't take the time to ask what the connection was; he had seen a lot more curious things in his courtroom.

The lawyer went through practically the same thing with Miles and Emma; another divorce was granted. Now, Miles and Katherine were twice divorcees.

The foursome walked out of the courtroom in a celebratory mood. Miles had planned to buy lunch for everyone; however, he had one stop to make first. He went up to one of the guards in the hallway and asked for directions.

"Where do you apply for a marriage license?"

"Right down that hall; make a left at the water fountain," the guard said as he pointed in the direction of the County Clerk's office. Away Miles and Katherine raced to fill out the necessary forms. Since there were no new children involved in either marriage, there was no waiting period. They could get married as soon as they got their blood tests and found a minister.

Miles and Katherine ate their lunch filled with the same anticipation they had the first time.

"I know a minister; I'm sure he will marry us," Katherine told Miles. "It's the same minister that married me and John, but that doesn't matter to me, does it matter to you?" she asked Miles.

"I guess not, if it doesn't matter to the minister." Miles was skeptical.

"It shouldn't matter to him if it doesn't matter to us," Katherine said, and she meant that; if she was okay with it, that's all that should matter to anyone.

Miles found himself in the office of a Lutheran minister for their first pre-marital counseling, a far cry from the southern Methodist church where he used to drive a bus. At the same time, if it made Katherine happy, he was willing to go along with her plans.

   Pastor Brown remembered Katherine; he wondered what happened. She hadn't continued to go to church so he lost touch of her.

   "Katherine, what happened with you and John?"

   "Well, Pastor Brown, he was a very cold man. He paid more attention to his dog than he did me," Katherine explained. "Our relationship simply didn't work any more; all we did was argue."

   "Miles, I don't know you, but what happened with your marriage?" the pastor asked.

   "Pretty much the same thing; we simply couldn't get along anymore." Miles didn't like having to answer those kinds of questions.

   "Now, I understand that you two have been married to each other before. I don't need to remind you that couples who remarry find that they have the same difficulties as before; the same personalities have the same reactions to the same problems," the minister said with some trepidation.

   "We've talked it all out, pastor; we will be able to make things work this time," Katherine persuaded. She talked herself practically breathless until Pastor Brown agreed to marry them. Katherine was not about to take *no* for an answer.

   The date was decided upon, one month to the day from when the divorces were final. Katherine wrote to all of the relatives in the south, her side and Miles'. Everyone was happy to get the news; however, nobody could make the trip; this time, not even Dennis.

   "That's was okay; who needs them." Katherine wasn't going to let anyone rain on her parade.

   It was going to be a very small wedding. Harry, Larry, Gladys and the kids would be there; even Mrs. Pepper and Jerry planned to attend. Katherine was going to get to see her beloved friend again.

   Katherine's eyes sparkled like blue diamonds as they shown with happiness; her face was donned with a wide smile almost every day. She was sure she was going to be happy for the rest of her life.

   Katherine shopped for her wedding dress; she decided on a beautiful, dusty blue, lace sheath. Katherine almost always chose a sheath because she had a figure that could wear it. The dress came with a lace, bolero jacket with three quarter length sleeves; the scoop neck would look nice with a string of pearls. Katherine selected a small headpiece with lace and tulle accents; again, she had her shoes and purse dyed to match. To complete her perfect ensemble she ordered her favorite corsage, white carnations tipped in blue; Miles got a boutonnière to match.

Miles had a presentable suit. The fact that he got married to Emma in it didn't matter. If there wasn't enough money to buy a new suit, then the one he had would do nicely; Katherine could overlook that kind of thing. She let nothing or no one get in the way of the one thing she had been chasing from the time she was born.

Pastor Brown stood in front of the couple he was about to marry. As he looked at Miles and Katherine, he couldn't help but feel apprehensive about their union. Since he couldn't convince them to reconsider their actions, he at least advised them to wait a while longer before taking this step. He was going against his better judgment; he hoped, no, he prayed, they would be okay. The pastor could see that the couple looked happy; he looked out over the pews and could see that the children and other family members looked happy. It was something that everybody wanted to happen; he took solace in their intense hope for the future; this delicate little family needed each other so badly. Miles and Katherine were pronounced husband and wife once again.

A nice dinner at a restaurant finished the ceremony and Katherine enjoyed reconnecting with her very first in-laws; there was a lot to catch up on, but that could wait. Since Judy was old enough to watch the two younger girls, Miles took Katherine on her first real honeymoon to Niagara Fall

Katherine was filled with anticipation; she had her lover back. She hadn't really been made love to since Miles left; now her body trembled with eagerness. It felt like they had never been apart, like the past five years had never happened. She sat next to Miles and watched his sandy hair blow from the breeze of the opened car window. She was filled with hope and excitement for the future. They were meant to be together, it just had to work out.

The newlyweds checked into the motel. Before going out to take a look at the Falls, they felt powerless to do anything but consummate the very dream they made come true. Katherine's powder blue negligé lay softly crumpled on the floor beside the bed. She lay in the arms of the only man she ever really loved.

Katherine felt her body heat up as she responded to Miles' attentions; her capillaries tightened as she grew more and more aroused. Miles was a considerate lover that night; he remembered what gave Katherine pleasure and took his own delight within her parameters.

The romantic roar of the mighty Niagara Falls fell faint against the fervent moans of the two lovers. The Falls could wait until tomorrow.

Chapter 56

Miles, Katherine, and the two youngest girls were on their way down south to see the families they had left behind so long ago. What was even better than seeing their family was that they were going back as a family. As they neared the mountains, she could feel the warm, smoky, blue mist reach out and wrap around her; it pulled her close and welcomed her home. She had missed the hills of Tennessee; she already felt renewed. Even if it was just for a visit, she was going home.

Katherine broke down in tears as she hugged her aunt. Aunt Etta embraced Katherine; she hoped with all of her heart that it would work out for her niece. At the same time, Aunt June wasn't afraid to voice her concerns.

"Well, do you two think you can make it work this time," she screeched, her red hair had started to turn gray a little; at the same time, the fiery streaks were still evident. "That's what you get for moving up to that God forsaken country."

Miles and Katherine simply laughed it off.

The days were spent getting reacquainted with family members on both sides. And to Katherine's delight, Dennis and Alice came up to Tennessee to visit them too. Alice couldn't keep Dennis away when he really wanted to see his sister. They gathered at their aunt's house and had a great time catching up on all of the family gossip. Katherine asked about Alice's brother; even though she had been divorced twice, and she wasn't proud of it, she used Clovis as a way to measure her morality. Dennis told her he was working on his seventeenth divorce.

"She'd better not say a word to me, Dennis," Katherine whispered. Dennis simply shook his head.

Reconnecting with family was good medicine for Miles, Katherine and the girls; they reinforced some strong roots

"Miles, why don't you and Katherine move back down here," Bunn asked.

"Bunn, I can't afford to leave my job at General Motors. The benefits are simply too good to give up," Miles explained. "I would never get a job that good down here."

They had no choice but to go back to Michigan; beside, their life was rooted there now.

Things were good and Katherine was happy. She was ready for another trip. The three girls had been able to get reacquainted with their dad; however, the oldest daughter hadn't had that pleasure yet. Katherine, Miles, and the two youngest wasted no time packing up and heading out on Route 66, West to California; Miles wanted to see his oldest girl.

Carolyn anxiously awaited the arrival of her parents as a married couple; she would no longer have to admit that her parents were divorced; she would simply leave out the part that this was the second time around for them.

California was a long ways away. It was August and there was no air conditioning in the car; it was hot, very hot! The girls, being temperamental teenagers, Linda being prone to car sickness, and Katherine's constant nagging about Miles' led foot didn't help the atmosphere in the car. Plus, Miles and Katherine were in a bad mood to begin with.

"I can't believe they got married, can you?" Katherine gasped. "John and Emma got married; unbelievable."

"I don't k now what they were thinking." Miles was just as disgusted. "John is not suited for Emma; she must be crazy,"

"Why do you say that? Why do you care about her?"

"I didn't say I care; I simply said she's crazy," Miles explained.

"John's the crazy one; he won't be happy with Emma." Katherine didn't like the situation at all; the more she thought about it, the more irritated she got, so did Miles. They didn't want to admit that they were actually jealous.

"Why is John the crazy one? Emma is not that bad. She'll be good to him."

"What? She's not that bad? Well, do you miss her?" Katherine snorted at her husband.

"Katherine, don't go there, of course not. Let's just drop it." That was a good idea; Katherine tried.

"This is like a damn *Payton Place*," she mumbled.

The family finally got to California and the visit with Carolyn and her family went wonderfully. However, like all vacations, it was way too short.

The family got back to Michigan just in time for the girls to start school and for Miles and Katherine to face their financial woes. The two divorces had destroyed each of their economic stability; they were going to have to sell the house and move, again. Even worse, it led to another bankruptcy. True to Katherine's resolve, she handled the inevitable and moved on; she got busy and set up another new house.

Katherine found organizing a new home exciting and invigorating, especially if she could decorate at least one room in blue, which was usually her bedroom. She had become accustomed to being disrupted; oddly, she found it stimulating. Perhaps it helped to keep her mind off her nerves, which were always on the edge of breaking down.

Katherine had quit her job when she and Miles got married; but now, she was ready to help with their financial troubles

"I don't want you to work," Miles insisted.

"If I get a job, then you don't have to work a second job. You can be home at night with me," Katherine argued.

"I'd rather work a part-time job so you don't have to work. I'd like you to be home with the girls, and be there to make dinner."

"No, I'd rather work part-time. I don't want you gone at night. I want to be with you," Katherine protested.

"I want my wife home," Miles insisted.

"Miles, we talked about this. You said you wouldn't take a second job; you said you would stay home with me. You said it wouldn't bother you if I went to work, remember?"

"I know, but, I already found a part-time job. The garage on the corner needs a mechanic. They said I could work what hours I want."

"You already have another job!" She was viably surprised. "When were you going to tell me?"

"I was going to tell you, soon," Miles responded.

"Soon? When?"

"Don't worry, honey," Miles said as he snuggled at her neck. "It will be okay. I'll only work a few days a week. It won't be that bad, you'll see."

"I don't know about that, Miles." Katherine was clearly upset.

Katherine didn't want Miles to work a second job. That was one of their main problems the first time. She could feel her mind slipping back into the past, a place she fiercely did not want to go. Her stomach began to churn with old, familiar worries. She grabbed a cigarette and tried to ease her anxiousness.

For the rest of the year the couple bickered back and forth about Miles working a second job. However, a new, unfamiliar problem arose; one she never would have predicted; it threw her totally out of kilter.

When Miles left home for the first time, the two youngest girls were just babies. He had only seen them once a year there after; so, for all intense purposes, his mind still saw them as little girls; but alas, they were very much teens in the midst of hormonal mayhem.

"Stop yelling at her, Miles!" Katherine shouted at Miles when he tried to discipline his youngest daughter.

"She's not going to talk to me that way," Miles shouted back. He took his belt off.

"What do you think you are doing?" Katherine screamed.

"She needs to be taught a lesson. She's too smart for her own britches; she won't listen to me." Miles grabbed Barb's arm and began whipping the back of her legs.

"I won't stand for you doing that to her," Katherine yelled; she grabbed the belt out of Miles' hand. "You're not going to beat her." Miles actions hit way too close to home for Katherine. Once again, she turned into a lioness protecting her young.

"I'm not beating her; I'm just teaching her a lesson. She has to listen to me," Miles ordered. "You baby her too much."

"I don't baby her. You're thinking of her as a little girl. She grew up when you were gone; she's not that little girl anymore. It's not her fault you missed twelve years of her life," Katherine lectured. "Leave her alone."

Katherine was furious with Miles' rough punishment. She had guided them through all of the hard times; she cared for them, and protected them. Even though they were Miles' children too, he had given up the right to have any say about their discipline. Even though he was back in their lives now, and Katherine wanted him there, he had forfeited certain parental rights. Katherine and Miles could have differences about money, their relationship, part times jobs, and even sex; but, nobody had dominion over her girls except her! Unfortunately, Miles didn't understand that; sadly, the first crack appeared.

Miles continued to work a part-time job at the local garage; he still loved the automobile and had to be near it. Katherine sat alone most nights and smoked her cigarettes. Her stomach began to knot up with worry, a feeling that was way too familiar. As she puffed away, she wondered if she had a reason to worry. She wondered if she had been foolish to believe Miles' promises; had she been misguided at taking the chance.

Katherine stared at the walls; however, she didn't see them; her mind's eye was back in the south where she sat alone at night wondering where her husband was;

a lonely time that she didn't want to revisit. She resisted acknowledging a truth was all too real; Miles hadn't changed at all.

Miles walked in around midnight as Katherine shot dirty looks at him.

"What's the matter?" Miles had the audacity to wonder why she was so pissed.

"Where have you been? I thought the garage closed at 9:00."

"It does, I stopped by the bar with the guys for a little while."

After Miles had a few beers in him he was exceptionally playful. He tried to give Katherine a hug; he was ready for sex. More than that, he was ready for his favorite sex, the kind he learned in Germany.

"What are you doing, Miles?"

"Come on, Katherine, give it a try, you might like it," Miles coaxed.

"I told you before, I don't want to do that, it turns my stomach," she shot back at him.

Miles' drunkenness made him angry. "Why are you so cold? Emma wasn't cold; she would have that kind of sex with me," Miles bellowed. That was the worst thing he could have ever said.

"Emma liked it! Well, why did you leave her then," Katherine screamed back.

"I don't know, maybe I shouldn't have." Miles grabbed a beer from the refrigerator. "All you do is bitch anyway. You can't be positive about anything. I'm getting tired of it." Miles' remarks hurt terribly.

"Well, maybe I'll just kill myself." Katherine reverted to her old threat in an attempt to get her husbands attention.

"You're too mean to die," Miles mumbled as he fell on the bed about to pass out.

"Oh, no you don't; you're not gong to sleep in bed with me. You go sleep on the couch." Katherine threw his pillow at him.

Miles slept on the couch that night, and many nights after that. Another inherit truth was revealed; Katherine hadn't changed either; thus, the second crack appeared in their marriage.

Katherine would not surrender to Miles' sexual needs; at the same time, he ignored his wife's need for attention; the circle began to spin. They hated to admit that just maybe the attorney and the preacher had been right. Their same old problems began to resurface; they each had the same old reactions to the same old problems.

For a while, Katherine wasn't positive about Miles' activities, though she was suspicious.

"Where have you been?" Katherine barked at Miles.

"I worked late; now back off," Miles yelled back.

"Were you out at the bar with other women?" She quizzed.

"Katherine, are you trying to pick a fight. I said knock it off."

"You promised you wouldn't do that anymore; if I would only marry you, you wouldn't do that. Huh, that's a laugh." Katherine stared at Miles. Her sadness at the path their marriage had taken was obvious. She had wanted it to work so badly; she not only felt sad, she felt stupid.

Katherine became uncontrollably suspicious; she picked at Miles mercilessly, which only kept him away from the house for longer periods of time. Finally, he had enough and he moved out. Katherine was devastated. Again, she was left alone. Questions tormented her; she wondered why Miles couldn't have changed his ways, why he didn't love her enough to change for her; it was the ultimate betrayal.

Not being able to keep her one true love, her soul mate, for a second time was an unspeakable sorrow Once again, Katherine sank into the darkness of unattainable answers. Why couldn't someone love her? Why did she have such bad luck? Her self-pity flourished.

Miles had been away from the house for several months without Katherine knowing where he was. This time he didn't stop by the house periodically to give her money, the way he did the first time; there was no communication at all. She grew edgy and resentful. She sat in her rocker and smoked.

Katherine's dream of living the rest of her life with her one true love had sadly slipped into the fog of broken dreams. What was she going to do? She stared until the room became a void of blue nothingness. She wondered why she saw blue. She always loved blue, it made her happy; this sad, lonely place shouldn't be blue. She shook her head freeing herself from the void; and, so she could light another cigarette.

Katherine's curiosity got the best of her. She wanted to know where Miles was staying; she just had to know; it drove her crazy. She didn't like being in the dark about any thing. Katherine covertly rode up and down the neighborhood streets and peered into strange driveways.

Katherine's sadness changed to anger; she became consumed with her mission. Once she accepted the inevitable, her inherent survival skills kicked in. Despite her bad nerves, her slight frame, and her sourness at life, she was never stronger than when she was determined to *even the score*; she had learned that the hard way.

After their first break-up, Katherine had not bad-mouthed Miles in front of the children; however, all restraints were off this time. If anyone even so much as said a nice thing about Miles she was ready to give them the worse chastising of their life, even her girls. He didn't deserve anyone's niceness anymore. She was hurt, mad, and staunchly unforgiving!

Katherine sat at the table and drank a cup of coffee after work. Her thoughts were interrupted.

"Mom, I found him." Linda was excited and out of breath.

"Who?" Katherine questioned.

"Daddy."

"Oh? Where?"

"I took a short cut home and went down Washington Street. I saw dad's car parked in a driveway there," Linda explained

"Where's Washington Street?"

"The street right behind the garage where dad works."

Surprisingly, it was only a few blocks away from their house. She couldn't get over his nerve; but then she never could.

Katherine couldn't stand it. After dinner she went for a ride.

Chapter 57

Katherine pulled into her driveway almost sorry that she knew. Not knowing where Miles was allowed her to deny the truth, it made it easier to give him the benefit of the doubt; but now, having seen Miles' car parked in the driveway of another woman's house made it all too real. It hurt like hell. Scorn raced through her head. All the promises he had made her, all the plans they had for the future, and it happened again; he turned to another woman!

The betrayal was devastating as she tried to go about living. Her thoughts were erratic and inconsistent. She was furious; she hated what he had done to her again; she was jealous that another woman was in his arms. She wanted to cry but her anger wouldn't let her. The disdain that raged in her was fierce, not because she hated him, but because she loved him.

Just when she thought she was able to definitely end the relationship, her aching heart kept alive the possibility that she could take him back. The little bit of the dream, which was still left, allowed her to hedge toward giving him one more chance; if he wanted it; if he could stay away from other women. She had taken him back many times during their first marriage, but now, she was stronger, more aware of how to live on her own; she had more pride. At the same time, she wanted, and needed, his love more than anything else in the world.

Katherine hadn't talked to Miles in months; as each day passed she got madder and madder until she finally got mad enough to go see a lawyer. In fact, she was so pissed she gave the lawyer the address of Miles' girlfriend as the place to serve him with divorce papers. Katherine wasn't going to be disgraced any longer; she wasn't going to sit home and wait for her husband to finish with his whore.

After the visit to the attorney, Katherine reverted to her rocking chair; cigarette in hand, she mumbled to herself.

"Miles, you shit ass, why did you do this? Why the hell couldn't you be faithful? You ruined everything." She could feel her face heat up as she gritted her teeth with contempt. She couldn't stop the tears, which ran down her cheeks.

Her scorn for him was not hate; it went much deeper than hate could go. It went to the very bowels of her soul, where the agony of betrayal and hurt paled in comparison to the anguish of failure. Nothing would ever hurt that bad again. After only a short four years of what was supposed to be forever, their ivory tower crumbled; Katherine was single again. Again she had to write to Aunt Etta with the bad news; again Aunt June shook her head with, "I told you so."

Katherine's stomach began to hurt worse; more nicotine helped to dull the pain that the cigarette smoke couldn't choke out.

Katherine got a letter back from her aunt.

"… I'm sorry to hear about you and Miles. Honey, I feel bad that you've had so much hurt. I don't know why that is. I've prayed to God to give you some happiness.

I tried to raise you with love; Lord knows you had such a difficult childhood. Perhaps I spoiled you too much; all I wanted to do was make you feel loved."

"Is that a letter from Aunt Etta?" Katherine's daughter asked.

"Yes, she feels that maybe she spoiled me too much, that I didn't feel loved enough by her. Imagine that, she's the only person who did show me enough love."

Katherine certainly didn't want Aunt Etta to feel any blame for her misfortunes; if there was any blame to be had, it was life itself.

"Aunt Etta became an old maid because of me. She gave up love in order to keep me." Katherine's guilt weighed heavily on her shoulders.

Dennis felt equally sad at his sister's hard luck. He had seen her struggle through emotionally difficult times; he knew she was a difficult person to live with, but why couldn't she find the one person who could see the goodness in her, that could love her just the way she was, imperfections and all; someone who could love her unconditionally. Dennis had seen Katherine's blue eyes sparkle when she was happy; he had seen the funny side of her. He, like his aunt, never understood why she couldn't find the right man. Dennis also agonized over his sister's sadness, which he kept secret from his wife.

Katherine's nerves were in bad shape; however, being the paradox that she was, she dug deep down and found the strength she needed to keep her head on straight and take care of business. She still had two girls at home, though they were older teenagers; she still had to support them. Like before, Miles did not pay any child support; it was up to Katherine to be the soul supporter; and she did just that. Her ability to stretch a dollar was phenomenal; as a result, with a bit of sacrifice Katherine forged ahead toward proving that she did not need a man to take care of her.

Katherine's continued perseverance paid off. Her self-esteem got a big boost when she landed a very good job; one she had applied for several months back when she realized she might be alone again. She got assigned to the dietary department of the local hospital, with much better pay than she was used to. The job would turn out to be her greatest a source of security and pride.

Even though Katherine got a decent check from her job, it wasn't enough to keep the house that she and Miles had bought. Katherine packed up her girls and belongings and headed for a place that tested her fortitude beyond what was even fair.

"Mom, do we have to go back there?" Katherine's daughters protested.

"That's the only place I can afford. There is no other choice; you will simply have to adjust," Katherine ordered the girls.

"It's not a nice place any more. It's trashy now," the girls complained. Katherine knew they were right, but what could she do? She couldn't afford to stay in the house; she could only afford a small, single house in the *project*; a huge blow to her pride as well.

"There's no sense complaining; I don't like it either." Katherine admitted; after all, it was just as hard on her as it was on them.

During the years she had been gone away from that neighborhood, it had deteriorated terribly; now, it was considered the slum of the area. Katherine hated to move back there; it was a step backwards. Life was supposed to be a series of moves up the ladder, not down. She hated to be exposed to the stigma of living in that part of town; she hated to expose her girls to it; nevertheless, they were simply going to have to suck it up and manage; she expected nothing less.

Katherine's son-in-law, Chuck, Judy's husband, had become quite a successful property owner; he had bought several duplexes and single family homes in the project. He let Katherine rent one of his places for a price she could afford. He was a good man and the one positive male figure in her life; he became the son she never had.

Katherine, along with her girls, was resilient. She knew living in that part of town was only a temporary set back and was in no way a reflection on her class; she would not allow that. At the same time, it was hard for Katherine to slide down the rungs of social status. She would never forget the rub burns caused by the questioning looks from people wondering why she was back on that side of town. Proudly, she held her head high and professed that once she got out of there, she would never let it happen again, ever.

During her lonely nights, Katherine worked on ways to make ends meet while her roller coaster ride through life kept her nauseous with its highs and lows. She hoped it was time for the ride to pull into the station and give her some calm; however, the ride was not over.

Chapter 58

Katherine climbed up on the stool to reach the top of the giant, hot, coffee urns. It was a dangerous job, but she managed. She cleaned and prepared the steam tables, another hot job; but, her favorite job was running the cash register. She became extremely proficient at ringing up the customers and her speed became her trademark.

Katherine was a perfectionist when it came to procedure; she certainly wasn't going to give anyone anything to call her down about. She hated being confronted; if you were the unlucky person that did it, you would have to endure her wrath forever.

Katherine, her name quickly shortened to Kathy by her co-workers, didn't particularly like her schedule, which was afternoons and sometimes a split shift, four hours in the morning and four hours in the evening. However, it didn't matter whether she liked the schedule or not, she needed the job; consequently, she allowed her life to revolve around her schedule. The inconvenience was worth it; she suddenly felt a security she had never felt before. Katherine no longer had to depend on the government, or a man, for support; she was now self-sufficient.

Katherine quickly got acquainted with the other workers and the gaggle of eclectic women had some adjusting to do to each other. Even though the group was certainly diverse to begin with, Katherine threw a monkey wrench into the mix. There was Agnes, a redhead that Katherine thought was a smart ass; there was Darla, a mild mannered woman who was married to a French Canadian man, whom Katherine found to be very attractive when he came in to see his wife; there was Laura, a heavy set woman who was from a similar background as Katherine, and seemed to instantly understand and accept her for who she was;

there was the boss, Ms. Phelps, a black woman that Katherine found to be very condescending and just as prejudice as anyone. Perhaps it was Katherine's southern upbringing and Ms. Phelps inter-city influence, but their relationship was destined to clash. And then, there was Princesses Katherine, who was quickly dubbed *the bitch*. Where Katherine's family, in order to keep peace, overlooked her difficult nature, even babied her, the co-workers felt no obligation to do so. Hence, the doctors, nurses, and visitors were privy to some interesting lunch and dinner hours.

During her evening shift, Katherine meticulously cleaned the steam table after the dinner line had closed. Out of the corner of her eye, she saw a figure walk into the cafeteria; she didn't look up, she simply kept wiping. She assumed the person would see that the steam table was empty; consequently, she didn't feel the need to announce that dinner was over. Her peripheral vision allowed her to see that the figure continued to stand at the counter. Before she could stand up and inform the visitor they could get something at the vending machines, the male voice spoke.

"Hey, how have you been?"

Katherine recognized the voice at once; she froze. Finally, she stood up and looked at him face to face. She stared at him not offering any response.

"I bet you didn't expect to see me here?" the man said with a big grin on his face.

"What are *you* doing here?"

"I came to see you," he said with a grin.

"Are you visiting someone in the hospital?" Katherine wiped her hands.

"No, I came to see you."

In her wildest imagination, she never expected to see her ex-husband, John, come to see her. She knew how pissed he was when she divorced him.

"What do you want?" Katherine asked.

"Can we talk?"

"I don't have anymore breaks. I get off at 9 o'clock." Katherine pointed at the clock, which read 7:30.

"I'll wait." John walked over to a table and sat down.

"You'll wait?"

"Yea, I'll wait," he said with a grin.

Katherine was surprised; he must have something important to talk about if he wanted to wait an hour and a half. She went about her business of cleaning up the cafeteria for the morning staff, all the while she wondered why in the world John was there to talk to her. She found that she was interested in what was going on with him and Emma; she turned up her nose with scorn at the thought of that woman; even so, she was curious. Katherine wondered what Emma would think if she knew her husband was there to talk to the women who stole her ex-husband; even though Emma's ex-husband was her first husband first, and Emma's present husband was also her ex-husband. Katherine sighed with disgust at the mess. "Yes, a real *Payton Place*," she mumbled.

Oddly, the two women, who had so much in common, still had never spoken to each other. As the web of their relationship grew more entangled, Katherine became more engrossed.

When she finished closing up, Katherine meandered over to the table where John sat; she was good at doing that if she wanted to convey her mistrust at someone's intentions. She tossed her cigarettes on the table as she lit the one she held between her fingers. She took a big drag and sat down.

"What do you want?" she spoke as the smoke came wafting out of her mouth.

John paused with a sheepish grin on his face. He stalled until he got up his nerve.

"I heard you and Bob got a divorce." He waited for her reaction.

"How did you know that?" Katherine asked with a sneer on her face. She wondered who blabbed.

"News travels fast at that corner gas station. Someone got wind of it there and passed it on to Emma," he explained. Obviously, Emma was keeping score also.

Katherine turned up her nose at the thought that Emma knew she lost Miles once again; how humiliating. The shame stung like a swarming bee getting past her guard and lingered throughout their conversation. She had a snarl on her face, which had become normal; her smile had disappeared some time ago. She explained what happened.

"Yah, he hadn't changed. He couldn't stay away from other women. I wasn't going to put up with that shit again."

John wasn't surprised. He had reminded Katherine of that very trait while he tried to save his marriage to her. He wanted to say, "I told you so," but he didn't.

"Not only that, but he had a problem with the girls. He still saw them as little, like when he left; he couldn't handle them as teenagers," Katherine explained.

Katherine felt bad that John had brought up all the unhappy memories. "So, what do you want?"

John sat across from Katherine and looked at her, he noticed she hadn't let up on her smoking; he also noticed there was less sparkle in her eyes; however, he forgot about all that so he could get to why he was there.

"Well, I have something to tell you," John said mysteriously.

Katherine stared at him with questions oozing from her faded, blue eyes. "What?"

"Well," John paused. "Emma and I are getting divorced."

"You are?" Katherine asked in a most curious way. "Why?"

"We were never right for each other. We just got caught up in the rebound, that's all," John explained.

The truth be told, Emma was a very passive woman, not much emotion. Dare he admit he missed Katherine's spirit, even though at times it was hard to cope with? Yes, he had to admit it; however, he didn't tell her that. He didn't want to sound romantic; he knew she wouldn't buy it.

They talked a little while longer; Katherine was drawn in while John divulged the problems with his marriage and how he and Emma never quite connected.

"What about her son?"

"I had very little contact with him. You know, Emma said that Bob had very little contact with him too."

"That's what Miles said, but I didn't know if it was really true," she said.

"Well, it was true," John confirmed.

That made Katherine feel a little better; Emma's son had always been a barb in the fulfillment of her motherhood; it irritated her, it made her feel guilty; it made her feel that Miles had the son he always wanted in Emma's son. John's information made her feel vindicated. Even though the second marriage to Miles had come and gone, it made Katherine feel better to know Miles' marriage to Emma had not been the perfect love nest she thought it was.

"John, why did you feel the need to tell me about your divorce?" Katherine interrogated.

John fidgeted in his chair. "I guess I'm here because I miss you."

"You miss me?" Katherine chuckled.

"Yes, I miss you. We had some good times," John recalled.

Katherine puffed away on her cigarette. She tried to recall the good times; maybe there were some in the beginning.

"Do you think we could spend some time together?" John asked.

"I don't know, John. I don't know if it's a good idea," Katherine rationalized.

"Well, why don't we give it a try; maybe things can work out for us."

When Katherine went home that evening, she felt just a little bit better; her blue eyes were just a little bit brighter at the thought that someone was interested in her; that someone wanted to love her.

Over the next few months Katherine saw a lot more of John. The girls knew that John was getting a divorce from Emma, Katherine had told them; but, they had no clue just how close their mother and he were getting.

"Mom, why are you going out with John? Wasn't he doing weird thing before, isn't that why you left him?" Their mother didn't have an acceptable answer for them; she only knew that she liked the attention he showered on her.

Actually, Katherine was cautious about rekindling her relationship with John; at the same time, John was so relentless in his pursuit that she eventually allowed her caution to lay at the wayside. Besides, her caution had no right to interfere with her chance to find love once again, and that went for any person who may get in the way; that would have been considered disloyal, something she couldn't abide.

The sun was warm and inviting while Katherine and John sat on her patio; they had seen each other for several months. The two younger girls lay in the sun out of ear's shot of their conversation.

"I don't know, John. I would have to ask them."

"Well, go ahead; ask them."

"Girls, come over here," Katherine called out.

John intently watched the slim, teen figures, in their two-piece bathing suits, sway over and step under the aluminum awning. The girls were clearly aware of his stare.

"John wants us to get married again," Katherine announced. "I told him I would have to check with you two." The girls stared at their mother. Katherine knew what they must be thinking; however, she negotiated away her misgivings.

"John said he would never do those things again. Would you two be okay with it?" It never occurred to Katherine that she should have talked to her daughters in private first.

Perhaps Katherine lost some respect from her girls that day; however, the teens knew there was only one answer they could give their mother if life was going to be tolerable. They couldn't be the ones who stopped her from having the love she hungered for.

"Yea, I guess so," each one answered.

Katherine saw her daughters hold their heads high; she required them to be as tough as she was; she expected it. After all, this was her change to get the one thing that she always wanted.

With getting the absolution she sought, Katherine felt free to get serious about John's proposal; however, she hesitated a little while longer. She remembered their past problems; she heard John's promises; she pondered whether it right to remarry him. All the while, John smothered her with attention.

It didn't take very long for her to decide; three months, almost to the day, after divorcing Miles, she remarried John. She didn't dare ask Pastor Brown to marry them; she was too embarrassed. They chose an Episcopal church a few cities away, which had been suggested by Jeanette. At that point, the kind of church they got married in meant very little to Katherine.

"Judy, will you be my maid-of-honor? Luigi, Jeanette's husband, is going to be John's best man."

"Of course, Mother."

All the children privately knew it would never work; at the same time, none of them wanted to be accused of interfering so they kept quiet. Their parents were all on their own with this one.

Once again, Katherine found wedding bliss dressed in blue; a nicely tailored suit with a frilly white blouse was her choice. It accented her eyes, which were much more vibrant than when John saw her in the cafeteria; her corsage of white carnations tipped in blue graced her shoulder. John bought his bride a fine, half-karat, round cut, diamond wedding ring; the brilliance of the stone fascinated Katherine, which cemented her long time love of the gem. Throughout the dinner reception, Katherine admired the ring; every movement of her hand caused each facet to reflect in her eyes and shoot blue rays of hope out over the wedding party. At that moment she was happy.

Katherine's relatives hoped she would be happy this time, but doubts of her judgment flew throughout the family. Aunt Etta prayed that her niece would find what she was looking for.

Alice, wasted no time voicing her opinions about Katherine; Dennis couldn't' say much because his sister kept giving his wife ammunition. At the same time, Dennis reserved judgment of his sister; how could he criticize her for wanting what everybody else wanted? He, too, prayed that his sister would be happy this time.

Katherine anxiously awaited a response from her aunt; however, it had been slow in coming. She thought her aunt was upset with her; in actuality, Aunt Etta's health was beginning to fail. Katherine couldn't even conceive of the possibility that anything could be wrong with her aunt; she was certain that Aunt Etta was disgusted with her. Her guilt at hurting her aunt continued to eat away at her stomach.

Once again, John refused to live in the project, which suited Katherine just fine.

He moved Katherine and her girls back to the other side of the railroad tracks, keeping them out of the lower class. However, because of their endless financial upheavals, John and Katherine could only afford a small bungalow, which was terribly cramped for four people.

The close quarters made it too tempting for John. It didn't take long for the girls to be intimidated by their step-father's stares; the shadows moving near the crack at the bottom of the bathroom door taunted them. Disgustingly, John's perversions had returned.

"Mom, I'm getting a job," Katherine's youngest daughter told her.

"Barb, you're only fifteen."

"I know, but I can handle it."

"I'm going to work too, I can get something in the evenings when I get home from classes," Linda said; she commuted to a near by college.

"That's a tough schedule, girls. Are you sure you can do it?"

Katherine was proud of her girls and their independent nature; at the same time, she felt a hint of a twist in her gut, which she chose to ignore.

Unfortunately, Katherine's exhausting denial of the past placed her right in the middle of the same state of affairs. A brand new Cadillac boldly sat in the driveway; John and his dog, Tippy, a toy Manchester Terrier, sat together in the easy chair and watched a brand new, state-of-the-art, color television set. Just as before, Katherine was denied the affection she so hastily entered the marriage to get.

"You're sitting with that damn dog again. How come you can show that dog so much attention and you don't show me any?" Katherine rushed over to the television and snapped it off.

"Get away from that T.V. before I break you arm!" John yelled.

Katherine should have known better than to be surprised, after all, she had learned a hard lesson from re-marring Miles; however, she *was* surprised.

Worse than being surprised, Katherine's suspicions grew.

"Girls, can I talk to you? Is John bothering you?" Katherine watched her daughters cast their eyes toward the floor.

"Well, does he stare at you?"

"Yes, mom. He sneaks around, he stares at us; he's even started making lurid remarks. Yes, he is bothering us."

"He promised he wouldn't do that; damn it."

"What did you expect, mom? People like that don't change."

Katherine was embarrassed to get a scathing from her daughters; however, she made no apologies for attempting to have love; at the same time, she was mad.

"John, you promised that you would leave the girls alone. They tell me you've been staring at them." Katherine boldly confronted him. "What do you have to say?"

Katherine became even more infuriated when he didn't say anything.

"Don't you have anything to say?" Her requests turned into demands. "Answer me, damn it!"

John simply shrugged his shoulders and cowered away to his sanctuary in front of the T.V.

Tension was at a stifling level; Katherine's disillusionment worsened. She watched John like a hawk in the little house. Soon, John became disenchanted as well. They both realized very early they had made a big mistake.

"This isn't going to work, John. I can't take the pressure. My nerves are shot and my stomach is killing me."

"You're right, Katherine; it's not going to work. I'll move out." Ironically, John rented the same little hut at the Niagara Motel that he had rented the first time he left.

Luckily for Katherine's nerves, the break-up was amicable and quick; however she was alone once more.

"How dare him; he had me served papers at work, that shit ass." Katherine complained to her daughters. "That was embarrassing. I hope I never see him again."

Katherine was livid for days. She didn't like having the tables turned on her; she didn't like being made to look like a fool.

Nobody was surprised that John and Katherine's marriage lasted only two years. Now at 50 years of age, Katherine had been married and divorced four times. It didn't matter that it only involved two men. Each break-up was just a traumatic as the one before. It was still four failures; it was still four heartbreaks.

All the girls loved their mother; they were grateful for her sacrifices to raise them, for which they were reminded of many times. Their unconditional acceptance of their mother, despite her bad decisions, afforded her a compassionate cushion for when she fell off the back of her Knight's white horse. Since Katherine couldn't ask God for guidance, he mercifully gave her four loving and forgiving daughters to support her.

What Katherine's family and friends, who were very few, found frustrating was her inability to learn from her mistakes. She was the epitome of *love is blind*; her craving for love was so strong that she was willing to try again and again, even though the odds were noticeably stacked against her. She never gave up hope that somewhere on the road of life, love was out there for her. She could not turn away from the path, though tattered and obscure, marked *Love, this way.*

Katherine spent many hours in her rocker as she puffed away on her cigarette. She thought about her girls. They never again mentioned John and what he did; from the time the divorce was final, their lips never spoke his name. In her bemused mind, Katherine thought the whole ordeal must have been forgotten. At least that was the only way she could ease her guilt for bringing that man back into their lives. She should have known better than that. Those kinds of things are never forgotten, and her daughters hadn't. However, Katherine not knowing for sure, and too ashamed to ask, would forever be burdened by her culpable decision.

Katherine wasn't as worried about being on her own this time. Her job afforded her the security she needed to be a single woman; unfortunately, once again she couldn't afford to keep the house she and John bought. That meant another move and a vow to never trust a man again.

Chapter 59

"Mom, I have something to tell you," Katherine's youngest daughter announced. "I'm getting married."

"Married? Barbara, you're so young. You're just going to turn eighteen. You should wait a little while."

"Mom, we've dated for three years; we don't want to wait," Barb explained.

Katherine was the closest to her baby daughter; perhaps she over compensated for the attention she lacked from her father; thus, it was going to be hard to let her go.

"He wants to marry me. Mom, he loves me." Katherine wiped away her tears; that was something she understood.

"You're not going to invite your father, are you?"

"No!"

Katherine retired to her rocker in her newly acquired townhouse. She had a hard time letting her daughters go; each one took a piece of her heart when they left, and Katherine didn't cope well with the emptiness.

At the same time, the girls were born with an astute understanding of their mother's makeup; they knew they would never be able to give her enough attention to satisfy her needs, even if it meant staying home and becoming old maids; it would never be enough. They stood by their mother during her difficult times; at the same time, they would have drowned in her sea of neediness if they hadn't kept some space from her.

Katherine sorely resented being placed second next to her sons-in-law and grandchildren. She even felt slighted as having to share their attention with the new in-laws. Because they refused to put her first, Katherine had the audacity to feel snubbed and unloved by the girls. If they heard it once, they heard it a million times, "I was the one that stayed to take care of you; your father abandoned you." Katherine could strategically place guilt when needed.

Katherine and her family sat in the middle pew at church; it was Mother's Day.

"What are we going to do after church?" Katherine asked.

"We'll have lunch at Rose's and then we have to go to our in-law's."

"Well, what am I going to do all afternoon? You're going to leave me alone?"

"You can come with us," Judy suggested.

"Why do I want to go over there? That's not my family," Katherine retorted.

"Well, we have to go see Chuck's mother today," Judy huffed; Barbara echoed her sister's sentiment.

Katherine pouted through the entire church service. She couldn't be happy that the girls were in church with her, or that they were going to have lunch together; she made sure the girls had a guilt-ridden afternoon at the in-laws.

The ache in Katherine's gut for attention was so strong she couldn't imagine anyone needing it more than her; nobody had to cope with the kind of hurt that she had to; nobody needed love as badly as her; she didn't understand.

Katherine, in all her determination to survive, forged on with life, working at her job and mourning the loss of love. Her bitterness grew more and more impenetrable; time spent with her was genuinely depressing. The girls understood their mother's moods and they overlooked the way she was; unfortunately, for Katherine to keep a friend was totally impossible. It seemed no one could cope with her negativity; most potential friends were seen running away from her in order to save their own sanity. Katherine's inability to recognize her condition kept her from changing it; she was determined to stay in the dark, lonely world that she knew so well.

Katherine got a welcome reprieve from her loneliness. Sam ventured up north to see his daughter; Lillian had passed away a few years back. The fact that Sam wanted to see her was good medicine. While they passed their time with small talk, Katherine had a gnawing in her gut. She wanted so much to confront her dad about their rocky past. She had always said that she wanted to ask him, "Why?" She had grown just resentful enough to finally do it.

"Dad, what went wrong with you and my mother?" Katherine asked. "She never wanted a divorce from you."

"Kat, your mother was messed up. She was very difficult; she had a lot of ..." Sam was interrupted.

"Dad, now don't you say anything against my Mother. I don't want to hear it. Just because she had some problems didn't mean you should have left her, and us. She died of a broken heart because of you," Katherine spit at him like a bad taste that had stayed in her mouth far too long. "And, you shouldn't have let Lillian be so mean to me. Why did you do that?"

Sam was stunned; he needed a moment. "Katherine, I don't remember Lillian being so mean."

"You don't remember! You mean you don't want to remember!" Katherine finally let it all out. "Ask Dennis, he'll tell you that I'm right. Lillian beat me; she wouldn't buy me shoes to go to school. God, dad, you don't remember that?"

Sam remained silent.

"I just want to know why?" Katherine needed an answer to sooth the burn in her soul.

"Katherine, I don't have an answer. I feel bad that you've carried this around for so long. I just don't remember it being that bad."

"Well, it was!"

"I'm sorry, Kat. I always loved you," Sam told his daughter. He was clearly upset with Katherine's revelations.

Katherine didn't care if he was upset; he should be. She didn't say anything more; being able to voice her feeling after so long was a huge release; she felt vindicated; her shoulders felt a little lighter. She bragged to her daughters.

A few years later, Katherine's last unmarried daughter announced her wedding plans. Katherine tried to be happy for her daughter, but all she could think about was now she was really going to be all alone.

For Katherine, the happiest part of Linda's wedding was that Dennis and Alice traveled to Michigan for the celebration; she was thrilled. Even though Katherine and Alice irritated each other with the same old gibes, the visit with her brother was worth it.

One of Katherine's most noticeable attributes was that she always looked younger that her chronological years; however, Dennis thought she looked drawn; her eyes looked weary. The blue wasn't as bright as he remembered. He felt sad for his sister. He had hoped that somehow his sister would have found happiness. His hopes were now deflated with what appeared to be her destiny.

Despite everything, Katherine planned a quaint little reception for Linda and Norm at her townhouse. It wasn't a very big place but it worked out just fine. The small wedding party gathered for punch and tea sandwiches; Katherine had even ordered a beautiful, pink and white, three-tiered wedding cake. She didn't have much money; however, she still managed nicely. She thoroughly loved planning a party and this one was the perfect rouse for her troubled heart; with the wedding celebration and a visit from her brother, she had a purpose.

It was a hot July evening with no air conditioning in the complex; nevertheless, the wedding party, and its hostess, celebrated into the night; the heat never bothered Katherine anyway. Everything was just perfect except for one irritation. One of the guests, a very large man, began eating just about all of the tea sandwiches; Katherine fumed to the point of being irate; she pulled her daughter aside.

"Tell him to stop eating all of the sandwiches. There won't be any for anybody else," Katherine complained. "God, he's just shoveling them in his mouth, one right after the other. Make him stop!"

Katherine and her girls were not big eaters; consequently, she always made just enough food for what was needed for each person. If there were four at home for dinner, she made four pork chops; if there were three for dinner, she made three pieces of cube steak; that went for even if there was a husband in the picture. Consequently, when a larger person was around and ate a lot of food, she saw it as gluttony; it made her sick. This large friend of Norm and Linda's not only made her sick, he also made her mad as hell!

"Tell your friend to stop eating all the sandwiches, damn it; they're almost gone," she angrily whispered to her new son-in-law, who practically ignored her.

That irritated Katherine even more. She decided to take matters into her own hands; she followed the large fellow around the buffet table trying to insert some subtle remarks.

"Save some for everyone else," she picked; she wasn't a very subtle person.

When he paid no attention, she huffed away. Her disgust was evident to everyone, except the large fellow. If it hadn't been so irritating to the mother-of-the-bride, it actually would have been very funny.

When the reception was over, and the bride and groom had left for their honeymoon, and just a bit of clean-up was done, Katherine retreated to her steadfast, blue rocker with a cigarette in one hand and a tissue in the other; she cried. She didn't cry because her last daughter had married or because she worried about her daughter's future; Katherine cried for herself.

Chapter 60

The solitude in which Katherine now found herself was unnatural; the only thing that had kept her going all of those years was raising her girls; now they were gone and she didn't like it. At the same time, losing Linda's rent payment caused even more hardship.

"I'm having a hard time making ends meet," Katherine told her daughter. "The rent is going up and that doesn't leave me very much for the rest of the bills."

"Well, let me talk to Chuck; I'll see it there's anything we can do."

A few days later Katherine got her answer.

"Mom, I think I've come up with a plan to help you. I'll refinance our house to get enough money to buy this little house down the street from us. I can then sell it to you and you can give me payments that you can afford. How's that?" Chuck asked his mother-in-law.

"Can I see the house?"

"Yea, let's go see it," Chuck responded.

"This is a nice little house. I like it. Okay, let's do it." Katherine was excited. The thought that she could afford her own home was empowering. All the papers were signed and Katherine moved into her little solitary world of security; she had a good job, a nice car, a light blue Monte Carlo that she dearly loved; and now, a small house of her very own. The only thing she didn't have was a man; her infamous words resounded to whom ever would listen.

"I don't want a man; I'm done with them. The last thing I need is another man." She finished her lament as she summarized her love life. "My first husband couldn't leave other women alone; my second husband was a Frenchman, but he didn't know how to make love," at this point she paused, "but I don't think a woman ever forgets the man that she had her children with."

There was always a far-off look in her blue eyes, almost hollow, as if she was envisioning her ivory tower now too distant to ever reach again. Katherine tried to ignore the ache in her heart.

In the years that followed, Katherine functioned well as a single, independent woman; she learned to manage the loneliness. The passing of time allowed her to adjust to her new, single lifestyle. She was even able to keep her nerves under control; providing she got the attention from her daughters that she demanded, which they obliged for their own sanity. Unfortunately, it was not always stress free.

"Why are you letting your son choose where we eat? I don't like that place; I'd rather eat there," Katherine complained to Judy, who had taken her mother to Florida with them.

"I don't want that place, mama, it looks too ordinary; this place looks more interesting," Judy's youngest son yelled.

"We're going to go to that restaurant over there, Mom."

"Why?"

What does it matter?" Judy was exasperated with the bickering.

"Because, I wanted to go to the other one! Why does he get to choose the restaurant?" Katherine was used to getting her way; in fact, she was used to having priority over the family group, any group for that matter. She sulked in the back seat like a spoiled child; her need to be catered to had not changed. Consequently, Katherine wasn't about to willingly give up her control.

"So, what are you doing on Saturday?" Katherine asked Barbara.

"I'm going shopping with my mother-in-law."

"What? Why don't you go shopping with me?" Katherine grumbled, full of jealously. The thought that she might loose the only love she really had, the love of her daughters, scared Katherine to death; it showed its ugly head by turning her blue eyes green with envy at their relationships with other mother figures.

"Mom, I go shopping with you all the time. She asked me to go with her; I can't tell her, *no*. She's my mother-in-law."

"She hangs all over you; she acts like she is your mother," Katherine hissed.

"That's not true; that's just her personality," her daughter explained.

"She acts like you're *her* daughter; she doesn't even acknowledge me. Don't I count?" Katherine clearly felt scorned.

Trying to convince their mother that having a relationship with someone else didn't mean they loved her any less was an exhausting undertaking for the girls.

However, that was their mother and they couldn't change her. Loving Katherine didn't mean that you approved of her ways; it meant you understood them.

Despite all of the dysfunctional rousing that went on between Katherine and her girls, the little family unit stayed loyal and dedicated to each other. With no extended family near by, they were all each other had.

Katherine loved her new found independence. She was a petite woman and her small frame was deceiving when it came to handling her own affairs. In all temperatures she mowed her own lawn, raked her own leaves; in all temperatures she shoveled her own snow. The neighbors marveled at this small woman's persistence. When a large snow fell, she shoveled at midnight so it wouldn't be so hard at 5 am when she got up to shovel before going to work. In all of her weaknesses, she was a very tough little lady; that had to be respected.

Near Katherine's tenure of living alone, she had adjusted nicely. She had her own space with no one to tell her what to do, which she wouldn't allow anyway. Her misfortunes in love still weighed heavy on her chest, but not as much as her cigarettes. Katherine's panic attacks had mercifully stayed at bay; however, in her lonely nights, when the buried hurts in her heart worked their way to the surface, she pondered what she did to chase love away, what she did to deserve to end up alone. Another puff on her cigarette dulled the pain.

"Katherine, why don't you come to Bingo with me tonight? I think you'll enjoy it." The invitation came from one of her co-workers.

"Bingo? I don't know. I've never played Bingo before."

"Oh, there's nothing to it. I'll show you what to do," the worker encouraged. "Bring enough money to buy your chips and daubers."

With that, Katherine became quite the player, and a very lucky player at that. It served to fill many lonely hours. In addition to the bingo playing, she and another co-worker occasionally attended the local singles' club. Katherine had dated a few guys from the club from time to time. However, she was always uncomfortable at those kinds of places; they made her feel cheap. The relationships never panned out anyway; the guys in her age group always seemed to be a bunch of moochers. Nothing turned Katherine off more than a moocher. She had worked too hard in her life; she had cut her grass too many times at 98 degrees; she had shoveled her snow too many times at minus 5 to accept a slacker. She was comfortable being her own woman and having her own space; time had been healing.

Katherine answered a knock at the door. Her shock was evident.

"What are you doing here?"

"I thought I would stop by to see you."

"Why? It's been years since we've seen each other," Katherine scolded. "By the way, aren't you married again?" Resentment resonated in her voice.

"Yes, I'm married," he said as he turned up his nose. "It's not much of a marriage, though; it's more like a friendship."

"Oh?" Katherine felt a familiar interest. "Well, what do you want, John?"

"I thought we could go out for coffee; we could talk," he said with the same charm that attracted Katherine the first time they met.

Katherine looked at her twice ex-husband; her mind raced with indecision. Should she go? It's just for coffee; then again, he's married. At the same time, the feeling of delight that someone wanted to be with her crept into her empty soul. John waited for an answer while Katherine hesitated.

"No. I don't think that is a good idea, John."

"Why not? It's just for coffee."

"No. I don't want to; we're apart now, it's for the best that we stay that way," Katherine philosophized.

"I know that you're still mad at me because of what I did. But, you're alone now, no kids around to be a temptation."

"God, John, is that what it takes for you to be good? Besides, you're married," Katherine stressed.

"Well, I can always fix that, if there was a good reason too."

"There's no way I'm going to do that; no way!" Katherine was surprised at his gall.

"Are you sure; just a cup of coffee?"

"No."

As John walked away, Katherine wondered if a cup of coffee would be so bad. Should she go with him to see what he wanted to talk about? It was flattering that he still thought about her; she contemplated it for days.

A few days later John was back at Katherine's front door. "Hi. I thought I'd ask once more. Would you like to go for coffee or something?"

"John, what are you doing? I already said no."

"I thought perhaps you'd changed your mind," John said with his characteristic grin.

"No, I haven't changed my mind. It wouldn't be right. I don't want to get involved. No!"

"Okay; can I call you some time?" John sounded desperate; Katherine noticed, but she stood strong.

"No, John. Let's just leave it alone." Katherine watched John walk back to his Cadillac.

Katherine sat in her blue rocker and had a cigarette. She blew out the smoke with more ease than she had felt in years. With a smile of gratification on her lips, she smashed out her cigarette.

Katherine drove in from playing bingo. She rushed through the door to answer the ringing telephone.

Chapter 61

"Hello."

"Hi Kathy, this is Marianne."

"Hi," Katherine said back.

She was very short when she didn't feel particularly close to the person she was talking to. Marianne was an in-law of one of her daughters, one Katherine didn't particularly like; she was jealous of the closeness Marianne had with her daughter. Some niceties were exchanged and then Marianne got to the point of her call.

"We know a man that belongs to our sportsman club. He's been going to the Saturday night dances at the club for years; now he is widowed. What if I give him your name and phone number? Maybe he could bring you out to the club. I know you like to dance," Marianne explained, excited about the possibility of being a matchmaker.

This caught Katherine totally off guard. She hadn't thought about going out with another man for a very long time. She had resigned herself to that part of her life being over. However, the spark of intrigue started to flicker; the blue in her eyes began to glow.

"Oh?" Katherine questioned in her most curious way.

Marianne proceeded to tell Katherine all about Albert, Bert for short; Katherine listened intently. After some more conversation, Katherine agreed to let Marianne give her number to newly widowed, Bert.

After the women hung up from their conversation, Katherine felt a familiar twinge in her stomach. The muscles in her face perked up to allow a smile; her eyes suddenly brightened up with the thought of possibility. The spring in her step revealed there just might be a little space left in her jar of *Lovers*.

She didn't tell anyone about the potential suitor; however, she was in an awfully good mood for the next few days. In fact, she was in such a good mood that her co-workers wondered what was up with her.

The call finally came. "Hello," Katherine answered.

"Hi, this is Bert. Marianne said I should call you." Bert sounded like a pleasant fellow. "I know this is awkward. I don't know what all Marianne told you, but I'm a widower. My wife died of cancer last year."

"That's not very long ago, Bert. How are you doing?" Katherine asked.

"I'm doing okay. I get lonely, but I have two daughters who help keep me busy."

"Oh, I have four daughters," Katherine informed him; she felt good that they had something in common. "One lives in California, the others live close to me."

"Are you a widow?" Bert asked Katherine.

"No, I'm divorced. Actually, I've been divorced twice," Katherine said. In her mind, since it only involved two men, it was the same as two divorces. There was a brief silence.

"I'm Lutheran; we don't believe in divorce."

Again, there was silence. Katherine didn't know what to make of that. She tried to explain the faults of each man and the circumstances of each break-up; still, Bert seemed hesitant. *Well you shit ass,* Katherine thought; *if you don't like it then don't call back.* They talked a little while longer and then hung up; Katherine was miffed. She didn't like being judged, especially by someone she didn't even know.

There must have been something that attracted Bert to Katherine because he did indeed call back; he invited her to go dancing at the club on Saturday night. He was very upbeat and never mentioned her divorced status. Katherine let her reservations slid and allowed herself to feel positive. She finally told her girls about her new friend.

"That's great, mom. Go and have a good time," the girls encouraged their mother.

They saw a glimmer of happiness in her they hadn't seen in a long time. They sincerely wanted her to find happiness with a nice man; one who would be good to her, who would be a companion for her in her later years.

"Katherine, why don't we meet before Saturday night? After all, we don't want to be stuck for the whole evening if we don't like each other," Bert said in a phone conversation.

"That's probably a good idea," Katherine agreed; she got a kick out of his candidness. He was right of course, they might not feel comfortable together; he simply chose a quirky way to say it. She agreed to meet with him.

"Why don't you come over to my house for dessert? I'll make an apple pie; it never occurred to her to make a carrot cake.

"Sounds good."

Katherine opened the door to reveal a fairly tall, slightly pudgy, 220 pound, half bald man. His big smiled made his cheeks plump up, almost like Santa Clause, and his eyes actually twinkled. He and Katherine were nervous to meet this way, without anyone present to do the introductions.

"Come in, Bert," Katherine shyly invited. "Don't mind my dog, Chanté; he's just a little rambunctious." Katherine had gotten the male, toy poodle to ease her loneliness, and it helped. The apricot pedigree was overly attentive to Bert; in fact, the dog was so enamored that he began to hump Bert's leg immediately. Katherine was disgusted with the dog's behavior; however, not as disgusted as Bert. He tossed Chanté off is leg as Katherine grabbed the dog and threw hi in the bedroom and slammed the door. After her apologies, she and Bert ate apple pie and got relaxed with each other. The date was cemented.

Nervously, Katherine got ready for her night out.

"Mom, have a good time tonight. Now be careful and don't ride with him if he's had too much to drink," Linda told her mother, like all adult children in role reversal.

"Oh, for heavens sake, Linda." Katherine chuckled; she wasn't ready for the reversal just yet.

Bert arrived and off they went to the dance like a couple of teenagers on their first date. It was kind of cute.

Katherine was almost giddy; she had a man interested in her and she was going to get to do one of her favorite things, dance. Once they got to the club, Bert and Katherine greeted Marianne and her husband. They didn't sit with them however, Bert and his wife had always mingled with a different group; all were friends, they simply sat within their own click. It was exceptionally brave of Katherine, being a shy person, to enter a world of strangers. In spite of her timidness, Katherine began to meet the people around the table.

Katherine and Bert danced well together. All the cares of the world could not touch Katherine as she twirled around the floor; she was light and free of her trials and tribulations. Her hair was done up in fashionable curls on top of her head, very princess like, and her blue eyes shown with hope. The pleasure went on until the club emcee announced it was time for their honored tradition.

"Grab your partner; we'll do the Texas Star."

"What's he mean?" Katherine asked the people at her table.

"Square dancing," a couple of people shouted in unison as they jumped up and practically ran to the dance floor. This was obviously a popular activity at the club.

"Square dancing," Katherine exclaimed as she turned up her nose. Of all the dancing she had done over the years, square dancing was her least favorite. It invoked some unpleasant memories and she wasn't happy.

"Come on, Katherine, let's give it a try." Bert grabbed her arm.

Bert and his wife had always square danced; in fact, it was one of their favorite things about the club.

"Well, okay; but I haven't done this in years. I don't particularly like it," Katherine said; Bert ignored her comment.

Unfortunately for Bert, Katherine never made it through the first do-si-do. She headed for the table to get a glass of beer. Square dancing was not her thing and it was never going to become her thing.

"Okay, maybe we can try some other time." Bert tried to understand; all things considered, the evening went very well.

The new couple talked almost daily. They made dates to meet for coffee or dinner; sometimes Bert stopped over to the house for a visit. They were as giddy as young lovers.

Bert lost his wife of forty years to cancer. His two daughters helped care for their dying mother who had been in hospice care in the home. The oldest daughter was quite the anal Lutheran; at times, her actions could raise the question, "is that what Jesus would do?" The younger daughter was far less up tight and more accepting of her father having a girlfriend. Both girls had been very close to their mother, especially the eldest; both simply tolerated their father.

All and all, things were going well for Katherine and Bert. After only a few months, Katherine began to drop hints to her daughters about possible marriage. Katherine didn't believe in wasting time on dating. "Long engagements are a waist of time. If you love each other, then you go ahead and get married." That had always been her philosophy.

Bert and Katherine decided the girls should meet; a get-acquainted cookout was held. Katherine's girls were not opposed to their mother possibly getting married again; their non-judgmental personalities accepted Bert and his daughters into their lives. Bert's youngest girl felt pretty much the same way; however, the oldest daughter was terribly unwelcoming. The very idea of another woman, and her children, being in her mother's house angered her; she was furious with her dad. In addition, she was sure the new girlfriend was only interested in her dad for his money.

Bert had retired from one of the auto companies and lived comfortably on his pension. He had been in the stock program, contributing since the beginning of his employment; he had *a lot* of money. Naturally, Bert's daughter didn't know Katherine well enough to know that she would never marry a man for his money; love and companionship was what she was after; money was only needed for existence. However, the oldest daughter wasn't about to give Katherine the chance to prove that her intentions were honorable.

The daughters were amiable with each other during the few times they were together; conversely, they avoided cementing any real ties. Katherine's girls had learned that closeness was a very risky business; casual friendship meant easier parting of the ways; Bert's girls were simply not interested.

Katherine was used to her daughters staying out of her relationships, but Bert's girls were right in the middle of things. Whether they meant to or not, they were rather cruel to Katherine. The oldest one, and clearly the one having the hardest time, never missed the opportunity to inform Katherine of some of her dad's less attractive qualities.

"You know, Katherine, my dad isn't the easiest person to live with. You'll see," she snarled. "He gave my mother a very hard time. He had to always be in charge; he had to always tell her what to do, and he was always tight with his money. We had to sleep upstairs in the attic with no heat. He was afraid he would have to spend some of his precious money. And another thing, he really only wants you for sex."

Katherine was taken aback by all of this new information. Could he really be that bad? He didn't seem to be such a nasty person. She wondered if the daughter was simply mad at her dad for having a girlfriend or was there some truth to her accusations. Katherine tried to give her new boyfriend the benefit of the doubt.

The younger daughter was easier to get along with and Katherine was more comfortable conversing with her. However, when her dad wasn't looking, she would echo the same sentiments as her sister, just not as hateful.

"Katherine, my dad can be difficult. I hope you take some time to get to know him. My sister told me that she mentioned his sexual appetite. Well, it's true."

These comments had Katherine concerned; however, the dating continued.

"Katherine, why don't we get married this summer?"

"This summer? That's awfully soon, Bert," Katherine pondered.

"I know, but we're not getting any younger. So, why not?" Bert hugged Katherine; it felt good to have someone hold her close again. At that moment,

Katherine forgot about all the tid-bits Bert's daughters had so generously relayed to her. She allowed herself to envision being loved again; she stayed true to her philosophy.

"Okay, let's get married."

Bert contacted his minister and quickly got the required three premarital meetings scheduled.

"Reverend, like I told you on the phone, Katherine has been divorced twice; will God forgive her for that?" Bert wasted no time addressing his concerns; if he knew there had been four divorces, all hell would have broken loose. "Where does that leave me? If I marry a divorced woman, does that affect how God sees me?"

Katherine glared at Bert. She couldn't believe what she heard; she was horrified.

"Katherine, tell me about the problems with your first two husbands," Rev. Miller asked; he wanted details. She figured the details were her business, but she gave them up.

"Well, my first husband ran around with other women; he neglected me and the children. My second husband paid me no attention," Katherine explained. She didn't tell the minister the whole truth about John, which she should have done in her own defense; however, she was unable to speak the words. "Both divorces were granted on the grounds of mental cruelty."

"And did you try to work out your problems?" the Rev. asked, rather condescendingly.

"Yes, I tried to work out my problems. Both times I tried; I stayed in the marriages for years and tried to work things out." Katherine defended her life; and got more irked by the minute.

Although God may be the almighty judge, Bert and Rev. Miller took on the job with regards to Katherine's fitness to marry a devout Lutheran. She left the meetings feeling guilty and shamed. She didn't like that; Lord knows she had enough guilt to deal with, she didn't need anyone to validate it for her; she didn't need that degradation. Bert and the Reverend were the first ones who had dared to confront her so blatantly about her mistakes; she was livid.

"What the hell was that all about?" she confronted Bert when they got outside.

"I told you, we don't believe in divorce. The Reverend wanted to make sure you had a good reason; he wanted assurance that it wouldn't happen again."

"I wasn't the only one in the marriage, you know. Was I supposed to stay and take their crap?"

"Well, yes; you're supposed to stay and work it out," Bert preached.

"I tried to work it out. They wouldn't try." Katherine pouted all the way home; the nerve of these two chauvinists.

Katherine's wedding date approached; Bert seemed nervous; he drank more. Katherine still had her two beers at night and only moderate social drinking. Up to the engagement, Bert had only drank moderately too. However, something was different. She attributed his increased drinking and edginess to being a nervous groom, which she thought was not uncommon.

As Bert got more secure in their relationship, he began to let his guard down; he wasn't the restrained boyfriend anymore. He was much more boisterous, especially after he had a large amount of alcohol.

"What's wrong?" Katherine asked Bert as he came barreling in the house late for a home cooked meal; he was obviously agitated.

"I don't know about your divorces. I don't know if I can marry a divorced woman," Bert slurred. "Divorce is a sin; you're a sinner!"

Katherine was stunned by his behavior.

"My wife and I were able to have a good marriage. We didn't get a divorce when things didn't go well. She was a good woman." Bert taunted his fiancé.

Katherine tried to settle him down; however, he was too obnoxious to listen, he continued his jabs.

"Bert, just go home. You're not going to stay here and talk to me that way. Just go home," Katherine ordered.

Bert finally said all that he wanted to say; he left Katherine's house with the dinner still on the table, uneaten and cold.

Katherine retired to her rocker; her staggered mind spun in circles. "Now what do I do?" she mumbled. "I can't believe he did this."

Bewildered, Katherine couldn't talk about the incident for days. Finally, she voiced her concern to her daughter.

"Mom, you don't have to get married right away. You can postpone the wedding for a while. Don't rush into this," Linda told her mother.

"Everything is already planned; I've even ordered the damn invitations." Katherine was disgusted she had to deal with the new situation.

"Well, it's better to waste the invitations than to make a big mistake, isn't it?"

"I don't know; I hate to change all the plans. Maybe once we get the wedding behind us he'll settle down," Katherine contemplated.

"Mom, I don't think you should take that chance. I would postpone it for a while; give yourselves time to get to know each other better. Bert's only been widowed a year; maybe he needs more time." Linda pleaded with her mother.

"I'd be too embarrassed to postpone the wedding." Katherine wrung her hands with uncertainty.

"Mom, you have to find out about this drinking thing; you have to know if it's a problem before you marry him."

"He's probably just nervous. He's so damned worried about my divorces."

"And that's another thing. If he doesn't like it, why does he want to marry a divorced woman? You can't let him judge you that way."

"He says he'll get over it; he says he loves me." Katherine's inability to let go of the one thing she sought couldn't be argued with.

"I don't know, Mom; I think you should wait a while."

Katherine worried and fretted for days about Bert's change in personality; she even tried to talk to him about it. He insisted he was sorry for his behavior and that it was just premarital nerves. His daughter's warnings swirled around in Katherine's head. "You don't really know our dad," echoed in her ears.

Katherine was so torn; should she heed the advice of her daughters and postpone the wedding; should she believe Bert when he said that it wasn't his normal behavior?

"Damn it," Katherine mumbled to herself. She rocked, smoked and thought. She was irritated that she was put in this position; all she wanted was to be with someone. Her stomach hurt.

Even though Katherine was leery about the way Bert showed himself that day, she simply couldn't cancel. She gave her groom the benefit of the doubt and the wedding plans went on as scheduled. At the same time, Katherine's hopeful smile had changed to a cautious grin.

Linda was not happy with her mother's decision.

"Mom, I'm not saying that you should never marry Bert; just wait a little longer; get to know him better, that's all. Make sure his drinking is not a real problem."

"We already have the church and the hall scheduled; we have the food ordered. Everything is all set." Katherine reiterated that she couldn't call it off; she would simply be too humiliated.

"So what, mom, it's better to be humiliated than to get into something that could be really bad," Linda counseled. "And another thing; look how Bert talked you into selling your house. You really didn't want to do that." Katherine could see that her daughter was exasperated as she continued to lecture. "And worse than that, he told you that you couldn't bring Chanté into his house. That was just plain cruel."

Katherine had actually wanted to keep the house and rent it out; a survival plan in case the benefit she awarded Bert didn't hold up. Bert didn't like that; he saw it as an obstacle in the way of his dominance.

Demanding that she get rid of her dog was terribly inconsiderate. Chanté had been a source of comfort for her during some very lonely times. How could Bert expect her to simply give him away? It was indeed cruel.

Doubts swirled around in Katherine's head; however, something wouldn't let her cancel. She couldn't miss the opportunity that this marriage might work out, that she just might have love in her life; that she just might not have to be alone. She was willing to sacrifice some things very dear to her in order give it a chance, to possibly fix the tumult of her past, even vindicate it. She looked for a good home for Chanté.

Katherine went home to an empty house; her daughter's words resonated in her head as she tossed out Chanté's chewed up bed. "Mom, don't do it!"

Chapter 62

"Here's a nice one," Judy said, as she held up a floor length, blue, lace sheath. Katherine had decided to go formal for this wedding.

"I don't know." Katherine turned up her nose at the dress. Judy was surprised; after all, it was her favorite color. Katherine continued to shift through the racks of dresses. A pink chiffon frock caught her eye.

The dress fit Katherine perfectly. The empire waist accented a flowing skirt; the bodice was lace and the dress came with a matching lace bolero jacket, which tied at the neckline with a dainty bow. With Katherine's hair and eye coloring, and her Flame red lips, she looked pretty as a picture. She made her decision; yes, this time she would go with pink; maybe it would change her luck.

Katherine continued to make all the arrangements; Bert gave her pretty much carte blanche. However, true to his daughter's warnings, he made Katherine split the costs; she agreed.

The hall was rented and a hundred guests were invited. Katherine was finally going to have the big wedding she always dreamed about. She tried to cover up her doubts as she fussed with all of the little details; it worked. The wedding was going to be exactly what she always wanted.

Katherine's past weddings were simple, the bride, the groom, and an attendant for each, no formality involved. This time, Katherine was going to have it all. Judy was the matron-of-honor, Bert's brother was the best man; the rest of the girls were matrons-of-honor with their husbands as the groomsmen, which amounted to ten in all. To add the final, formal touch, Katherine's son-in-law, Chuck, walked her down the aisle. A yearning inside Katherine had finally been put to rest. It was the wedding of her dreams.

The wedding guests gazed as Katherine walked past them; she was beautiful in flowing, pink chiffon with her bouquet of white carnations tipped in pink. Her big smile revealed the hope that was in her heart.

The guests looked on as the bride and groom exchange vows; they watched Bert place a beautiful, sparkling, 1 ct., round cut, diamond ring on Katherine's finger; she swooned with enchantment. Her love of the gem had grown in its passion, and this stone was a fine addition to her collection. The couple kissed and they were off to celebrate.

The bride and groom, along with the rest of the wedding party, sat at the bridal table; Katherine gazed around the reception hall thrilled that all of this was for her. She watched as the D.J. shifted through his romantic ballads to start off the dancing; she was anxious for the bridal dance. Katherine had chosen *After the Lovin'* by Englebert Humperdink for that occasion; she couldn't wait for the spotlight to be totally on her.

The D.J. stepped up to the microphone. "Can I have the happy couple up on the dance floor, please?"

Katherine and her groom moved to the center of the floor. She was on cloud nine as she twirled around the room; for the moment she forgot about her misgivings; she was lost in the euphoria of finally having her very own bridal dance, her very own choice of song, her very own big wedding. It took her five trips to the altar, but she finally got it.

"So, where are you two going on your honeymoon?" one of the guest asked.

"Hawaii," Katherine answered, elated as the words left her mouth. She had dreamed about going to Hawaii for a long time; she couldn't wait to leave.

Even though she had a significant fear of flying, she wasn't going to let that get in the way of realizing part of her dream. She was sixty years old and she figured this would probably be her last chance to have all the things that would make her happy. Nothing was going to get in her way, not even her aviophobia.

The newlyweds stayed until the last guest left. Bert had not over indulged, which pleased Katherine; the entire evening was a delightful success. Katherine was optimistic when they got to their hotel room.

"Wasn't that a wonderful reception?" Katherine asked her new husband.

"Yes, it was real nice," Bert said as he got into bed. Katherine hadn't even had time to put on her new negligé when Bert was ready to collect his conjugal rights.

Katherine had always been a willing bride, and she was going to have to get a lot more willing.

Bert was exceptionally quiet during the flight over the Pacific; however, Katherine didn't think much about it; she was too busy making sure the plane stayed in the air; she had a whisky sour to calm her nerves.

Hawaii came into view; Katherine peered down at the breath-taking, blue water, which surrounded the island. She could hardly believe she was actually there. Bert didn't bother to look; he had already been to Hawaii. He and his first wife had gone there on a vacation just a couple of years before she died.

"Wow, look at that view!" Katherine exclaimed.

"Mary liked to sit by the window and look at the water," Bert said with a hint of guilt in his voice. Katherine stared at him; she didn't like the mention of his dead wife on *her* honeymoon.

From the instant they stepped off the plane, Bert and Katherine were not alone. They rode in the limousine to the hotel, Mary rode with them; they walked around in the hotel lobby, Mary walked with them; Katherine clung to Bert's arm, Mary clung to the other one. Bert couldn't hold back as they toured the city.

"I remember that restaurant," he said, "Mary loved that one."

Katherine looked at her new husband. Again, she let the remark slide; however, her irritation started to simmer.

"Oh, I remember that park. Mary loved to sit there and watch the waves."

"Bert, why are you telling me that? Why are you talking about Mary? I don't want to know about all the things you and your first wife did."

"Well, I can't help but remember when we were here," Bert said inconsiderately.

"If that don't beat all; we're here on our honeymoon and all you can do is talk about your first wife."

"My only wife," Bert said under his breath.

Katherine stopped in her tracts. "What?

"Nothing. I'm just pointing some things out to you that Mary and I did."

"Well, I don't want to know what you did with your dead wife."

"Stop referring to her as my dead wife."

The excitement, which Katherine had been filled with, was gone; Bert had started her honeymoon as an insensitive bastard. Katherine was jealous beyond words that all Bert thought about was Mary; her blue eyes took on a sea, green glow; even her skin had a green hue. She no longer felt like a happy bride; and she certainly wasn't interested in any ménage à trios, even if the third person was a ghost.

Their first night in paradise was strained to say the least. Trying to get in a romantic mood after such a shaky start was gong to take some extreme concentration. At the same time, Bert's testosterone allowed him no trouble; he was ready. His bride being perturbed was not a good enough reason to deny him; he became quite forceful.

With Katherine's petite frame, it was easy to over power her. She wasn't used to such aggressiveness, neither of her other husbands had been that way. Even though Miles had been passionately assertive, force was never involved. Miles and John understood *no* means *no*; Bert didn't; he forced himself upon Katherine.

Katherine finally understood what his daughters had been talking about when they shot their warnings at her. Bert's sexual appetite was insatiable, and romance had nothing to do with it.

"Bert, let's take a break. Your weight is heavy on me."

"Well, that's no problem. We can try some different positions."

Katherine didn't like the sound of that. She didn't want anything to do with different positions. She managed to get Bert to take a break; however, he wasn't happy.

After a few nights of experiencing Bert's ability in the bedroom, he, like John, didn't measure up to Miles. Katherine was mindful as she compared Bert's lovemaking to Miles'; she was sure Bert had compared her to Mary.

It was a terrible shame that the rhythmic sway of the palm trees were ignored, that the warm, gentle breeze, which blew off the Pacific, was not felt. Their irritability prevented them from enjoying the infectious beat of the island music, and from smiling at Don Ho's slightly intoxicated sounding rendition of *Tiny Bubbles*. Unfortunately, all the delights and romance of paradise eluded the couple. They went about sightseeing, minus the thrill.

"Let's buy a case of these grapefruits. We can divide them between the girls," Katherine suggested as they walked around a tourist market.

"Do you really want to get that? It looks bulky to take back on the plane," Bert protested.

"Yes, I would like to take some back. I know the girls like them," Katherine insisted. Bert gave into Katherine's wish and grabbed the flimsy box of the citrus.

As they walked back to the hotel, the poorly fastened box burst open and grapefruits rolled all over the place, all over the sidewalk, into the street, everywhere. Kindly bystanders offered to help pick them up.

Katherine was so easily embarrassed that this episode threw her into a tizzy. Bert was so easily riled that he became quite agitated.

"God, what a mess. You weren't holding the box very well."

"This wouldn't have happened if you hadn't wanted the stupid grapefruits in the first place," Bert yelled back.

Katherine's flare for the dramatic kicked in and the only way she could handle this spectacle was to flee the scene. Away she dashed; she headed for the hotel by herself. It was not wise for Katherine to take off in a strange city all alone; however, the need to make a point did not always allow her the prudence to think clearly.

She walked briskly; her anger had her wound up. She was more than angry; she was hurt from Bert's continual reference to his first wife; Katherine's over reaction to the grapefruits simply allowed her a release.

"How dare him constantly talk about his first wife?" Katherine talked to herself as she raced from stop sign to stop sign. She never imagined her honeymoon would turn out like this. In her fantasy, it was going to be the most wonderful honeymoon she ever had; it was supposed to prove her misgivings were wrong.

"Huh." Katherine fought back her tears as she walked along unfamiliar streets. Her feet started to hurt. She got turned around and began to get frightened; she couldn't find the hotel.

Katherine's breathing became rapid. "Where is the Paradise Palms Hotel," she asked a souvenir stand clerk. Katherine was pointed in the right direction and arrived back at the hotel long after Bert had; of course an argument ensued.

Katherine resorted to one of her spiteful ploys to punish her badly behaved lover: she withheld sexual favors until she felt he had learned his lesson. She had used this trick many times with Miles and John; however, little did she know just how dangerous this maneuver would be with Bert.

It was the second night that Katherine had rejected her husband.

"I'm not sleeping on the couch again, damn it," Bert yelled.

"You're not sleeping with me until you can behave yourself. God, we're on our honeymoon and look how you are acting. You're supposed to be nice to me," Katherine complained. She slammed the bedroom door.

Bert began to drink; he talked and yelled incessantly all night. He shot hurtful remarks at Katherine; he was determined to claim her attention. Short of busting down the door, he kept Katherine awake by reaching into the broken box and throwing grapefruits at the bedroom door.

"Open that damn door," Bert shouted; he hurled another piece of fruit, which splattered juice all over the walls.

"Stop that!" Katherine screamed. "I'm going to call the hotel manager if you don't stop."

It was a nasty scene; instead of having beautiful dreams about paradise, Katherine suffered with nightmares about the horrible mistake she just may have made.

Morning dawned and the newly weds agreed to try to salvage what they could of their honeymoon; they even managed to share a bed again; but sadly, happiness was not part if it.

All Katherine's dreams for the future had been shattered with the way Bert had acted. Instead of making memories with his new wife, he relived his old ones with Mary. Of all the places for him to miss his first wife, of all the places for him to realize his guilt of being with another woman, during their honeymoon was the ultimate blow; Katherine was devastated. The honeymoon that started in paradise, ended in hell.

Their plane ride home was silent. Katherine's sadness was obvious as she sucked on a mint; she wanted a cigarette in the worse way. Beginning a marriage with contention was depressing. It was hard enough to make a relationship work; having one that needed fixed from the start felt too much like being in a battle with expendable soldiers; and she didn't want to be the one left lying in the field. Katherine wasn't sure how long she could keep up the fight.

However, one thing about Katherine, she was a fighter; she wasn't ready to give up yet. While the hum of the jet engines calmed her anger, a thought came to her. Maybe she and Bert should talk to the minister; it might help. Katherine was always willing to get some help. She had actually dragged Miles and John to a marriage counselor. She didn't give up easily.

Once they got home and settled in, Katherine found the right time to suggest her idea. Bert hit the ceiling.

"No way, no how."

"I think it might help us," Katherine insisted.

"No! I don't need any damn marriage counseling, especially from the minister. You can forget it, bitch."

It was hard on Katherine being called names so blatantly; she wasn't used to it. She decided to forget her idea for the time being.

Bert started drinking excessively from that moment on. To Katherine's grave misfortune, a large amount of alcohol turned him into Mr. Hide; and, he was just as ugly as Stevenson's character.

Katherine's dislike for drinkers only added fuel to Bert's fire by nagging him about it. Their personalities clashed worse than the Titans and neither had the tenacity to solve the riddle.

Many mornings Katherine went to the cafeteria with no sleep. As difficult as it was, her job was one security she was not willing to give up.

"I've got to get to bed, Bert. I've got to work tomorrow," Katherine said as Bert continued to suck down the beer.

"Go ahead, I'm not stopping you."

Katherine tried to go to sleep; her eyes popped open with the sound of tapping on her window.

"What the hell?" She looked out her bedroom window and saw a man clad only in his tee shirt and briefs run away. Katherine lay back down only to be disturbed again, and again.

"What the hell are you doing?" Katherine flung opened the bedroom door.

"I'm not going to let you sleep. I don't care if you have to work," Bert slurred.

"You're crazy!" Katherine shouted as she retreated to the bedroom. She lay in her loneliness feeling sad; all she wanted was to be happy with someone; to be loved by someone. She didn't know what to do about this bizarre man.

Bert slept while Katherine tried to drag herself through the day. She could do that as a younger woman; however, being in her sixties made it that much harder to function with no sleep. She may have accused Miles and John of mental abuse, which turned out to be a bunch of legal jargon; she now was being subjected to real mental abuse first hand.

Katherine's unsettled state of mind was challenged even more. She picked up the telephone to here Linda on the other end.

"Mom?"

Katherine heard urgency in her daughter's voice. "What's wrong?"

"Dad died last night."

There was silence on the other end. Katherine was stunned. *Dead*, she thought. She couldn't believe Miles was dead.

"What happened?"

"Apparently, his wife went to bed and left him sitting in his easy chair watching football. She found him the next morning just where she left him, already cold. His heart simply stopped," Linda explained.

"His heart stopped? He was only sixty years old."

"I know; it's too bad. I'll call you when I find out the arrangements."

Katherine felt a strange concern; an unexpected sadness.

"Maybe I'll go to the funeral home with my daughters." Katherine discussed her thought with Bert. "But, I don't want to see Violet, Miles' last wife."

The ugly, green-eyes monster in Bert shot obnoxious remarks at Katherine.

"Why do you want to go to the funeral home? Do you want to see your old lover?" Bert disgustedly sneered.

"Don't be ridiculous. I would like to visit with Lula; I'll probably never see her again," Katherine explained.

"I could tell you still loved him; I knew it all along."

"How?"

"By the way you talked about him; it was obvious from the start." Bert guzzled down another beer. "Why don't you just climb up in the casket with him?"

"You're sick!"

There was no better way to describe Bert than just plain ugly! Katherine didn't know how to cope with this kind of man. She wondered how he could even think to say the kinds of things he would say. It sickened her.

Katherine had an unexpectedly hard time coping with the death of her one true love; in her alone time she thought about Miles. Things were so rocky with Bert, that for the first time, she thought only about Miles' attributes; his faults paled next to Bert's. Time had softened Katherine's memory; she missed Miles.

She never went to the funeral home; she never said goodbye to Miles, and she never had closure with his family. Miles died on October 5; a few more wrinkles showed up in Katherine's face by the time he was laid to rest.

Bert's irritation flourished as he taunted Katherine. "Why don't you get rid of that damn car?" He vehemently hated her Chevrolet.

"No. I'm not going to get rid of it; I love my car."

"It's a piece of junk. GM products are a piece of junk." Bert went on and on about the slug of a car until Katherine covered her ears and tried to block out his spitefulness.

"Don't cover your ears. Listen to me," Bert shouted as he grabbed Katherine's hands and tried to lower them from her ears. A scuffle ensued.

"Ouch, you're hurting my fingers." Her hands had been bad with arthritis for years, having them squeezed hurt like hell.

"Look what you did to my mother's ring. You bent it right on my finger; I can't even get if off."

Bert ignored her and sought refuge in the basement. Katherine struggled with lotion to pry her bent ring off her finger. It finally slid past her swollen knuckle. Katherine sat at the kitchen table with a cup of coffee. She needed to talk to someone.

"Mom, you should think about leaving Bert. You have to think about your safety." The girls were furious with Bert.

"I don't know what to do. Maybe I can get him to go to AA; that might help." Leaving had crossed her mind a time or two; however, it was so early in the marriage, she thought she would give it more time. She didn't want to be divorced for the fifth time. "I'll talk to Dr. Cash tomorrow. He runs the AA group at the hospital."

"Well, you have to decide what you want to do, but I don't like it," Katherine's daughter told her.

Katherine felt a twinge of optimism as she thought her idea might help them work things out.

"No way in hell am I going to AA! Forget it!" Bert shouted.

"I think it might help. You have a drinking problem," Katherine bravely shouted back.

"What are you talking about, you bitch? I don't have a drinking problem; I didn't have any problems until I married you," Bert yelled. "There's no way I'm going to AA. You can forget it." Bert ranted and raved all night as he called her every name he could think of.

Katherine decided not to pressure Bert on that subject; he became too volatile when she brought up the subject. However, the following year of staying together in their antagonistic turmoil weighed heavily on their health. Katherine had always been complemented on her youthful looks; to her dismay, all the wrinkles that had kept from gradually showing on her face, like most people, began to surface all at once. Her increased anxiety and lack of sleep only added to her rapid aging, and it was no doubt starting to creep into her arteries.

As for Bert, he was rushed to the hospital with chest pains.

Chapter 63

"Katherine," the cafeteria manager shouted, "you have to get to the emergency room right away. Your husband has been brought in."

"What? Is he okay?"

"I don't know; go ahead, you can leave. I'll cover for you."

Katherine rushed through the halls and burst into the waiting room.

"Where's Bert?" Katherine asked the desk nurse.

"He's been taken to radiology for some tests. He'll be back soon."

While Katherine waited for her husband to come back, and some word from the doctor, she called Bert's daughters. They hurried right over. Katherine greeted her stepdaughters at the emergency room door; while the youngest hugged Katherine, the older one simply glared at her stepmother.

"What happen to dad?"

"I don't know yet, I haven't had a chance to talk to the doctor."

The three women sat in the waiting room; they were quiet as they anticipated the appearance of the doctor. Very few words were exchanged between the females. Finally, the doctor summoned the women to Bert's triage cubicle.

"Bert has had a mid heart attack. Luckily, the tests show there was little to no damage to the heart muscle. However, a lot of things can affect the heart; his weight is a factor; stress can also be a problem. Does Bert have a lot of worry or stress?" the doctor interrogated. Before Katherine could say a word, the oldest daughter let loose.

"It's all her fault," she screamed and pointed her finger at Katherine. Tears streamed down her face. "It's all her fault that my father is in this hospital having a heart attack; the gold digging bitch!"

Katherine was stunned. The doctors and nurses were stunned. The whole surrounding area was deathly quiet. Once Katherine got past the shock, she became embarrassed; everyone was embarrassed for her. Bert lay on the emergency room gurney and never told his daughter to stop attacking his wife like that. Perhaps he felt the same way.

"Well, like I said," the doctor tried to gain some control, "I don't think there is any damage, but I would like to keep him over night for observation and a few more tests." The doctor ordered a room for Bert.

Katherine had worked at the hospital for a long time and she knew just about everyone who worked there; she was humiliated.

"How dare her say that to me. I didn't cause Bert's heart attack," Katherine told one of the nurses. "If anyone should have a heart attack, it should be me!" It was all Katherine could do to hold back the tears.

"Bert, I'll be up to see you when you get to your room, okay?" Katherine wasn't going to stay there and be accused like that; she went back to her job to close up for the day.

Katherine wasn't used to such outbursts from children; she had plenty of name calling from men, but she had never suffered an attack like that from a child or stepchild. She was totally incensed. But more than that, again she was on the receiving end of being belittle Whatever she did, whatever she said, it all came back to slap her in the face. She simply didn't understand it.

After she closed up the cafeteria, she had a cigarette before going to see Bert. As she puffed away, she sat quietly alone. That wasn't the first time she had been attacked in a hospital and blamed for something; it wasn't the first time she had a finger pointed at her and told it was her fault. She couldn't understand why everyone always turned on her.

Katherine took one last drag on her cigarette before she smashed it out in the ashtray and went up to the fifth floor. She was mad but she tried to contain her feelings; she knew she shouldn't confront Bert about his witch of a daughter right then; after all, he just had a heart attack.

As Katherine entered the hospital room, she was surprised to see Bert's younger daughter still there.

"Kathy, don't mind my sister. She's just upset, that's all."

Katherine gave her a look to let her know she did not appreciate being embarrassed.

"I'm upset too. She didn't need to attack me like that, and right in front of everyone. She should be ashamed of herself; she's thinks she's such a good Christian."

Bert still said nothing about the scene in the emergency room; however, he said plenty.

"I don't see why I have to stay in this stinking hospital. I'm okay. Those doctors don't know what the hell they are talking about."

"That's not nice, Bert. These doctors are good. They're just trying to help you," Katherine defended. "You'd better listen to them."

"Huh, I don't have to listen to them; I'll do what I want."

The girls went home while Katherine stayed a little longer to keep Bert company; although, she wasn't in the mood to be a very good companion. She was still pissed about the emergency room incident. Bert knew she was upset; however, he still did not chastise his daughter. Like it or not, that let Katherine know where she stood when it came to a disagreement in the family. That was not good.

Katherine took Bert home the next day; as they walked up the back steps and into the kitchen, Katherine got an eerie feeling of déjàvu; Bert walked past the trash can and threw away the pills.

"I'm not taking any damn heart pills. Those doctors don't know what in the hell they are talking about," Bert grumbled.

"You're not the doctor, Bert. You'd better listen to them,"

"I said, I'm not taking any pills," Bert snapped back.

Katherine didn't say anything else; she simply watched this stupid man take a huge risk with his life. She could have nagged at him to take the pills; however, she made the decision, and a good one, not to say anything about his heart problem or taking the meds. It only would have caused more trouble; besides, if he wanted to die, he could.

However, their arguing continued. Finally, Katherine convinced Bert that a visit with Rev. Miller might help. She actually threatened that she would leave him if he didn't. With Bert's aversion to divorce, he finally agreed.

Since Bert and Katherine had not attended church regularly, the first part of their meeting was spent catching the minister up on all that had happened. Bert's told about his heart attack and Katherine recapped their dreadful honeymoon.

"The whole time he talked about his dead wife," Katherine complained. Then she got into an area where Bert didn't want to go.

"I don't have a drinking problem," Bert screamed back at Katherine.

"Bert," The Reverend scolded.

"I don't know why we're having these problems. Mary and I never had these problems," Bert said to the minister.

There was a long pause and a raised eyebrow from Pastor Miller. "Now Bert, you know that's not entirely true."

Katherine's head straightened up. Finally, some vindication!

Bert looked sheepishly at the floor; he avoided both the eyes of the minister and Katherine; he didn't want to acknowledge that the minister was well informed about his and Mary's relationship; what's more, Bert hated that Katherine was going to hear about his sorted past.

"Bert, you know that you and Mary had your problems. This isn't all Katherine's fault."

Katherine's posture relaxed as a heavy portion of guilt lifted off her back. Finally, someone agreed it wasn't all her fault. After that acknowledgement was made, the minister moved on to suggestions for the couple to try to make things better in their relationship. Interestingly enough, most of the suggestions were geared toward Bert. The pastor knew the real Bert; he took no exception to what Katherine hold him.

"Now Bert, it takes time to adjust to a new relationship; Katherine is not Mary. You have to be tolerant; let Katherine run the house, let her shop where she wants; you must be patient," Rev. Miller encouraged. Bert looked at the minister and gave a slight gesture that he would try. Bert had not said anything back to the minister in his own defense; at the same time, he hadn't agreed with him either.

When they got to the car, Bert let lose. "He doesn't know what the hell he is talking about. Mary and I did just fine," Bert yelled; he wasn't going to admit that he was just as much an asshole with his first wife as he was with his second.

Katherine let him vent; she knew she was the lesser of the two problems. Bert continued to fuss while Katherine went to answer the phone.

"Katherine, this is Dennis. I have some bad news. Dad died last night."

"What happened?" Katherine gasped.

"Dad and Stan were ready to get into the boat and go fishing when dad dropped dead right there on the dock, his fishing pole still in his hand," Dennis explained.

"What are the arrangements?" Katherine was hardly able to believe that her dad was dead. Of all of life's dirty tricks, death was the hardest for her to cope with. Dennis gave her the arrangements and she and Bert planned a trip down south.

The drive down was hard on Katherine; she relived all of her troubled times while growing up with her dad and Lillian. Bert didn't understand, nor did he care.

They arrived in Chattanooga the night before Sam's funeral. That evening she introduced Bert to the family; everyone had a very nice first impression of him; however, so had Katherine. The next day at the funeral, Katherine sat in the front row with her two brothers and two half-brothers; she cried her eyes out. All of her hurts, all of her disappointments, and all of her remorse rolled down her cheeks and dropped onto her lap. The father she wanted to love, and she wanted to love her, was gone. Her four brothers were surprised at her sobbing lament; however, they knew from whence it came.

After the Williamson children laid their father to rest, they managed to have a nice visit and everyone got better acquainted with Bert. The family seemed to like him. Katherine bit her lip and thought *if they only knew*. She wasn't going to tell them what he was really like; however, she resented the good impression he made.

Katherine and her brothers gathered at their father's house for one last time. A picture on the mantle caught Katherine's eye. As she got closer she was disgusted to see that it was a picture of Lillian lying in her casket. Sam had taken the picture and he pined in front of it daily. Katherine remembered having such a hard time with her stepmother that she couldn't understand how her dad could love this woman so much; it wasn't within her sphere of understanding. Even though she thought it was morbid, she found herself wishing that she had a man who loved her enough to gaze at her from beyond the grave. It was a love she would never understand, or know.

Katherine wanted to see Aunt Etta before she left Tennessee; however, she was leery. Before her and Bert left Michigan, Katherine had called her aunt to see how she was doing. Aunt June answered the phone.

"Katherine," June screeched in a much higher pitch than normal. "We had to put Ettie in a home. She doesn't know who she is. It's a shame, Katherine, such a shame. She doesn't know anything."

"What's the matter with her?"

"The doctors say its hardening of the arteries. It's terrible, Katherine, just terrible."

Katherine had been upset for days after learning of her aunt's condition. Now she didn't know if she wanted to see her like that. She thought perhaps she wanted to remember her aunt as the loving caregiver that hugged her, smiled at her, read Bible passages to her, and sang as she taught the piano to her; Katherine was torn.

"Katherine, there might not be another chance to see Aunt Etta. You'd better go see her now," Dennis encouraged.

"I know, Dennis, but I don't know if I want to see her that way." Katherine grimaced.

"I think you should visit her," Dennis said again; Katherine finally gave in.

She stayed only a couple minutes when she saw that her dear aunt was not aware of anyone in the room. She couldn't stay any longer and see this wonderful lady, who had given up a life of love to become an old maid for her, who was the closest thing to an angel she would ever know, laying unaware in the nursing home bed. Katherine walked away, her eyes bulged with tears of apology.

Bert and Katherine arrived back in Michigan with the stress in their relationship still alive and well. A few more trips to the minister's office afforded some drastic attempts to save the marriage. Rev. Miller suggested that Bert sell his and Mary's house and he and Katherine buy one that would be theirs together. That suggestion staggered Bert; he never thought about selling his house. He would have to think about that.

However, the more Katherine threatened to leave if things didn't change, the more Bert considered the move. They found a very nice brick, ranch in Wayne and very close to the hospital where Katherine still worked. Not only was Katherine happy that she did not have to live with Mary's ghost anymore, she was thrilled she had such a beautiful home; one like she had always wanted. She hoped this attempt at making things better would work.

Again Katherine lost herself in decorating the house. Again Bert was his old spiteful self; he made her split the costs of the home furnishings. Bert had hundreds of thousands of dollars between his bank account and his stocks, and Katherine had the little bit of equity she had gotten when she sold her small house. However, for Katherine, love was far more valuable than a bank account.

True to her quest, and in order to keep the momentum of reconciliation going, Katherine didn't fuss over that stipulation. She wasted no time in going through Penney's catalog; she ordered a blue bedspread and curtains for the bedroom and a blue shower curtain and matching rugs for the master bathroom. She felt renewed with Bert agreeing to buy a house with her. Perhaps the move was just what they needed.

It did help for a while; Katherine didn't feel like she was an intruder, and Bert couldn't remind her how Mary used to run the house. Sadly though, Bert soon settled into his old ways of drinking while Katherine was at work. There was only one logical solution.

"Bert, I was thinking about retiring. That way, we can be together during the day. What do you think about that?"

"I think that sounds like a good idea." Bert actually seemed encouraged about Katherine's decision.

Reluctantly, but filled with hope, Katherine turned in her retirement papers. It seemed one by one she gave up her sources of independence; she had given up her house, and now her job, her real source independence. Months of thought had gone into her decision; and again, she grabbed at the chance to save her marriage, she and Bert paid a visit to the Social Security office.

Along with her regular benefit, Katherine was informed that she would receive part of Miles' benefit. Even though he was married to someone else at the time of his death, she had been married to him enough years to be entitled to part of it. That was a wonderful surprise to Katherine; she finally got something from Miles; Bert was pissed. However, there was no way Katherine was going to forfeit the benefit rightfully afforded her; Bert kept his mouth shut, for once.

It may have been admirable for her to keep trying; unfortunately, and not surprising, Katherine's willingness to give her all for love didn't work. Bert continued to drink and shout obscenities; he repeatedly taunted Katherine throughout the night until it sent her fleeing to an apartment, her first attempt to free herself of the arduous stress that wore her down. Her leaving left Bert in a drunken stupor for days; that was something he simply couldn't handle. The thought that this separation might lead to a divorce was beyond his ability to manage. He could do all the horrible things he wanted, but being divorced would send him straight to hell.

Katherine's daughters supported their mother's decision to leave Bert; in fact, they were relieved. They had worried about her safety for a long time. However, to the daughter's distress, after Bert gave Katherine some space, he began to call and visit her at the apartment.

"Mom, what are you doing? Are you going to let Bert come over? You must have an awful short memory," the girls scolded.

"He promised that he would stop drinking; he even said he'd go to AA."

"Do you actually believe him?" they rebuked.

"If he agrees to go to AA, I will give him a chance," Katherine told her girls. Her determination to save her marriage gave Bert the benefit of the doubt once more.

After some serious coaxing, Bert talked Katherine into moving back to the house with him. And, he actually held up to his word and went to AA; once!

"Those people don't know what they are talking about. I don't have a drinking problem anyway; I can stop if I want to," Bert bellowed. "I'm not going back."

"Bert, you have to keep going if you want it to help," Katherine coaxed.

"Help what? There's nothing wrong with me; except you," Bert roared.

Katherine was disillusioned once more. She scheduled a meeting with Bert's AA coach.

"You know, Katherine, it's not your fault Bert drinks; he has a problem and he tries to blame everyone else. When he yells obscenities at you, don't take it personally. It's the booze talking; he probably doesn't even remember what he said," the coach advised Katherine.

"I can't ignore it; I can't take him saying those things to me. I can't live that way," Katherine confided in the counselor. "How can I not take it personally?"

"A lot of the times alcoholics don't know what they are saying. The brain changes; they're not the same people when they are sober."

"I don't think I can cope with it. He's simply too mean."

"Well, you have to do what you think is best," the coach advised.

When Katherine's next cry for help came, the daughters were there to help their mother move out again. This went on for the next three years. All the girls were discussed with their parents. Bert and Katherine were very close to being the poster children for the ridiculous. Their continuous back and forth antics were hard on everyone's nerves; the demand for their constant shift in loyalty and acceptance was far beyond what the girls, and their families, could offer; however, it was expected.

Katherine's hope of a kind and loving husband, and Bert's fear of a divorce kept them trying to make their marriage work for seven, long years. Finally, and to everyone's relief, their violent, vulgar marriage was over; they conceded to a divorce. Katherine gave the relationship all that was in her capacity to give; sadly, it wasn't enough.

The seven years of stress with Bert took a tremendous toll on Katherine's health. One year after her fifth divorce she had a strange sensation in her chest.

Chapter 64

In Katherine's lonely hours following the divorce, she rocked herself into a trance in her one bedroom apartment in the Senior Towers. She languished at the realization that she couldn't make her fifth marriage succeed, and it worked its damage on her susceptible mind and body. She cried as she suffered through a mixture of hurt, regret, anger, and the painful knowledge of once again failing in her attempt to be happy.

With watery eyes and angry sobs she spent her lonely evenings cutting up all of her beautiful wedding pictures. She couldn't bear to have the glossy reminders anywhere near her. The very presence of them sitting in a picture album in the same room seemed to radiate the throb of failure, and it hurt. She learned the painful lesson that a large wedding with all the fantasy trimmings was not assurance of a happy ending. How dare the fairy tales be so cruel as to plant those hopes in her head? The last bits of her heart, which had been spared from her past mistakes, were now broken.

Katherine went so far as to tear up her and Bert's marriage license and divorce papers. Any physical evidence of the failure was simply too hurtful for her to have around. However, eliminating the proof didn't erase the memories in her head; nothing wiped them away.

Katherine was lonely with nothing to do. Almost from the time she quit her job she regretted it. She never objected to working; in fact, it was where she found stability, it was where she had a purpose; but more than that, it was where she achieved success.

"I never should have quit my job," Katherine complained to her daughter.

"Well, mom, if you want to go back to work, I have something for you," Linda said.

"Oh?"

"Yes, Norm and I are buying an ice cream shop in town," she said excitedly.

"An ice cream shop? I can to that. When can I start?"

"Not so fast. It's still in the works. It will take a few months."

Katherine was elated; it was perfect. It was close to home, the hours were flexible, and she would get to see more of her daughter. So, at 69 years old, Katherine became the ice cream shop's first employee.

She loved going up to the shop to work, it motivated her, it gave her a reason to get up in the morning; just like her cafeteria job, she was the most dependable employee there was. It helped Katherine beyond explanation; it gave her broken soul a change to mend. However, the physical damage could not repair itself.

"I don't feel right, Linda. There's a burning in my chest."

"Do you think it is heartburn?"

"I don't know; I usually don't have heartburn," Katherine said.

"Have you had it for very long?"

"It's been like that for a few days," Katherine explained.

"Why don't you go by the doctor's office on your way home," Linda suggested.

"Maybe I will." Katherine rubbed her chest.

The technician hooked Katherine up to the EKG machine; the doctor nearly flew into a panic when he looked at the irregular rhythm that printed out on the graph.

"Mrs. Mangrum, I'm going to call an ambulance to take you to the emergency room."

"What? I can't go to the hospital. My car is here," Katherine protested.

"I don't care about your car, Mrs. Mangrum; you're having a heart attack. You need to get to the hospital right now." The doctor couldn't believe that she was more concerned about her car than her life.

The rescue attendant rolled Katherine down the narrow hallway of the doctor's office. Before the bed was pushed out the door, Katherine made the attendant stop at the office window.

"Can you call my daughter and tell her to come and get my car?" Katherine yelled out from beneath the blanket; she couldn't bear the thought of leaving her precious, blue, Monte Carlo all alone in the doctor's parking lot. She had given up her dog, her house, her job, and her marriage; the car had to be protected.

"I'll call her," the office clerk yelled back.

The emergency room got Katherine stabilized and then admitted her for further testing. A heart specialist informed her that a catheterization had been ordered to take a look at her arteries; he suspected some blockage. The doctor was right.

"Katherine, three of your arteries are completely blocked, you are going to need open heart surgery immediately.

"I can't do that right now. I'll go home and think about it for a few weeks." She couldn't accept the fact that she was in such eminent danger.

"You're not going to be here in a few weeks if you don't get the surgery right away. The blocked arteries are cutting off the blood supply to your heart; you are going to die if you don't have the surgery now." The doctor warned Katherine in no uncertain terms.

After more coaxing from the doctor and her girls, Katherine finally signed the consent papers. Before she could fill out her menu request for her noontime meal, she was whisked into an ambulance, which headed for a more experienced hospital in Detroit.

It was a surreal forty-five minute ride. Katherine lay on the gurney as she glanced at the attendant, who rode in the back with her. Occasionally she looked outside at the passing billboards alongside the expressway; she wondered what more could happen to her. She was even more convinced of life's unfairness as they passed the airport; an airline ad for finding romance in Hawaii whizzed by.

"What a laugh," she mumbled.

"What's that," the attendant asked.

"Oh, nothing; I'm just talking to myself. My girls are going to meet us at the hospital. I have wonderful girls." The attendant smiled at Katherine just to let her know that he heard.

Katherine got settled in and calmed down; the family was back bright and early the next morning for the surgery; however, she had already been taken to pre-op.

"Can't I see my daughters before I go?"

"We're ready to get you prepped. No one can come back here." The nurse turned when she heard some commotion.

"We're going to see our mother before she goes in," a trio of voices bellowed through the swinging doors. Katherine was delighted to see that her girls insisted on being able to see her before she was cut open.

"I love you all." Katherine looked up from the gurney; her eyes started to water.

"We'll see you on the other side, mom."

The girls, and their husbands, nervously awaited the doctor's appearance. They spent hours reminiscing about what their mother had put them through; however, they mostly found humor in her sarcastic expressions and abrupt candor, which could sometimes be very offensive; but, nonetheless, comical. She had been born with a sense of humor, just like her mother; however, the road of life had twisted her humor into a strange sort of stand-up-comedic act about a hard luck survivor. A fair amount of people had gotten the chance to experience this expression; afterwards, they walked away from her shaking their heads and chuckling to themselves. If they had been lucky enough to be privy to her story, they agreed that indeed she suffered a great deal of bad luck; however, she was a survivor.

The family walked single file into Katherine's ICU room. "The doctor said everything went well, mom," Judy whispered as her mother began to awaken. "They had to take some veins out of your leg, but it will be okay." Katherine nodded and went back to sleep.

It only took three days and Katherine was back to complaining about being inconvenienced by the intravenous lines and antagonized by all of the blood draws. It was mind-boggling that she was irritated by the monitors, needles, and beeps instead of being glad that all of these contraptions and procedures were responsible for keeping her alive.

"I hate this food. Bring me something else when you come back tonight," Katherine demanded. Again, the girls spoiled their mother by bringing her fast food hamburgers, her favorite, instead of making her eat the hospital food; Katherine's finickiness about food always caused a problem. The girls gave in to her demands.

"Here you go, mom, here is a hamburger."

"I don't want it." Katherine pushed the food away. "The doctor was just here, I had a heart attack."

"What?"

"He said that probably the day after the surgery, one of my new arteries closed up."

"How do they know that?"

"I guess from the blood tests."

"What are they going to do?" the girls inquired.

"Nothing! He said I would be fine with the two he fixed." Katherine was beside herself with angst; though it was understandable, her pessimism was difficult for the staff to handle.

She should have been observed a few days longer; instead, the doctor released Katherine early. She went home to recover at Judy's house. She couldn't be alone for a while; plus, she needed someone to force her to do her walking regiment, which was crucial for her recovery.

"Mom, you have to walk. It's important for your recovery," Judy coaxed.

"It hurts. I don't want to do it," Katherine yelled. "I can feel the wire in my chest. The doctor told me that he wired my breast bone back together; I can feel it. It hurts I tell you!"

Not only was Katherine annoyed with the pain, the fear of having another heart attack made her frustratingly difficult to deal with. Her fears were not uncommon; at the same time, Katherine's neurosis heightened her fears ten fold.

Again, she took on the role of the child and fought her daughter every step of the way; she even threw tantrums about not wanting to do her exercise plan. It was surprising she recovered as well as she did.

However, mentally Katherine faltered. The edge of the cliff, which she had been teetering on for years, was now dangerously close to not holding her anymore. The strength she needed to recover from heart surgery drained her last little bit of balance. What she had been able to fight off for seventy years, now over took her; Katherine fell into the pit of depression, complicated with panic attacks.

After Katherine got back to her apartment and had to be alone, her daily routine consisted of constant calls her daughters in a manic, scared, hysterical state. The girls spent literally hours talking, either on the phone or in person, to their mother trying to calm her down, trying to convince her that she was not going to die, which was Katherine's greatest fear; it was a drain on everyone.

"Mom, we think you should see a psychiatrist," the girls counseled their mother. "It might help you to work things out and calm you down."

"I don't need any damn psychiatrist."

"You need some help, mom. Maybe he can give you something for your nerves."

"I'll go if you can find a good one," Katherine finally gave in.

The search was on; Katherine and the girls tried to find a good psychiatrist, which they found to be quit a formidable task. However, they kept up the search.

Katherine wanted to get back to the ice cream shop. She needed a purpose to keep going, a purpose to keep fighting the panic. Making chocolate milk shakes for her favorite customers was the perfect incentive. At the same time, it wasn't easy.

"Linda, I can't breathe; I don't think I can drive to the shop." Katherine whined; the terror in her voice was obvious.

"Try to calm down, mom; you're going to be okay."

"I think I'm going to die!"

"Mom, you're not going to die. It's the panic attack making you feel that way. You have to get your mind on something else."

"Okay, bye." Katherine hung up clearly unsure if she was actually going to be okay.

Katherine slowly pulled into the parking lot of the ice cream shop. It took all her fortitude to get behind the wheel of her car feeling like she couldn't breathe; one couldn't help but be amazed, even astounded, by her courage.

"I don't know how I got here; I'm in bad shape," Katherine whimpered.

"Just sit there until you feel like you can get up," Linda coaxed.

"Well, you've got customers coming in; I'd better get up there." With that, Katherine headed up to the counter to greet her devoted milk shake drinking public. For the moment she was in control.

While the girls admired their mother's courage, it didn't make it any easier to handle the endless attention she required. Katherine called at all hours, and as many as twenty times in a day. Something had to be done, and quick.

In the middle of Katherine's difficulty, she was faced with an added worry. Barb, her baby, had contracted Multiple Sclerosis. Dave, Barb's husband, decided to stay home and care for her, which made their income dwindle to Barb's social security benefits. Living in Michigan was too expensive so they moved to Missouri. Katherine pined over her baby girl's condition at great lengths, which only added to her stress. It was a normal reaction for a mother, but any little bit of added stress only made matters worse for Katherine.

Katherine's girls continued to search for a doctor while Katherine did some searching on her own. She spied the shingle of a clinical psychologist in her town, Dr. Pampimm; she made her own appointment.

"Mom, if you make an appointment in the evening, I can go with you," Judy said.

"That's okay; I think I can go by myself."

"If you're sure, because I will go with you," Judy reiterated.

"I can go alone," Katherine reassured her daughter.

Katherine walked into the dim lit office of Dr. Pampimm. She was nervous; secretly she didn't think he would be able to help her; nor, did she want to be there in the firs place.

"Please, sit down," the doctor invited. He asked the usual introductory questions.

"Well, Mrs. Mangrum, she went back to using Miles' last name, why are you here?"

"My nerves are shot," Katherine chuckled nervously.

"How so?"

"I don't know; that's why I'm here." Katherine's boldness continued to show itself.

"Okay, why don't you tell me about yourself; tell me about your family."

After Katherine told the doctor about her open heart surgery, she started at the beginning.

"My mother died when I was twelve; she died of a broken heart."

The doctor raised one eyebrow. "A broken heart?"

"Yes, my dad left her for another woman."

"I'm not so sure people die of a broken heart," the doctor remarked.

"She did!" Katherine shot back. The doctor continued to listen.

"I went to live with my aunt until my father and stepmother talked me into going to live with them. That was a mistake; my father let my stepmother beat me. He never raised a hand to stop her." Katherine sniveled as she pulled at her throat. The doctor closely observed Katherine's behavior.

"My oldest brother never paid any attention to me; he borrowed my inheritance and never paid it back," Katherine explained.

"How long ago was that," the doctor asked.

"About fifty years ago; and he still hasn't paid it back!" she complained. The doctor stroked his goatee and wrote down some notes.

"My brother, Dennis, was always nice to me, but I can't stand his wife. She always stopped Dennis from helping me as much as he would have liked too," Katherine continued. She cleared her throat as if she was having some trouble breathing. Obviously her nerves were getting worked up as she talked about all the things that bothered her.

"Are you a widow?" the doctor asked.

"No," Katherine answered, almost to embarrassed to start on that subject. "I'm divorced; I was married five times to three different men." The doctor raised the other eyebrow.

"Why did you marry the two men twice?" Dr. Pampimm asked, clearly fascinated with his new patient.

"They both promised to change; I believed them."

"What about your fifth marriage?"

My last husband was an alcoholic; he was mean. He promised to change too; I gave him a few chances. I finally realized it was hopeless."

Dr. Pampimm wrote more notes. He watched and listened; he picked up on every gesture, every inflection in her voice, every nuance of blame, and who she placed it on.

"What do you hope I can do for you?" the doctor asked Katherine.

"I just can't settle myself down. I pull for my breath; it feels like my throat is going to close up, like I'm going to smother," Katherine answered with desperation in her voice. "I hope you can help me with that."

The doctor watched Katherine's body language; he listened to her slant on every event that shaped her life. Unfortunately, there were certain personalities that were rubbed the wrong way with Katherine's demeanor; Dr. Pampimm's happened to be one. He didn't like her; her narcissism annoyed him.

Katherine watched the doctor twitch in his big, brown, leather chair. She waited for his suggestions.

It wasn't clear why he prescribed the particular treatment that he did. It wasn't clear if he was just being nasty and wickedly unprofessional, or if he was simply some sort of New Age therapist; but Katherine left his office stunned and disgusted. She sat in her car on the verge of tears; she was sickened by what the doctor told her to do. What had she gotten mixed up in? What kind of doctor was he? She drove home vowing never to set foot in Dr. Pampimm's office again.

"How did you like that doctor?" the girls asked a few days later.

"He's weird; he doesn't know what the hell he is talking about."

"What do you mean?"

"You know what that shit ass told me to do?" Katherine finally confessed.

"What?"

Katherine had to turn away from her daughters to speak the words. "He told me to put a man's thing, you know, his penis, in my mouth. He said that would take away my throat problems." Katherine grimaced like she had just tasted something nasty.

The girls were momentarily speechless. "What!" they gasped. "Are you sure you heard him right?"

"Yes, I heard him right! That is what he told me to do. Can you imagine that?" Katherine snarled.

"No! That is disgusting for a doctor to tell a seventy one year old woman to put a man's penis in the mouth as a form of treatment. What's wrong with him? Is he some sort of New Age therapist or something?" the girls quizzed.

"I don't know what he is. All I know is he's nuts."

The girls discussed confronting the doctor, but decided not to. They simply became more earnest in helping their mother fine a credible therapist. From then on, one of the girls went with her to that kind of appointment, and insisted on being present during the sessions, which Katherine had to agree to; of course she did. She wasn't going to run the chance of being told to put any other man parts in her mouth again.

The world of psychiatry seemed to be almost impenetrable to those who needed it the most; it was frustrating and exhausting. Though there were literally hundreds of psychiatrists in the phone book; however, an appointment could not be had in the tri-city area. Katherine became disenchanted with that field of medicine; there seemed to be no one available to help her.

Finally, at long last, some help came. "Mom, my boss gave me the name of a reliable psychiatrist." Judy was an x-ray technologist at the hospital where Katherine worked. "His name is Dr. Patt, and he comes highly recommended." Their search was over; the three women could finally exhale.

Dr. Patt turned out to be wonderful; he was kind, and gentle; he had a pleasing voice, and he was pleasantly attractive. He was everything Katherine needed in a therapist.

Dr. Patt listened as Katherine went through her repertoire of life's events.

"Mrs. Mangrum, you have to let those things go. They're in the past; they happened a long time ago. Everyone has had bad things happen them. You can't change it; you have to move on," he urged.

The doctor tired to reason with his new patient. He had just met her so he had no idea how deeply those events were burned into her very being; they were just as much a part of her as her eyes, or her hands. She couldn't let those things go any more than she could let her memories go.

"I can't, doctor. I don't know how."

"Like I said, everyone has had difficulties in their life. You can choose to let them run your life, as you obviously have, or you can choose to let them go and learn from them."

Katherine listened as she fought back the tears.

"Those things didn't happen because you were a bad person; they just happened, and it's time to let them go." The more Dr. Patt talked, the more he could see that Katherine was not going to be able to do it herself.

"I'm going to prescribe some medication; this will help. Now, it won't work right away; it takes two to three weeks to feel any relief," the doctor explained.

"Well, that is what I need, some relief." As much as Katherine hated taking medicine, she was willing to accept his treatment if it would indeed give her relief.

Gradually, very gradually, Katherine started to feel better. Despite the ache in her chest where her sternum had been sawed apart and wired back together, she called her daughters less; she complained less; she even started to smile again. Dr. Patt had given her what she needed; her life was bearable again.

Katherine managed to get to work every day, rain or shine; she was more reliable than the mailman. Her reputation for the best chocolate shakes in Wayne grew and she again adjusted to her solitary life.

Through her therapy, Katherine had come to workable terms with a few things; she developed a comedic routine about her bad luck with love; she made sure that she told everyone who would listen that from now on she was through with men. Though she made light of it; she wasn't about to let outsiders know about the many pieces that made up the whole of her broken heart; to let them know would only admit defeat, and she wasn't about to be defeated.

Each time Katherine battled through her darkness and began to see a little light bursting through her tunnel of despair, fate seemed to search her soul to see just how much she could really take. Destiny wasn't satisfied yet.

Katherine called Aunt June to check on Aunt Etta. She got no answer. Katherine tried a few more times; still she was unable to reach Aunt June. Finally, her curiosity got the best of her and she decided to call her cousin, Johnny, whom she hadn't seen in many years; however, she remembered him fondly as the boy who she was raised with; as a youngster she was as close to him as her own brothers. She dialed Johnny's number and heard his southern draw on the other end.

"Katherine, how in the world are you?" Johnny said, surprised to hear her voice.

"I'm fine, but I've been trying to call your mother to see how Aunt Etta is doing," Katherine explained, "but I can't get an answer."

There was silence on the other end. Katherine began to feel uncomfortable. Why wasn't Johnny saying anything? Finally he spoke.

"Katherine, I'm sorry to have to tell you, but Aunt Etta passed away a few months ago."

"What? She passed away! Why didn't anyone call me?" Katherine yelled in her cousin's ear. Again there was silence.

Johnny suddenly realized his negligence. "Katherine, I don't know what to say. I'm sorry. It just happened; it was a small funeral and the family got it over with quickly." Johnny tried to explain why they overlooked calling her.

"But why didn't anyone call me?" Katherine demanded. "Did anyone call Dennis or Raymond?"

Johnny had to further admit his mistake to say that neither Dennis nor Raymond had been contacted.

"No one called Dennis either?" Katherine exclaimed; she wasn't ready to let Johnny off the hook.

"No, Katherine. I didn't call him either!" he confessed.

"Why?" she demanded. Katherine insisted on getting an answer; however, Johnny had no answer for her. He felt terrible. He continued to use the quickness of the funeral as the reason. He must have forgotten that Aunt Etta raised Katherine as a daughter and looked after Dennis as a son. It was a reprehensible disregard on the part of the family. She would never forgive them.

Katherine couldn't help herself, she had to call Dennis. He was just as upset and intended on calling Johnny the moment he hung up. The two siblings talked about their aunt and how she stood by them, how she took on the role of their mother; they talked about how they had been prevented from saying good-by to the woman who had been their protector and defender. Not being able to be at her aunt's side and pay her the respect that she deserved was devastating; Katherine would have to take her burdensome guilt to the grave with her.

Katherine was depressed for weeks; the girls understood their mother's depression; it was a horrible oversight by her family. They ached for their mother; the heartbreak Katherine felt for not being able to send Etta to heaven with her gratitude was felt in their own hearts. Katherine's daughters were actually beginning to feel mad at life for continuously widening the cracks in their mother's heart.

Keeping Katherine from slipping back into her depression was going to be a big job; the girls worked to keep her busy, they tried desperately to thwart off another spell. Katherine, herself, worked to keep her mind on other things. True to her ancestral strength, she kept going. However, it was months, and possibly never, before Katherine stopped crying about missing her aunt's funeral. Her heart ached as her eyes cried blue tears for the woman who had loved her unconditionally.

Chapter 65

"I think I'll move." Katherine informed her girls. She had become so used to being uprooted and upset that calm periods were dull; she was the personification of *some people don't feel alive unless they are hurting*. She was restless.

"Absolutely not!" her daughters ordered.

"Why not?"

"Mom, you have moved twelve times; haven't you had enough? Besides, you'll never find a better place than the Senior Towers. The rent is low, the complex is nice, and our friend pulled some strings to get you in," Judy insisted.

"I'm bored."

"Things are running smooth for you; your nerves can have a deserved rest." Linda hoped her mother to would appreciate the calm in her life. However, Katherine needed something to handle, something to manage. That's where her successes were.

"You're not going to move, mom. The Senior Towers are right in the middle of town; you'll never find a better place. We're not going to move you again."

"Don't tell me what to do; I'll move if I want to," Katherine shot back. However, the girls would not talk about it any more.

Katherine pouted for a few weeks. She needed something exciting to occupy her mind; finally she came up with the perfect idea.

"I'm going to buy a new car."

She did need one; her blue Monte Carlo was old and it needed a lot of work. The girls were surprised she was willing to let her prized procession go, but they also thought it was a good idea; it was a good compromise.

Katherine had persisted in her thriftiness and she was certain that she could afford the payments. She didn't have a lot of money; however, she had some equity from when she sold her little house; she had insisted that the money be put in an account in just her name, even though Bert had protested. In addition, the judge had awarded her, after seven years of marriage to wealthy Bert, $3,000.00 as a property settlement, which covered the home furnishings, which she left in the house when she moved.

She frugally guarded her little nest egg with tender loving care, and she was cautiously boastful about her balance. Even though it wasn't that much, it was the most money she had ever had. So, with the trade-in from her Monte Carlo, Katherine signed the papers for her new car.

"There is no blue on this chart."

"No ma'am. That is not one of the colors for this year's model," the salesman told her.

"There's no blue? There should be blue on this color chart," Katherine complained.

"Well, there isn't," the man insisted.

"Well, I don't like that." Katherine turned up her nose. "I guess I take white."

Despite the color, Katherine proudly drove her Buick round town; it was her pride and joy. She babied her new car and she carefully looked it over for dents and dings every time she went out to go somewhere. She wouldn't even smoke in it, nor would she allow anyone else. Every night she walked to the end of her corridor, which had a window that faced the parking lot. She gazed at the new car; she tucked it in; she said good-night to her proudest possession.

Rain pelted down on Katherine as she hustled from the side door of her apartment building to the parking lot. She didn't want to be late at helping Linda set up the ice cream shop. She held her rain bonnet on her head as she arrived at the spot where she parked her car the night before. Katherine lifted her head to see where she was. She stopped and stared at an empty parking spot. Confused, she looked around the lot. At first she thought she had parked in a different spot and perhaps forgot. Standing silent with the rain dripping off of her bonnet, she panned the parking lot for her white Buick. She was oblivious to the rain showering down on her as she walked up and down the rows of parked cars. She refused to believe that her car wasn't there; it had to be there, she parked it right there in the lot last night when she came home from bingo. Katherine kept looking sure that she would spot it somewhere among the other cars. She even walked over to a near-by municipal parking lot just to make sure she hadn't parked there and forgotten about it. It was as if the car had taken on a life of its own and wanted to play a game, like some mischievous little child; however, Katherine wasn't amused. Finally, soaking wet and frantic, Katherine ran into her building. She burst into the manager's office.

"My car has been stolen!"

"Are you sure?" the manager asked.

"Yes, I'm sure. It's not in the parking lot; it must be stolen."

"I'll call the police," the manager said while Katherine paced franticly.

"I can't believe this. Why did this have to happen to me?"

"Try to stay calm, Katherine. The police will be here soon."

"I guess this place isn't safe anymore," Katherine confronted the manager. "I don't know if I want to stay here if this is what is going to happen."

The police drove up and Katherine flew out the door before the manager could defend the apartment complex.

"My car was stolen last night. I parked it right here; now it's gone!"

"Ma'am, can I see your license and insurance? Can you give me a description of the car?" the officer asked.

Katherine handed over the information, "don't you guys watch this lot? How can someone just walk up and steal someone's car?"

Though offended, the officer kept his composure. "Yes, we watch this lot, but we can't be here every minute. We'll put out a stolen vehicle report. We'll let you know if anything turns up."

Katherine filed a report with her insurance company and waited for her poor car to return. She smoked an extra pack of cigarettes every day while she worried about her Buick; whether or not it was it hurt, if it was still in the city, and why it hadn't made its way back home where she could take care of it. She would give it a mother's scolding when it finally showed up.

At the same time, Katherine surprised everyone; Nietzsche would have been especially proud of her. She was the embodiment of his encouragement, "that what doesn't kill us only makes us stronger."

"Mrs. Mangrum, we found your car," a policeman announced on the phone.

"Oh, where did you find it?"

"It was found abandoned by the side of the road in Garden City," he informed her.

"Garden City? That's three cities away. What's it doing over there?"

"I'm sure I don't know; but we had it towed to a storage yard; you have to go over and identify the car and sign papers to release it to your insurance company."

"Okay." Katherine got directions to the yard; she and her daughter went to claim her precious property.

"My car is supposed to be here," Katherine snapped at the clerk, disgusted that she had to be at this grungy junk yard.

"Well, your car *is* here," the burly gal barked back. That only made matters worse; Katherine swelled up and complained about the junkyard woman's attitude, not acknowledging that she was just as bad. She entered the grimy yard in search of her car.

At the end of a row of jalopies sat her regal, white Buick. It was out of place among the lowly piles of scrap metal; she rushed towards it as if to comfort the poor car. The wheels were gone, the driver's window was broken out, indicating the point of intrusion, the radio had been ripped out, and it appeared that just for meanness, the seats had been slashed.

Katherine wanted to cry; it was a travesty that her brand new car had been so abused; she felt violated. However, she was relieved knowing that the Buick bump shop would send a truck over to rescue her vehicle.

The way Katherine handled the whole situation was admirable. Accepting difficult circumstances and seeing them through to the end stimulated her need to find closure in a situation; something she was unable to do with grievances of the heart.

"Mom, I have to run over to the hospital for a few minutes. Do you want to go with me; you can visit the people in the cafeteria?"

"Yeh, I'll go. I don't have anything else to do until I get my car back."

As they walked in the hospital together, a nurse called out. Katherine waited impatiently while Judy and the woman whispered in the corridor.

"What did she want?" Katherine asked.

"Stop here a minute, mom. I have something to tell you."

"What?"

"John died last night. I suppose he couldn't fight the damage done by the tuberculosis any longer," Judy explained.

Katherine had little to say.

"If you want to go over to the funeral home, I'll go with you," Judy offered.

"I'll think about it. I'll talk to you about it later." The two women went off to their own directions.

Judy stopped by the cafeteria to pick up her mother when she was finished with her errand. "Did you think about it? Do you want to go to the funeral home?"

"I thought about it. No! I don't want to go." Katherine had the same reaction to the memorial visit that she had for Miles. She didn't want to see certain people, especially John's last wife, which he managed to stay married to for the rest of his life. Both Miles and John died while married to other women, whom they have been married to longer than her. She didn't need that slap in the face.

"Are you sure?" Judy asked again.

"Yes, I'm sure." Another part of her life was dead. Katherine was downhearted for days. She couldn't explain it; she wasn't particularly sad that John had died; however, he had been part of her life; he had once loved her. She rocked and smoked until she was able to let him go; and she did.

Katherine got her car back as good as new and her life was again calm and smooth; too smooth.

"I don't like it here. The management is bad and the people aren't friendly. I want to move!"

Chapter 66

▼

"Mom, I think you should go see the doctor," Linda said as she and her mother set up the ice cream shop, "I don't like the sound of the cough."

After a few more days, Katherine ended up in the hospital, her lungs weak from her long time smoking habit.

"Your mother has pneumonia; the x-ray shows that one lung is completely diseased. It's going to be hard to clear up the infection with the condition their in," the doctor explained. "We're going to try an accelerated antibiotic treatment; we'll see if we can get this to go away quickly."

Unfortunately, Katherine's weak body couldn't handle the strong antibiotics; a dangerous chain reaction was set in motion.

"What happened? This was supposed to be a routine treatment," the girls interrogated the doctors at their mother's bedside.

"The increased antibiotics, which killed the bad bacteria, at the same time, killed much of the friendly bacteria," the doctors explained. "That is what caused the acute diarrhea."

That wasn't much conciliation when the girls looked at their mother's small, frail body, which had shrunk to 95lbs.

"What about her mouth?" the girls asked.

"In addition, the excess antibiotics had caused a horrendous yeast infection in her mouth."

"I can't even eat; it hurts so badly," Katherine complained. Her refusal to eat only added to her condition as she lost almost all of her body fat and muscle tone. In a short few weeks she became unable to walk on her own. The pneumonia had cleared up but the damage to her viability had been done; she was too weak to go home. The doctors called for a consultation.

"Mom, the doctors don't feel you can go home alone; it wouldn't be safe."

"Where do they want me to go?"

"Well, the new way for patients to rehabilitate is to go to a nursing home for a few weeks."

"Oh no; I'm not going to any damn nursing home."

"Mom, you won't have to stay forever; it's just until you get better."

"No, I won't go; absolutely not, I'd rather die."

However, Katherine's girls knew better than that; they knew she was not ready to give up yet. They knew better than anyone just how much strength was in that little frame of a woman. They had seen her go through too much to think she was done with this life just yet. Katherine simply needed a little push to get back on her road to recovery. The girls and their husbands began a regiment of being at the hospital at meal times in order to encourage Katherine to eat.

"We're not going to stop nagging you until you eat at least half of your meal."

"I can't eat. My mouth hurts, and my stomach hurts," Katherine complained.

"Well, you have to try or we're not going to leave you alone," they vowed.

They sat by her bedside and pumped food into her shriveled body; she looked like she should be laying in a casket rather than a hospital bed; however, they encourage her to keep up the fight. It worked. Slowly, very slowly, she began to gain some strength.

To everyone's surprise, there was a hint of a glisten in Katherine's undefeated, blue eyes. That glisten was all the girls needed to see. If their mother was still willing to fight, then they would make sure she got the chance.

"Mom," Judy said excitedly. "I found out about an accelerated rehab center at Allenwood Hospital."

"Oh?"

"But, the patient has to be referred by a physician in order to be admitted. I'm going to talk to the doctors; maybe they'll sign for you to get in."

"It's not a nursing home?"

"No, no. It's part of the hospital. However, like I said, you have to be willing to work hard; you have to cooperate."

"I'll cooperate," Katherine huffed.

Katherine had been in the hospital going on three weeks; the doctors had been warning Katherine that she was going to be discharged.

"Have you found out about that center you told me about?" Katherine asked her daughter. "They want me out of here."

"I'm still working on the doctors. They don't think you are strong enough for the program," she explained.

"Why do I have to go anywhere; why can't I stay here?"

"Mom, there's nothing more they can do for you here. You need to be rehabilitated; you have to go somewhere else. I'll talk to the doctors again; see you tomorrow."

Katherine picked at her evening meal; she was upset no one came to see her.

"Okay, mom, the doctors finally agreed to refer you to Allenwood. An ambulance will take you to the center later today," Judy said, extremely relieved.

It was a nice facility. The rooms were set up to accommodate six patients with a pull curtain to separate them; there was a common bathroom. Katherine was irked; she wanted a private room.

When Katherine arrived at the rehab center, the therapists were surprised at just how weak she actually was; they were used to their patients being ready to get up and get started; Katherine was not ready for that yet. However, the nurses and therapists got right to work with her daily regiment.

The work was very hard and Katherine complained about every little thing, from a stomachache, to diarrhea, to a heavy chest; she complained the loudest when it was time for her therapy. Unfortunately, every time she complained, the doctors ran another test or gave her another pill. Instead of telling her it would take time for things to work out, or try to understand her complaining nature, they kept her quiet by feeding her neurosis with medication; however, it was never enough. A consultation was called with Katherine and the family.

"Your mother is being quite impossible. She always finds an excuse to skip her therapy."

Katherine pouted; she didn't like being tattled on.

"We are thinking of asking her to leave," the head nurse said.

"No, don't ask her to leave yet," the girls begged. "Give her a little more time."

"We have other patients to tend to; we can't spend all of our time babying her. It's not fair to everyone else," the nurse scolded.

"We know, she just needs a little more time."

"Okay, we'll try a little longer, but she has to cooperate!"

"She'll cooperated, won't you, mom?" The girls gave their mother a look that made her agree.

"However, we do have a question about her mouth. What is going on with all those blisters? It's horrific. It's understandable why she is irritable." The girls defended their mother's complaint about that particular problem.

"That's the yeast infection. When it gets that bad, it takes a long time to go away. We are giving her a daily mouth wash. That should help. It will just take time."

Katherine continued to be uncooperative and nasty; she was such an anomaly of traits. She was strong when it came to emotional traumas; however, physical disturbances knocked her for a loop. She was so afraid of death that any ailment meant the possibility it just might be at hand. So much of her worry space was occupied by her emotional ills that she couldn't spare any on her body; it just had to stop causing her problems.

"Okay, Katherine, it's time for your walk. Let's get up," the perky therapist announced.

"My back hurts; I can't do it today."

"Now, we'll have none of that. You've got to get up. Do you want to be in that bed forever?"

"No, of course not," Katherine grumbled.

The word spread quickly through the ward that Katherine was the worse patient they ever had; she had everyone mad at her. In fact, some aids refused to even be assigned to her. Another consultation was called.

"Mom, okay, listen; the nurses told us that a family member is going to have to stay here with you or you'll have to leave."

"Why?"

"You're causing the therapists to spend too much time with you; they have other patients." They explained. "You're not ready to go home yet, so you'll have to go to a nursing home for the rest of your rehab."

"I'm not going to any nursing home." The words *nursing home* scared Katherine; after that she shaped up. She survived six weeks at the rehab center, six weeks of arguing with the physical therapists, six weeks of wanting her bed mates moved and six weeks of whining about the food; everyone else survived as well. Finally, Katherine got to go home.

A twenty-four hour in-home care company was hired because Katherine was still weak and couldn't be alone yet.

"Are you going to get my lunch?" Katherine snapped at the caregiver.

"You're supposed to get up and help yourself. That's how you're going to get better."

"Well, what am I paying you for?" Katherine demanded.

"I'm here to make sure you are safe, but you also have to help yourself."

"I'm not going to pay you to just sit there while I make lunch." Katherine was furious. "Don't come back tomorrow. I can do this much by myself."

Katherine was not willing to drain her precious bank account on the lethargic lumps that sat around all day and ate her food. Her stubbornness was just what she needed to get her over the hump for recovery; she gained strength daily. Once more, Katherine stopped short of walking through death's door; she was still in charge and she was not ready yet.

"Glad to see you back, Kathy," one of the regular ice cream customers called out. "Make me one of those chocolate shakes, and put some love in it."

Katherine smiled to know she was missed. Too bad fate was in the mood for a joke.

Chapter 67

Katherine stood in front of her bathroom mirror as she got ready to go to work. She quickly picked through her hair; she had cut her locks and coiffed a short, curly perm. As she tossed her curls with the pick, she seemed to be able to see right through her normally thick hair.

"I think my hair is falling out," Katherine told Linda. "Look how thin it is."

Within a few weeks, clumps of light brown curls lay in Katherine's bathroom wastebasket; she winced at seeing her scalp. She was off to see the doctor.

"What?" Katherine questioned.

"Telogen Effluvium." The doctor explained what had happened.

"Extreme physical trauma and chronic emotional stress can shock the hair follicles and throw them into a dormant stage. Large amounts of medicines can also affect the roots," the doctor told her. Between the excess medicines and intensified anxiety, Katherine's poor follicles needed a rest.

"It's not uncommon, Katherine. It takes several months after the initial trigger factor for the hair to actually fall out," he explained. "But, don't worry; this condition is not permanent. Your hair will grow back."

"Don't worry? What am I going to do?" Katherine screeched.

"You can always wear a headscarf." The doctor was from India and thought his suggestion was perfectly logical.

"A headscarf? I'm not going to wear a headscarf."

Within two weeks of noticing the thinning tresses, all of Katherine's hair fell out; a merciless side effect, especially for a woman. Katherine's daughters, and the other workers at the shop, were sure that she would have a melt down. They were sure that she would hide in her apartment until her hair grew back; they were bracing themselves for her anticipated grumpiness. After all, so much of a woman's vanity lies in her hair, and Katherine was no exception. She was always very particular about her appearance and her hair had always been her crowning jewel.

"Do you think I could get a wig?" Katherine asked her daughter.

"Of course; we can go to the mall tomorrow."

Katherine and her daughter headed toward the wig department; Katherine removed her rain bonnet; she had turned down the loan of a neighbor's babushka.

"I like this one." Katherine gazed at herself in the mirror. "I think this one looks rather stylish." She turned in all directions to get a good look.

"Yes, it looks great," Judy said; she marveled at her mother's fortitude.

"Good, I'll take it."

Everyone was amazed at how Katherine handled the loss of her hair. It was curious how she could handle certain problems just fine, but others threw her for an emotional loop. That was simply one more thing that made it difficult to understand her, and especially difficult to help her; the inconsistencies were exasperating.

In her own spunky fashion, Katherine made it through another ordeal; by the same time the following year it was as if nothing had happened at all. In fact, her head of new, healthy, shinny hair had replaced her over-permed and color treated curls. She even started to notice the middle-aged mailman who always came in the shop on his break; she thought he was kind of cute.

"Too bad he's married," she complained to her co-worker.

Katherine's girls marveled at their mother's endurance and chuckled at her expectation that she may find romance again. As much as Katherine's pessimism dominated her personality; she always left a little room for the possibility of love. The girls found themselves hoping they had inherited her strength, her courage, and her verve. Katherine was a marvel of resilience in its purest form.

The sureness of time began to rear its ugly head and Katherine's trusty companion, the one that had always lifted her up from every low point in her life, finally betrayed her. Her cigarettes had weakened her lungs and they finally succumbed to disease and emphysema. Katherine knew she should stop smoking, but she couldn't let go of the crutch that continued to help her manage life.

"Hello, 911," the operator announced.

"I can't breath, I can't breath." Katherine struggled to tell the operator where she lived. They were there in two minutes.

By the time Katherine's daughters met outside the triage treatment room, Katherine's heart rate was up to 220. The girls were dismayed. They couldn't help but think that things had run too smoothly for too long. How silly of them to think their mother would get a little reprieve from turmoil; that would be too much to ask.

Katherine lay on the gurney with the ventilator shoved down her throat. She tried to ask questions; however, the ventilator tube only allowed her some unintelligible grunts. She could hear some commotion outside her cubby.

"We want to see our mother."

Katherine became agitated when she heard her daughter's voices. She stretched out her arm as if reaching for her life force. Finally, the nurse let them in.

Katherine had made it known that she didn't want to be kept alive hooked up to tubes or machines; at the same time, this episode did not suffice as that kind of situation. She hadn't stroked out; she was not unconscious from some other condition. She was still very much alive; she wasn't ready to die yet; as Katherine's searching eyes met their's, they knew it. There would be no rest for Katherine in death, or for the girls in life, if she had been allowed to die before she was ready; and she wasn't ready.

"You're going to have to leave now," the nurse said as she shooed them out of the room. "You don't want to see this."

Katherine's frightened eyes followed them to the door. The girls peered through the crack in the door and saw the crash cart being prepared to send jolting volts of electricity through their mother's struggling body. One jolt was all it took to get Katherine's heart back to the normal 60 beats per minute. The doctor called them back in.

"Time will tell if she'll be okay. We'll keep her in ICU for a few days."

Katherine wanted to grab her daughter's hands; however, she couldn't because her wrists were bound. She wiggled her hands to let them know she needed them to touch her. When she felt the warmth of the children she seemed to relax; it was as if the life she had given restored hers.

The doctor and Katherine's daughters locked eyes for a few second, all having the same thought, *how much more can this frail, little lady take?* They finally broke their stare but clearly continued to feel a certain melancholy for Katherine. They would try as hard as they could to keep fate off her back; however, it would ultimately be her own perseverance that would keep her going.

By the second day, the ventilator had been removed and Katherine was fidgety and irritable. She didn't know why she had to be in ICU with no phone or T.V., and limited visiting hours. She wanted to go home. Katherine was in a foul mood when Judy and Chuck visited her. She was too well to be in ICU and the atmosphere annoyed her. A man, who definitely needed to be there, occupied the room next to her; his condition caused involuntary, guttural moaning.

"God, what's wrong with him, he sounds like he is dying," Katherine complained, and not very discreetly.

Well, it was ICU, and the poor man was dying; however, Katherine was oblivious to the reality of the situation; all she knew was she didn't want to listen to the sounds that he made; she wanted to be moved, and more accurately, she wanted to go home. She got both wishes; Katherine was moved to a regular room for a few days and then released. Weak, but determined, Katherine fought through another bout with her looming destiny. She won another round.

At 80 years old, she still mixed her signature chocolate shakes at the ice cream shop, and flirted with the mailman. Her determination was nothing less than admirable. However, it was obvious that her mind was losing some of its sharpness. The lack of oxygen getting to her brain, due to her lung disease and hardening of the arteries, a condition that Katherine had always described as the Tomas' demise, affected her alertness.

She spent more time sitting in her rocker, her blue eyes peering through the cigarette smoke, drifting back over her sorrows. It would have been a blessing if her aging mind could have drifted back to when she felt happy; unfortunately it always stopped short of that kindness and landed right in the middle of all of her heartaches. She was still aware enough to realize that her dreams would never come true, and the nicotine couldn't cover the taste of bitterness that still lay on her tongue.

Katherine got up to answer the phone.

"Mom, I have some bad news. Uncle Harry died," Linda announced.

"He did? Oh, that's too bad," Katherine answered.

"Do you want to go to the funeral home?"

"Yes, I'll go." This time she wouldn't be kept away.

The news made Katherine remember the last visit she had with Harry. She arrived at her niece's house for a family reunion, the first one she had been invited to, a year ago.

"My God, Harry, you look just like Miles," Katherine said. One glance at him opened the floodgates; torrents of memories came rushing at Katherine. Her tired mind took her back nearly fifty years, to a time when she was happy, to a time when she was with her soul mate. She talked only about times gone by.

"Katherine, that's all water under the bridge; lets talk about something else," Gladys suggested when Katherine wouldn't stop talking about the past.

The visit was bitter sweet for Katherine. She got to renew some old relationships, but she was also reminded of the family that she lost, of people she missed, and of the one man she would always love like no other. Her broken heart was evident.

Gladys knew Katherine had pined for Miles ever since he left; she also knew that Miles suffered a great deal of guilt because of his decisions and mistakes; she new he regretted how his and Katherine's relationship ended up. Gladys was the only one that knew Miles missed his soul mate too; she always felt his pining for Katherine was what killed him. Gladys never spoke of her feelings; perhaps if she had it would have given Katherine a little reprieve from her guilt; if she had known Miles missed her too perhaps her soul would have felt less burdened.

"You know," Gladys said to the group, particularly Katherine and Linda, "I was watching the History Channel the other day. The program told about a pair of Greek lovers, Paris and Oenone.

"Mother, please," Gladys' daughter said.

"No, now listen." Gladys particularly wanted Katherine listen to her tale.

"The ancient text tells that Paris, a warrior in the battle of Troy, was married to Oenone, but became infatuated with a beautiful woman from a neighboring tribe. Paris left Oenone for this woman, leaving his devoted wife embittered, but still in love with him. Eventually, Paris' new lover left him, just as he had left Oenone. He found another love; but alas, was left alone again, leaving him rejected and lonely."

Katherine was not a history lover, especially, ancient history; however, she tried to focus on Gladys' story.

"Paris had sowed his wild oats and went crawling back to his first wife. Oenone was still bitter; sadly, she would not have him back."

"Why sadly?' Katherine interrupted. "Why should she take him back if he kept running around on her?" While everyone held their breath, Gladys finished the story.

"Eventually, Paris died in a flaming battle. When Oenone found out that her one and only love had died, she took her own life. She couldn't bear being in the world without Paris in it too."

Katherine didn't understand the analogy. She wasn't going to kill herself over a man like Oenone had; however, she didn't realize that her broken heart slowly and methodically weakened her vitality. Just as Oenone had pined away for the loss of Paris, Katherine pined away for the loss of Miles, her one true love.

The two modern lovers experienced a need for each other so strong that it held up to the most ancient of tragic love stories.

"It was so good to see you." Gladys hugged Katherine and whispered in her ear. "We're still sisters-in-law."

It took Katherine days after that visit to stop the hurt all over again. What seemed like a good idea at the time, to reconnect with family, only added to the bewilderment of her weakening mind.

Katherine and her daughter arrived at the funeral home; they stood at the casket and stared at Harry. "He looks just like your dad, doesn't he?"

"Yes, he does."

Katherine felt a gentle tap on her shoulder. She turned to see a kind face from the past; one that she had wondered about, one that she had longed to see so many times over the years.

Jerry Pepper gave her a hug. It was all Katherine could do to keep from crying. She hugged him as tight as she could. She thought if she hugged him tighter she could make up for all the years she grieved the loss of him and his mother; Katherine knew Mrs. Pepper had passed away some time ago. She squeezed Jerry hoping she could feel the touch of his mother through him, hoping she could feel the gentle kindness and the unconditional acceptance his mother had given her. With teary eyes she held on to Jerry a little longer.

"It's so good to see you, Jerry. It's been a long time."

"It sure has, Katherine. How have you been?"

"Oh, you don't want to know," Katherine chuckled. "Harry sure looks like Miles, doesn't he?"

"Yes, he resembles him a lot."

"I remember when you and your mother came over when I lived in the project; you guys used to ...," at that moment, Linda interrupted her mother.

"Jerry doesn't want to hear about all of that stuff, mom. Besides, we'd better get going. We have a long drive."

"Okay."

Katherine quietly told Harry good-by. If she could have, she would have told Harry that she never fell out of love with his brother.

CHAPTER 68

▼

"Mom, we're gong to sell the ice cream shop," Linda announced one day.

"Oh?" Katherine inquired.

"We've done it long enough and we have a buyer; so, it's time."

"What will I do?" Katherine asked. "I liked working there. It gave me something to do."

"You have other things to do."

"What?"

"You have bingo." Linda hoped to discourage Katherine from being depressed.

However, Katherine was depressed; she had enjoyed going to the shop and making the ice cream treats; she missed talking to the customers. In addition, she missed seeing her girls; Judy had moved to Florida; and now, she didn't see Linda every day. With no job, and no chaos in her life, she was board and lonely.

To fill her time, Katherine drove to bingo a few times a week; however, a couple of fender benders had her nervous. She began to feel unsure about her driving sense; the third incident convinced her that it was true.

As Katherine pulled into a parking spot at Bingo, she misjudged the distance and side swiped the car in the adjacent parking spot. She knew she did it; when she got out she looked at the other car and found just a small dent. Katherine looked at her car and saw a similar small dent.

"Oh well," she mumbled, "maybe no one will notice." She chose to keep it to herself. Katherine went into the Bingo hall and bought her usual twelve playing cards and two packs of paper specials. She found her favorite spot and spread her cards out in front of her. She placed her red plastic chips on one side of the cards, which were used to cover the hard cards, and her blue dabbers on the other side, which were used to dab the paper cards. Katherine confiscated an ashtray from the next table and positioned it where she could place her lit cigarette comfortably.

Katherine patiently waited to daub her first number when there seemed to be a commotion coming from the check-in table, which was near the front door. She could see a policeman talking to the manager of the hall; curiously, they looked in her direction. Katherine assumed they were looking past her at someone else. She was wrong. The manager, the policeman, and a strange woman walked toward her; they stopped right in front of her.

"Do you own a white Buick?" the policeman asked.

Astonishingly, and unexplainably, Katherine said, "No."

Katherine was not above being a little white liar when she was caught in the act.

"Excuse me," the strange woman said.

"I saw you hit that car. You looked at your bumper and then just came in here like nothing had happened," the woman shot back at Katherine, proud of herself for being the stoolie. "I called the police."

Katherine sat at her table with her bingo cards all spread out in front of her; the numbers on the cards became eyeballs that witnessed her shame. She didn't know what to do next. Everyone stared at her. With no escape, she finally confessed.

"Yes. I have a white Buick."

"Why did you lie?" the policeman asked.

Katherine didn't answer.

"Okay. Will you come outside with me, ma'am?" The policeman helped her up from her chair.

Katherine gathered up all of the Bingo paraphernalia and followed the officer outside; he took out his citation pad.

The office took pity on her. "Ma'am, I could write you a ticket for leaving the scene of an accident. However, I'm not going to do that; I'm going to write you for not reporting an accident; it still requires a court appearance though."

"I have to go to court?" Katherine grimaced; she gave the stool pigeon a dirty look.

"I'm afraid so."

Katherine didn't go back into the Bingo Hall; she and her naughty car cowered home in disgrace.

"Now just relax and answer the Judge's questions," Katherine's son-in-law, Norm, told her. He was the only one available to go to court with Katherine.

"Okay," Katherine shot back; her body language radiated her pissy mood. "I don't know why I had to come here. I agreed to pay the ticket."

"Shhh," Norm hushed.

"Don't shush me; I'll say what I want," Katherine scolded her son-in-law.

"Mrs. Mangrum, my report says that you hit a car and you didn't report it," the judge read. "Tell me what happened."

"I guess I hit it; I didn't see any damage, Katherine explained. "I guess there was a little scratch on the other car."

"Mrs. Mangrum, how old are you?"

"Eighty-one," Katherine replied.

"How are your driving skills?"

"Not too bad; I'm still a good driver,. I don't know why the policeman had to write me a ticket." Katherine's irritability showed.

"You knew you hit the car but didn't report it; that's why," the judge retorted.

"I didn't see any damage," Katherine answered.

"Shhh," Norm whispered as he nudged his mother-in-law's arm. He tried to avert her crabbiness before she got the judge mad.

"Don't shush me."

However, she started to shift her weight as she stood in front of the podium; she knew her ability had slipped.

"Well, I'm not going to take your license away, but I want you to seriously think about your driving skills," the judge said, half scolding and fully concerned.

"Thank you, Your Honor." However, Katherine still didn't think there was anything to be concerned about, and it showed. She huffed out of the courtroom and over to the clerk's window and paid her fine.

"I can't believe she was thinking about taking my license away. I can still drive okay," Katherine complained to Norm.

"Maybe you shouldn't drive at night anymore," Norm said. Katherine gave him a dirty look.

Katherine was disgusted with the judge; however, she was more disgusted with herself; she was fully aware that her driving skills had seriously slipped. To her credit, she only drove a few more months; her lack of confidence made her hang up her car keys.

Perhaps the lack of purpose, or more accurately, the need for chaos, exacerbated her weakening mind, and chaos was what Katherine got. The panic attacks were back; it was sad that a woman of 81 had to go through such a horribly difficult and frightening time. The calls to her daughters at all hours resumed; the frantic rocking resumed, the chain smoking occupied her shaking hands. Aside from the exhausting attention that she needed, Katherine was pitiful. The search was on for a credible physiatrist. Finally, one agreed to see her.

"I'm not going to take that medicine," Katherine bluntly told the doctor.

"I can't help you if you don't take what I prescribe," he lectured.

"I'm not going to take it!"

"If she's not going to take the medicine, then I can't help her," the physiatrist told Katherine's daughter. "Don't bring her back."

"Mom, if you don't cooperate, the doctors can't help you," Linda scolded.

"I don't know what he prescribed," Katherine argued. "I don't even know him. I'm not going to take all that strange medicine."

"Don't come back; I can't help her," the doctor interrupted.

The two women went home disheartened and frustrated. The need for help was so fierce that being rejected was nothing short of being lost in the snake pit of disregard, their desperation unacknowledged.

During one of her visits, Judy asked around and found out where Dr. Patt had relocated; again she begged for an appointment. Maybe he could get Katherine back on a healing path like he did before.

The doctor was over booked for the next several weeks; however, the request came with such desperation that he agreed to see Katherine on his lunch hour. He had been the only physiatrist that had shown true compassion for his burdened patient, and Katherine trusted him explicitly.

"Come in ladies; I'm going to grab some lunch as we talk, okay?"

"Sure."

"Katherine, what's going on with you?"

"I can't make it stop, doctor. I feel like I'm going to die," Katherine whimpered.

"What has happened since I last saw you?"

Katherine's daughter informed Dr. Patt about her trials.

"What else, Katherine?"

"I lost my oldest brother a few years ago." Katherine began to cry.

"How old was he."

"Eighty seven," Katherine blubbered.

"Eighty-seven! Why are you crying that way over someone who lived to be eighty-seven? He lived a long life. I don't understand why you are so upset," Dr. Patt queried.

Katherine couldn't understand why the doctor didn't understand her sorrow. Though Dr. Patt had been the most supportive and kind doctor she had seen, he didn't understand the complicated, intertwined threads of unresolved relationships that still bound Katherine's resolve. No one would ever understand the depths her choking ropes went to gripe her tortured soul. He could tell her to calm down and understand that life ends somewhere around the age of Raymond, if you were lucky. At the same time, the finality of Raymond's death assured Katherine that she would never get the love from him that she had always wanted. The doctor's words were futile.

"I think this medication will help you, Katherine," Dr. Patt said as he handed her the prescription. "When you are out, your primary doctor can order a refill."

This time Katherine wasn't as impressed with Dr. Patt.

"How dare he eat his lunch while I paid for his time?" Katherine was absolutely livid about him being so unprofessional. "What does he mean that my primary doctor can give me the refills? Doesn't he want to see me anymore?"

Katherine continued to get worse. At the same time, she added fuel to her out of control fire, she decided that it was time for her to quit smoking. Her continuous respiratory problems were evidence that she should indeed quit smoking, but her timing couldn't have been worse. Her diminishing mental capacity prevented her from using the nicotine patches properly. Katherine found herself in a vicious circle of cravings and compensation. When she needed a cigarette, her weakened constitution allowed her to keep adding patches to her arm to calm her desires. The added supply of nicotine made her feel fine; so, off came the patches until the midnight hour of want came back. Back on went the patches, and, "just one little smoke won't hurt," she convinced herself. Of course it did! The overdosing of nicotine played havoc with Katherine's fragile mind and body. She was thrown into a full blown nervous breakdown.

The darkness that consumed Katherine terrified her; the inevitability of her own mortality lurked in the shadows; she was scared. The medicines Dr. Patt had prescribed did not work because she was mixed them up, and sometimes double dosed. For many years she had been able to stay centered on her bumpy road; now the path had become rough and obscure; she had lost her way. It was becoming unsafe for her to live on her own; her most valued and protected privilege had deserted her.

The girls were desperate to get their mother some help. Of all that life had put her through, having to experience the horror of a breakdown at her age was appalling; life having forsaken her this way was shameful. She had managed to be strong enough to get through her childhood, through the loss of love, through her break-ups, even through her aching arthritis. However, she needed help to get through this; more help than just a visit to a psychiatrist. A trip to Katherine's family doctor had him extremely concerned.

"Stop the nicotine patches; the way you are using them is doing more harm than good. You can go back to smoking," the doctor ordered. He was exasperated with Katherine's condition. "It's not going to make any difference now. However, we have to get your meds under control," the doctor said. "You can't do it by yourself; you need monitoring. I recommend you go to the ward at St. Ann's Hospital for a few weeks. That's the only way you can get straightened out."

"Ward? You mean the nut house? I'm not going to any mental hospital. I'm not crazy," Katherine resisted.

"No, you're not crazy. Your meds are out of control. Going in the hospital is the only way to get them straightened out, that's all," the doctor explained.

"No, I'm not going in any hospital!"

Katherine had been thrown down and trampled on by eighty-one stampeding years; she felt crushed. After all she had been through, after all she had been able to survive; how could she end up in a mental hospital now?

She didn't want to think about it, she couldn't think about it. She would simply try to pay more attention to how she took her medicines. The doctor agreed to give her one more chance.

Katherine tried; she tried as hard as her mind would let her. There was no change. Katherine continued to mix up the timetable for her seven medications. It was sad to watch her aging mind fight for its dominion.

Her doctor and daughters finally convinced her that the hospital was the only way to keep from disappearing forever into her dark void of chaotic disorder. Katherine agreed to sign the papers with the idea of being in the hospital about a week.

"Don't tell anyone at my apartment building where I am. It's none of their business."

"Okay, mom, we won't."

Silently, Katherine rode to the hospital, along with her dark, little secret. It was a trip Katherine had been on the verge of taking ever since she was a very young girl; it was a trip Aunt Etta had been able to keep her from taking; it was a trip Miles manage to save her from; she had always been able to stay just out of the reach of its imprisoning grip. Somewhere along the way she lost her footing; now she was in the embrace of her greatest defeat, the loss of herself.

Chapter 69

It didn't take long to do the paper work.

"Okay, we're finished; you can go now," the ward nurse told Judy and Linda. "There is no visiting allowed for the first two weeks while the patient is being evaluated."

"They can't come to see me?" Katherine protested; the nurse ignored her.

"After that, you can visit two days a week for a half hour at a time," the nurse instructed.

"Why such short visiting hours?" the girls asked.

"We find that influence from family members slows down the patient's treatment. Its better if the family stays out of the way."

The nurse showed the girls out. Katherine watched as the door was bolted. She followed the nurse down the long hallway. It wasn't a dark hallway like the ones normally portrayed in the old psychological movies; however, it might as well have been; Katherine could see nothing bright about where she was. She saw no light at the end of her hallway; forlorn, she wiped away her tears.

Katherine's room looked like a normal hospital room.

"There are two beds in here. Do I have a roommate?" Katherine snarled.

"Yes."

There were two small dressers, one for each patient. The rooms were quite bare; there were no pictures on the walls and no vases of flowers; there was nothing that could be thrown or smashed. Katherine looked around the room and saw the uneven curtains, which hung at the windows; she noticed there was no television.

"Where is the television?"

"It's in the social room. If you want to watch T.V., you'll have to watch it there," the nurse barked.

Katherine didn't like that a bit. She didn't want to socialize, especially with these people; she wanted to watch television all alone like she was used to doing at her apartment.

"Where's the phone?"

"We don't have phones in the rooms. There is a house phone down the hall; however, you have to get permission to use it," the nurse instructed.

Katherine was pissed. She didn't want to be there in the first place; but, now she was being deprived of her freedom, her own T.V. and the use of a phone. Her strong will and independence was irked at being denied of her wants. She wondered how in the hell this was going to help her.

Very quickly Katharine was scheduled for sessions with the physiatrist. He listed the medications she had been taking. He talked with her for a while and wrote some notes on his pad. He could feel the fright coming from her glassy, blue eyes; he could see the trembling of her hands and the working of her mouth, probably due, in part, to her meds, but mostly from her anxiety. He could also tell she was not happy to be there.

"I don't know why I have to be here. I'm not crazy," she spit at the doctor.

The doctor tried to ignore her comment and went about his evaluation.

"How long do I have to be here?"

"Let's not focus on that right now. Let's work on getting you better," the doctor answered in his physician's way of avoiding the question.

That irritated Katherine; she didn't like being put off; however, she stopped asking. The session wasn't long and it was time for dinner; another irritation.

Katherine had hoped she could eat her meals in her room by herself; not a chance. Everyone had to go to the community dinning room, which actually was the social room, which was converted during meal times. She didn't like to be made to socialize; she wanted to do it on her own terms, which most of the time was never. In addition, Katherine hated the food; being a picky eater made this kind of situation pure hell.

Katherine was not cooperating with the scheduled social and meal times. The nurses didn't say much to her, they simply observed and took notes. They gave her a little more time to adjust.

The first week went slow. Katherine walked the halls; she was lonely; she wanted to talk to her daughters; she wanted to know when they could visit. She felt restrained. Even though she had signed herself in, she felt like she was being held against her will. She wanted to leave, and now.

"I'm ready to go home. I can manage on my own," Katherine argued with nurses. "I can manage my meds by myself."

She was a pathetic soul insisting on her own dominance. Her favorite phrase became, "this place is like a prison." For all intense purposes, that's exactly what it was.

The doors were locked, the windows were barred; she wasn't free to come and go as she pleased, she wasn't allowed to eat when she wanted to; she wasn't allowed to watch T.V. in private. She began to resent the fact that she allowed her daughters to talk her into doing this. If she could only tell everyone she had changed her mind. She tried, but no one listened.

The first two weeks had been completed with no change to Katherine's condition; it was too soon. However, she was cognizant enough to know that it was the first day she could have visitors; she had only asked the nurses twenty times a day every day for two week.

Katherine stood next to the locked, double doors. She listened; there was no doorbell, no buzzer or knock. She heard nothing; she started to pace. Finally, the nurse walked over to the door and let the visitors in.

Katherine grabbed her girls and squeezed with all her might. Her tears flowed freely with the joy of being with her children again. When the emotions subsided, Katherine's mood changed.

"I want out of here!"

"Mom, let's not talk about it right now. Let's just have a nice visit," the girls said as they tried to change the subject. "Why don't you show us around?"

"I don't want to show you around, I want out of here!"

"You have to give it some more time; please, mom, don't act like this. Show us your room."

Katherine pouted, but she took them on a tour. First, she showed them her room, where she informed them that the bed wasn't comfortable and her roommate was noisy. They moved on to the social room, which was converted to the dinning room, at which time she complained about the food. The girls weren't surprised about that. Then Katherine started in on the other patients.

"They're all crazy. They talk to themselves or to somebody who isn't there, and they don't talk to me. They're not friendly at all; half of them try to walk around in their pajamas."

However, Katherine was right about one thing. She had been admitted for a much different reason than most of the other patients. Her primary problem was discovering the right medicines for her and then getting them regulated. She didn't have the same problems as the bi-polars and schizophrenics. It was very hard for Katherine to be confined to such a ward; it was equally hard for her girls to see her there.

"We know its hard, mom; but it's necessary in order to help you," they insisted.

"When do I get to go home?"

"We don't know; hopefully in a few weeks," they replied.

"A few weeks? I'm ready now. It was only supposed to be one week," Katherine argued. "I've already been here two weeks."

"It takes time. You have to be patient." The bell rang indicating that visiting time was over. The nurse gave a stern look in their direction.

"Don't go," Katherine whimpered when the girls got up to leave.

"We have to; we'll be back."

They had to turn their heads so their mother wouldn't see their tears. Katherine let her tears be seen. Her watery, blue eyes reached out to hold on to her children, who were the very purpose for her being, the very essence of her life. She didn't want them to go; she didn't want to be alone.

She missed her favorite television programs, she missed her favorite nighttime snack of a toasted, cheese sandwich, Cheez-it's, and a glass of Pepsi; she missed her bed, and she missed seeing her white Buick out the corridor window. She wanted to go home.

The girls left their mother sitting on the bench by the door. It was a picture out of place. A woman of eighty one years, shriveled up with life's inflicted wrinkles, bent over from osteoporosis, aware enough to cry from loneliness, shouldn't be perched on a bench by the door in a mental ward for a week waiting for another visit from her children. It was a paradox of ambiguities that landed Katherine in that place; a place where she never imagined she would ever be. She stared off into space as she sat dejected, her shoulders gradually slumped lower and lower, like a balloon loosing its air; she lost concentration and let her mind go blank.

Chapter 70

▼

"Hi, mom, you look great."

"I feel pretty good," Katherine replied; there was even a hint of a smile.

"The doctors must be getting your meds regulated nicely," Linda said.

"I guess."

Something had worked; either Katherine had found a way to adjust or the medicines had helped, probably both. Whatever it was, there was improvement, slight, but it was there. The visit was far too short and the girl's attempt to stay longer was squelched by the ward nurse, a clone of Nurse Ratched.

"Your mother is doing well; then again, her transition is at such a fragile state she could easily backslide," the nurse lectured.

"We don't want that to happen; we'll go." The three women hugged as if transferring each other's life forces to the other. Katherine held on the tightest.

Katherine let the girls go easier each time. She felt less anxious; finally there was a little light at the end of her hallway. In fact, her sense of humor had even emerged and talking with her co-admittees became commonplace. Comically, she sounded very much like an inmate.

"What are you in for?"

She wasn't so sure about some of the ambiguous answers; she was sure, however, that some of them, including her roommate, were indeed crazy.

Katherine had journeyed far in her life; not only in distance and real estate, but from wanting love and finding it, to loosing it and seeking it out again. She had traveled through marriage, motherhood, loneliness, and fear. Now her travels consisted of a long hallway and the reminiscences of the paths taken.

However, there was a change; there was an obvious calm about her. Calmness was definitely what Katherine needed; her frazzled nervous system needed a rest. Sadly though, the reason for the calmness, whether it was the medicine or submission, caused the light in her laughing, passionate, hopeful blue eyes to dim.

Just as Solomon sang, "… for love is strong as death, passion fierce as the grave. Its flashes are flashes of fire, a raging flame."

The love and passion she had wanted so fiercely in her life had kept her fighting against all odds, even the grave; but now, her raging flame had dimmed. She knew better than anyone what Solomon sang about; she had felt it stronger than the King himself. It was that passion that had kept her going for so long, attesting to its power.

Even though Katherine's depression allowed her to feel like giving up, her passion kept up the fight. The doctors were encouraged with her progress and scheduled a meeting with her and her daughters.

"Your mother has made good progress. We feel she can go home; however, not alone. We suggest you look for a facility, perhaps an assisted living situation. She needs to be monitored with her medication."

"I can take care of myself," Katherine insisted.

"Can we see if she can do it on her own," they questioned; they knew what their mother's reaction was going to be.

"I don't think it is a good idea. If you let your mother go home knowing that it is unsafe for her, you could be charged with parental neglect if she gets hurt or overdoses," the attending social worker inform them. "She is simply too forgetful to safely handle her meds by herself. A recent CAT scan showed some shrinkage of the brain, indicating the beginnings of Dementia. No, she can't be alone."

"I'm not going to any nursing home!" Katherine augured.

"Mom, you don't have to go to a nursing home. We'll check out some assisted living facilities. We'll bring you some pictures."

"I don't want any damn pictures. I want to go back to my apartment!"

Chapter 71

The frantic search was on. Finally, an assisted living facility was found; it was close to home, brand new, affordable, and the only one that allowed smoking. The girls visited their mother armed with pictures.

"See how nice it is. It's brand new; everything is beautiful," the girls boasted.

"I want to go back to my apartment," Katherine insisted.

"This place is very nice. You won't have to worry about cooking or cleaning; there will be people around to look after you, and they will help you with your meds. It's great," they continued.

"I want to go back to my apartment," Katherine demanded.

Oak Manor was a one story, sprawling facility. A forest green canopy at the entrance protected slow moving residents and gave them time to get into their wheel chairs or situate their walkers. The beautifully carved, wooden doors opened up into a reception counter on the right and an exquisite sitting room on the left. The quality of the furniture far exceeded that at Katherine's apartment building, which was nice in itself; in addition, the baby grand piano was the focal point of the arrangement. It sat at one end of the room all polished and ready for its marvelous tone to be sent out to caress every door, and bring calm and pleasure to the residents inside; however, nobody entertained the piano's offer. The baby grand's gift was lost on the lost.

The wide carpeted hallway forked at the end of the corridor and Katherine's prospective apartment was to the right. She would be one of the newest tenets so she was placed very near the reception desk. The girls liked that. The facility had a theatre room, an exercise room, a laundry room, and a huge dining room, all outfitted with high quality equipment and furnishings.

There was a light whisper of lavender in the air, nothing like the bold oder of urine smelled in a nursing home. Oak Manor was new, very nice, and the girls felt excited, which was more than they could say for their mother.

"Is this a nursing home?"

"No mom, this isn't a nursing home, far from it. It's a new assisted living complex; it's very nice and the people are great," her daughters explained.

No matter how hard the girls tried to convince Katherine of the pleasantness of the facility, she only heard nursing home. She wasn't interested.

"Look, mom, you don't have a choice. The doctors won't release you to live on your own. They'll keep you here if you don't go to this facility. You don't want that, do you?"

"Why can't I go home?"

"You need a little help with your meds," the girls tried to explain.

"I can handle it myself," Katherine insisted. "I'll be extra careful with my pills."

Nevertheless, their hands were tied; letting her live alone was like allowing her to kill herself; she could accidentally overdose or maybe fall and be left to lay until someone found her. There was always the danger that she would fall asleep with a cigarette in her hand. No, Katherine could not live alone any more.

Great pains were taken to make Katherine feel comfortable in her new home. Even the special touch of getting blue accessories for her bathroom was not over looked. The finishing touch was in place when Katherine's car was placed in the complex parking lot.

Katherine loved getting out of the hospital but she hated where she had to go.

"Look, mom, we've arranged this apartment just like your old one."

The girls had meticulously placed everything in as close proximity as she had in her other apartment.

"See your rocker is next to the sofa, just like before, your television is at the same angle to the rocker, just as before. Look, all of your favorite pictures are hung, and all of your nick-knacks are sitting on the same tables."

"Mom, come and look out the window at the end of the corridor; see, there's your car."

Katherine saw her car and went back to the apartment. "When can I go back to my apartment?"

Though Katherine was weak and frail, she was mad as hell that again she was being forced to do something against her will. The little bit of fire she had left still showed a spark. She gave everyone concerned a very hard time. She was very lucky that the facility administrator was tolerant.

"Katherine, now you're supposed to do as much for yourself as you can. This is not a nursing home. Doing some things yourself is good therapy," the worker explained. "Now, this pull cord is only for emergencies."

"You mean I'm paying all this money and I have to do things for myself?"

The worker ignored her.

Katherine got herself in big trouble; she pulled the emergency cord when she needed to go to the bathroom, or when she needed her laundry done, or just to get a visit from someone. The frantic mode the staff went into when a cord was pulled halted all scheduled activity in the facility as they rushed to help the resident in need. The staff didn't appreciate arriving at Katherine's apartment armed with emergency equipment and being asked to take out the garbage.

"Katherine, you have to stop pulling that cord. It is for emergencies only," the exasperated staff told her.

"I thought I was supposed to pull it if I needed help," Katherine surmised.

"Yes, but emergency help, not domestic help. We're not here to do your chores for you," they explained.

"What about my pills. When is someone going to unlock the box; it's time for my medicine," Katherine argued.

"When it is time, the aid will be down. I am putting a sign on the cord to remind you that you do not pull it unless you have a medical emergency; okay?"

"Okay," Katherine answered; however, she tested their patience a few more times.

Just when the head administrator was about to tell Katherine's family that she wasn't adjusting to their system and she would have to leave, Katherine got the drift that she had pushed the staff too far. Finally, she stopped her shenanigans with the emergency cord; there was a little more peace in the complex. By the end of the first month of Katherine's occupancy, everyone knew the resident in apartment 225.

Katherine sat in her blue rocker and thought about her life; however, her memories stopped short of delving into her deep pool of regret; a true blessing. When her family or the staff, talked to her, all Katherine recalled were her four daughters and her lost loves, particularly the father of her children. As frail and weak as she was, she still had a comedic retrospect about her journey; it sounded like acceptance, which she had fought to have her whole life, and a release from guilt, which she had longed to be free of since she was a little girl. It was not uncommon to find Katherine standing at the counter talking to the aids about her three husbands and five failed marriages.

"The last thing I want is a man. I'm done with them," she joked. It was obvious, though, that her eyes still had a longing in them when she spoke about the father of her children.

The next two years found Katherine struggling with a broken wrist and a fractured pelvis. With the advancement of her osteoporosis, everyone was amazed beyond words that she recovered from the two falls; her petit frame, along with her perseverance, had an unmatched resilience.

Katherine's advanced emphysema and lung disease kept her in and out of the hospital with congestive heart failure and respiratory problems. She continued to fight her way through near death episodes, astounding the doctors with her strength. The point was, she just wasn't ready to go yet; and she wasn't about to do anything she wasn't good and ready to do.

The last time Katherine pulled the emergency cord, there was for a good reason; she could not breathe. Her congestive heart failure had gotten to of point where the excess fluid was crowding out the function of her heart and lungs. The EMS unit came and rushed Katherine off to the emergency room.

Katherine's daughter arrived at the hospital to find her mother hooked up to a ventilator. All that could be heard was the machine as it rhythmically pumped her lungs up and down; it provided her with life giving oxygen and saved her from her greatest fear; death.

After a few days, the miracles of modern medicine brought Katherine around and the ventilator was removed. However, her blood oxygen was so low that she required a large amount to be pumped through a nose tube. After a few more days of monitoring, the diagnosis was confirmed.

"Katherine, you're too weak to go home. I am sending you to rehab. If you get strong enough there, you can go home," the doctor explained.

"Is this a nursing home?" Katherine asked.

"Yes."

"Do I have to live here forever?" Katherine asked her daughters once she got settled in her room.

"No, Mom, you're in the rehab section; when you are better you can go back to your apartment at the Manor."

The resident doctor had a consultation with Katherine and the girls.

"We're not going to start rehab on Katherine right away; she can't spare the calories. Her heart has to work so hard to beat that it burns more calories than she can spare; exercise would simply exacerbate the problem."

"Do you think she'll get strong enough to start rehab," Linda asked.

"We'll just have to wait and see," he replied. "Maybe in a few days."

In Katherine's spunky fashion, she still had enough wits about her to complain about the uncomfortable bed, the bad food and her strange roommate; and, of being tired of lying in the bed.

"Okay, Katherine, you're going to do a little rehab today," the therapist told her.

"Oh, okay," Katherine said; she was willing to give it a try.

Unfortunately, Katherine's visit to the rehabilitation room sent her to the hospital in respiratory distress. The emergency room called the family and they got to the hospital just as the doctors were putting Katherine on a ventilator.

"Why is she on a ventilator?" Linda demanded.

"She signed a DNR order when she went into the nursing home," Katherine's daughter shot at the nurse.

The nurse scrambled through Katherine's papers, which the nursing home had sent over with her.

"Oh, I'm so sorry," the nurse gasped apologetically. However, since the ventilator was already in place, it couldn't be removed until she was able to breathe on her own; of course they wouldn't know that unless the ventilator was removed.

Though Katherine didn't want to be kept alive by machines, there was still a life force present in her weary body; though the ventilator was taped to her mouth and the sound of the machine pulsated to the rhythm of a heartbeat, there was still determination in Katherine's blue eyes; it wasn't her time yet. A weak later Katherine was back at the nursing home. No more rehab was scheduled.

The girls, their husbands, and the grandchildren visited Katherine often. However, one afternoon was particularly poignant for Katherine. Norm sat at the foot of her bed; they were all alone. Some small talk was had and then Katherine got up the nerve to ask a question that had been on her mind. She looked directly at her son-in-law; courageously, but softly she asked.

"Am I dying?"

Norm looked at the floor. He couldn't look at her; he couldn't answer. Katherine looked closely at the bowed head and saw a hint of a nod. She looked away and let out a breath; she wiped away a tear. At least she got a straight answer.

"Was it the cigarettes?" Katherine quietly asked.

"Well, mom, they didn't help, that's for sure," Norm answered. Katherine stared into space, acknowledging that she finally understood their danger.

The warm sun ushered in the first day of October and Katherine was rushed back to the emergency room. It had only been two days since her epiphany. Although she wasn't ready to give up the fight, her lungs offered no air for the battle. This time, however, the emergency room honored her request of no ventilator.

Katherine's daughter rushed through the automatic doors at the emergency entrance.

"Where is my mother?" Linda asked.

"Over there." The doctor said solemnly.

Katherine was in terrible distress when her daughter rushed up to her. The only thing that was done for her was an oxygen mask strapped to her face to try to alleviate her struggle to breathe. As Linda bent over to kiss her mother, Norm went to call their minister.

Katherine reached up to get a hug from her daughter; she wanted to speak.

"Don't try to talk, mom. You have to keep the mask on."

Katherine lay on the gurney; she was uneasy and uncomfortable. She was in too much misery to even realize this just may be her last trip to the E.R. She wasn't thinking about anything except being able to breathe.

Katherine had been in the emergency room so much in the last two years that the doctors and nurses knew her and her condition; and they knew her prognosis. The doctor on duty ordered privacy for Katherine and her family; curtains were drawn and other patients kept at a distance. Respect was afforded the dying.

As Katherine struggled to breathe, she sucked in the life sustaining oxygen and looked around at the people there with her; her daughter, her son-in-law, and her minister. If she knew what was about to happen, she didn't let on. The Reverend started praying.

If the soul is seen through the eyes, then there was something missing in Katherine's blue gaze. Her eyes were absent of depth, of subsistence; they were transparent, like a light blue marble, a purie, glassy and clear. The life of her soul was slipping away and her translucent blue eyes searched for direction.

The doctor peeked through the curtain curious at what Katherine's heart rate was. From the look on his face it was obvious that he was surprised she was still alive. A few minutes passed. The small group kept vigil as they stared at irregular peaks on the heart monitor; they waited, but waited for what; did they wait for the peaks to become more regular, or for them to stop all together? There was a peculiar air in the curtained cubby; an odd sort of game was being played. The rules seemed to be that the participants watched the peaks become smaller and more irregular until they were no more. But, if there were no more peaks, it wasn't the end of the game; it was the end of a life.

As Katherine held her daughter's hand, the rhythmic beeps on the heart monitor ceased and the dreaded flat line appeared. It was very odd; Katherine was still awake. Her eyes met the eyes of those standing near by; her blue corneas miraculously faded to a translucent light cerulean; however, she was still wide awake. The doctor was summonsed to the cubical; he stood with the other three as they stared at the monitor. To everyone's surprise, the rhythmic peaks appeared on the screen again; she was back, apparently she was never really gone. Nobody said a word; evidently the heart simply took a rest so it could beat again; Katherine's little way of saying, "nope, not yet!"

About four minutes later Katherine flat lined again; and again her heart resumed its life-sustaining beat; astonishingly, it was fairly regular and slightly stronger; the self imposed rest worked.

It was obvious Katherine's body was ready to go, but not her unwavering spirit. She held on to the precious life she had always feared loosing.

"Katherine, I'm sending you up to the fifth floor." The doctor had to recant his gut feeling.

Chapter 72

▼

It was just a matter of time, days, or perhaps hours. The local funeral home was called and arrangements were made; an appointment was scheduled with the Department of Public Works to pick out a burial plot in the city cemetery.

Katherine had voiced her desire to be buried next to Miles; alas, there was no plot available next to him. However, there was a plot to the side of Miles' third wife. Of course, that was not going to work. Besides, it wouldn't be fair to the surrounding neighborhood to subject them to any ghostly cat-fights. An available space two plots away from Miles was decided upon by the family.

Katherine laid in her hospital bed an obvious anomaly to the rules of physics; she should have been dead days ago. There was no medical reason for Katherine being alive; perhaps it was as simple as she was not ready to go yet; perhaps she needed a little more time to find her redemption. Death would have to wait.

Katherine was very different now. There were no complaints about the bed being uncomfortable; there were no complaints about the food being bad; there were no complaints about life being unfair. She talked a little when her family visited, but even short visits robbed her of her precious, fading energy.

She wasn't hooked up to any I.V.'s, she had no machines attached to her, she was in no distress; her pain had ceased; she actually looked peaceful. One visit with her children was perhaps the most enlightened Katherine had ever been in her life.

"Well, I've had a good life," she softy confessed.

"We're glad you feel that way, mom." The tears were hard to hold back.

"I got to do a lot of things I wanted to do, I got to go a lot of places."

"You did. I think you went more than me," Linda said; Katherine smiled.

"I know I made a lot of mistakes; but I did the best I could. I raised four wonderful girls; and, I loved your father," Katherine sighed.

And there it was; the admission that validated her worth, the absolution that released her soul. She realized her blessings and accepted her misfortunes. Katherine's final lesson was to realize that forgiveness, for others as well as for herself, was all she needed to feel worthy.

"We love you, mom." Mother and daughters embraced.

"Katherine, I have to take your vitals now," the nurse interrupted.

Katherine grinned at the nurse. "Did you see my roommate's doctor? He's kind of cute."

"You go girl; I admire the fact that you're still looking," the black nurse cackled. Katherine grinned bigger; in fact, everyone grinned. That was the real Katherine underneath all the hurt.

Sunday morning, while Norm and Linda sat in church, praying for God to surround Katherine with his love and comfort, praying that she would not have to linger in a nursing home, the doctor left a message on their answering machine.

"This is Doctor Rallie. Your mother expired this morning at 10:38."

Franticly, they rushed to the hospital. On the way Norm had an epiphany.

"What's the date today?" he asked.

Linda looked at him. With the surprise of awareness she answered.

"Oh my God, it's October 5, the same day that dad died." The car was silent all the way to the hospital.

Katherine's children and the minister gathered around her hospital bed. A calming peace hung over her bed; a hint of a smile shown on her face. The minister prayed for Katherine to have a peaceful journey into God's hands; at the same time, her children knew she was with the one meant to guide her.

Katherine never looked lovelier lying in her pale, sapphire casket. She lay peacefully in a light blue, chiffon dress; she had requested that a small corsage of white carnations tipped in blue be placed in her hands; it was done.

Katherine's blue eyes would have sparkled if they could have seen that the funeral home beautician had been given a bottle of her favorite hair color. She would have beamed if she knew that a bag, which contained her blue eye shadow and #15 Flame Red lipstick, had been left to finish her preparation. Katherine had always been meticulously groomed and she would have taken delight in her last appearance. In fact, she looked as lovely lying in her casket as she did on any one of her wedding days.

The casket was designed with a small ledge where a delicately painted angel rested; the saintly sentinel looked down at Katherine with assurance that her troubles on earth were indeed over. In addition, there were four angels, one at each corner of the coffin, which surrounded Katherine with protection from any further hurt.

Katherine's four daughters stood at the casket as proof that their mother's life, despite her pain and problems, had purpose and honor; it indeed had worth. They had been her four angles on earth; they never left her, they never abandoned her and they unconditionally loved her.

The talk at the fashionable tea, which followed the funeral, was filled with eerie fascination about Katherine passing away on the same day as Miles. Some mourners were sure that Katherine waited until October 5 to leave; others were sure that Miles came for her on the anniversary of his death. Either way, there was quiet contemplation throughout the gathering that afternoon. Most everyone there knew she had never gotten over losing Miles; despite their stormy periods, he had always been her one true love; her soul mate.

The small group of mourners wrestled with the bitter-sweetness of Katherine's passing. They were sad because life was over for her; then again, they knew she had longed for a love that somehow always eluded her.

Katherine's inter battles with guilt, resentment, and bitterness plagued her life, but her spunky strength defined it; to know her was to know that.

Following the funeral, a small procession slowly made its way to the cemetery. When the minister had concluded a short prayer, the funeral director and the gravediggers motioned for the mourners to head toward their cars. It was the cemetery's procedure for the family to leave before they placed the casket in the ground. The girls would not hear of it. They had to stand by their mother to the very end; just as they always had.

It was a tranquil autumn day; the warm sun reflected against the blue, metal casket as Katherine made her way to life's final affair. The girls watched the cemetery workers lower the casket into the ground; her journey was finally over.

Before the girls left their mother lying peacefully in her coffin, they stepped over a few plots to glance at their dad's grave. Again they marveled at the date, October 5; a rare comfort was felt. All the hard times, all the turbulent times were forgotten. Even though they were going to miss their mother terribly, they couldn't dismiss the feeling that she was finally in the arms of the one who shared her soul.

The final question, which lay quietly on everyone's heart, those who knew her, those who disliked her, and those who loved her was this; after the heart stops beating, does it stop breaking?

Yes it does.

978-0-595-41918-0
0-595-41918-6

Printed in the United States
79778LV00003B/1-24